Blessings to you

Patrick Evans

Joy in the Morning

PATSY EVANS

Cover Design by Kendall Evans

WESTBOW
PRESS®
A DIVISION OF THOMAS NELSON
& ZONDERVAN

Scripture taken from the King James Version of the Bible.

WestBow Press books may be ordered through booksellers or by contacting:

WestBow Press
A Division of Thomas Nelson & Zondervan
1663 Liberty Drive
Bloomington, IN 47403
www.westbowpress.com
1 (866) 928-1240

ISBN: 978-1-9736-3785-1 (sc)
ISBN: 978-1-9736-3784-4 (hc)
ISBN: 978-1-9736-3786-8 (e)

Library of Congress Control Number: 2018910045

Print information available on the last page.

WestBow Press rev. date: 11/09/2018

To Bob

Acknowledgments

A number of people have been instrumental in my writing this book. First, I want to thank my husband, Bob, whose love, patience, and encouragement made the completion of the book possible.

Another person to whom I am enormously grateful is Dr. William Mitchell, Professor Emeritus of English Literature at Oklahoma Baptist University. Dr. Mitchell read and, in some cases, reread my manuscript and responded to each segment with suggestions and encouragement to keep pushing forward.

Jim Couch, MD and Martin Hullender, MD were extremely helpful with medical input concerning congenital anomalies and information regarding medical knowledge about such conditions during the late 1950s.

Renee Gunkel, an Altus, Oklahoma, attorney-at-law, read and critiqued excerpts that dealt with legal actions. Her guidance in the use of correct legal language and appropriate courtroom procedure was invaluable.

Contributing significantly was William Park, a former actor who played the parts of Gus in *Cats* and the phantom in *Phantom of the Opera* on Broadway National Tour during the 1990s. His input, based on his intimate knowledge of the theatrical world, offered a unique perspective to the sections dealing with the New York City theater scene.

My granddaughter, Kendall Evans, created the background for the book cover design. Her contribution gave my work a specialness that only a grandparent would know how to appreciate.

Other friends and acquaintances allowed me to impose on their time: Barbara Davis and Maureen Uphues, friends and retired teachers, helped with proofreading; Jim Fowles and Dan McNeill, native New Yorkers, gave input about neighborhood and city life in New York City; Phyliss Jones and Dena Prosen came to my rescue several times in resolving computer technology issues.

To all of these and the many other friends and family members who saw fit to overlook my inadequacies and to believe in the work of grace out of which this writing was born, I express my sincere gratitude.

PREFACE

A few years ago, for the benefit of my grandchildren, I wrote a series of essays about my childhood memories. These essays are mainly about family members and friends who made memorable impressions on my life. This book, which began as one of those essays, evolved into a work of fiction.

Thinking about Aunt Ruth and Uncle Terrell McBride, carried me far back to early childhood and to vague images of two children, a boy and a girl, who were born to them. Both children were born with physical and neurological anomalies, but I don't remember ever hearing a term used to identify their particular medical conditions. Since I was younger than they, I recall only certain characteristics I have carried with me through the years.

The thing that impressed me most, however, was not the children themselves but the attention given them by my aunt and uncle. For as long as they lived (the boy, Terrell Pat, to age fourteen and the girl, Bobbie Ruth, to age eight), Aunt Ruth and Uncle Terrell patiently addressed the daily needs of each child. Their children were the center of their universe, and they did what their love for their children compelled them to do.

Although the story told in this book is entirely a work of fiction, Bobbie Ruth McBride serves as the model for Joy Marie Buffington.

This novel, therefore, is a tribute to Aunt Ruth and Uncle Terrell, both now deceased, and to all parents who have experienced or are experiencing the challenges and the blessings of ministering care to children with special needs. It is my prayer that all of us will be blessed with the ability to see God's perfection in imperfection.

CHAPTER 1

Even at 5:30 a.m., the air was warm in Dallas, Texas, and promised to usher in another August scorcher. Ann's daddy had taken her to the airport and had stayed with her for a while, but when her plane was delayed, she insisted he return home to beat rush hour traffic.

Her destination was New York City to fulfill a dream that had been building in her since she was fifteen and saw her first live musical. *People of the Land* was still a vivid memory, and her love for the theater had grown from a gentle breeze into a tornado spinning inside her.

For the past year she had looked forward to this move, to being truly on her own, making her own decisions, and not having to explain her actions to anyone. As she watched Daddy walk away, however, the finality of it hit her, and she had a strange longing to crawl back into the car and let him take her back to the house she had called home all her life.

Alone with her thoughts, she felt the strong arms of nostalgia carrying her back to the uncluttered innocence of childhood. She could see Sheppy and Feisty, her collie and Boston terrier, dancing and wagging their tails impatiently as they faithfully waited for her to step off the school bus. Then she would run as fast as her legs could carry her, both pooches yipping at her heels, and collapse in the front yard to embrace their ecstatic slurping of every inch of her exposed skin. She would climb the steps to the front porch where Mother's hug carried the promise of an after-school snack with the aroma of freshly baked cookies wafting around her and clinging to her hair and clothes.

Dozens of visions from her childhood randomly invaded her mind—Daddy teaching her to ride her bike, going to movies with friends, roller skating at the portable rink that came to Bonner Valley every summer, and folding back the covers and melting into the comfort of her bed. She smiled as she remembered family trips they had made. The three of them would ride along singing hymns or popular songs, their voices strangely mellowed and synchronized by the wind from the car's open windows.

Suddenly she was jolted back to reality by a voice on the loud speaker announcing the boarding of her flight. She resented the interruption to her reverie, but it was a pipe dream anyway—a melancholy flashback to a time that could never be again.

She lifted her tote bag to her left shoulder and placed her purse handle in the crook of her left arm. Then she picked up her hanging bag and moved into the line of passengers waiting to present their boarding passes. An attendant with a painted smile took her boarding pass, ripped off the stub portion, and returned it to her. With stub in hand, she inched along the crowded ramp to the plane where a stewardess took her hanging bag, unfolded it, and placed its hook over the rod in a compartment with other hanging bags. She glanced at the stub to confirm her seat location and was pleased to see she had an aisle seat near the front.

After placing her tote bag into the overhead storage area, she settled into her seat next to a middle-aged man reading a book. She was grateful he seemed not to notice that she had taken the seat beside him. She wasn't in the mood for making polite conversation with a stranger.

Ann had been crushed when her mother had died suddenly near the end of her freshman year at the University of Texas. She and her mother had been closer than most mothers and daughters, maybe because Ann was an only child or maybe because of the kind of person Eve Jernigan was. She had the ability to make the people around her feel good about themselves. She had always told Ann, "When you're visiting with other people, talk about them and their interests instead of talking about yourself; not only is it the gracious thing to do, but you might find a treasure hiding inside that person." Mother believed you could find good in everyone if you got to know them well enough and looked for it hard enough. She had been Ann's best friend, her confidante, her encourager, and most ardent supporter throughout her school years, even after Ann announced her desire to make the theater her career.

At first, Daddy had resisted her plans and thought she would forget about the theater once she got to the university and realized all the other options open to her. Even now, he was apprehensive about her pursuing such a competitive and unpredictable profession, but Mother's attitude had been that she should go for her dreams. How she missed Mother's smiles, hugs, and words of encouragement and wisdom!

Daddy had been married to Nora for almost two years, and after their wedding, Ann had found a lot of excuses not to go home. She had visited them a few times, but it was difficult seeing the house that had her mother's fingerprints in every nook and cranny occupied by another woman.

Everything in the house had remained the same. The furniture, the dishes, the cooking utensils, and even the bedspreads and decorative pillows had been carefully chosen by her mother. Ann had been in shock the first time she went home after they married. She couldn't believe Nora would be using Mother's things instead of replacing them with at least *some* of her own.

Even the pictures on the walls were the same, with one exception: Not a single photograph of any member of Daddy's family could be seen anywhere in the house, not even of Ann; they had all been replaced with Nora's family pictures. A picture of Daddy and Nora was now hanging above the fireplace where one of Mother and Daddy and Ann had hung. On the wall where a portrait of Ann used to be was a picture of Nora's daughter and two sons.

Ann wanted Daddy to be happy, and she guessed he was, but

Nora wasn't a warm, fuzzy human being; in fact, she was aloof and bossy, and Ann felt her presence in *their* house was resented by Nora and awkward for Daddy. That's why this day was so important. It was her escape from what had become an unbearable humiliation. It was the closing of one phase of her life and the christening of another.

Following her graduation from the University of Texas in the spring of 1955, Ann had accepted the invitation of Aunt Lil, her mother's sister, to move back home to Bonner Valley and live with her and Uncle Ben. They had lost their only child to pneumonia when he was two years old, so Aunt Lil had always felt Ann was part hers. She was a sweet, gentle soul, but she was a worrier who treated Ann as if she were still six years old and had to be sheltered from the harsh world. Aunt Lil couldn't imagine why Ann would want to move to a dangerous place like New York City. Sometimes Ann wondered how Mother and Aunt Lil could have had the same parents; they were nothing alike.

When Dr. Blanchard, Daddy's dentist friend, learned Ann was coming back home and wanted to work a year to save money before moving to New York, he offered her a job as his receptionist. Helen, his regular receptionist, wanted to take a year off following the birth of her first baby, so the timing was perfect! Since Aunt Lil and Uncle Ben refused to let her pay any rent, she had few expenses. She was able to save almost all her salary.

Daddy had covertly paid the deposit and first month's rent on Ann's apartment and had paid for having some of her things sent ahead and placed in her Brooklyn apartment. He had told her it was their secret since Nora didn't do things like that for her kids and wouldn't understand.

The aisle was still glutted with passengers searching for their seats and overhead compartment space. As Ann watched them file by, she became aware that an older woman had stopped beside her and was struggling to stow her carry-on. A tall, agile young man, maybe still in his teens, came to her rescue and placed the woman's bag in the compartment. A toothless smile brightened her wrinkled face as she turned to face him. "Thank you, young man," she lisped. "You are a gentleman."

"You're welcome, ma'am. I'm glad I could help," he replied.

Then she turned her smile toward Ann and pointed to the seat next to the window. Ann returned her smile, stood, and stepped into the aisle. The man beside her continued reading his book, seemingly oblivious to everything going on around him.

"Excuse me, sir," the old woman said, and waited for the man's acknowledgment. The man glanced up at her and mumbled something under his breath. Then he pulled his long legs to one side, still half blocking her access. Ann wondered if he was a grouch by nature or if maybe he flew routinely and had become callous to the common courtesies of airline travel.

Soon after the aisle cleared, the stewardess began her routine explanation of the plane's features and the mandatory safety procedures. Ann could hear seat belts clicking around her and glanced furtively to see if the woman and man had fastened theirs. They had. That's when she saw something she hadn't noticed before—a purplish mark on the man's right hand over two of his knuckles and dipping down between his pinky and ring finger. He indifferently looked beyond the woman and out the window as the plane backed away from the gate. Then he returned his attention to his book. The old woman watched the buildings and loading equipment go out of sight as the plane turned and slowly taxied into position.

Except for the roaring of the jet engines, silence prevailed as the plane sped down the runway, lifted from the ground, and soared into the clouds. When the seat belt sign went off, Ann released herself and settled into a more comfortable position. She wanted to sleep, but instead she took a note pad from her purse and began jotting down things she needed to do. There would be time to nap after her mind was settled about the responsibilities that lay ahead. She would be too busy unpacking boxes and getting settled in her apartment to get out again today, but tomorrow would be a busy day about town.

She had already decided to take a taxi from LaGuardia to avoid having to struggle with her luggage on a busy subway. With her shoulder tote and hanging bag in tow, she walked directly to the nearest taxicab among those waiting to be pounced on by the passengers streaming from the airport. The driver met her, took her bags, and placed them on the seat beside her. She gave him the address and he pulled away from the curb.

Ann had made this trek six weeks ago to look for an affordable apartment that wouldn't be too far from a subway station and a grocery store. Since she had returned her car to Daddy, she would have to walk or take public transportation everywhere she went. The thought of lugging bags of groceries for several blocks or juggling them on the subway gave her nightmares.

She had found a furnished living room/bedroom combination with a small kitchenette and a three-quarter bath on the third floor of an apartment building among a whole section of old row houses that had been converted into apartments. There was no elevator, but she had decided going up and down the stairs would be good exercise anyway. Her enthusiasm built as she fantasized about the new life that awaited her. Even the hardships of being without a car and having to trudge up and down two flights of stairs every time she left her apartment seemed exciting. She felt like a pioneer.

CHAPTER 2

A nn awoke to a room flooded with light, looked at her watch and saw it was already 9:30. She had planned to get an early start today, but she must have been more physically drained than she had realized. Her body was telling her go back to sleep, but she didn't give in to the temptation.

She looked around at her new surroundings and was pleased with her accomplishments. She had opened all seven boxes of her personal effects, mostly clothes, and had put everything away last night before slipping into her pajamas and falling into bed without even removing her makeup or brushing her teeth.

Since she had no food in her apartment, she took a quick shower, dressed and was on her way. She had several things on her *To Do* list and a few things on her *To Buy* list, and she hoped to draw a line through everything on both lists before this day ended.

After locking her apartment door behind her, she dropped the key into her bag with some loose change and a money clip holding several bills. She skipped down the stairs and stepped into bright sunshine from the building she now called home. She was captivated by the excitement of living in this magical place.

Her first stop was to pick up a newspaper at the stand down the street from her apartment. It was a perfect day for finding her way around the city, but first she would have a cup of strong, hot coffee with a pastry while she read the news, giving special attention to the jobs section. She folded *The New York Times*, clutched it to her chest, and headed for the little pastry shop she'd seen the day she leased her apartment.

At twenty-two, Ann was full of dreams and ambitions. Broadway with all its grandeur summoned her. Like most young would-be actors, she envisioned sought-after roles followed by rave reviews and, somewhere down the line, curtain calls and flowers at her feet. She was ready to take the giant leap from university stage productions and community theater to the big time. She knew it was a gamble, but it was one she had to take.

Living in New York City would be a financial drain if she didn't discipline herself. The money she had saved while working for Dr. Blanchard should be adequate for her living expenses for a while, but she was anxious to find some kind of part-time work.

She made her way to a little out-of-the-way table near the rear of the pastry shop where she could read the paper and enjoy her pastry and coffee with some degree of privacy. After scanning the front page, she turned to the ads section and a job opening soon caught her eye: *Wanted: part-time caregiver for elderly woman. Call Buffington at MA4-4242.* It wasn't exactly the type work she had envisioned, but she could at least look into it. She wanted something part-time that would afford her the time she needed to explore ways of breaking into the wonderful world of musical theater.

As she finished her coffee and sat mulling over her agenda, she decided to call the number about the job. *I have to start somewhere,* she reasoned, *and I need to find something soon so I won't use up all my savings.* She tore out the ad and put it into her bag, leaving the rest of the paper on the table as she left.

Back on the sidewalk, she walked the half block or so to the phone booth she had spotted earlier. She pulled the ad from her purse, closed the door behind her, fed a coin into the slot, and dialed the number. A female voice answered, "Buffington Transport. This is Vicki." Ann explained why she was calling, and Vicki immediately replied, "I'll put you through to Mr. Buffington."

"This is Nelson Buffington."

"My name is Ann Marie Jernigan, Mr. Buffington, and I'm

calling regarding your advertisement for someone to care for an elderly woman."

"Yes, Miss Jernigan, or is it Mrs. Jernigan?"

"It is Miss."

"I need someone to stay with my mother from 7:00 a.m. until 1:00 p.m. on Mondays through Fridays. Your duties would be helping her with bathing and grooming each morning and preparing her breakfast, lunch, and dinner. You could have breakfast with her if you wish, and then lunch would be for three people: Mother, you, and Richard. Richard is my son who stays with Mother in the afternoons. You would also need to prepare an evening meal for three people and put it in the refrigerator for my sister to heat later in the day. You would need to make her bed each morning and clean the kitchen following meal preparations.

"I assume you have a car. You might need to take her to appointments occasionally. Her appointments are usually in the afternoons. Richard takes her when he can, but he is often tied up. Therefore, we would depend on you to take her at those times. You would, of course, be paid for the extra time she is in your care.

"Now about your qualifications: How do you feel about elderly people, Miss Jernigan? Do you like them? Have you ever cared for an elderly person before? Sometimes older people have needs they are embarrassed to discuss. Could you be sensitive and discreet in dealing with someone under such circumstances? Do you have references? I hope you—"

As Mr. Buffington continued jetting through his interrogation and injunctions, Ann was stunned by the arrogant, presumptuous tone of the voice at the other end of the line, and she pictured Mr. Buffington as a pompous bully who expected everyone to rush to meet his expectations without considering what might be expected of him in return. He was evidently accustomed to barking orders to subordinates, and she had no desire to become one of them.

She didn't really care how he might receive her terse retort. "I have friends and acquaintances of all ages, Mr. Buffington, and I seldom meet anyone of any age whom I don't like. I have never been employed as a caregiver to an elderly person—or to any person, for that matter—but I do know how to cook and clean, and I feel confident I could competently and discreetly assist your mother with her personal needs. I do not own a car, nor do I have a New York driver's license, and I have no immediate plan to acquire either.

"Now I would like to ask you a few questions, Sir. What is the status of your mother's health? Is she emotionally and mentally stable? To what extent does she require assistance? Does she have an agreeable disposition, and does she approve of having a stranger come to her home to assist her? And finally, how much would I be paid for my services?

"If you choose not to entrust the care of your mother to someone who has no professional experience and who would be unable to drive her to appointments, then I wish you well in finding the right person. I have recently moved to this area and do not have a telephone at this time, so if you are interested in speaking with me again, please let me know when *I* might call *you*."

A long pause followed Ann's calm but commanding discourse. She thought Mr. Buffington had hung up on her, and she wouldn't have been surprised if he had. But it didn't really matter to her, since she considered this call a waste of time anyway. Then as she was moving the receiver away from her ear to place it back on its hook, she heard a voice, but it was more subdued and less condescending than the voice she had heard earlier.

"Miss Jernigan, evidently, I have offended you. I didn't intend to be so forceful in stipulating my mother's needs. I suppose my directness with you is a product of my profession. I live in a corporate world where everybody is always in a hurry to get things done, and people are impatient with lengthy conversations, particularly when they involve simple business arrangements. Could you come to my office so we could get acquainted? I think we could better assess our individual perspectives if we meet personally."

"That would be fine, Mr. Buffington."

His invitation for an interview took her by surprise, and she agreed to it before even thinking it through. After their verbal clash, she thought the door had slammed shut on her dealings with Mr. Buffington. When he opened the door, however, something piqued her curiosity and lured her in.

"I will put you back with my secretary and ask her to work out a time that will be convenient for both of us. Is that satisfactory?"

"That will be fine," Ann replied.

Ann was pleasantly surprised by the seeming change in Mr. Buffington's attitude, and as she listened, she felt her resentment for him ebbing away. Maybe she had misjudged him. Later, though, as her mind replayed his words, she wondered if she had jumped to the conclusion that he was apologizing when that wasn't the case at all. He had never said he was sorry; he had simply explained his position. His words, *particularly when they involve simple business arrangements* flashed into her mind. It was as if he was telling her that her *business* with him wasn't worthy of the time it would take to carry on a courteous conversation with her.

The more she thought about it, the more she felt his *apology* carried undertones of sarcasm and derision. On the other hand, he had asked her to come for a personal interview—something he wouldn't have done had he not been at least *considering* employing her. Although her feelings about Mr. Nelson Buffington were ambivalent at best, she was willing to give him the benefit of the doubt.

His secretary came back on the line and gave her the office address and asked if she could come in day after tomorrow at 10:30 a.m. Ann was happy not to have to carry this burden of uncertainty through the weekend. As strange as it seemed, she was anxious to meet this man whose brashness had so unsettled her.

Ann opened the directory that dangled from a cable next to the phone and thumbed through the first few pages to find the number to call about getting a telephone in her apartment. She dialed the number and arrangements were made for her phone to be installed on Thursday of next week. She supposed she could live a few more days without a phone, but she did need to call Daddy and bring him up to date on things.

"Rosemont Dairies. This is Jernigan."

"Hi, Daddy. I don't have a phone in my apartment yet, so I'm at a pay phone and can't talk long. How are things going?"

"Hi, honey. I'm great, but how are things with you? I was expecting you to call yesterday. Was your flight delayed long? What time did you get there?"

"I boarded the plane about forty-five minutes after you left and got to my apartment about 4:30 p.m. New York time. The flight went well, and the delay didn't mess up my plane change."

"And had all the boxes we sent ahead been put in your apartment? I worried a little bit about doing that."

"Yep, they were all there. I checked with Mr. Yancey, the building superintendent, and he said they came last week. He signed for the delivery just as he had told me he would. I even got everything unpacked and put away last night, so I'm pretty much settled in. I still have to deal with getting rid of the boxes, but I just stacked them all in one corner. I got so busy working last night that I forgot to eat supper, but I'd had lunch and an afternoon snack on the plane so I wasn't really hungry. I don't have any food in my apartment, but I'm going to that little neighborhood market I told you about and stock up.

"By the way, I'm going for a job interview day after tomorrow. It's just part time, but that's really all I want for now. Wish me luck. I have to go, Daddy. The operator just came on and told me I have thirty seconds left to talk. I love you, and give my love to Aunt Lil. I'll call you when I know something about the job."

"Okay, honey. Glad you called, and I'll look forward to hearing from you in a couple of days. You take care of yourself."

"I will. Bye, Daddy."

It was noon, and suddenly the sidewalk was teeming with people on lunch break. Ann shook off her despondency and joined the flow of pedestrians in a hurry to get to their various destinations. She hastened her step, and in less than an hour was exploring the little market Mr. Yancey had recommended.

Kaminski's was a small space so packed with canned, boxed and bagged foods that the aisles had to be navigated single file. Under the awning in front of the store and on each side of the door, a section about the size of a card table displayed fresh produce. At the rear of the store, a refrigerated area with dairy products and drinks of various kinds occupied about one-fourth of the back wall. The meat market took up the rest. Their specialty was Polish sausage, which they made in store. The aroma of cooking sausages filled the small market and drifted out the open door, and Ann could feel herself gaining weight just inhaling the heavenly scent. Along with her other purchases, she bought a quarter pound of the sausage.

Outside again, this time with each arm curled around a large paper bag, she hastened along the sidewalk and back to her apartment. A woman with a little boy happened to be leaving the building as she was ready to enter, so the woman held the door for her. Ann thanked her as she edged the bags sideways through the opening.

On the landing of the first flight of stairs, she decided to give her aching arms a rest. She had just put the bags down when a boy who looked to be sixteen or seventeen came bounding up the stairs. He stopped on the landing and asked her if she needed help with her groceries. She gratefully accepted his offer. He lifted both bags as though they were filled with feathers and carried them all the way to her apartment. She went ahead of him and unlocked her door, and he set the bags on the small kitchen counter. She took a fifty-cent piece from her purse and extended it to him. He wouldn't take it, so she thanked him and told him maybe she could return the favor someday. He smiled sheepishly and left.

She was surprised that New Yorkers with their hustle-and-bustle lifestyle would take time to help a stranger. Maybe she had been wrong about them.

CHAPTER 3

Ann emptied the grocery bags and put everything away. Suddenly she was famished. She spread her feast of sausage, cheese, bread, and kosher pickles before her on the little drop-leaf table and thought about the one thing she still wanted to buy before this day ended—an electric percolator.

The Woolworth's across from the phone booth she had used would probably stock coffee pots. It was only 1:30, so she should have plenty of time to make her purchase and get home before the work day ended. As exhilarating as Ann found New York City to be, the one negative she found was continually having to maneuver through swarms of people. Growing up in a small town did have its advantages.

The Woolworth's was about a forty-five-minute walk, but the beauty of the day overcame her sense of urgency and slowed her gait to a leisurely stroll as she took in the sights and sounds of her neighborhood.

Three teen-age boys sat idly on the steps of the apartment building next door. Two women, each with a baby stroller, leaned against an iron railing and chatted while their offspring slept peacefully. Up ahead, two little girls and a little boy were playing hopscotch. As Ann approached, they all three stepped aside, scowls replacing the laughter she'd heard just seconds earlier. She stopped and smiled at them. Then she hopscotched her way through the chalk-drawn pattern on the sidewalk. When she heard their giggling, she knew she'd won them over, so she looked back at them, smiled and said, "That was so much fun. Thanks for letting me play with you." Another round of giggles followed her down the sidewalk, and Ann thought, *Children's laughter is the same whether you're in Brooklyn or in Bonner Valley.*

Woolworth's was crowded with parents and children buying school supplies for the upcoming academic year. Ann headed directly to the small appliances section and found the electric percolator. She decided she needed some dish cloths and dish towels, so she added a half-dozen of each to her purchase and started for home.

Back in her apartment, the boxes stacked in the corner seemed to be staring at her. She broke them down and stuck two of the best ones under her bed for future use; the rest she tied together with the twine that had secured them in shipping. Since her apartment was at the end of the hall, she thought it would be okay to drag them into the hallway and prop them against the wall until she could find out what she should do with them.

On Thursday, she left her apartment early to make sure she wasn't late for her appointment. She decided she could use any extra time she might have to reacquaint herself with the bustling metropolis called Manhattan.

Judging from the location of Mr. Buffington's office, she would be within walking distance of the south end of Central Park. Even if she didn't have time to make it there before her interview, afterwards she might grab some food somewhere and find a park bench where she could drink in the tranquil setting as she ate her lunch. She had been enthralled with Central Park when she came to New York City as a part of a study group between her junior and senior years at UT. It had been a trip for which she had received university credit, and it was just another enticement that had lured her to this area.

It was 9:22 when she stepped off the subway, and she decided it would rush her too much to go to Central Park before the meeting. She walked around the area for a while and then back to Mr. Buffington's office. Vicki, the receptionist, greeted her, and at precisely 10:30 escorted her into a large, bright office overlooking Madison Avenue from ten stories up. Mr. Buffington stood and shook her extended hand. "I'm Ann Jernigan, Mr. Buffington. It's nice to meet you."

"And I'm happy to meet you, Miss Jernigan. Please be seated." He gestured toward a large chair opposite his desk and then returned to his own chair behind the desk. He was taller than she had expected, not a handsome man but well-groomed and distinguished looking. His face looked familiar to her, but then she was always seeing someone that reminded her of someone else.

He leaned back in his chair and looked at her across the desk. "Well, Miss Jernigan, you're here in response to my newspaper ad for a caregiver for my mother. I remember our telephone conversation, and I'm happy we could meet personally to discuss things. I was thinking $200 a month might be sufficient for six hours a day, five days a week. How does that sound to you?"

Ann tried to hide her astonishment at the amount of the salary, but inside she was excited that Mr. Buffington would pay so much to a part-time caretaker who was obviously not the ideal person for the job. "That's very generous, Mr. Buffington, but I would like to know more about your mother, especially how she feels about having a stranger come into her home to help her."

"Yes, I understand. Mother is eighty-seven years old, and both her body and mind are slowing down. She has fallen several times recently, and my sister and I are concerned about her safety. She didn't break any bones but had some bad bruises each time. I think the falls have shaken her confidence in her own ability to walk without assistance. She now uses a cane.

"Her mind has always been sharp, but recently she has been uncharacteristically forgetful. She forgot to turn off the water at the bathroom lavatory one morning, and another time she left water boiling on the range. My sister discovered each situation before any damage was done, but these incidents have caused us to feel we need someone with her during the day.

"My son is a graduate student at New York University, and he goes to her house every day after his classes. I may have told you in our telephone conversation that he arrives about 11:45 a.m. and stays until about 6:00 p.m. My sister spends nights and weekends with her.

"As I indicated, I want someone to be with her in the mornings and help her with bathing and dressing, as well as with meal preparation. She does know about and approve my getting someone to help with these things. Have I answered all your questions, Miss Jernigan?"

"Yes, I think so . . . well, there is one other thing. Where does your mother live?"

"Here in Manhattan, but her house is four blocks from the nearest subway station. Would that be a problem for you?"

Ann chuckled. "I walked farther than that every day going to classes at the university. I like walking; I can get where I need to go and get my exercise at the same time."

"Oh . . . well . . . that brings up another question. Are you a university graduate?"

"Yes, I received my Bachelor of Arts from the University of Texas a year ago."

"It seems you are overqualified for this job. Why are you seeking such employment?" He paused and then explained, "The thing I'm getting at is this: I don't want to employ a caregiver for my mother only to have her leave for a better-paying job in a few weeks."

"I can't make a guarantee about how long I could help with your mother, Mr. Buffington. I will say that, for now, my plan is to remain employed on a part-time basis; however, that could change. I do promise that unless something unforeseen and beyond my control occurred, I would give you adequate notice to find a replacement."

"I appreciate your candor, Miss Jernigan." He leaned forward and seemed to study Ann's face, his demeanor turning more serious. "You have a forthrightness about you, Miss Jernigan, that engenders trust and confidence that you will fulfill your responsibilities. How soon can you begin work?"

Ann was taken back by his sudden decision to hire her. Her conversation with him had squelched her apprehensions, and she found herself telling him she could begin on Monday of week after next. When she entered his office, she certainly didn't expect to leave as an employee of this man whose manner she had found so abrasive in their earlier telephone conversation. "I just moved into my apartment a few days ago," Ann explained, "and I need some time to take care of few things before I begin work. Will that time be all right with you?"

"Well, of course, I'd rather have you begin right away, but I've managed so far, so I think I can wait another week or so. Let's see, today is August 16; that would make your first work day on August 27. On that morning, I will pick you up at your apartment; then I'll take you to my mother's house and introduce you to her and help you find your way around the house. I'll also point out the nearest subway stop. How does that sound to you?"

"I like that plan. I'll leave my address with your secretary, and I'll be waiting on the sidewalk for you if you will give me a time."

"How about 6:15? Does that sound all right?"

"Yes, I'll be in front of my apartment building at that time."

This time, it was Mr. Buffington who extended his hand for the traditional handshake to seal their agreement. As her hand met his, she noticed a discoloration on the hand he was offering. It was a purplish mark over two knuckles and between his ring finger and little finger. She almost gasped but caught herself, quickly shifted her eyes to his face, and returned his smile. *It couldn't be! Was it possible that two men could have identical birthmarks?* As she left his office, her head was spinning at the overwhelming evidence that she had just been employed by the obnoxious man who had sat beside her on the plane.

CHAPTER 4

As Ann approached the park bench clutching a cola in one hand and a hot dog in the other, her thoughts were anything but serene. She wondered if she had been too hasty in accepting Mr. Buffington's job offer. Questions about this man and everything related to her dealings with him hammered at her brain and clamored to be answered: *Why would he hire me when I fail to meet many of the criteria he set forth? Are his mother's needs more extensive than he has disclosed, and he is desperate to find someone willing to take on such a demanding task? Why would he offer me such generous compensation for a half-day, five-days-a-week job that requires no particular training or skill? Is he indeed the man I encountered on the plane?*

Mr. Buffington was an enigma, a seeming dichotomy of charisma and boorishness, but she had hoped to come away from her interview with him feeling some sense of direction. Instead, she felt bewildered.

When Ann arrived back at her apartment, a letter from Daddy was in her mail box. She read it quickly before going up the stairs. He was writing to tell her that Aunt Lil had fallen and broken her hip and was in the Bonner Valley Hospital. He said she was getting along all right, but he thought a note from Ann would be a great encouragement to her. He included other tidbits of Bonner Valley news and reminded her to call as soon as she knew the results of her job interview. He had stuck a $10 bill in with the letter, and Ann felt a warmth go through her as she tucked the envelope and its contents into her purse. It was almost as if Daddy had folded a hug in that $10 bill and had sent it to her from 1,400 miles away.

She thought about going to a phone and calling him right then, but what would she tell him—that she had been offered the job and had taken it but was afraid she might have made a mistake? No. She needed time to think things through before she told him anything about the job or about Mr. Buffington. She even wondered if she should call Mr. Buffington and nix his offer of employment before it went any further.

As she took out her key to open the door to her apartment, she happened to glance toward the end of the hall where she had placed her unwanted boxes. They were gone. She hoped Mr. Yancey wasn't upset with her for putting them there.

That night, Ann took the events of the day to bed with her, her mind in a vise of confusion and turmoil. She scolded herself for jumping into the first job that seemed to fit her needs. *I should have looked at ads for several days before making such a decision*, she told herself. She beat her pillow and called herself names and fumed and fussed until she was physically and emotionally exhausted. Finally, she reasoned: *Okay, I made an error in judgment. This isn't the first mistake I've ever made, and I'm sure it won't be the last. It isn't the end of the world!* Still, her mind wouldn't let go of her inner tumult.

Mother had always told her God loved her and wanted to be part of her life, but that He wouldn't force His way in; she had to invite Him. She remembered praying as a child, but as she had grown older the practice of prayer had been greatly neglected.

Given her present situation, Ann felt a powerful urge to pray. She found herself pouring out all her pain and frustration in a whispered heart cry, "Lord, please help me. Please give me peace in my mind and heart about this job and about Mr. Buffington. Please take away these feelings of uncertainty and fear." The word *fear* caught in her throat, and the sound of her own voice admitting she was afraid choked out the words that were to follow. Suddenly she realized *that* was the real problem—*fear*. She was *afraid* she might have made a mistake about the job—*afraid* because of her insecurity about Mr. Buffington—*afraid* of running out of money and having to admit she couldn't do this on her own—*afraid* of being a failure and having to limp back to Bonner Valley like a puppy with its tail between its legs.

Then, as she analyzed her fears, she could hear her daddy's words, *Get up, Annie. If you quit trying just because you fall, you'll never learn to ride that bike. Don't let your fear whip you.* Her mind carried her back to the images of falling and getting up many times, and then in one magical moment, she was riding. She didn't even know how it happened—at what point Daddy turned loose of the bike and sent her off on her own.

Those memories sparked a peacefulness that covered her like a warm blanket, melting her doubts and producing a confidence to face and conquer her fears of inadequacy and failure. She had reached a decision: in the future, she wouldn't allow herself to panic when things didn't go as she wanted. She realized she'd been too anxious to prove herself in the arena of life-on-her-own. If nothing else good came out of this experience, at least she had learned not to make impulsive decisions.

Two days slipped by, and Ann suddenly remembered she hadn't called Daddy. He must be frantic by now. Aunt Lil also must be wondering why she hadn't heard from her.

She quickly showered, dressed, and checked her purse to make sure she had enough change to call Daddy. As she was going down the stairs, she heard someone call her name; it was Mr. Yancey. He told her he had taken her boxes away and that any time she needed to discard bulky items, he would take care of it for her. She was relieved to know she hadn't tarnished her good standing with Mr. Yancey. She liked him. He reminded her of her daddy, not in appearance, but in his easy-going manner.

Since today was Sunday, Daddy wouldn't be at the plant. She couldn't be sure he would be the one to answer the phone at the house, but she decided to chance it rather than call person-to-person. She was relieved when she heard her daddy's voice.

"Hi, Daddy; I thought I'd better check in with you."

"Hi, sweetheart. I'm glad you called. Did you get my letter?"

"Yes, I got it. I'm sorry I didn't call sooner. I just wanted to wait until I was sure about the job before I called. By the way, thanks for the money. You didn't have to do that, but I really appreciate it. How's Aunt Lil? Is she still in the hospital?"

"Yeah, but she's going home tomorrow. She's doing all right. I hope you'll write to her though. You know how she feels about you. What do you mean about wanting to wait until you are sure about the job? Don't you know yet if you got the job or not?"

"Yes, I got the job."

"Then the interview went all right?"

"I think it went well. Mr. Buffington, the man who interviewed me, is sort of hard to read. He seems really nice at times and not so nice at other times, but it's his mother I'll be working with."

"Then I'm talking with an employed young lady?"

"You certainly are. At least, I will be a week from tomorrow. That's when I actually start to work. I guess I could start sooner, but I need to be home when someone comes to install my phone. I just hope I *like* the job. I'm a little bit uncertain about that, but the salary is fabulous for the amount of time I'll be working. He's paying me $200 a month! Doesn't that sound great?"

"Yeah, it does. Maybe I'd better change professions."

Ann giggled at his little joke. "I'll keep you posted on how things go. I'm supposed to get my phone on Thursday, and that will make it a lot easier for me to call you. Well, Daddy, I hate to end our conversation, but I don't have any more change, so I'm going to have to hang up. I'll put a note to Aunt Lil in the mail, but if you talk to her, tell her I said hello and that I love her. I love you, Daddy. I don't think I even asked if everything is all right with you."

"I'm fine. You take care of yourself, honey, and let me have your phone number as soon as you get it. Then I can call you, and that will simplify things for both of us. Bye, sweetheart."

"Bye, Daddy."

Something in her daddy's voice made her wonder if he was really all right. It wasn't anything he said or even the way he said it. She just sensed something wasn't quite right.

CHAPTER 5

A few days later, Ann decided to make another trip into Manhattan, this time to check out the theaters. Off-Broadway was in its infancy when she was in New York in the spring of 1954, and a visit to this venue was not on the agenda for her study group. She was anxious to see some of the shows and hoped to get to meet some of the cast members. It would be less expensive than Broadway, and she had heard that in some of the theaters, cast members followed the curtain call by going into the audience to greet people. She hoped that was true.

Ann exited the subway station and leisurely strolled to the Rosso Theater. The marquee read, *Working the Crowd*. She purchased a ticket for the 2:00 p.m. performance and then decided to go back to the little coffee shop she'd passed. She should have time to have a cup of coffee and get back to the theater before curtain time. As she sat relaxing, her thoughts turned again to her new job and to Mr. Buffington, but the distraught feelings she'd had earlier were virtually gone. She was surprisingly chipper today and excited to be attending the theater.

When the curtain dropped on the third act, the audience applauded enthusiastically. The applause finally died, and the house lights came up. As it became evident this wasn't one of those theaters where cast members came into the audience, people from all over the theater began moving toward the aisles.

Ann rose to leave. As she did so, she noticed a girl, still in costume and makeup, emerge from a side door. The actress seemed to be searching for someone and was reluctant to leave until she had

23

found that person. Ann hesitated and then decided to go to the girl and congratulate her on her performance. She hoped she could get acquainted with the actress and maybe even ask her about casting and auditions. She wasn't sure how the girl would receive a stranger approaching her in this manner, but what did she have to lose?

"Hello. My name is Ann Jernigan. I'm so happy to have an opportunity to meet someone from the cast." The young actress seemed startled by the sound of a stranger's voice, and she turned abruptly toward Ann with an expression reflecting a combination of bewilderment and anger. When she gave no verbal response, Ann struggled to say something—*anything*—to escape the awkwardness of the girl's reaction: "The performance was . . . uh . . . outstanding. All the cast did . . . did such fine work. The . . . the staging and choreography were very impressive." Her tentative words sank into a sea of silence—elusive, meaningless. The girl's furrowed brow and vacant gaze sent Ann's mind racing. *This girl has a problem. How do I get out of this gracefully? Should I just leave?* Gathering confidence, Ann made one last effort to break through the invisible wall: "If you have time, would you please sign my program?"

The girl's eyes softened, and a faint smile came to thin lips expanded by bright red lipstick to make them look full and seductive. Her delicate features were lost in heavy makeup intended to give a hard, cold countenance to her innocent face. She took the program and asked, "What is your name again?"

"Ann . . . Ann Jernigan. I appreciate your willingness to take time to sign it for me."

"I'll be happy to. I apologize for being so distracted. My fiancé was supposed to be here, and I was looking for him. I broke the rules by coming out here still in costume, but when he didn't come backstage, I was afraid he'd leave and I wouldn't get to see him. I guess I wasn't very polite to you." She scrawled *To Ann—All my best!* over the bottom half of the program and signed it *Charlotte Patton*. She returned the program to Ann, lowered her eyes and mumbled, "I guess Tom's a no-show."

Ann was surprised that Charlotte Patton would speak so openly about her personal life to a complete stranger, but she took it as a sign that she might be willing to discuss musical theater with her. As Charlotte turned to walk away, Ann reached out and gently touched her arm, "If you don't have other plans, could I visit with you for a while after you get changed? I am an actress—at least an actress want-to-be—and I really don't know how to get started."

Charlotte looked at Ann questioningly for a moment; then with a conciliatory shrug, she nodded her head, "Sure, why not? I'll meet you in front of the theater in twenty minutes. I'm starved, and we can go to a little restaurant nearby. Hope you don't mind visiting while we eat."

"Oh, of course not. That would be great! I'll be waiting, and I'll buy dinner."

"Well, I can't beat a deal like that."

Charlotte disappeared back through the side door from which she had entered the auditorium. Ann thought about how lucky she was that Charlotte had come into the audience area at all, and even luckier that she was getting to visit with her. She felt bad for her that her fiancé hadn't come to see her perform, but it had turned out to be an opportunity for Ann to visit with someone who was involved in musical theater. It was step in the right direction, even if it was a baby step.

The sound of heels clicking on the sidewalk drew Ann's attention. Charlotte had evidently gone out a back door somewhere and was approaching from Ann's left. In the light of day, Ann was struck by the beauty of the face that had been hidden behind heavy makeup. The defensive, defeated person she had met following the performance had evolved into a charming young woman. "Harold's is far from being a swank restaurant, but they have really good food. Are you hungry?"

"I certainly am. I didn't have lunch today. What's their specialty?"

"Mainly soups, salads and sandwiches, and they sort of cater to those of us who can't afford to gain weight. I love their chef salad, and they make wonderful chicken noodle soup. They make their own dressings—low fat, low sugar but amazingly tasty."

"Sounds like my kind of place."

Harold's had a number of empty tables, but Charlotte motioned for Ann to follow her to a secluded little table in the back of the room. As they were taking their seats, Charlotte said, "I almost always sit at this table; most people don't even know it's here, and those who do usually prefer a larger one. I love that it's private and quiet."

A young man Charlotte called Donnie took their orders and then exited abruptly, leaving them alone. "Another reason I sit here," Charlotte explained, "is that Donnie rushes the order for me because he knows my schedule."

After a few moments, Ann ventured, almost apologetically, "Charlotte, I really appreciate—"

Before Ann could finish, Charlotte interrupted, "My friends call me Charlie. I'd like it if you'd call me that."

Ann smiled broadly, feeling Charlotte's invitation was a gesture of friendship—sort of an olive branch to mend an uncomfortable first meeting. "Okay. As I was saying, *Charlie*, I really appreciate your willingness to visit with me. I moved to New York earlier this month hoping to get into musical theater, but I don't know where to begin. I'm just a green kid from Texas, and although I performed in several musicals while I was at the University of Texas, as well as in community theater productions, I'm really unsure of myself here in New York. Do you have any advice?"

"What was your major?" Charlie asked.

"Vocal music with a minor in dance. I did have some classes that incorporated various aspects of theater, and in community theater, I played some straight acting parts. I don't really know how much any of that matters."

"Well, I don't know that I'm the best one to advise you, but I can tell you it requires patience. I've been in New York for three years, working in restaurants and hotels and going in for auditions at every opportunity, yet I'm still plugging along with minor parts, usually as part of the chorus, as I am in *Working the Crowd*. At least I'm on stage and getting paid for it, so I feel fortunate. A lot of people never make it that far."

"Is there some type of organization for people like me who are just trying to get started?" Ann asked.

"Well, subscribing to *Upstage*, a weekly newspaper for actors, will alert you to casting calls by various theaters and acting companies. Beyond that, I don't know of anything."

Just then Donnie returned with their food and placed it before them. They thanked him and continued talking between bites.

"Ann, my advice is to jump in and see what happens. Look for casting calls and every time you have opportunity to try out for a part, go for it. You won't get paid for it at first, but if you're good, you'll eventually attract some attention."

Ann and Charlie finished their meal and visited for a while before Charlie had to return to the theater and get ready for the evening performance. They had a lot in common. Charlie was from a small town in the state of Washington and had been heavily involved in community theater in Seattle. She was a college graduate and had majored in modern dance and minored in vocal music. Their credentials were very similar.

As they parted to go their separate ways, it was Charlie who suggested they meet in front of the theater again on the following Wednesday at 5:30 p.m. "Maybe I can have more information for you by that time. You caught me off guard today, but I'll have more time to think between now and next Wednesday."

Ann was flabbergasted! She couldn't believe someone she had met only this afternoon would volunteer to assist her in this way. She felt good about the affinity she had with Charlie. Once they got beyond the anxiety of that initial contact, Ann sensed a budding friendship.

On Thursday morning, Ann bounced out of bed early, and by 8:00 a.m., she was eagerly awaiting the arrival of someone from the telephone company to install her phone. She was sipping coffee when she heard a knock. She opened the door to a short, stocky man with

Arnold monogrammed on his shirt. She asked him in, and they exchanged information about the telephone installation. In less than an hour, Arnold picked up his bag of tools and handed Ann her telephone directory. "Your number is written inside the first page of the directory, and your installation charge will appear on your first bill." With that explanation, Arnold was out the door.

She opened the directory and found the number: BR 3-2104. She dialed Daddy's office.

"Rosemont Dairies. Paul Jernigan."

"Hi, Daddy. Yea! I finally have a telephone!" she exclaimed. "Are you ready to write down the number?"

Daddy chuckled, "Great! I'm ready."

As he wrote the number, Ann declared, "Now I expect *you* to call *me*."

"I certainly will—probably more than you want me to."

"That's impossible. Oh, by the way, I went to the theater yesterday, and I got to meet one of the cast members. In fact, we had dinner together. She's really nice, and I'm supposed to meet her again next week. Her name is Charlotte Patton, but she likes to be called Charlie. We hit it off really well, and I think she will be a lot of help to me in getting some auditions."

"That's great, honey, but be careful. I know you tend to trust everybody. I just don't want anybody to take advantage of you."

"I know you worry about me, Daddy, but I'm really not as gullible as you think I am."

"I really don't think that. It's just a daddy's nature to worry about his little girl, even if she is all grown up. I love you, sweetheart, and I'm glad you have your phone. Lil is home and doing well. You know she's a fighter, and it takes a lot to get her down. She got your card and really appreciated it. I'll give her your phone number, so you'll probably be getting calls from her too."

"Okay, Daddy, I'll let you go. I just wanted to touch base. Call me."

"I will, sweetheart."

"Tell Aunt Lil I love her. On second thought, I'll call her and tell her myself. Bye, Daddy."

"Good. She'll like that much better. Bye, hon. I love you."

Ann sensed a sadness in him. It was something she couldn't pinpoint, but he seemed to be forcing cheerfulness.

Trying to ignore these vague concerns, she concentrated on dialing Aunt Lil's number. Aunt Lil was excited to hear from her, as Ann had known she would be. After all, Aunt Lil was the closest thing Ann had to a mother, and the bond between them was strong. Her thoughts turned again to Charlie. She could hardly wait for next Wednesday.

CHAPTER 6

On Monday morning, Ann was waiting outside her apartment by 6:05. She wanted to make sure she was there when Mr. Buffington came to take her to his mother's house. She was anxious to start her new job, but in a way, she dreaded this first day. She didn't know what to expect, but she tried to convince herself that Mrs. Buffington would be a sweet little lady who would graciously receive her and be thankful for her help. Although she knew this might be far from an accurate description, she was determined to keep a positive attitude.

When Ann saw Mr. Buffington drive up, Ann hurried to meet him. "How are you today, Miss Jernigan?" Mr. Buffington asked as he opened the passenger door for her.

"I'm well, thank you and looking forward to meeting your mother."

"And she is anxious to meet you. I told her I thought she would like you—that you were a very mature young woman. Mother places great importance on maturity. Don't get me wrong, she appreciates humor and enjoys teasing so long as it's in good taste; she just doesn't like it to be demeaning or sarcastic."

Ann felt she had just been forewarned as to how *not* to conduct herself, but it was a warning she appreciated. "I'll remember that, sir. I certainly don't want to make a bad first impression.

"I feel strongly that the two of you will become friends. She may be distant for a while, but she will like you. I'm sure of that."

"I'm glad you're so optimistic, sir," Ann laughed, "and I certainly hope you are right. Our working relationship will be much more comfortable for both of us if we like and respect each other."

"Yes, and you have just mentioned another quality she values—respect. And I might add another—genuineness. She has an uncanny gift for spotting a fraud. If you're honest and genuine, she will admire you even if she doesn't always agree with you."

Mr. Buffington seemed to be making a great effort to acquaint her with his mother's likes and dislikes, and she didn't quite know what to make of it. Was he afraid she might do or say something that would spark his mother's disapproval?

The conversation died while Mr. Buffington navigated through heavy traffic, but when they turned onto a side street, he pointed out, "You'll notice the subway station is on this corner. We're almost there." He drove two blocks, turned a corner and drove two more blocks. then he pulled to the curb in front of the third house on their right. He got out of the car and moved to the passenger side to assist Ann. She was impressed by his attentiveness. This seemed to be a different man from the one whose manner she had earlier considered so insufferable. If he was indeed the man who had occupied the seat next to her on the airplane, he must be a Jekyll and Hyde.

The beautiful tree-lined median was a distinctive feature of the upscale neighborhood, and although there was no lawn, patches of ground cover, ivy growing on trellises, and flowers in planters nurtured a natural world atmosphere. "What a beautiful home," Ann commented.

"I grew up in this house. Although many years have passed since then, I still think of this house as home."

Mr. Buffington unlocked the door, walked into the foyer and held the door open for Ann to enter. He called to his mother, and a shrill, grainy voice answered from a nearby room, "In here, Nelson. Come on in."

As they moved from the foyer into a rather small sitting room, Mrs. Buffington, wearing a robe and house slippers, laid aside the newspaper she had been reading, and greeted her son with a loving squeeze as he leaned forward and gave her a peck on the cheek. "I've brought Miss Jernigan to meet you, Mother. You remember I told you she would be coming today to begin helping you each morning with bathing and dressing and also with your meals. Won't it be good to have someone pampering you like that? Taking Ann by the arm and ushering her between himself and his mother, Nelson Buffington said, "Mother, this is Miss Ann Jernigan; Miss Jernigan, this is my mother Sarah Buffington."

"It's so nice to meet you, Mrs. Buffington."

"And it's a delight to meet you, Miss Jernigan." The crackle in her voice was gone, but the high-pitched, almost musical quality Ann had heard earlier seemed to be her natural speaking voice. She was a tall, slender woman with large brown eyes and, for her age, amazingly taut olive skin. Ann envisioned the beautiful young woman she used to be.

"Well, Nelson, you didn't tell me she was pretty as well as smart."

Ann smiled modestly at Mrs. Buffington's compliment and responded, "Thank you, Mrs. Buffington, but I could make the same comment about you."

Mrs. Buffington chuckled softly and retorted, "That might have been true a long time ago, but those days are long gone. All my mirror shows me is skin draped over bones, but I'm thankful to still be here. Did Nelson tell you I am eighty-seven years old?"

"I don't think he did," Ann lied, "but if that's true, I'll just say you certainly don't look your age. I would have thought you were much younger." As soon as the words left her mouth, she remembered Mr. Buffington's warning about his mother's ability to spot a fraud, and Ann wondered if Sarah Buffington thought her words were insincere flattery. But why should she worry? She was being honest.

"In my mind, I *am* younger. I'm just having trouble convincing my body," Mrs. Buffington chuckled.

Ann could see that Mrs. Buffington was still mentally sharp, even if she did occasionally forget to turn off the water or remove a pan from the stove. She was far from senility, and Ann knew she would have to be on her toes to stay ahead of this proud, outspoken woman.

"I will have to leave soon, Mother, to meet with a 9:00 o'clock appointment, so I will show Miss Jernigan the rest of the house now and give her the menu for the week. We will be back in here in a little while. Do you need anything before we leave?"

"No, I'm fine. I'll continue reading the paper while you're gone."

"As you can see, Miss Jernigan, this is the room where Mother spends most of her waking hours, but her bedroom is adjacent to it through this door." He gestured to his left and led the way into her bedroom and adjoining bathroom. Ann followed him as he continued his explanation of where she could find his mother's clothes and the things she would need for her shower.

Next, they went into the kitchen where Mr. Buffington showed Ann the menus for the week and gave her a quick tour of the storage areas for various types of food and kitchen utensils. "I'm giving you a lot of information at once, Miss Jernigan. Do you have any questions?"

"I think I can figure it out, with your mother's help."

"Well, if you have any questions, don't hesitate to call me at my office."

"I'm sure I'll make it fine, sir."

When Mr. Buffington was gone, Ann and Mrs. Buffington were alone in the parlor. Ann broke the silence: "Well, Mrs. Buffington, Have you had your breakfast?"

"No, have you had yours?"

"No, but I'm not a big breakfast eater. Do you want to have breakfast before or after you shower and dress?"

"I'll have breakfast first."

"What would you like to eat?"

"I'd love bacon, eggs and toast, but I will enjoy it more if you will eat with me."

"Okay, maybe that will be a good way for both of us to start our day."

"Where did you grow up, Miss Jernigan? I can tell you're not a New Yorker."

"Now, how did you figure that out?" Ann giggled the words out of her mouth. "I grew up in a rather small town in Texas."

"I knew you were from somewhere in the South. I love your Southern way of talking."

"Well, in some parts of Texas, people speak with that charming slow drawl, but in North Texas where I grew up, the speech of most people is lacking in that quality."

"That's not true of you, Miss Jernigan. Your voice is delightful."

"Thank you, Mrs. Buffington. That's good to hear after having several people tease me about the way I talk, but I sometimes have trouble understanding native New Yorkers. I guess it's all a matter of regional dialect."

"Yes, but your voice has a cultured, resonant sound. Do you happen to be a singer?"

"What a nice thing for you to say! Yes, I majored in vocal music at the University of Texas. It's good to know my efforts paid off in some way."

"What are you doing in New York City? Do you hope to launch a singing career?"

"I want to be in musical theater. I'm hesitant to tell people that because their facial expression usually tells me they think I'm not living in the real world."

"Oh, I don't look at it that way. If we don't have the ambition and initiative to work for what we want out of life, then we have to settle for something less important to us. I believe in shooting for the stars, and if you don't make it, you still have the thrill of the effort and the satisfaction of knowing you tried."

Ann felt goose bumps rising on her arms. Mrs. Buffington's words sounded so much like what her mother had told her. She liked Mrs. Buffington and felt herself connecting with this woman whom she had known for less than two hours and who was old enough to be her grandmother. What an unexpected delight!

Ann made the bed and stood close by as Mrs. Buffington took her shower and dressed for the day; then they returned to the parlor. "I didn't sleep very well last night, and I think I will lie down on the sofa for a little while," Mrs. Buffington said. "You just go on with whatever you need to be doing, Miss Jernigan."

Ann watched as Mrs. Buffington gingerly sat down and stretched her body out on the sofa, and for the first time, she noticed a lack of confidence in the older woman. "Let me put this pillow under your head," Ann said as she tucked a puffy little throw pillow behind Mrs. Buffington's neck. "You know, I'm not used to being called *Miss Jernigan*," Ann said, "I'd feel more comfortable with *Ann*."

"All right, I'll call you Ann. Later, Ann, I'll probably need help getting up. Sometimes I lose my balance for a little while when I stand."

"We certainly don't want you to fall, so don't try getting up by yourself. Call when you need me. That's why I'm here—right?"

Mrs. Buffington laughed softly, "Right."

Before Ann could say anything else, Mrs. Buffington closed her eyes, and Ann knew if she wasn't already asleep, she soon would be.

CHAPTER 7

Ann tip-toed out of the room, and as she entered the kitchen, the phone rang. After the first ring, Ann answered, "Buffington residence."

"This is Richard Buffington, Sarah Buffington's grandson. I apologize for not remembering your name, but I assume you are the woman who is staying with Grandmother in the mornings."

"Yes, I am. My name is Ann Jernigan. I understand you will be here for lunch about 11:45 and will spend the afternoon with your grandmother."

"Well, that's what I'm calling about. My class has been canceled, so I will be there sooner than that. I have to go to the library for a little while, and then I'll be on my way. I should be there by 11:00."

"Okay, we'll expect you then. Thanks for calling. I can have lunch ready a little earlier."

"That sounds good, but I don't want to rush you."

"It isn't a problem. I'll have it ready about 11:30."

"I appreciate that. Thanks."

Ann glanced over at Mrs. Buffington to see if the phone woke her. When she saw she was still sleeping, she went back to the kitchen to begin preparing the two meals.

Later she heard the front door open and a deep male voice call, "Grandmother, I'm here." Richard had arrived and seemed to be a jovial young man. When he heard no response, he called again, "Grandmother, did you hear me?"

Sarah Buffington answered, "Yes, Richard. Come on into the parlor." Her sluggishness divulged that she had been awakened by the sound of his voice. She squinted at her wristwatch. "Is it already lunchtime? Where did the morning go?"

Richard laughed as he approached the sofa where she had now brought herself to a sitting position, "I'm a little bit early today. I called about 9:30 to let you and the lady who stays with you know my class had been canceled and that I would be here earlier than usual. Didn't she tell you?"

"No, she didn't. I wonder—"

Ann entered the room smiling ruefully. "I'm afraid I'm guilty, Mrs. Buffington, but you were sleeping and I didn't want to disturb you."

She walked over to Richard and extended her right hand. "I'm Ann Jernigan. I spoke with you on the phone."

Richard appeared stunned for a moment but soon regained his composure, shook her hand, and stammered, "I'm Richard . . . uh . . . Richard Buffington. It's a pleasure to meet you, Miss . . . is it Jernigan?"

"Yes, but your grandmother calls me Ann. You may call me that too." His gaze followed her as she walked over to his grandmother. "Would you be more comfortable in your chair, Mrs. Buffington?"

"Yes. Thank you, Ann." Sarah Buffington took Ann's arm, and Ann guided her to her chair.

"If you and Richard would like to eat early today, lunch will be ready in about fifteen minutes."

"Well, I'm sure Richard is starved," Mrs. Buffington declared.

"You know me, Grandmother. I'm always ready to eat."

"He never eats breakfast," Sarah Buffington said, tossing a reproachful glance at Richard. "I tell him he should, but he thinks he's smarter than I am."

Ann disappeared into the kitchen, and when she returned, Richard and his grandmother were laughing and talking. Ann was impressed by the manner in which they interacted.

"Well, if you are ready to eat, I'll help you to the bathroom to wash your hands, Mrs. Buffington," Ann said as she extended her hand to help Mrs. Buffington out of her chair. When they reached the bathroom, Ann asked, "Do you want some privacy in the bathroom or do you need me to help you?"

"Privacy please. You had better wait for me though, and if I'm not out in five minutes, come on in. You may have to pick me up from the floor."

"Well, if it isn't too much trouble, call me *before* you fall," Ann called as she closed the bathroom door behind her.

Mrs. Buffington let out a cackle and retorted, "Don't be sassy."

When Ann heard the lavatory water, she called, "Are you ready for me to come in?"

"Yes. I don't have my cane, so I guess you'd better let me hold your arm."

Back in the parlor, Mrs. Buffington moaned, "I slept the morning away; what a waste of time!"

"Sleep is never a waste of time," Ann declared. "It's your body's way of telling you it needs rest."

"Since you were sleeping, Mrs. Buffington, I couldn't ask whether you want to have lunch in the kitchen or the dining room. I set the kitchen table. I know it's small, but I think it will be large enough for three people if we don't clutter it with serving dishes. I'll just serve your plates and bring them to the table if that's all right with you."

"That's exactly the way I would do it, Ann."

They ate in silence for a few minutes before Richard asked, "Where are you from, Ann?"

"A town in Texas called Bonner Valley. It's not too far from Dallas. I have only been living in New York for about two weeks, so I'm still learning my way around."

Richard laughed, "Well, I've lived in Manhattan my whole life and I'm still learning my way around."

When they had finished eating, Mrs. Buffington and Richard went into the parlor, and Ann cleared the table and cleaned the kitchen. Back in the parlor, Ann found Mrs. Buffington in her chair. She had a ball of yarn in her lap and a wide band of knitting draped over the arm of the chair and cascading into a basket on the floor. Her fingers were busily adding to the pile. Richard was sitting on the sofa reading the paper. "It's only 12:45, Mrs. Buffington. I have another fifteen minutes before I leave," Ann said. "Is there anything else you'd like me to do?"

"I can't think of another thing, Ann. You might as well leave for today. I'll have to admit I wasn't sure I would like somebody banging my pots and pans around and making a mess in my kitchen, but you have proven your competence, and you've been gracious and delightful company. I'll look forward to seeing you tomorrow morning. By the way, I'll have Olivia—Olivia is my daughter and she stays with me at night—I'll have her leave the door unlocked so you can come on in when you get here. You run along now, dear, and I'll see you tomorrow."

Richard folded the paper and placed on the sofa beside him. Then he stood and volunteered, "I'll walk you to the subway, Ann. I need the exercise." Turning to his grandmother, he said, "You'll stay put while I'm gone for a few minutes, won't you, Grandmother?"

"Where would I go?" his grandmother teased.

He followed Ann out the front door. "I wanted to talk with you, Ann, out of range of Grandmother's hearing—not that there's anything secretive about what I have to say; it's just that Grandmother sometimes makes a big thing out of something insignificant." He paused, inspected his shoes for a moment, and then spoke softly, "I know you must have noticed my surprise when I met you, and I want to explain. I guess I assumed you would be an older woman, and when I met you, I . . . well . . . I just didn't expect to see such—" he hesitated, looked away, and then shyly divulged, "such an attractive young woman working as Grandmother's caregiver. I apologize if my gawking embarrassed you. It wasn't intentional."

Ann smiled at him. "There's no need to apologize. If I understood you correctly, you just paid me a compliment," she giggled. "I do understand your surprise, though. I guess most women are out there vying for opportunities to climb the corporate ladder, but I didn't want a full-time job right now. This job fits my needs, and I think I'm really going to enjoy your grandmother; I like her a lot."

"Yeah, most of the time she's a sweetheart, but she can be extremely intimidating if she isn't happy with a particular person or circumstance. You're seeing her good side because she likes you, and I don't see any reason for that to change."

"I hope you're right." They continued strolling along in silence for a while before Ann said, "I understand you're in graduate school. What are you studying?"

"Marketing. My BA is in business management. My dad owns a transport company, and he's paying for my post graduate work in exchange for my signing a two-year contract with him. I think he's trying to bait me; he hopes when the two years are up, I'll decide to stay with the company, but right now that's not my plan. What about you? What brought you all the way to New York from Texas?"

Ann didn't want to do too much explaining, so she answered, "Oh, I fell in love with New York City when I came here between my junior and senior years at the University of Texas, and I just decided I wanted to live here."

"You're a university graduate? I guess you know you could make a lot more money doing something other than taking care of my grandmother," Richard chuckled.

"I'm not so sure of that. Your dad is paying me well. I have no complaints."

"What was your major?"

"I majored in music, so you see that doesn't give me much of an edge in the business world. Does that help explain why I chose to work with your grandmother?"

"Well, I'm glad you did choose to do that so I could meet you," Richard said.

"Richard, you really don't need to walk all the way to the station with me; I'm a little bit concerned about leaving your grandmother alone for so long. I think you should go back to the house."

"Maybe you're right, but I hope we get to visit more later. You take care."

"You too," she replied. "I'll see you tomorrow."

Ann hastened her steps to the subway, her mind alive with thoughts about her first day on the job and about her unexpected fondness for Mrs. Buffington—and for Richard.

CHAPTER 8

The next day went by quickly and smoothly as Ann settled into her role as Sarah Buffington's caregiver. She visited with Richard briefly during lunch, but he seemed quiet and distant, and she didn't push making conversation with him. He didn't even to say good-bye to her when she left at 1:00 p.m.

On Wednesday morning, Ann and Mrs. Buffington were eating breakfast and visiting casually when Mrs. Buffington abruptly halted their chitchat and commanded, "Stop calling me Mrs. Buffington! You're making me feel like an old woman! Call me Sarah!" Her voice was stern and authoritative, but Ann was coming to realize this tone of mock austerity was typical Sarah Buffington. It was her way of teasing, and Ann admired the candor and wit of this proud lady who had always been self-sufficient and was fighting hard to remain that way.

"No woman as quick-witted and spry as you are should feel old, so *Sarah* it is."

"How old are you Ann?"

"I'm twenty-two."

"That means I'm only sixty-five years older than you. We could be sisters!"

"Great! I don't have any sisters, so I'll just adopt *you* as my sister," Ann teased.

"Your big sister. That means I give the orders," Sarah declared.

They both laughed at their silly bantering, and after breakfast, Sarah returned to the parlor and began reading the newspaper while Ann cleaned up the kitchen. Then they repeated the showering, dressing, and grooming routine. Ann made the bed, and they went back to the parlor where Sarah slowly lowered herself into her chair and picked up her knitting from the basket beside her.

When Ann was sure Sarah had everything she needed, she went to the kitchen to prepare lunch and dinner. Richard arrived and was once again the carefree young man she had met two days earlier. Yesterday's doldrums were gone.

"Hey, Grandmother, how's my favorite girl today?"

Her eyes never left her knitting as she retorted, "Your grandmother is just fine. I don't know how your favorite girl is."

Richard laughed, "I knew you'd have a comeback, Grandmother." He turned to Ann, who had just entered the room, and remarked, "I never get the last word with her!"

"I know exactly what you mean. She's too sharp for me," Ann said.

Sarah guffawed at their accolades, but Ann knew she delighted in having them praise her astuteness. It had always been her forte, and Ann could tell she was afraid of having it slip from her grasp.

Instead of going into the parlor with Sarah when lunch was over, Richard began helping Ann clear the table. She objected when he took a dish towel from a drawer and began drying the dishes. "This is my job, Richard. You go visit with your grandmother."

"I'll have plenty of time to visit with her this afternoon. I want to visit with you for a little while. What would be the chances of a guy taking you out to a movie or something some evening?" He looked at her with an impish grin.

"Well, it would depend on who the guy is and which night it is. I'm a busy girl, you know." She giggled and hoped he understood the irony of her last statement. "No one in the world has a schedule as free as mine," she admitted. "I don't become bored easily, but I've been pretty close to it since all my family and friends chose to stay in Texas when I moved to New York."

His silly grin turned into a shy smile. "I'm the guy, and how would tomorrow evening fit your *unbusy* schedule?"

"Tomorrow evening would be fine."

"Okay, good. Give me your address and I'll pick you up about 6:45. Does that sound all right to you?"

"That sounds perfect. You may have trouble finding a place to park, so I'll meet you outside in front of my apartment building."

They finished the dishes together, and she wrote her address and telephone number on a pad she kept in her purse. When she handed the paper to Richard, he smiled and said, "Oh, this is in Brooklyn. I'm familiar with this area, so I won't have any trouble finding you."

Ann led the way into the parlor where Sarah was lost in her knitting. She was laboriously manipulating the yarn, her fingers moving slowly and clumsily as she struggled with the needles. Ann noted the difference in this performance compared with yesterday when her fingers had rapidly gobbled up the yarn from her lap. "Sarah," Ann called.

Still grasping the knitting needles, Sarah lowered her hands and looked up at Ann blankly. Her mind had obviously wandered, and the cunning Sarah had been replaced with an innocuous, naïve child.

Richard was standing behind Ann, and she turned to him, her expression telling him something was wrong. Richard moved around Ann and squatted down beside his grandmother's chair. She had not resumed her knitting, and when Richard placed his hand on hers, he found them limp and clammy. "Grandmother, say my name." She looked at him but didn't respond. "Grandmother, do you know who I am?"

"Yes," she whispered.

"Who am I?"

"Ri—char—" she said softly, the word broken and trailing off at the end.

"Would you like to lie down?"

"Yes," she whispered.

Richard replied, "Grandmother, I'm going to carry you to the sofa, and Ann is going to call Dr. Anderson." Sarah was silent. He told Ann she could find Dr. Anderson's phone number on the list of emergency numbers in the kitchen desk drawer, and Ann disappeared into the kitchen. Richard lifted his grandmother's limp body, and when he had her situated on the sofa, he placed a pillow under her head and covered her with an afghan. "Is that better, Grandmother? Are you comfortable?" She didn't answer but closed her eyes, and Richard slipped into the kitchen to join Ann. "Did you call Dr. Anderson's office?"

"Yes. I spoke with his nurse and described Sarah's condition to her. She said she would call right back after she had a chance to talk with Dr. Anderson, but she said she was almost sure he would want her taken by ambulance to the hospital. Richard, do you think she will be all right?" Ann's voice betrayed her concern.

"I don't know, but I think the fact that she is responsive and knows me is a good sign. I'm afraid she's had a stroke."

"I thought of a stroke too, but I don't know much about the symptoms of stroke. I'm so glad you are here. I don't know how I'd deal with this if I were alone."

The phone rang and Richard answered. It was Dr. Anderson himself, so Ann went back into the parlor to check on Sarah.

Ann touched Sarah's forehead but detected nothing unusual. She spoke to her, and Sarah opened her eyes. "Are you feeling any better?" Ann asked softly.

"Tired," Sarah answered. Then she closed her eyes again. Ann pulled a little foot stool close to the sofa and sat down beside her. She felt helpless, but at least she was there in case Sarah roused and needed something.

When Richard came back into the parlor, he motioned for Ann to go into Sarah's bedroom. He followed her and spoke in muted tones, "Dr. Anderson's thinking is in line with ours concerning the possibility of a stroke. He is sending an ambulance, and it should be on the way now. She has a little suitcase on the top shelf of her closet; would you pack it for a hospital stay?"

After Ann packed the bag, she joined Richard, who had walked back into the parlor and was crouched down beside his grandmother. She appeared to be sleeping, so he didn't disturb her.

Ann set the bag down beside the sofa and asked Richard if he had called his dad or his aunt to let them know what had happened.

He said he had called his dad and that he was meeting them at the hospital.

"I'm going to ride in the ambulance with her, and I'll decide what to do after I find out more about what's going on with her. There's no need for you to stay longer. I've imposed on your time by having you stay this long."

Ann looked at her watch and saw it was almost 2:00 o'clock. With all that had happened, she had completely forgotten she was supposed to meet Charlie after the matinee today. She hated to stand her up, but she didn't want to abandon the Buffingtons. "Are you sure you don't want me to be on standby in case you need me?"

"No, you go on home. I have your address and phone number, so I'll call you when I know more."

"I do want you to keep me informed about your grandmother's condition, but I just remembered an appointment this afternoon. It isn't anything important; it's just that I don't know how to get in touch with the friend I'm supposed to meet to let her know I won't be there. If you'd rather I would stay home and wait for your call, though, I'm sure she will understand."

"Oh, no. That's not necessary. I'll call you tonight. What time do you think you'll be home?"

"Probably about 7:00 or 7:30."

"Okay. I'll call you sometime after 7:30."

The doorbell rang and Richard greeted the medics. "I'm Richard Buffington, and if you'll follow me, my grandmother is resting on the sofa; she's very weak. Did Dr. Anderson give you any information about her?"

"Yes, he said it was a possible stroke. We know what to do."

"Will it be all right if I ride with you? I'd like to be there when you take her in."

"Absolutely. Just let us get her into the ambulance first. A medic will be working on one side of her, but you can sit on the other side. It might help her to know you are with her."

"Thanks. I really appreciate that."

When the medics went out the front door with Sarah Buffington on the gurney, Richard grabbed his briefcase and went out behind them. Ann picked up Sarah's little suitcase and followed him outside. "Don't forget this, Richard," she called as she held the bag in front of her.

"Thanks, Ann. I guess I'm not thinking straight right now. I appreciate your help, and I'll call you tonight."

"I'll be waiting to hear from you. You said you're optimistic, Richard; so am I. I'm expecting to hear a good report. Take care."

Richard looked back at her as the attendant held the door for him to get into the ambulance, and Ann could see the strain in his face. She sensed that Richard and his grandmother had a special bond, and she was reminded of the relationship that had existed between her and her mother. Her heart went out to him. She watched the ambulance until it was out of sight. Then she walked slowly to the subway station, dazed by the events of the day.

CHAPTER 9

Ann was unable to find a seat on the subway, so she propped her body against a pole and held on to keep her wobbly legs from giving way beneath her. She glanced at her watch as she exited the car. It was 3:58, and she had over an hour to kill before she would meet Charlie in front of the theater. Her whole body felt tired and heavy as she plodded along 47th Street, still trying to digest all that had happened over the past few hours.

She had passed a little outdoor coffee shop before her mind processed that this would be a good place to rest for a while. She went back and found an unoccupied table at the edge of the area. As she lowered herself into the chair, she felt an outflow of the tension and weariness that had been trapped inside her. Despite the chair's merciless iron frame, it was good to find relief for her trembling legs.

Almost immediately, a timid voice asked, "What can I get for you?" Ann looked up into the face of a teenager with a dimpled smile and red-rimmed eyeglasses framing blue-green eyes. Her dull brain finally realized she was expected to order.

"Oh . . .um . . . a glass of iced tea, please."

The teenager disappeared and soon returned with her order. She fished in her purse for change and found two quarters. She handed them both to the waitress and told her to keep the change. She knew she had vastly over-tipped, but right now she didn't care. She just wanted to be alone for a little while and get a grip on her emotions before she met Charlie.

Waiting outside the theater and watching as the audience filed out, Ann decided her respite at the coffee shop had been a life saver. It had not only given her time to relax physically, but it had also helped her recapture rational thinking that had taken flight when she was faced with a crisis. She wondered how she would have reacted to Sarah's sudden illness if Richard hadn't been there. She admired the way he had taken care of the situation. He seemed instinctively to know the right things to do.

Before long, Ann heard the familiar clicking of heels on the sidewalk. She looked in the direction of the sound and saw Charlie approaching. Ann waved and Charlie returned her greeting with a smile and a quickened pace. "It's so good to see you again, Charlie. I've been looking forward to our get-together today."

Without breaking her brisk stride, Charlie circled her arm in Ann's, pulling her into cadence with her. "Me too," she answered. "Believe it or not, I don't have many friends among the cast and crew. Maybe it's just my insecurity speaking, but they all seem a little uppity. Are you ready for dinner?"

"I'm ready," Ann said.

"Is Harold's okay with you again today? It's the best place I know that is close enough to give me time to relax and eat and still get back to the theater for the next show."

"Absolutely! I hope we can get that same little table we had before. I felt we could talk there without everybody around us listening in."

"Yeah, me too," Charlie agreed. "Have you had a good week?"

Ann sighed deeply and hesitated a moment before answering, "Yes and no. It's a long story, and I won't burden you with it."

"Hey, you really have me curious now! What has happened? Have you had an audition? It's no big deal if you were turned down for a part. That happens all the—"

"No," Ann interrupted, "I haven't really had time even to think about auditions or anything related to the theater." Ann went on to explain her new job with Sarah Buffington and what had happened earlier in the day. "The doctor thinks she may have had a stroke. It was such a shock that this happened because, despite her frailty, she's usually so full of life. She's really a great lady!"

"Oh, what a horrible experience for you! What did you do? Will she be all right?"

"Thankfully, her grandson Richard was there, and he took charge. He's optimistic that she will be okay. He's supposed to call me tonight to give me a report. Well, enough about that. Let's talk about something more pleasant. How has your week gone?"

"It's had its ups and downs. I'll tell you about it over lunch."

At Harold's, Charlie led the way to the same little table they had last week, and Donnie came and took their orders. For a while after he left, they sat quietly. Charlie seemed lost in her thoughts, and Ann remembered back to last week when Charlie's fiancé had failed show up for her performance. She wondered if Charlie's pensiveness had something to do with him.

Suddenly Charlie's mind returned to the present and she announced, "Well, we all got a pay raise this week; I'm happy about that."

"Wow, that's great! Well, it sounds like you *did* have a good week."

"Yeah." Then with a dramatic flair, Charlie tossed her long brown hair over her shoulder, stretched both arms into the air and belted out, "Oh, what a beautiful day!" They both burst into laughter, and Ann wondered what the people at other tables thought of Charlie's impromptu performance; they would have to be deaf not to have heard it.

As suddenly as Charlie's elation had been born, it died, and her sagging shoulders and desolate expression now told a different story. Her words came haltingly, "But my whole week hasn't been great. Tom and I had a . . . we . . . he . . . broke off our relationship."

"Oh, I'm so sorry, Charlie. I know that was painful."

Charlie was silent for a moment; then seeming to slough off her despondency, she straightened her back and declared, "Yes, it was, but I guess it was really best. He never understood why I have to work so much. To him, it seemed I never had time for us to be together. He knew from our first date what I do professionally, and if he had really loved me, he would have been able to accept my crazy work schedule.

I guess it's better to find out how he feels now instead of later. By the way, I have something for you."

Charlie pulled a paper from her purse, unfolded it and placed it on the table before Ann. "I brought you the names of some acting companies and theaters, and I included the name and telephone number of the director of each one. I also listed contact information for Zach Minelli, my agent. Zach is one of the few who is taking on inexperienced clients. You may or may not want an agent at this stage of your career. Sometimes it's better to wait and see how successful you are on your own. Some people have a knack for selling themselves and had rather go about it that way." Ann skimmed the page as Charlie was talking, and when Charlie looked at Ann, she saw tears welling in Ann's eyes. "Ann, what's the matter? Did I say something that hurt your feelings?"

"Oh no, Charlie, just the opposite," Ann said softly, "I'm just amazed that you, with your busy schedule, would take time to do this for me. We have known each other for only a week, and you've gone out of your way to help me. I don't know how I can ever thank you."

"Oh please! You're making it sound like I spent hours getting this together. It took me all of fifteen minutes. I'm glad you appreciate it, but it was no trouble at all, so get that miserable look off your face."

A whispered thank you escaped Ann's lips.

Donnie brought their orders and they continued visiting as they ate, sharing their hearts with each other the way good friends do. Ann felt as if she had known Charlie forever. She walked back to the theater with her, and they made small talk and giggled along the way.

Before saying good-bye, they agreed to meet again next Wednesday after the matinee. When they had parted last week, Ann had sensed the beginnings of a friendship, but she couldn't be sure Charlie wasn't just being benevolent—helping a struggling want-to-be actress the way she might pick up a stray puppy because she didn't want to see it starve. Today, though, she got the impression that Charlie wanted her friendship as much as she wanted Charlie's. She hoped that was true.

CHAPTER 10

Ann had been anxiously watching the clock, and when the phone rang at 7:35, she pounced on it.

"Hi Ann. I have good news. Dr. Anderson said Grandmother did have a stroke but that she should fully recover without any long-term effects. She has some memory loss, but he said that's not uncommon. She doesn't remember the ambulance ride or being in the emergency room or even what happened at the house this morning. He says those memories may never come back, but since she doesn't seem to have trouble remembering other things, we shouldn't worry about it. He's hospitalizing her for a few days to do tests to determine treatment to prevent another stroke.

"My dad is here, and he said to tell you he would call to let you know when you need to return to work. I guess there's no need for you to go to the house if Grandmother isn't there."

"Oh, of course not. I'll just wait until I hear from him. Thank goodness she's going to be all right! By the way, Richard, about our date tomorrow night, I know you'll want to be with your grandmother as much as possible and that you lost valuable study time today, so I'll just see you after Sarah goes home from the hospital."

"I don't think the fact that Grandmother is in the hospital should change anything. Unless something else happens between now and then, I want us to plan on tomorrow night. Same plan unless I call you otherwise. Okay?"

"Okay, if you really want it that way. I just don't want you to feel obligated to do that."

"Obligated? I'm not taking you out because I feel obligated! I'm taking you out because I want to be with you. Got it?"

"Yes," she said softly. "Thank you for calling and I'll see you tomorrow night."

"I'm looking forward to it. Bye for now."

Ann sat for a long time thinking about Sarah and Richard, playing the morning over and over in her mind. She remembered the distraught look on Richard's face when he had looked back at her as he was getting into the ambulance. It was good to hear him cheerful again. Within a few hours, things had gone from being terribly wrong to being right again. For her, things were right not only because of the good news about Sarah, but also because of her friendship with Charlie.

She remembered the list Charlie had given her, took the paper from her purse and looked over the names and telephone numbers. *No matter what Charlie said, I know it took a long time to gather and type up all this information*, she mused.

She decided to call Daddy. She hadn't talked to him since she had started her job, and she knew he was interested in finding out how things were working out. She had a lot to tell him. As she dialed the number, she hoped Daddy would be the one to answer. She knew from past experiences that immediately after Nora's hello, she would call, "Paul, Ann's on the phone." Then she would put the receiver down and Ann would hear her footsteps walking away. Never in Ann's memory had Nora been willing to carry on a conversation with her, and it wasn't because Ann hadn't tried.

"Hello."

It was unfamiliar male voice. Thinking she might have a wrong number, Ann inquired, "Is this the Jernigan residence?"

"Yeah, who's this?" was the curt reply.

"Well, who is this?" Ann countered.

"I asked you first, Missy," snapped the surly voice at the other end of the line.

"I'm Ann Jernigan, and I would like to speak with my father, Paul

Jernigan." Ann's blood was beginning to boil. *Stay in control*, she told herself; *don't let this guy rattle you.*

"Oh, he ain't here."

"You still haven't told me who you are."

"I'm Johnny Rhodes, Nora's son. I don't know when Paul will git back. He just left and didn't say nothin' about when he'd be comin' back."

Ann wondered if Johnny was eating. His voice was louder than necessary, but his words sounded garbled and squishy.

"Well, then please ask him to call me when he comes home, and I hope you have a good visit with your mom."

"Oh, I ain't visitin'; I live here."

Ann was speechless! *He lives there? He lives there, but I wasn't welcome to live there the year before I moved to New York?* When she regained her composure, she asked, "Oh? Are you in between jobs or something?"

"Naw, Paul gave me a job at the plant, and I didn't have no place to live, so Mom said I could come live with her and Paul."

Ann wanted to end the conversation quickly to keep from saying something she might regret. "Well, again, please have my dad call me when he returns."

With an air of mock servitude, Johnny pitched his voice into a high falsetto and whined out the words, "I'll most certainly do that, Ma'am, I'll most certainly do that."

She returned the receiver to its base without responding to his blatant accusation that she had somehow suggested his inferiority.

It was almost 10:00 o'clock when her daddy called. His voice sounded tired. "Hello, honey. I'm sorry I wasn't here when you called. How are you?"

"*I'm* just fine, Daddy, but *you* sound awful. Are you sure you are all right?"

"I'm okay, sweetheart, just a little weary."

"Daddy, I'm going to come right out and ask you this, even though it's none of my business. Is Johnny living with you and Nora?"

"Yeah, for now. Listen, honey," he whispered, "it's a long story, and I can't talk about it right now. I need to talk to you, though. Could I call you from the plant at my lunch break tomorrow? Oh, that won't do . . . you'll be at work and . . . well . . . I'll just—"

"No, Daddy, it's okay," she interjected. "I'll be home tomorrow. I'll be here all day, at least until after I hear from you."

"Okay. I'll call on my lunch break. That will be about 1:00 o'clock New York time. I need to call collect, but I'll send you some money for your phone bill. I intended to do that anyway. Hon, I need to get off the phone, but I'll talk to you tomorrow. Don't you worry about me. I'm okay. I love you, sweetheart."

Don't you worry about me echoed in Ann's mind. Daddy's voice had been somber, and she knew something was wrong. She struggled to sleep, but her mind was cluttered with questions about her daddy's predicament.

CHAPTER 11

She grabbed the receiver after the first ring shattered the quiet at 1:40 p.m. The operator asked if she would accept a collect call from Paul Jernigan. She answered in the affirmative and was greeted by Daddy's futile attempt to sound casual: "Hi, honey. I'm a little later calling than I'd planned to be, but I had some interruptions."

"That's fine, Daddy. As I told you last night, I don't have to go anywhere today. You still sound tired. Is everything all right with you?"

"Yeah, I'm okay, but I need to talk to you about something. I hadn't intended to tell you about this right now, but after your conversation with Johnny last night, I know I need to explain. I don't know how to tell you this except just to come right out and say it. I'll soon be telling Nora that our marriage isn't working and that I plan to file for divorce. I don't know how she'll react to it, but I've come to realize she doesn't care much for me anyway. I don't know how all this will turn out, hon, but the main thing I want to tell you is that I plan to go tomorrow and try to change the name on the deed to the house. I want to take my name off and put the deed solely in your name."

"But Daddy, it's *your* house, and it should be in *your* name."

"Well, I know, and we may do something about that after all this divorce thing is settled, but let me explain why I want to change it. Texas is a community property state, which means Nora will—or could—get half of everything I have. I haven't seen a lawyer yet, but I'm hoping there's some type of disclaimer on that law in the case of

55

a second marriage where children from a first marriage are involved. It may be that the law pertains only to property and money acquired during the marriage; in that case, she couldn't get the house anyway since I already owned it before we got married.

"I'm just going to have to check all this out, and I don't plan to say anything to Nora about it until I've done that. I don't even know if deeding the house to you is legal without Nora signing off on it too, which, of course, she won't do. I just have a lot of things to sort through, sweetheart, but I'm getting there, so I don't want you to let this worry you."

"But I do worry about you, Daddy. I'm sorry you're having to deal with all this, but to tell the truth, I'm relieved. Several times, I have detected in your voice that something was wrong, and I've been afraid you were sick with some terrible illness."

"No, honey, it's nothing like that. Now about Johnny living with us—I didn't even know Nora had told him he could live here until he just showed up at the house with his belongings. I realize now I should never have hired him. He doesn't like taking orders or following instructions, and everybody at the plant resents him. He came in acting like he owns the place. If he keeps behaving the way he has been, I'll have to let him go.

"Since I've told you this much, I might as well tell you what has brought this thing to a head. Several days ago, I found out Nora has been seeing another man, and that explains a lot about her actions toward me lately. She isn't aware I know about her affair, though, and I'm not going to say anything to her about it until I check out a few things. I don't want to make her look bad in the eyes of the people in town, so I'm trying to handle this discreetly.

"I probably shouldn't be telling you all this before I say something to Nora. I guess I'm being unfair to her to go about things in this way, but she certainly hasn't been fair with me, or with you either, for that matter.

"I just want you to know I'll do everything in my power to protect your rights in this thing. My will states that the house and everything else I have is yours after my death, but I made that will right after your mother died, and I don't know how valid it is now that I'm married to Nora. I guess I didn't do a very good job of taking care of business before I jumped into a second marriage. I just never dreamed it would turn out like this."

"Oh, Daddy, a lot has been going on with you that I didn't know anything about."

"Yeah, well, even before I found out about this other man, I knew something was wrong. I just didn't know what it was. Now I know. I kept thinking things would get better, but I've just been kidding myself for a long time. Nora has been using me, and I guess I was blind to it. I thought I knew her, but she isn't the woman I married.

"I didn't mean to unload on you like this, kiddo, but you're all I've got, and I'm not going to let anybody do anything that will hurt you—not if I can prevent it. I think I let that happen to some extent anyway, but I can't undo what's been done. I can only tell you that's all going to change."

"I hurt for you, Daddy, because I know your heart is broken."

"Well, I'd be lying if I said I wasn't hurt by it, but after I got past the initial shock, a lot of things came into focus. I'm especially sorry for the way Nora acted toward you. I guess for a long time, I didn't see what was happening. I noticed that you weren't coming home very often your senior year, but I thought that was because you were overloaded with work at school. When you decided to move in with Lil and Ben last year, I just thought you felt it would be unpleasant to live here with another woman running things in the house that held so many memories of your mother.

"Quite a while before you left for New York, I began to think about how Nora had acted toward you, and I was embarrassed by it; then I started resenting it. In the last few days, my eyes have really been opened. I know she made you feel unwelcome, and I'm sorry I let that happen."

"Daddy, I love you, and you don't need to feel guilty about anything that has happened. I have always known you loved me, and that's all that matters to me. I just want you to be happy. I wish

I could be there to help you through this. Do you want me to come home for a while? I know it would be awkward for me to stay in your house, especially with Johnny there, but I could stay with Aunt Lil and Uncle Ben."

"No, honey. All I want from you is understanding. I can handle the rest of it. I already feel better just getting all this out in the open. It has been bottled inside me while I've tried to hide it from you and everybody else. Living with a secret gets pretty lonesome."

Ann had surprised herself by keeping her emotions in control as her daddy bared his soul to her in a way he had never done before. Listening to his last statement, however, produced that aching in her throat that always came when she was trying to choke back tears.

"I'm so sorry, Daddy. I wish you had told me sooner. I don't know of anything I could have done to help except listen when you needed to talk, but at least I could have done that. I wish you could come up here for a visit. I think you need a hug from me, and I know I need one from you."

When Ann heard his sigh and muffled chuckle, she knew her daddy was back. The heavy-hearted man she had been listening to had reverted to the daddy she had always known.

"Yes, you're right. I do need a hug from you; in fact, I need a lot of hugs from you. I can't come now, but as soon as I get all this behind me, I'll come to see you. I guess I'd better get off the phone, hon. One of the guys needs to see me about something, but I'll keep in touch."

"Okay, Daddy. We'll talk later. I hope things go all right when you talk to the lawyer. I love you."

"I love you, too, honey. I'll call when I have some news. Bye, sweetheart."

"Bye, Daddy. Take care of yourself."

He didn't reply, but she knew he was doing the best he could. She had a strange feeling as she returned the receiver to its cradle. It was a mixture of sadness and relief and even a type of happiness. She wasn't happy that Daddy was getting a divorce, yet she knew in her heart that she could never have that feeling of belonging and family togetherness with Nora. It was the prospect of having that feeling restored that brought her happiness. *Divorce* had always been a dirty word in her family—the profanity of something sacred. She hoped Daddy wouldn't feel like a failure because his marriage to Nora didn't work out as he had thought it would. He deserved happiness.

CHAPTER 12

Richard had called and asked to change their date to 6:30. It was already 6:25, and Ann wanted to be outside when he arrived. She quickly locked her door behind her and hurried down the stairs. As she exited the building, she pulled her sunglasses from her purse and slipped them over eyes. It was an unusually warm day, and she decided to wait in the shade of the porch. Soon she caught sight of Richard's red convertible, top down, crawling along the street with a handsome young man at the wheel. She waved and virtually flew down the stairs. Richard double parked, got out of the car and walked around to the passenger side just in time to open the door for her.

She was looking forward to this evening with Richard, but her daddy's difficult situation was lurking in the shadows of her mind like distant rumbles of thunder. She didn't want this distraction to ruin their date, so she forced herself to concentrate on what promised to be a pleasant evening.

"Well, that was good timing; I just now came outside to wait for you," Ann commented as she got into the car.

"It's good you didn't come out earlier. It's too hot to be outside today. Maybe it will be cooler after the sun goes down." Richard moved to the driver's side and slid under the wheel. "How are you this evening?" he asked as he nudged his way into the line of traffic.

I'm fine," she replied cheerfully. "How are you?"

A grin spread across his face as he glanced at her. "I'm great *now*."

Her heart did a little flip-flop, but she didn't want to make more of his comment than was intended, so she directed the conversation to what she knew would be safe territory. "And how is your grandmother? Any more news?"

"She seems to be all right. She ordered me out of her room a little while ago because she was afraid I would keep you waiting, so I'd say she's back to her normal self."

"Sounds like it," Ann giggled. Then turning serious, she added, "I'm so thankful the stroke didn't leave her impaired in any way."

"Me too," Richard sighed. "We're very lucky. Changing the subject—I wanted to come earlier so we can go to dinner. What time did you have lunch?"

"It was about 2:30, I think."

"What do you say to a movie first and then dinner?"

"Sounds good to me," she answered.

"There's a murder mystery playing at a theater not far from here, so we can make it for the early showing. How do you feel about murder mysteries?"

"I love them if they're not too gruesome."

"This is a Cagney movie. Maybe it will be all right.

"You asked about Grandmother. Dr. Anderson thinks she can probably go home day after tomorrow. Of course, we don't know what time she'll be dismissed, so Dad said to tell you he would call you."

"That will be fine. I'm ready to go back to work any time. It's strange, I've known your grandmother less than a week, but I feel as if I've known her forever. I really enjoy being with her."

"Well, I think she feels the same about you; I'm glad you two are hitting it off so well."

As the movie started, Richard reached over and took her hand in his; then with a histrionic flair, he whispered, "I'll hold your hand so you won't be scared."

Ann giggled quietly, "Thanks. That's a good idea." Amused with themselves, they exchanged knowing glances and chuckled at their adolescent behavior.

When the movie was over, he released her hand, stepped into the aisle, and ushered her in front of him. Then, taking her hand again, he escorted her through the crowd and out to the car. Backing out of his parking spot, Richard asked, "Do you like Italian food?"

"I don't know that I've ever had anything Italian other than spaghetti and meat balls, but I like that."

"There's a great little Italian restaurant near here. They have all sorts of Italian cuisine, and they serve this wonderful hot garlic bread they bake at the restaurant. You can usually smell it baking even before you walk in the door."

"Oh, you've said the magic words. Hot bread is my downfall. That sounds wonderful."

As they perused the menu at Ascoli's, Richard teased, "With all these choices, surely you don't plan to stick to spaghetti and meat balls."

"No, I think I'll be adventurous and have lasagna. I've never eaten it, but at least I know what that is, which is more than I can say about some of the items on this menu."

After they finished eating, they lingered at the table and continued chatting and laughing together. The anxiety Ann had felt earlier had melted away, and she was truly enjoying herself. She felt at ease with Richard, and she sensed the feeling was mutual.

Riding along on the way back to her apartment, Richard asked if he could see her again tomorrow night. "How would you feel about an evening of dancing?" he asked. "There's a supper club in Manhattan I think you would enjoy. It doesn't have the status of a lot of the other clubs, but they have good food and a great band."

"I'd love that. I haven't been dancing in ages."

In the next block down from Ann's apartment, a car pulled away from the curb, and Richard accelerated and quickly maneuvered into the vacant spot. He went around to the passenger side, opened Ann's door, and took her hand to assist her.

They walked along silently for a while, hand-in-hand, an invisible blanket of warm, moist air settling over them. Ann thought about how different the neighborhood seemed at night. It was almost midnight, and the pedestrian traffic was virtually gone. Somewhere a siren wailed. Traffic hummed and horns blared on nearby streets. An el train ripped the air, quietly at first, and then grew to a thunderous crescendo that quickly faded into the blackness. Lights pulsated on the tops of skyscrapers, and off in the distance a search light made its predictable cycle.

"It's still warm, but it's actually a pretty nice night," Richard assessed.

"Yes, it is. If it weren't so humid, it would be a perfect summer evening, but I guess we can't order weather with just the ingredients we like," she chuckled.

Conversation lulled for a few minutes before Richard launched into a new subject: "You told me you graduated from the University of Texas and that you majored in music. What exactly do you plan to do with that degree? Do you want to be a teacher?"

"Well, to be more specific, I majored in vocal music and minored in dance."

"Aha—so you're a singer and dancer. I think I'm beginning to see your real reason for moving to New York City. What you said about falling in love with New York—that isn't really why you moved here, is it?"

"No, I guess not, but I didn't lie to you; I just didn't tell you the whole truth. I had just met you when we had that conversation, and I didn't want you to think I was living in a fantasy world."

"Believe me, I would never think that about you. I guess your ambition is to perform professionally, but how do you go about getting the opportunity to do that?"

She laughed and admitted, "I don't know. I'm just sort of feeling my way along and trying to figure that out. I went to an off-Broadway musical last week, and I met one of the cast members, a girl named Charlotte Patton. Charlie—which is what she likes to be called—and I got together right after the matinee, and we really hit it off. We met again yesterday, and she gave me a list of several acting companies and theaters, along with the names of people to contact. I plan to start by following up on her leads."

"But Ann, do you really think you can trust her? You just met her last week. Do you know anything about her except that she's an actress?" The urgency in his voice was not only puzzling but also frustrating to Ann. What gave him the right to censor her choice of friends?

"Yes, I do trust her. What would she have to gain by leading me down a wrong path? And Richard, I just met you earlier *this* week. Can I trust you?"

He coughed into his fist and became silent. Ann didn't know how to interpret his reaction. She didn't want to offend him. "I do trust you, Richard, but do you see my point? I trust you because of what I see and sense in you as a person, not because of what I know *about* you. It's the same with Charlie."

"I understand what you mean, but I don't think you can compare your acquaintance with *her* to your acquaintance with *me*. You know I'm part of a respected family. You don't know anything about Charlie's family background, do you?"

"Well, I don't walk up to people and ask for their pedigree before I'm willing to be friends with them, if that's what you mean."

They both laughed. Then he suddenly came to a complete stop, took both her hands in his and turned to face her. After staring into the darkness for a moment, he shifted his gaze and looked into her eyes. "I don't mean to be critical. How you feel about Charlie isn't any of my business. I just don't want you to be disappointed if she lets you down."

Then he did something that completely surprised her: He put both his arms around her, drew her close to him and whispered into her ear, "I would never do anything to hurt you. I'm just concerned. I want what's best for you." He stepped back, gently cupped her face in his hands, and leaned forward and kissed her softly on the lips.

The breath instantly left Ann's body; she paused before speaking, "Richard, I like you, and I have really enjoyed being with you tonight. I don't know exactly how to say this—I'm not trying to discourage a relationship between us, but maybe we shouldn't rush things."

He laughed quietly, "I hadn't planned to do that, but walking along in the moonlight with you . . . I . . . well . . . I'm sorry if I was out of line."

A coy smile came to her lips, and she weighed his flimsy excuse before responding, "You certainly know how to say sweet things, and it was a sweet kiss. I guess you noticed I didn't put up much resistance, so maybe it was no more your fault than mine."

A frown furrowed his brow as he declared, "*Fault!* I'll plead guilty to . . . well . . . maybe to a mistake, but not to a fault. That kiss meant too much to call it a *fault*." Then he smiled at her with a boyish innocence that melted her heart.

She giggled. "You're really a mess, you know that? You have a clever comeback for everything I say. I think some of your grandmother must have rubbed off on you."

They continued walking along, enjoying a silent camaraderie. As they approached Ann's apartment building, she said, "Thank you for the movie and the nice dinner, Richard. I enjoyed the evening very much."

He didn't respond but took her hand as they climbed the steps to the porch. When they reached the outside entrance, he gathered both her hands in his and looked deeply into her eyes. He spoke softly, sincerely, "I loved being with you tonight, Ann, and I'm looking forward to tomorrow evening. I'll call you later about the time." With that, he released her hands, danced his way down the steps, and walked briskly back to his car.

Back in her apartment, Ann threw her purse on the bed, plopped into her comfy chair, and kicked off her shoes. She smiled as she thought about how completely Richard had assuaged her fears. While she was with him, her concern for her daddy had been abandoned to her subconscious; but now that she was alone again, those disturbing thoughts surfaced and vied with the exhilaration she'd felt for the past few hours.

She crawled into bed and switched off her lamp, still basking in the pleasure of the evening. She resolved not to stress over things she couldn't control. *Wait until you hear from Daddy,* she counseled herself. *It's silly to worry about things that may never happen.*

CHAPTER 13

Ann decided to call Daddy at the plant. She knew he usually took his lunch and ate in his office rather than going across the street to Tyler's café with the other guys, so she waited until his lunch hour to call.

"Rosemont Dairies. This is Jernigan."

"Hi, Daddy. How are you today?"

"I'm fine, sweetheart. I'm glad you called."

"I'm not calling about anything in particular," she admitted. "I just wanted to hear the sound of your voice. Are you sure you are all right?"

"I'm okay, hon. After I got off the phone with you yesterday, though, I got to thinking that I didn't ask how you are. I guess I was too busy explaining my situation."

"I'm all right, Daddy. In case you wondered why I wasn't working yesterday, it's because Sarah Buffington, the woman I take care of, is in the hospital. She will probably go home tomorrow, so I'll go back to work either tomorrow or the next day. Has anything happened that you want to talk about?"

"No, not yet. I haven't had time to do anything about the house, but I'm taking the afternoon off to check into it. I'll call you as soon as I know something. I'm sorry to hear that Mrs. Buffington is in the hospital. What's the problem? Did she fall or something?"

"No, she had a stroke, but it was evidently a light one. She doesn't have any paralysis or other long-term effects from it. She's a very feisty little woman. She probably put up a fight and refused to let the stroke win," Ann jested. "I really like her, Daddy. She's such an optimist; in that respect, she reminds me of Mom."

"You remember I told you about my friend Charlie, the actress I met when I went to the theater?"

"Yeah, I remember—the girl with a boy's name."

"That's the one," Ann giggled. "Well, Charlie gave me a lot of information about getting auditions and other things I can do to get into some shows." She sang her next statement: "Things are looking up for me."

"Well, I'm glad you're getting some ideas about how to get started with your career. I'm proud of you, Ann, for working so hard to get what you want. Sometimes people limit themselves by not being willing to take a few risks. I've been guilty of that in my own life and in my attitude about your career."

"I know you're proud of me, but it makes me feel good to know you think I made the right decision by trying to have a career in the theater. I don't know if I'll make it or not, but at least I'll have the satisfaction of knowing I tried."

"Good for you, honey. I hope you'll become a successful actress because that's what you want, but if that doesn't happen, you'll be a success at something else. To some degree, success is a state of mind. Your mom's saying was *You aren't a failure unless you decide you're one.*"

Soon after she hung up the phone from talking with Daddy, Richard called. He would arrive at 7:00, but he wanted to come up to her apartment because he was bringing something to her. He told her it could take a while for him to find a place to park, so not to be concerned if he wasn't right on time.

At 7:14, she rushed to answer four rapid taps on her door. "Hello, Beautiful," said the biggest bouquet of red roses she had ever seen. Then almost immediately, Richard's smiling face peeked around the profuse cluster of blooms and buds.

"What on earth?" she cried, astonished at the incredible sight before her eyes. "They're gorgeous!"

She took the flowers and asked him to come in. "I don't have a vase large enough to hold this huge arrangement," she lamented. "Sit down while I find something to put them in." She remembered the small plastic trash can in her bathroom. It was about the right size, and roses similar to the ones in the bouquet were painted on the side. She put the flowers and some water into the pretty little trash can and set them on her chest of drawers atop one of Aunt Lil's hand-made doilies. Richard seemed impressed with her improvisation.

"Thank you so much, Richard. Now, how did you know the rose is my favorite flower?"

"Maybe it was ESP. Roses just popped into my mind. I wanted to do something to show you how much I appreciate you and to tell you I *really, really* like you."

"Well, they're beautiful, and I will enjoy them for many days to come."

"Are you ready for dinner and dancing?" Richard asked.

"I'm ready," she replied.

Later, at Trudy's Supper Club, they were led to their table by a fast-talking, wiry little man. He seated them and placed menus on the table before them. A waiter took their orders for iced tea and ginger ale, and Richard told him they would wait a while before ordering dinner. They were relaxing and talking when they heard strands of "Stardust."

"Would you like to dance, Ann?"

"I'd love to. You didn't exaggerate; the band is really good."

They had just finished their meal when a tall, olive-skinned man in his mid-to-late twenties approached their table. Richard stood and shook hands with him. Then he made introductions: "Ann, this is Bill Lambert, an old high school buddy; and, Bill, this beautiful lady is Ann Jernigan. Ann has recently moved to New York from Texas," he continued, "and I'm having a great time acquainting her with my favorite haunts."

"Hello, Ann." Bill said, "I hope you're enjoying New York."

"It's nice to meet you, Bill. I'm definitely enjoying New York."

"Well, I haven't seen you for a long time, Richard. The last I heard, you had just graduated from NYU. What have you been doing lately?"

"I'll finish my MBA in May. Then I'll be working for my dad, at least for a couple of years."

"Good for you. Sounds like things are going well for you."

"Yes, it's okay. I'm anxious to finish up this degree. I'm a little bit weary of classes and studying. What about you? I heard you got a degree in pharmacy."

"Yeah, I'm a pharmacist at a drug store in Queens. I decided one degree was enough for me," he chuckled. "I still remember that picnic we had in Central Park back in high school," Bill said. "Since you have the company of this young lady, I guess that's all behind you now."

Richard's body noticeably stiffened and his jaw tightened. He didn't reply. An eternity of silence froze the air before Bill finally said, "Well, it's good to see you, Richard, and it's a pleasure to meet you, Ann. I know Richard will show you a good time."

Richard mumbled something inaudible and avoided eye contact with Bill.

On their way back to Ann's apartment, conversation between them seemed strained. Ann could tell Richard was fighting some private war he was either unable or unwilling to share with her.

When they reached the entrance to her apartment, he turned to face her, clasped both her hands in his, and pressed his lips across her fingers. The gesture didn't seem romantic. Instead, he reminded her of a child desperately needing to be comforted. "I've enjoyed being with you tonight," he whispered. "I'll talk to you tomorrow." He released her hands, and she watched him slowly descend the steps and get into his car. He didn't look back.

CHAPTER 14

One cool Wednesday in early October, Ann had gone into Manhattan to meet Charlie for their regular weekly get-together. Once again, she had some time to kill and decided to make her usual stop at the little sidewalk coffee shop near the theater. Her heart was soaring as she pondered telling Charlie her big news. She had landed a part in a production of *Country Love* at the Archer Theater, and she was beyond ecstatic. She would be playing Liz, the naïve country cousin of leading lady, Evangeline. She felt this was one time when her southern drawl was an asset and may even have helped her get the part.

Her attention was fixed on some birds that had swooped to the stone surface beneath a recently vacated table. She was watching them search out crumbs when she heard a male voice. "Aren't you Ann Jernigan?"

She looked up into the face of the voice, hesitated, and then replied, "I'm sorry. Do I know you?"

"If you're Ann Jernigan, we met a while back at Trudy's Supper Club. You were there with Richard Buffington. My name is Bill Lambert."

"Oh yes, Bill, I remember you now." Her mind flashed back to their meeting at the club and the exchange between Bill and Richard that had seemed to put a damper on the whole evening. She wasn't sure she wanted to have a conversation with this man.

"Do you mind if I join you?"

"Well . . . uh . . . I won't be here long. I'm on my way to meet a friend."

"I don't have long either, but what I want to tell you won't take long."

Ann was dumbfounded. What could Bill Lambert possibly have to tell *her*? "Have a seat." She dubiously scrutinized him as he slid the chair away from the table and sat down.

He leaned forward and spoke softly, "First, I want to apologize. That night at the club I said some things I shouldn't have, and I could tell it really upset Richard. I didn't intend it that way, but now I realize what I said was out of line. The second thing is hard to talk about." He leaned closer to Ann and whispered, "I don't know how serious you are about Richard, but there's something you need to know if you plan to continue to date him.

"As I said, this is hard to talk about. There was an incident involving Richard and a girl he was dating in high school. We were on a double date and had taken a picnic lunch to Central Park. Marianne and I were walking ahead of Richard and Sherry, and we heard Richard screaming at Sherry. We turned just in time to see her slap him. Richard just stood there glaring for her for a minute. Then he doubled up his fist and hit her—really hard—on the side of the face. The blow knocked her to the ground, and she seemed addled for a minute. Marianne rushed to her and tried to help her up, but she shoved Marianne back and got up and ran away. Marianne chased her and called to her but couldn't catch up with her.

"Richard didn't say a word to us. He just stuck his hands in his pockets and stomped away. We were shocked by what had happened and didn't know what to do about it, so we didn't do anything. We just left. I guess at that age we were pretty naïve, and we decided it was none of our business—that it was something between Richard and Sherry.

"But that's not the end of the story. Sherry's parents formally charged Richard with assault and, long-story-short, Richard's dad pulled some strings and got the charges dismissed. At school, though, it created a scandal, and from that time on, Richard was on the black list of all the girls.

"That was eight years ago, and Richard's moved on since then.

71

Maybe nothing like that will happen again, but I thought you needed to know about it."

It was unbelievable! This couldn't be the Richard Buffington she knew. Yet Bill had told this outlandish story with such conviction that she had trouble dismissing it as simply a scandalous tale. On the other hand, could she trust Bill Lambert to be telling the truth? She knew nothing about him. Judging from his behavior when she had met him, maybe he had a vendetta against Richard brought about by some previous altercation.

"Well, that sounds nothing like the man I know. Richard has always been a perfect gentleman with me. I don't know why you would make up something like this, but let's just say I have trouble believing your story."

Bill pushed away from the table and stood to his feet. His countenance changed and his dark eyes flashed. "Whoa here," he declared as he stood and looked down at Ann. "I'm just trying to alert you to something that could spare you some trouble down the line. If you don't want to believe it, that's your business. You seem like a nice lady, so for your sake, I hope Richard's done a lot of growing up over the past eight years. I have to go, but here's my phone number at work and at home if you ever want to get in touch with me." He pulled a pen from his pocket, circled a number on a business card and wrote another on the back. He handed the card to Ann and walked away, leaving her stunned and perplexed by his bizarre accusation.

Ann walked on down the street to the theater, Bill Lambert's words still ringing in her ears. She had been robbed of the eagerness she'd felt earlier to share her big news with Charlie.

Suddenly Charlie appeared from nowhere. "Well, where do we go today? Back to Harold's?"

"Oh, Charlie, I didn't hear you walk up," Ann said. "What did you say? Oh . . . yes . . . Harold's is fine," she stammered, "wherever you choose."

"How about a burger today? There's a good burger place nearby, and their service is fast. I'll probably regret it, but I feel like indulging in something sinfully fattening. How about you?" Charlie wrinkled her nose, spread her lips in a devilish grin, and waited for Ann's response; but Ann's mind was paralyzed by Bill Lambert's assertions. "Okay? . . . Well? . . . Ann!" Charlie cried, grabbing Ann's arm.

Finally, Ann grasped the question. "Oh, yes, let's do that. A burger sounds great." Ann laughed in a weak effort to appear nonchalant, but Charlie saw through the façade.

"Ann, what's the matter? You're off in your own world today. What's bothering you?"

Charlie's words were like flipping a switch on Ann's emotions, and the tears began to flow.

"Oh, Charlie, I'm sorry," Ann blubbered. "I thought I was more in control than this. Just a little while ago I had a conversation with a man who told me some things about Richard that upset me. I'm very confused right now. I'll tell you about it sometime, but not now. I need to get my mind on something else."

"Okay, Ann. I'm not trying to get you to talk about it if you don't want to, but I'm a very good listener, and I'm here when you need me."

Ann smiled at Charlie and squeezed her hand. "I know." Strangely, her tears and Charlie's consoling words seemed to alter her perception of Bill Lambert's warning. She told herself that even if the things Bill had told her about Richard were true, the incident had taken place eight years ago. Almost every person alive would like to undo some past *indiscretion*.

"Ann, do you really want to go eat today? It's okay if you don't feel up to it."

"Yes, I do want to go. I feel better already. I need to be with you, Charlie, so I won't go home and feel sorry for myself."

The Burger Box was lively, and Ann was surprised at how quickly she recaptured that good feeling she always had when she was with Charlie. After they had ordered, Ann's countenance brightened and she announced, "I have exciting news. I got a part in *Country Love*. Rehearsals begin next week."

"Tell me all about it right now, Ann Jernigan," Charlie shrieked as she brought her fists down on the table. "What part did you get?

When does it open?" She seemed unable to contain her enthusiasm as questions spilled from her mouth.

Ann giggled at Charlie's exuberance. "Slow down, Charlie. I can only answer one question at a time. I got the part of Lizzie, and —"

Before Ann could finish, Charlie jumped in, "No! Your first acting experience in New York and you land a great part like that!"

"But it's a community playhouse—Archer Theater. I'm not in the big leagues like you are."

"Well, so what? It's still almost unheard of for a complete unknown to land such an important part in this city. That's a huge accomplishment." She stretched both arms into the air as if signaling a touchdown, threw her head back and chortled the words, "And you did it, girl!"

As they walked back toward the theater for Charlie to get ready for the evening performance, Charlie convinced Ann she must have made an impression on the director. Ann decided Charlie might be right—that what Ann had considered dumb luck was actually the director's recognition of her talent. Charlie's advice was to treat this role as the most important one of her life because it might be just that, especially if the performance happens to be viewed by the right person.

Ann's despondency evolved into optimism as she envisioned her performance as a catalyst for launching her career in musical theater, and the frightening storm cloud of Bill Lambert's allegations turned into a harmless shadow. Why should she believe anything Bill told her? He was probably jealous of Richard, and this was his way of getting back at him. It would take a lot more than Bill's snide indictment to shake her faith in Richard.

CHAPTER 15

Alone with her thoughts, Bill Lambert's words echoed in Ann's mind. She wondered why he would tell her such a sordid tale, and she decided she couldn't let it go without attempting to find out. After two days of torturing herself with unanswered questions, she took Bill's card from her purse and dialed the circled number.

"Spencer Drug. This is Bill. How may I help you?"

"Is this Bill Lambert?"

"Yes. Is there something I can do for you?"

"This is Ann Jernigan, Bill. I wonder if we could meet again. I have some questions about the conversation we had day before yesterday."

"Sure. Where would you like to meet?"

"Would that same little coffee shop be all right with you?"

"Yeah. I don't live far from there. I get off work today at 3:00 p.m. How about 3:45?"

"That's fine. I'll see you this afternoon," Ann replied.

The waiter had just placed Ann's iced tea on the table when Bill walked up. "I'll have one of those too," he said as he pulled out a chair and sat down across from Ann.

"Hello Ann. It's good to see you again. I felt sure you had taken offense to what I told you the other day and that I'd never hear from you again."

"Yes, I was shaken by the things you said about Richard. Whether or not that story is true, I can't imagine why you would tell me all those horrible things. I guess I can't understand why you would make a friend look bad, especially in the eyes of the woman he is dating. You and Richard must have been friends in high school; why else would you have been double-da—"

Before she could finish, Bill interjected, "Yes, of course we were friends. I still consider Richard a friend, although I'm sure he no longer feels the same about me. In hindsight, I made two major blunders: I should never have mentioned the picnic in Central Park to him, and I shouldn't have told you about what had happened. My comment to Richard was just one of those spur-of-the-moment things that pops into your mind and you say it before you think about how it's going to sound. That wasn't so with the things I told you, however. I just thought you needed to be aware that there is another side to Richard's personality. I honestly thought I was doing you a favor and that you would appreciate it. I know now that wasn't the case."

Ann was trembling inside, but she wanted to let Bill know how she felt. "I didn't mean to insult you by questioning your honesty, Bill. It's just that the Richard I know is a kind, considerate man. I just can't imagine that he would behave the way you described. A couple of days ago when you opened the conversation, you seemed genuinely sorry that you had upset Richard. How did you expect him to feel? How would you have felt if you had been in his place?"

Bill looked down for a moment and then shifted his gaze to Ann. "Yes, I know. I feel like such a fool that I didn't think about that before I spouted off. I know I hurt him. I would like to apologize to him, and I've thought about calling him and doing that. I just don't know if he would accept my apology. I've even wondered if it might make things worse instead of better."

"I don't see how it could possibly make things worse," Ann countered. "If you are sincerely sorry for what you said, I think he will respect and appreciate an apology. Apologizing is never easy, and sometimes it's risky. I guess it's a question of whether or not you're willing to take that risk.

"Another thing that has been bothering me besides your comment to Richard is the fact that you told *me* what Richard had done. You say you thought you were doing me a favor. You didn't even know *me*, but Richard was a friend. It doesn't make sense to me that you would tell a stranger something so incriminating about a friend. I have two questions: Was the story you told me true and, if so, what was your real motive in telling me?"

Bill's olive skin suddenly went pallid, and he put his hands over his face. He had the look of a trapped animal that found no way of escape. When he dropped his hands, he spoke quietly, credibly, "I don't know, Ann. I honestly don't know why I told you. I guess it was one of those things that just happened. I hadn't gone looking for you, and when I saw you sitting at that table . . . well . . . I guess I just thought I should warn you about what Richard could be like, or had been like on one occasion.

"Yes, what I told you was basically the truth, but I did alter the facts a little bit. Maybe it's because Richard was always the best-looking, smartest guy in our class, and I was a little bit jealous of the attention he got from everybody."

Bill paused as if he thought he had satisfied Ann's inquiry. In her mind, however, he still had some explaining to do. "And just how much *altering* of the facts did you do?"

"Everything I told you was just the way it happened except—" He paused and took a deep breath, "it was Richard instead of Marianne who rushed over to Sherry and tried to help her up. He ran after her and called out that he was sorry, but she just kept running. And the part about Richard's dad getting the charges dismissed . . . well . . . that didn't happen exactly like that. Sherry's parents were going to bring charges, but Richard and his dad went to them and apologized and they changed their minds.

"Richard and Sherry never dated after that, and some of the other girls turned up their noses at Richard. With most of the students, though, it was a forgive-and-forget type thing. I guess nobody ever knew what started it, but since Sherry always had a way of dramatizing everything and making a big deal out of nothing, I think most of the kids thought maybe she brought it on herself. Of course, that doesn't excuse what Richard did—and I think he would agree with me on that—but I shouldn't have brought it up to him or to you."

"Bill, this incident in Richard's life doesn't change how I feel about him. I believe in forgiveness and in giving people second chances—not in keeping on reminding them of their mistakes. Most people have done things they regret and look back on with shame, but they can't undo what has already happened. The only thing they can do is start from where they are and do the best they can from that point forward."

Ann stood and extended her hand to shake hands with Bill. His eyes never left her face as he stood and robotically shook her hand. "I'll call Richard . . . I will . . . and I'll apologize. I'm sure you don't want me to say anything to him about our conversation, and I won't. I wish, though, that I could figure out some way to let him know how lucky he is to have a woman care about him the way you do. Maybe I'll see you again someday, Ann, but if I don't, I want you to know you've given me a lot to think about."

"Thank you for meeting with me, Bill," Ann said. "I'll admit I'm still not sure how I feel about you, but I do believe you have been honest with me today. As I said earlier, I believe in giving second chances. I hope you will work on that jealousy thing; it's a miserable way to live. Good-bye, Bill."

CHAPTER 16

*B*y Christmas, *Country Love* was in full swing, and Ann's busy schedule of rehearsals and performances, in addition to her work with Sarah, left little time for anything else. She missed spending time with Richard, but he'd been patient with her obligations, and he'd taken her out to eat following several of the shows. Of course, she saw him every day when he ate lunch with her and Sarah, but that was not like the two of them having time alone. The musical was a short-term thing though, running only through the months of November and December, so it would close soon. Then maybe they could make up for lost time.

Ann was thrilled when her daddy called on December 10 to tell her he, Aunt Lil, and Uncle Ben were coming to New York for Christmas. They had booked roundtrip flights departing on December 22 and returning on Christmas Day, and they had made hotel reservations for three nights. Daddy told her he wanted to make sure they could see at least one of her performances, so he asked her to get tickets for them. Although Ann wouldn't have much time to spend with them, she was ecstatic to know they were coming for Christmas. It would be wonderful to have them with her at this special season. Thanksgiving with the Buffingtons had been a good time, but she had missed being with her family.

The three of them liked Richard. His Christmas break started before they arrived in New York, so he actually spent more time with them than Ann did. He took them sightseeing during the mornings, and at night he accompanied them to the theater or to take in the beautiful lights of New York City at Christmastime.

Daddy's divorce was now final, and Nora and Johnny had moved away from Bonner Valley. Daddy found out that Johnny had not been stationed overseas with the military as he had claimed, but that he had been in prison before he showed up in Bonner Valley. He had served two years for petty larceny, along with assault and battery against the service station owner who had caught him with his hand in the till. After learning this, Daddy decided Nora was afraid he would report Johnny to his parole officer if she didn't accept whatever Daddy was willing to give her. Daddy offered Nora what he considered a fair settlement and what his attorney called "extremely generous," and Nora agreed to it. Therefore, the divorce went through uncontested.

Ann felt good about Daddy. He seemed happier than she'd known him to be since before her mother had died. She was happy too. At last she seemed to have harmony between her professional aspirations and her personal life.

Her closeness to Sarah Buffington had grown into a tight bond, and the generational gap between them was a magnet that drew Ann into a deep respect for Sarah's experience and wisdom.

In October, Richard had told Ann he loved her and wanted to marry her as soon as he finished his MBA and started to work for his dad. She knew she loved him too, but she wasn't sure she was ready for marriage. In fact, she hadn't intended to fall in love with Richard; it just happened. She knew she couldn't keep him dangling forever, but she asked him to give both of them time to consider this decision. Could a marriage work between two people who knew exactly what they wanted out of life unless one of them was willing to forfeit his or her goals? She wouldn't expect Richard to give up his ambitions, but neither was she ready to abandon her goal of a career in musical theater. In her mind, there was still much to be settled between them.

Daddy, Aunt Lil, and Uncle Ben had to be at the airport by 9:30 a.m. on Christmas Day. Ann arrived at their hotel at 6:00 o'clock so they could all have breakfast together in the hotel restaurant. Breakfast was followed by a gift exchange and a time of sharing memories of past Christmases and other happy times.

"Do you have any plans to come home anytime soon, hon? I'd be happy to buy you a plane ticket any time you can get away."

"I don't know, Daddy. My schedule is sort of up in the air. Over the past couple of weeks, I've had a few agents wanting to represent me, including Zach Minelli, Charlie's agent. According to Charlie, that's a good thing. They think I show promise or they wouldn't be approaching me. Like any other business, it's all about the money, so they wouldn't want to be my agent if they didn't think it would benefit them financially. Zach would be my choice if I get an agent, and I already know I would have to be available for whatever opportunities he might find for me.

"There is one thing that might keep me from getting an agent right now—my work with Sarah Buffington. I enjoy being with her, and I really don't want to quit my job. Besides, I need to have some type of income. Hopes and dreams don't buy food or pay rent."

Daddy, Aunt Lil, and Uncle Ben all looked at one another and smothered their laughter. Was this their little Annie who used to go around with her head in the clouds, never concerned about where the money would come from to do all the things she wanted to do?

She saw their reactions and laughed because she knew what they were thinking. She agreed with them. She could feel herself becoming more practical and self-disciplined. "I know that sounds strange to you three, but when I moved to New York, I decided I had to take responsibility for my life. After all, I'm twenty-two years old. It's about time, don't you think?"

Suddenly, all the laughing and talking came to a halt. She looked at Aunt Lil and saw tears glistening in her eyes. Her daddy's lips were stretched into a taut smile of satisfaction. He had the look of someone who had just finished a long, arduous task and was pleased as he looked back at what he had accomplished. She knew that look—he was proud of her. She felt cradled in the warmth of their love as they all quietly savored this special time.

Finally, Daddy said, "Well, kiddo, we'd better get on our way. I know you have plans to have Christmas dinner with Richard's family. He's a nice guy. I understand why you like him so much. Tell him good-bye for us and give him our thanks for showing us all around the city. We really enjoyed it. Honey, you gave a great performance in the musical. I'm very proud of you. We're going to be looking to hear a lot of big things about you."

"Yes, we are!" Aunt Lil chimed in as she hugged her and gave her a kiss on the cheek. Uncle Ben patted her on the back and nodded his agreement. Daddy put both arms around her and hugged her with so much force he almost squeezed the breath out of her.

After they paid the restaurant bill, Ann followed them into the lobby. They had already checked out of the hotel, and their bags were waiting for them, all tagged and ready to be put into the taxicab. The hotel clerk called the taxi and told them to wait inside until it arrived and their luggage had been loaded. Ann waited with them.

When a taxi pulled up in front of the hotel and they saw their bags disappearing into its trunk, they initiated another round of hugs. Ann returned their waves as the cab pulled away from the curb. The sidewalks and streets that were usually bustling with pedestrian and automobile traffic were almost vacant. Ann watched the cab until it rounded a corner.

A fleeting pang of loneliness and isolation washed over Ann when they disappeared from view, and she became aware of the emptiness around her. It had been wonderful to be with them, and she was sorry to see them go, but she wasn't really sad. Their visit had satisfied her concern about Daddy's welfare, and now her thoughts turned to her New York *family*—to Sarah and Richard and Charlie—and to the excitement of being an actress. She might not be a professional yet, but she was on her way. She could feel it!

Ann slowly made her way back to the subway station. She had a long, busy day ahead, but she didn't have to be in a hurry. She'd be home by 9:30 at the latest. After today's show, she would be going to Sarah's where the family would have Christmas dinner together. As usual, Olivia was doing the cooking.

Since it was Christmas Day, the only show was a matinee, and Ann was especially excited about this performance. Richard was coming and bringing Sarah with him. Richard had been to several of the shows, but this would be the first and only time for Sarah. Today of all days, Ann wanted to do a good job. She wanted Sarah to be proud of her.

The theater was packed on this Christmas afternoon. When the curtain came down on the final act, the audience broke into a noisy demonstration with wild applause, cheers, and whistles. The audience grew even louder as each major cast member stepped forward to take a bow. When Lizzie stepped forward hand-in-hand with Al and Meg on each side of her, the cheers became deafening. The three made two sweeping bows before the audience broke into a chant: *Lizzie—Lizzie—Lizzie.* Finally, Al and Meg stepped away from Lizzie and stretched their arms in her direction to satisfy the audience demand. Lizzie bowed singly and the cheers mounted to a crescendo. Ann was dumbfounded. As her daddy would say, she had knocked the ball out of the park. Tears were streaming down her cheeks, but her bright smile concealed her emotions from the audience.

Ann had arranged with the theater manager to let Sarah and Richard remain inside the theater until she could join them and they could all go together to Sarah's house for the Christmas Day meal. When she walked into the auditorium, she saw Richard pacing near the rear of the theater. Sarah was still seated. Richard spotted her coming through the side door to the left of the stage and rushed to greet her. He put his arms around her. "Honey, you were spectacular. I've seen this thing five times, but today was the best yet! I don't know . . . it was different . . . you were different. I'm so proud of you! He laughed robustly, and his words echoed in the empty theater, "You stole the show!"

Ann saw Sarah, now standing, with a broad smile on her face, her dark eyes sparkling under the bright house lights. Ann walked over to her and hugged her. "Sarah, it means so much to me that you came today. I know it wasn't easy for you."

"What do you mean, it wasn't easy? I wouldn't have missed this. Richard had told me you were good, but you were better than good. You should be up there on Broadway!"

"I wish the producers and directors agreed with you," Ann chuckled.

"Well, if they don't, then they need to be in some other business."

With Richard on one side of Sarah and Ann on the other, they almost carried her up the unevenly spaced steps to where the floor leveled. Then Sarah balanced herself with her cane in one hand and held firmly to Ann's arm with the other as they made their way to the lobby.

"You two stay here while I go get the car," Richard instructed. "I'll try to double park long enough to come back in and help you."

Fritz, the theater manager, volunteered to help Ann, and when Richard drove up, they whisked Sarah along to the car. As Fritz closed the passenger-side door, he called, "Merry Christmas to all of you. Great performance today, Ann."

"Merry Christmas to you, Fritz, and thank you so much for all your help." Ann called. "It was so sweet of you to let Richard and Sarah wait for me inside the theater. I know I delayed you in getting home to your family."

"That wasn't a problem, Ann. Glad I could help."

As they pulled away from the theater, the afternoon rain turned to puffy flakes of snow. Sarah was in the front seat next to Richard, and Ann had the big backseat all to herself. She pulled her long overcoat tightly around her, wiped the vapor from the car window, and marveled at the wonders of nature. *I received four great Christmas gifts,* she reflected, *a special Christmas morning with Daddy, Aunt Lil and Uncle Ben; Sarah's attendance at the Christmas matinee; a good performance today; and now SNOW. Christmas Day couldn't be more perfect!*

CHAPTER 17

"Ann, you have to make a decision about our wedding," Richard barked. "It's almost March and you can't keep putting it off."

"Calm down, Richard. Why are you so upset?"

"I told you I was leaving that all up to you, but you're not doing anything about it. It isn't going to happen unless you at least come up with a date. I will graduate from NYU in June, so I thought we would get married soon after my graduation. Every time we start talking about wedding plans, though, you want to wait until later to discuss it. I don't care about the details, but we have to decide *something*." His tone had become demanding.

"We have talked about this, Richard. There are some things we need to settle before we make such an important decision. We have to consider our careers. It's important for me to remain in New York City, and your career could take you to other parts of the state, even other parts of the country.

"I'm afraid if either one of us gives in to the other, the one who does the giving in would eventually resent having to do that. At least I know that's how I would feel. That may sound callous, but I think you would feel the same way."

"But Ann, if we love each other, we can work this out. I will be working with Dad for at least two years because I signed a contract to do that. Anything could happen during those two years. Who knows, I might even decide I like it and want to stay. After all, it's a family company, and I know my dad's plan is for me to take over for him someday."

"That's not what you told me earlier, Richard. You said you wanted to work in the marketing field, and I got the impression you didn't want to have to answer to your dad all the time."

"Well, I've done more thinking about it, and I think I might want to work for him. Let's get married in June just the way we talked about earlier, and at the end of two years, we'll rethink our alternatives. If you do get your career started and are still happy with it—and I think that's probably the way it will be—I'll stay with the company. I may not have a choice in the matter anyway."

"What do you mean, you may not have a choice? You *always* have a choice. I don't want to force you into something you don't want to do."

"No, you don't understand. I know *you* wouldn't . . . but . . . well, my dad might." His voice trailed off to a whisper, and suddenly he seemed subdued and somehow cowed into submission.

As Ann read his body language, she was puzzled by his sudden transformation. He had always seemed forthright and confident. Now it was as if he had been stripped of his freedom, a vanquished king now reduced to serfdom.

"Richard, what's going on? There's something you're not telling me."

He cleared his throat, paused, and finally admitted, "Well, it isn't really anything for you to worry about. It's just that I don't think my dad will agree to let me quit after just two years with the company."

"What do you mean? He can't force you to stay. You're a grown man. You can choose to do whatever you want with your life."

Suddenly secrets were pouring from Richard's mouth—harbored feelings he had spoken to no one until now. "Oh, sure. I could defy him. I could go off on my own, but if I do, he will disinherit me— worse than that—he will disown me. I know that sounds far-fetched to you, but you just don't know him.

"He's been a great dad in many ways and has given me every advantage, but he has this domineering side I can't seem to shake. I just can't bring myself to go against him, and it's not really about the money. He's always been like a giant looming over me, dictating my every move. Of course, from his viewpoint, it's always for my own good, but I'm not sure it really is."

He became silent, put his arms around Ann, and held her close. She felt the depth of his love for her, but she could also sense the conflict that was ripping him apart. A frightening thought came to her mind: *If Nelson and I should disagree about something, whose side would Richard take?*

On March 2, The Archer Artistes opened with a new musical comedy written by the director of Archer, Bradley Dutch, and his brother Anthony. This time, Ann had the lead role. The Dutch brothers' *Pink Paper Rose* was brand new and untested, but they were hoping Broadway would take notice. Ann thought if it did gain the attention of the professional world, she might be swept into the arena of success along with the show.

Zach Minelli had called her several times to reiterate his desire to represent her. He told her he knew he could help her with her career if she would give him leeway to negotiate on her behalf. She had held off so far, mainly because of her work with Sarah. She didn't want to quit her job, but she didn't feel it would be fair to Sarah or to Zach if she tried to juggle both commitments.

Since her earlier conversation with Richard when he had adamantly demanded she set a wedding date, they had talked several times about what the future held for them. They had discussed whether their love could survive the seeming obstacles they would have to overcome. Richard remained resolute in his declaration that nothing and no one could cause him to abandon his love and faithfulness to her, no matter what.

Ultimately, they decided to put the wedding on hold. She asked him if he would be willing for them to wait a few more months for Richard to get settled into his new job and for her to continue pursuing a career on stage. Their thinking—or at least Ann's—was that this would give them time to test their love. It would give Richard time to know how he would feel about staying with the company beyond his two-year commitment, and it would give Ann time to rethink the practicality of her staying in New York City with only a hope and a dream to sustain her ambition.

After a three-week run, *Pink Paper Rose* faded and fell apart, but Ann's part in the play did garner some attention. Zach Minelli's talent scout friend, Jim Davies, had caught the show and called Zach. He told him casting was underway for a revival of *Flapperville* at the Pinwheel Playhouse, and he thought Ann might want to audition for a dancer spot.

Ann was thrilled when Zach notified her about the audition, and she told him to go ahead and set it up. She knew Zach's interest in this was to get her to sign a contract with him, so she told him she would sign a one-year contract with the option of renegotiating at the end of that time. She also told him the contract could not go into effect until three weeks after she learned the outcome of her audition. She needed time to give notice before quitting her job. Zach was pretty cavalier in accepting her terms. "I have no doubt you'll get in, and after that—well, it will just be the beginning of some great times for you, Ann."

Following the audition, Ann knew she had given it her best, but she could only hope it was good enough. She was on pins and needles for eight days before Zach called and announced, "You're in as a dancer, and you start rehearsals in two weeks."

Ann's head was in the clouds. She called Richard, Charlie, Daddy, and Aunt Lil in that order. When she called Richard, however, she asked him not to tell Sarah. She herself had to tell Sarah, and it wasn't something she could do over the telephone. She knew Sarah would understand and would support her decision. She wanted to make sure, however, that Sarah knew how deeply she cared for her and that nothing about their relationship would change.

CHAPTER 18

*T*he next day as Ann rode along with other passengers on their way to face another day on the job, her mind was busy planning what she would say to Sarah. She wanted to make her sentiments clear and positive. Sarah always saw the good side of everything, and Ann knew she would be happy and optimistic for her about this new direction in her life.

"Sarah, I'm here," Ann called as she walked into the foyer.

"Come on in, Ann. I have a surprise for you."

Ann entered the parlor and saw Sarah fully clothed and sitting in her favorite chair. "What on earth? Who helped you get dressed?" Ann queried.

"This is the surprise. Nobody helped me. When Olivia came in to check on me, I was already awake. I woke up early, so I just went ahead and showered. Olivia didn't know it, of course. I was in my robe when she brought me some coffee and then went on upstairs to get ready for work. After I had my coffee, I got dressed. I made it just fine. I don't want to do that all the time, but this time that's what I wanted to do, and I had a reason for it. I want to talk to you, Ann, and this way we'll have more time to visit."

"I should scold you for doing that, Sarah. You ran a risk of falling and hurting yourself. Since you're okay, though, I'm glad we'll have that extra time because I have something I want to talk to you about too."

About that time, Olivia came flying down the stairs rushing to get to work. From the foyer, she called, "Hi and Bye, Ann. I heard you come in, but I'm running late and don't have time to visit. Bye, Mother. I'll see you this evening."

"Bye, sweetie, you have a good day, and don't forget to bring me some yarn—brick red."

"I won't forget," Olivia called as she closed the door behind her.

"Ann, do you mind if we just have coffee and toast for breakfast. I'm not very hungry this morning." Sarah seemed preoccupied and anxious to move forward with some heavy agenda.

"That's fine with me." Ann had picked up the newspaper on her way in, so she unfolded it and handed it to Sarah. "Maybe you'll have time to scan the front page while I make toast."

"I'll do that."

Ann went into the kitchen to get things ready for their scant breakfast, and ten minutes later, she went back to the parlor to help Sarah to the table.

"Don't you think I can walk from here to the kitchen by myself? If I can shower and dress, surely I can do that."

"Well, aren't you feisty this morning? Okay, you walk with your cane, and I'll walk beside you. Will you permit me to do that, Your Majesty?"

Sarah chuckled. "Don't get smart with me. You know I love you like a daughter, and just listen to how you talk to me."

"You're the most loved and pampered lady I know. Your family adores you and so do I."

"Well, nobody ever tells me anything, but from what I've learned by eavesdropping, you'll be part of the family yourself before long. That's one of the things I want to talk to you about."

They didn't linger at the table the way they sometimes did after breakfast. Sarah wanted to go back to her chair in the parlor, and Ann pulled her chair close to Sarah's.

"You know, Ann, that little stroke I had got me to thinking. I'm an old lady and I could die any time, but that doesn't worry me. What worries me is what's going to happen to my family when I'm gone. I'm sort of the glue that holds them together. Oh, on the outside everything seems okay, but Nelson and Olivia don't really get along very well. When I die, they will inherit equally, but I'm leaving this house to Olivia. Nelson may fight her about it, but they both know how my will reads.

"William, my husband, gave each of them a sizable amount of money when they married. Besides that, when William retired, he gave Nelson $100,000 and control of the family business. The $100,000 wasn't for Nelson personally; it was given to the company as a financial cushion. Now I think it's only fair that Olivia should get the house. Besides, Olivia needs it and Nelson doesn't. Olivia was in a bad marriage, and by the time she got smart enough to leave him, he had whittled her dowry down to a toothpick.

"I've done a great deal of thinking about this. Nelson is a good business man, as was his father, and he's all right financially, but Olivia needs my help right now, and I'm going to help her. William wanted to give her enough money to make things equal when he gave Nelson control of the transport company, but he didn't trust that husband of hers. He refused to give her any more money for him to fritter away. Now that she's divorced, I'm going to do what William wouldn't do, and I'm going to do it while I'm still alive. That way, Nelson can't say anything about it; in fact, I don't plan to tell him about it. I still take care of my own financial matters, and regardless of what Nelson says, I will continue doing that until I go completely bonkers or they carry me to the cemetery.

"I don't want to burden you with all this, Ann, but I just want you to know what this family is like. Besides that, I trust you, and I know you won't go blab to Nelson or anybody else about what I've told you."

Ann was stunned. Evidently, Sarah was telling her things she had told to no one else, and Ann wasn't sure why. The words, *I just want you to know what this family is like* ran through her mind again. Was this a warning about some impending family split?

"I'm sorry about the friction between Nelson and Olivia," Ann said, "and I understand your concern. Family squabbles are painful. I've always wished I had a brother or sister, but when I hear about instances of sibling rivalry, I think maybe being an only child isn't so bad. Anyway, your secrets are safe with me, Sarah."

"You know, I'm not blind," Sarah said. "I've noticed those tender looks and words between you and Richard, so I've known for several weeks that you were crazy about each other. Furthermore, unless my hearing has failed me, I heard Nelson asking Richard if he had asked you to marry him, and Richard said he had. Now, if you and Richard are planning to get married, there are some things you need to know.

"When William was alive, he was the head of the family. He was strict with Nelson and Olivia when they were growing up, but he loved them, and they knew he loved them. His tactics were stern. I didn't always agree with his methods, and I told him so, but he did what he thought was right.

"The reason I'm telling you all that is to give you some insight into what Nelson is like. When his dad died—really even before that—he took on his dad's ways. I saw it in how he approached the business, and I saw it in how he dealt with his family. Joan, his wife, couldn't take it. She left him after almost twenty years of marriage, and two years later, she died of an overdose of pills. That took its toll on Richard. I saw that break-up coming. Nelson drove her away with his stubborn, demanding ways. Richard was fifteen when she left, and he chose to stay with his dad. This is a terrible thing to say, but it's my feeling that Richard stayed with Nelson because he was afraid not to."

Ann had been listening intently and was shocked by these new revelations. "What do you mean he was afraid not to? What would Nelson have done if Richard had gone with his mother?"

"Who knows? That's not really the point. The grip Nelson has on Richard—that's the point. Richard has been under Nelson's *rule* for so long, he doesn't know how to act or what to do without it. I know this is a harsh thing to say about my own son, but Nelson has crippled Richard by not permitting him to dream his own dreams. Now it may be too late for Richard to break loose and become his own person.

"Richard has always been a good boy, and now he's a fine man. He's smart and a man of admirable character, but he also has this . . ." Sarah grappled for words, "this inability to exercise his own conscience against his father's instructions. I could give you a lot of examples, but I won't go into all that. I just want you to be aware of it and to try to help Richard gain the strength to live his own life. I've tried talking to Nelson about what he's doing to his son, and I've tried to encourage Richard to live his own life, but I've failed on both counts. Ann, you are the best thing that ever happened to Richard. Maybe you're the one who can bring about a change in him."

Ann released her hands from Sarah's grasp, leaned forward, and kissed her on the cheek. "I love you, Sarah. Thank you for sharing all this with me. I know it wasn't easy for you to tell, and it wasn't easy for me to hear, but I appreciate the fact that you care enough to be candid about these things. You need to rest now. You've had a tiring morning. Tomorrow will be soon enough for me to discuss some other things with you. It's time for me to start lunch. Do you want me to get anything for you before I go into the kitchen?"

"No, dear. You go ahead and do what you need to do. I think I'll just sit here and finish reading the paper. I have my knitting close by."

Ann was shaken by the negative picture Richard, and now Sarah, had painted of Nelson. She loved Richard and couldn't imagine her life without him, but she was now concerned about what the future might bring if he was unable take a stand against his father.

Other indications of Nelson's insensitivity to other people's feelings flashed into her mind. She was now thoroughly convinced he was indeed the rude man who sat beside her on the plane when she moved to New York. On Richard's twenty-sixth birthday, Nelson had taken her and Richard to nice restaurant for dinner, and Nelson had loudly berated the waiter for failing to seat them at the table he requested. She also remembered his overbearing manner in her telephone conversation with him several months ago when she called about the job with Sarah.

Ann tucked all the things Richard and Sarah had said about Nelson into a distant compartment in her mind. She pondered them, but she was determined not to let them contaminate her relationship with the man who now owned her heart.

CHAPTER 19

The next morning, Ann finished cleaning up after breakfast and walked into the parlor where Sarah sat knitting, "Are you too tired for a short visit, Sarah?"

"Of course not. What's on your mind?"

"You know I told you yesterday that I have something to talk to you about. I have some news for you; in a way it's good news, but in another way, it's bad news."

"Well, you certainly have my attention. Which one are you going to give me first, the good or the bad?"

"I guess that did sound mysterious. I learned a few days ago that I have been cast as one of the dancers in *Flapperville*. It's a step up to a larger venue, and I'm excited about doing it. I'll actually be paid for performing," Ann laughed.

"Ann, how wonderful! I'm not surprised. I knew this would come someday."

"Well, that's the good news—now for the bad news: Zach Minelli, Charlie's agent, set up the audition for me, I just couldn't feel right about not hiring him as my agent; therefore, I need to keep my time open for rehearsals and for whatever Zach lines up for me."

Ann paused and studied the handkerchief she was twisting into a tight little rope. Tears formed rivulets down her cheeks, and her words stabbed the air, "I'm going to have to quit my job with you, Sarah."

"Shh, Ann. It's all right," Sarah whispered.

"But I really don't want to quit," she sobbed.

"I know, dear, and I wish you didn't have to, but we both know it's necessary." Sarah reached out and grasped both Ann's hands, and their tear-filled eyes met. "It's not like we're never going to see each other again. I'm not planning to exit the planet just yet, and I assume you will come for visits."

Ann smiled through the disappearing tears. "Of course, I will, every chance I get. I've never told you this, Sarah, but I've sort of adopted you as my mother. You and my Aunt Lil are the only women I feel that way about."

"Well, you know we've already adopted each other as sisters, Sarah chuckled. To be honest though, I think of you as my granddaughter, and after you and Richard are married, that's what you'll be. I don't believe in this in-law stuff; family is family."

"Oh, Sarah, I love you!" Tears again sparkled in Ann's eyes, but they were tears of gratitude for the shared love and oneness of spirit she felt with this dear friend.

"Ann, I'm very proud of you, and the thing I want most for you is for your dreams to come true. I'm going to miss having you spoil me like you do, but sometimes we have to make sacrifices. You go out there and show the world what you can do and, for goodness sake, stop being so sad. This is a happy time!"

For a while, the conversation died. There they sat in silence— two women, generations apart, engaged in a quiet communion that transcended the need for spoken words.

Ann looked at Sarah and smiled. "I'm going into the kitchen now to call Mr. Buffington's office."

"Why on earth do you need to call Nelson?"

"To get an appointment with him and tell him in person that I'm having to quit my job. I'll be right back. Maybe if I call now, he can see me today."

A few minutes later, Ann was back in the parlor reporting to Sarah, "I'm glad I called when I did. Vicki said Mr. Buffington would be out of the office for the next two days, but that he can see me at 3:00 this afternoon. I'll just stay here with you until then. That way, I'll get to spend more time with both you and Richard." Ann glanced at her watch, "Oh, speaking of Richard, I need to get our lunch ready. He will be here in about thirty minutes."

Sarah's mind seemed stuck on their previous conversation. "Nelson doesn't know yet about your acting job?"

"No, I didn't want to tell him until after I had told you. After all, you're the one who will be affected by it."

"Well, dear, don't be surprised if that pill doesn't go down easily for Nelson. He tends to think everything should work the way he wants it to."

"Oh, Sarah," Ann giggled, "he may be disappointed, but I think he will understand. I had a good visit with him one night when he took Richard and me out to eat. I told him about my desire to be an actress, and he seemed genuinely interested in it."

Sarah didn't argue the point. Instead, she straightened her back and declared, "Ann, I don't know squat about the theater business, but I know talent when I see it. You have talent, and I don't want you to let anybody—and I do mean *anybody*—talk you out doing what you want to do with your life. If you give up being an actress, you make sure you're doing it for the right reason."

The tone of Sarah's voice made Ann realize her words were an injunction not to be taken lightly. She wondered why Sarah felt the need to say those things to her, but she didn't question her.

When Ann arrived at Nelson's office, Vicki said she could go on in.

"This is a pleasant surprise, Ann. Is everything okay?"

"Everything's just fine, Mr. Buffington, and I will need only a few minutes of your time. I know how busy you are. I wanted to let you know personally, though, that I am having to give up my job as Sarah's caregiver. I wish I could continue because she's become very dear to me."

Nelson was silent. He stood behind his desk with his arms folded across his chest and looked at Ann impassively. She didn't quite know how to interpret his lack of response.

"My reason for quitting," she continued, "is that I have recently signed a contract with an agent who has lined up a demanding performance schedule for me. My other activities will have to work around rehearsals and performances. Since my schedule will be unpredictable, it would be unfair to Sarah for me to continue helping her. My last day of work will be two weeks from today. I hope you can find someone who will love Sarah as much as I do."

Ann wasn't prepared for Nelson's reaction. He angrily snapped, "I told you when you took this job, Miss Jernigan, that you were overqualified for it, and I distinctly remember telling you I didn't want to hire someone who would leave as soon as a better job came along. You're deserting Mother at a time when she really needs you, and I'm very disappointed. I thought I could trust you to live up to your word."

On the outside, Ann remained calm, but inside, she was trembling under the weight of his words. Her reply was slow and deliberate. "Mr. Buffington, I too remember our conversation. When you mentioned that you didn't want to hire someone who might soon leave for a better job, I told you I couldn't tell you how long I would be able to work with your mother but that I would promise to give you adequate notice to find a replacement. I am not leaving for a better paying job. You have paid me very well, and I have appreciated that, but this decision has nothing to do with money."

Nelson was slow to respond. "Well, I don't remember it that way. How much will I need to raise your salary to persuade you to change your mind?"

"You must not have heard me, Sir. It isn't about money. I moved to New York to try to have a career in musical theater. If I abandon that dream now, I will be breaking faith with my own goals and ambitions. You said you are disappointed in me. Well, I might say the same about you. I'm disappointed that you think I have not been honest and fair with you, and I'm disappointed that you think I'm such a shallow person that you can buy my loyalty. I have been and am loyal in giving not only care but also my love and dedication to Sarah. I owe you no apology, Mr. Buffington."

Nelson dropped his arms from their locked position and looked down. He inattentively played with some papers on his desk. Then he looked up at Ann and smiled.

"Now, Ann, we're going to be family soon. I don't want this bad feeling between us. You think things over for two or three days and then get back to me. If you still want to quit your job, I'll start looking for a replacement. I'm just thinking of Mother. I know how she feels about you, and I know she's going to be unhappy if you leave."

"But I've already told Sarah about it, and she understands. In fact, she encourages me to do exactly what I'm doing. I don't need more time to 'think things over,' Mr. Buffington. You need to start looking for a replacement now because my rehearsals begin on May 6.

"I, too, want us to have a good relationship. I love your son and plan to marry him, and I love your mother almost as much as I loved my own mother. I want to love you too, sir, if you'll stop hiding behind that tough-guy mask long enough for me to see the warm person inside you." The words just popped out of Ann's mouth. If she'd given it more thought, she wouldn't have been so forward with this self-centered, unpredictable man. She had no idea how he might react.

He paused and shuffled the papers again. Then he looked beyond her, and his words came slowly, "If you have already told Mother, and she thinks you're doing the right thing, then I guess I have to agree." His gaze shifted to her face, and she saw a softening of his countenance. "I'll never be able to replace you, Ann, but I hope I can find someone who will measure up to the standard you have set. I wish you well with your career."

He seemed to be thinking through some new idea that had just occurred to him, and he said more to himself than to Ann, "Since Richard will soon begin his job here, I will have to get someone to stay with Mother in the afternoons anyway. Maybe I should just hire one person to stay with her all day."

The moment Ann entered the hallway from his office, she vented her pent-up emotions. Nelson's rapid change of heart should have been reassuring, but she wasn't sure he didn't harbor bitterness toward her that might raise its ugly head again. She was hurt and angry and confused.

CHAPTER 20

As the days turned into weeks and the weeks into months, Ann was busier than she had ever been in her life, busy and happy with what she was doing. She loved dancing in *Flapperville*, and she enjoyed some of the people with whom she worked. It was true that a lot of these *show people* were flighty and aloof, but to her surprise, many of them were just ordinary, hard-working folks who were serious about their professions. Since she was the only *rookie* on the team, they helped her when she floundered and encouraged her when she was down.

Ann and Charlie tried to maintain their weekly rendezvous, although their busy schedules required some juggling of the times they could get together. Through Charlie, Ann became involved with a group who regularly visited and performed at a children's hospital in Manhattan. Ann had always loved children, and seeing these innocent little ones having to deal with the harsh realities of life and death broke her heart and drove that love and compassion even deeper into her soul.

Immediately after receiving his MBA on June 4, 1957, Richard started his job at Buffington Transport. Two months later, a new company was waiting to make its debut—Buffington Nationwide Movers—under the umbrella of the newly formed Buffington Transport, Incorporated.

Nelson asked Richard to become president of the new company, but in return, he expected another eight years in addition to his two-year commitment. Richard accepted his dad's offer. He told Ann, "It's too good to pass up. I will earn far more here than I could ever earn in marketing for some other company, and I'll be doing marketing with my job here. Dad has set up the corporation so that corporate owners are salaried according to rank. Since I am one of the owners, I won't have to wait for the moving company to turn a profit before I will have a substantial income."

"But will you *like* the work you'll be doing," Ann asked. "It's pretty miserable having a job you don't like—and for *ten years*! I want you to be happy."

"Well, I guess I won't know for sure until I try, but I'm really excited about it. As head of Buffington Nationwide Movers, I'll be able to run the company the way that seems best to me. I think I'll like that."

Ann didn't want to unfairly judge Nelson's motives in offering this position to Richard, and she certainly didn't want to put a damper on Richard's enthusiasm about working with his dad, but she didn't feel completely at ease with what had transpired. She was suspicious of the timing and convenience of all that had happened.

By October, Richard was settled into his job and seemed to be enjoying the challenge of starting a company from scratch and making it work. Nelson had laid all the groundwork by purchasing the moving vans and other equipment and by taking the steps to satisfy all the insurance and government requirements for interstate movers. From that point, Richard was on his own. He designed an advertising campaign and announced the opening date of service— August 15, 1957. He enthusiastically tackled a plethora of multi-faceted tasks, and he found immense gratification in using his own creativity instead of having to follow a work plan devised by someone else. Nelson's praise further bolstered Richard's confidence.

Not only was the rapport between father and son improving, but Ann had felt an increasingly comfortable relationship with Nelson over the months that had come and gone following their dispute about her quitting her job. She decided her suspicions that Nelson had *sweetened the pot* just to lure Richard into a permanent position with Buffington Transport were unfounded. On occasions when the family was together or when she and Richard were in a social setting with him, he was courteous and considerate, and he seemed to delight in introducing her as his future daughter-in-law. She knew he was still capable of being belligerent and manipulative, but he hadn't shown that side of his personality in a long time.

"I know you never thought you'd hear me say this, Ann," Richard commented one evening following her show, "but I really like my work. Dad seems happy with what I'm doing, and I think things are going well.

"When will you have time for a long lunch date? There's someplace I want to take you."

"Really? Where's that?" she asked.

"It's a surprise, so don't ask."

"Well, as a matter of fact, I don't have to be at the theater until 3:30 tomorrow afternoon. We could meet for lunch somewhere close to your office so you won't have to be away from work too long. I wouldn't want you to get in trouble with the boss," Ann teased.

"Okay. About 11:45 then?"

"Sounds great. I was planning to go see Sarah tomorrow morning, so I'll meet you there after my visit with her."

When Ann got to the restaurant, Richard was already seated and sipping a ginger ale. He stood and waved to her, and she quickened her pace to join him. "I ordered iced tea for you.

"Just what I need."

After they finished eating, Richard asked, "Are you ready for my surprise?"

"I can hardly wait!" she cried.

"Where we're going isn't far from here, so we'll just walk." He took her hand and ushered her along the busy sidewalk. Just as they turned the corner onto Fifth Avenue, she realized he was taking her to the jewelry store where he'd bought her Valentine's Day gift—a charm bracelet and a charm with two interlocking hearts.

"Richard, what's this all about? Another charm for my bracelet?"

"No, it's far better than that. I think it's time we become officially engaged, so I want you to choose an engagement and wedding ring set."

Ann gasped, "Oh, Richard!"

"Why are you surprised? We talked about this just two nights ago. I want everybody to know I have my claim on you," he laughed, "and I want to put a diamond on your finger to make it official."

An hour later, they left the store with a half-caret diamond solitaire on the ring finger of Ann's left hand and a gold band in a case in Richard's pocket. Ann could hardly contain her excitement, and Richard was like a little boy at Christmas time.

Ann couldn't wait to tell Daddy her big news, but she wouldn't be going home until after tonight's show. She decided to call from a pay phone on her way to the theater.

"Rosemont Dairies. This is Paul."

She smiled to herself as she anticipated Daddy's response. "Hi, Daddy. How are you today?"

"Well, hello, sweetheart. This is a pleasant surprise. I couldn't be better. How about you?"

"I'm great. I have news for you. I'm wearing a diamond on my finger. Richard surprised me by taking me to buy rings today."

"Oh, that's wonderful, honey. I know you're excited."

"*Excited* is an understatement! I can't keep my eyes off my hand. I'll have to take it off while I'm dancing, but it will go right back on my finger the minute the show's over."

Daddy chuckled. "I'll bet it will. Do you have a safe place to put it during the show?"

"Yes, we have lockers, and I have a bolt lock on mine. I'm not worried about that."

"That's good. You didn't answer me about the date. Have you set a wedding date?"

"No, not yet. We'll have to wait until I can get a break in my schedule and when Richard can take some time off. Oh, Daddy, I'm so happy. I just hope Richard and I can be as happy together as you and Mom were. If we can, I will feel truly blessed."

CHAPTER 21

wo weeks after Ann and Richard became engaged, the cast finished a matinee performance and were headed backstage when they were greeted with a prominently displayed notice:

Important Meeting Tonight!
All Flapperville cast and crew
meet on stage following tonight's show.
It is <u>imperative</u> that everyone be present!

Producer Austin Rice quieted the group. He assured them the meeting would not last long, but it was important that nobody skip out on it. "Okay, let's get right to the reason for this meeting. We're going to have to close *Flapperville* on the weekend following Thanksgiving. I know you—or at least most of you—were hoping the run would go a while longer. That was my hope as well, but something unexpected has come up. For the remaining five weeks between now and the end of November, we'll continue with our regular schedule. There will be more meetings later, so watch the bulletin board."

He paused and looked over the group as if signaling the end of the meeting. No one moved. "Why is it closing?" asked a male voice.

"I hadn't intended to tell you this until later," Rice said, "because it still isn't settled, but I guess you have a right to know. It appears the building is being sold. If the deal goes through, this won't be a theater anymore, and even if this deal doesn't go through, the owner won't renew our lease because the building will still be for sale. Our lease is up in December anyway, and our board of directors is looking into finding a new venue.

"I hope you won't let this discourage you. You're on your own to find employment, but all of you work well together, so I hope we can reassemble before too long. I'll keep in touch with everyone and fill you in on the progress we're making. Some of you may want to just take a break for a while and enjoy the Christmas season. This would be the perfect opportunity to do that."

When no more dialogue was forthcoming, low murmuring rippled through the group and they quickly dispersed. Ann's mind was spinning. She knew Zach would be trying to find another show for her as soon as he heard about what had happened, but she had other ideas in mind. She and Richard had talked about a Christmas wedding, and Richard had already told her he could arrange to be away from work for a couple of weeks if she could get a break in her schedule. She was bursting with eagerness to tell Richard about this unexpected opportunity.

Richard came on the line in his usual chipper mood, "Hi, sweetheart, what's up?"

"Am I calling at a bad time?" Ann asked.

"No, it's a perfect time. I have a lull right now. What's going on? Aren't you supposed to be at the theater?"

"I *am* at the theater," Ann answered, "but I wanted to ask you to pick me up after the show tonight. I have something I want to tell you."

"Of course, I'll pick you up. I was planning to do that anyway, but why all the mystery? Can't you just tell me over the phone?"

"No, it would take too long, and I don't have that much time right now. I'll just tell you this much: You'll like it."

"Now I'm really curious. This had better be good. I don't like being disappointed."

"You won't be," she assured him. "I love you, and I'll see you tonight."

"I love you too. Bye, sweetheart."

After the evening performance, Richard was waiting outside the theater. When Ann came into view he rushed to meet her. "Okay, now what's this big mystery?"

Ann threw her head back and laughed at his impatience. Then she circled her arm in his and drew him toward the door, "Buy me something to eat and I'll tell you all about it."

As they left the theater, Ann said, "Tatum's Steakhouse is within walking distance. Does that sound good?"

"That sounds great. I'm starving."

Tatum's was bustling with theater goers, but within fifteen minutes they were seated at a little out-of-the-way table for two that was perfect for their private conversation. As soon as they took their seats, Richard asked, "Okay, will you *please* tell me what's going on?"

She laughed and reached across the table and took his hands. "I think we may be able to have that Christmas wedding we talked about."

"That's great news!" Richard exclaimed, but what about the show?"

"*Flapperville* is closing at the end of November, and all auditions for another Pinwheel production are on hold."

"I'm thrilled you'll have this break, but I'm shocked. What has happened to cause them to do this?"

"It's a long story, and a lot of things are up in the air right now," Ann explained. After they gave the waiter their order, she relayed the information Austin Rice had given about the potential sale of the building and all the uncertainty of the situation.

"I'm not happy about the building," she said, "but I'm happy about having a break in my schedule at this particular time. The only thing any of us can do is move our things out and wait until this is all settled. We are free to seek employment elsewhere, but I don't want to do that."

Richard sat back in his chair, locked his fingers together behind his head, and sighed as if Ann's words had given him great satisfaction. "Well, sometimes there's relief in knowing you can do nothing to make a situation better. Just enjoy getting some time off. Let's plan our wedding and forget about theater stuff for a little while."

Ann's lips parted in a devilish grin as she chortled, "I like the way you think, Mr. Buffington."

CHAPTER 22

*E*ver since Ann had been doing the *Flapperville* run, she and Charlie had been forced to have their get-togethers over a late breakfast or resort to telephone conversations. Ann was anxious to tell Charlie what was happening at Pinwheel and to get her thinking about what might happen to the company known as The Pinwheel Players. She was also excited to tell her about the wedding plans she and Richard were making.

The next morning after Austin Rice had dropped the bomb about the theater, Ann called Charlie and asked if she would be free for lunch. They had to meet early so Charlie could get to work by 1:30 p.m.

"Hey, Ann," Charlie called as she approached, "you caught me half asleep when you called this morning, but the tone in your voice sounded like something was wrong. What's up?"

"What's *up* is that I'm about to be out of a job," Ann quipped. Then she laughed and said, "It's not quite that bad."

"What happened?"

"The way news gets around this town, I thought you might have already heard about it. Pinwheel Playhouse is going to sell, and our last performance will be the last day of November."

"What?" Charlie snapped, "That can't be! The landlord has to honor your contract until your lease is up!"

"Well, that's the problem; the lease *is* up—or soon will be—so the lawyer for the theater thinks it will be to our advantage to take the owner up on his offer to buy the remainder of our contract. I'm just not sure where this leaves The Players. We no longer have a theater.

All auditions are off, and everything is at a standstill until we can find another place to perform."

Ann and Charlie hashed around the theater situation until Charlie finally projected, "Well, don't worry about it, Ann. Zach won't have any trouble finding something for you."

"Oh, that's just it, Charlie. I don't want Zach to find anything for me, not just yet. I've been saving the good news for last. Richard and I are planning a Christmas wedding. We haven't actually gotten to the planning stage yet, but we do know it will be sometime around Christmas. My thinking is that we'll have something small and simple. We just don't have time to plan a big wedding and send out invitations and everything. I want you to be my maid of honor. Would that be possible with your busy schedule?"

"Are you kidding? I'll tell them I broke my leg or something. I wouldn't miss this!" They both laughed at her little tongue-in-cheek quip until their laughter turned to tears.

Richard came to the evening show, and he and Ann went for dinner afterwards. Ann was tired, but she was anxious to begin making plans with Richard. As they were eating, Richard brought up the wedding plans. "Well, what do you have in mind? You know, I told you several months ago that this would be your call. I've been wondering if you would want to go back to your home town for the wedding. If that's what you want, that's what we'll do."

"I thought of that too, and maybe under different circumstances, that's what I'd want. I grew up there and know almost everybody in town, so if we were to get married there, I'd want a church wedding so I could invite all those people I've known my whole life. But I don't have time for that. No, this is my home now, and it's where you grew up. This is where I want us to be married."

"How do you feel about eloping?" he chuckled.

"Richard, would you please be serious! I want something small— maybe a simple ceremony at Sarah's house for family only. I think Sarah would like that."

"I think that would be perfect. That way, we won't hurt any

feelings, and we won't have to pretend we enjoy visiting with a lot of people we don't even like," he teased.

"Then that's settled. Well, we do still have to talk to Sarah about it, but I know what her answer will be."

Richard's robust laughter filled the air. "Oh, Grandmother is going to love this. You'll have to keep a rein on her, though, or she'll do all the planning for you."

"I guess the next step is to set the date," Ann proposed, "but we'd better get Sarah in on that discussion, since it will be at her house. We need to talk with her before we make any further plans."

"Hey, I just had an idea!" Richard exclaimed, "Let's take her out to eat and talk to her then."

A big smile brightened Ann's face. "Richard, that's a wonderful plan. She will really enjoy going out!"

"Yes, she will. I'll call her early tomorrow morning and tell her I'll pick her up at 10:30. You can meet us at the restaurant at 11:15."

Ann wrinkled her nose and giggled, "Sarah will love this." Her excitement grew as she anticipated Sarah's pleasure in being included in their plans.

"Charlie is going to be my maid of honor. Who will you have for best man?"

"I think I'll ask Bill Lambert."

The sound of Bill Lambert's name momentarily struck Ann speechless. Did she hear correctly? Is he actually considering asking this Benedict Arnold to be his best man? She finally found her voice: "Oh, well, I had the impression you and Bill weren't close anymore."

"In high school, we were very good friends. We reconnected a few months ago and I think we're even closer now than we were in high school."

"Really? Well, you hadn't said anything about it, so I didn't know that had happened. Is this the same Bill we ran into at Trudy's Supper Club a while back?"

"Yes, that's the one. I know you noticed some tension between us that night, but he called later and apologized. There was this stupid incident I was involved in back in high school, and he had mentioned it that night at Trudy's. He knew his comment had upset me, and when he called, he was very contrite. He apologized for what he had said at Trudy's and for some other things too. He admitted to being jealous of me because I seemed to get all the breaks. That really surprised me. I had no idea he felt that way, and there was certainly no reason for it.

"It was like he was a different person. He'd always been sort of cocky and arrogant, but that was all gone. He was very humble and genuine, whereas back in high school he was . . . I don't know . . . sort of a fake. I knew what he was like, but I liked him anyway. He was fun to be with."

"Well, it sounds like he must have done some growing up since your high school days."

"Yeah, that's exactly what came to my mind, but I guess I've done some growing up since then too. By the way, he mentioned you one day when we met for coffee. It was strange. He doesn't really know you, but he was certainly right in what he said. He referred to you as a *priceless gem* and told me I'd better not let you get away."

CHAPTER 23

"Good morning, Grandmother, how are you today?"

"I'm just fine. This is a pleasant surprise. You haven't called in over a week. I thought you'd gotten so busy you didn't have time for me anymore."

"I always have time for you, Grandmother, and you know it. Have you had breakfast?"

"Of course not. It's only 7:00 o'clock. All I've done is drink coffee and read the paper. You know I'm slow getting around in the mornings."

"Well, you might want to eat light for breakfast, and tell Ginny you won't be there for lunch. I'd like to make a date with you to take you out for lunch. Ann's coming too; we want to talk with you about something. We'll make it an early lunch at about 11:15."

"I can't think of anything in the world I'd rather do than go out with you two."

"I'll pick you up at 10:30, and Ann will meet us at Halverson House. How does that sound?"

"It sounds exciting, that's how it sounds! I'll dress in silk and wear my best hat."

"That's all I needed to know," Richard chuckled. "I have to run now, but I'll see you later this morning."

Sarah was true to her word—not only a silk dress and her best hat, but white gloves as well. Ann was already waiting inside the restaurant when Richard and Sarah arrived.

"Are you trying to make me look shabby, Sarah?"

"What on earth do you mean? You look lovely, as always."

"Well, you look *beautiful*! You're the prettiest and most elegant girl in the place."

"Oh, Ann," Sarah chuckled, "you lie better than anyone I know."

"Will the two of you stop this! You're both gorgeous, and the waiter is waiting to seat us." Richard grimaced at his unintentional word play.

Ann was delighted that Sarah was obviously having a good time. *We need to do this more often*, she thought, *Sarah is loving it.*

When they had finished eating, they told her about their plans for a Christmas wedding and asked about having the wedding at her house. They knew what her answer would be, but they wanted to show her the courtesy of asking.

Richard had brought a calendar with him, so he spread it out on the table, and the three of them studied the month of December. "Ann and I are trying to decide on a date that will be sometime around Christmas but won't interfere with other plans," Richard explained. "Do you have a suggestion?"

"I had thought a day during Christmas week might work, but Richard says he would like to have it earlier," Ann interjected. "What do you think? Since we're having it at your house what would work best for you?"

"Well, all this takes me by surprise," Sarah replied, "but I don't know of any time that *wouldn't* be all right for me. What I'm going to say isn't necessarily a suggestion, but I was just thinking that Olivia cooks Christmas dinner at my house, so what would be wrong with having Christmas dinner and the wedding all as one big celebration. The only people we'd have to clear it with would be whoever performs the marriage ceremony and the two people who are standing up with you. According to what you've said, everybody else would be family."

Ann and Richard looked at each other. "Well, I don't think either of us had even thought of that possibility; at least, I hadn't," Richard commented.

"No, I hadn't either. What do you mean by *one big celebration*? Are you thinking that everyone who attends the wedding will also be included in the Christmas dinner?"

"Why not? Since our family is so small, I think it would be nice to have a larger group for dinner," Sarah declared. "Let's count up how many people that would be. Our family—counting you, of course, Ann—and your father and aunt and uncle would be eight. We would have your best man and maid of honor, plus the minister and his wife. That would be twelve all together, and the dining table can be extended to seat sixteen comfortably. I thought William had lost his mind when he wanted to buy that huge table, but I guess it's a good thing he did."

"The only thing about that," Ann said, "is that it will be a lot of work for Olivia to cook for that many people. I just can't impose on her like that."

"We can have the meal catered if we can find someone to do it on Christmas Day, or I might ask Ginny if she would mind cooking for us. I think her only family is a kitten. She might be happy to earn some extra money."

"Hey, I'm beginning to like the sound of this," Richard shouted. "What do you think, Ann?"

"It's okay, but there are a lot of *ifs* to work through. I don't really know where to begin."

"Let me begin by asking Ginny if she could help us," Sarah suggested. "Even if she doesn't want to do all that cooking, she would be a big help in serving and cleaning up. Then Olivia or I will call around about caterers. We don't have to commit ourselves to anything until we check things out.

"Ann and Richard, you two will need to check with your attendants to see if they can be free on Christmas Day, and I guess if the young man and woman have spouses or fiancées, we should include them. That would make fourteen people."

Richard tossed Ann a wink and a smile. "Didn't I tell you?"

"Not now, Richard," Ann whispered.

Sarah gave them a look that told them she knew they were talking about her. "What are you *not* telling me—that I need to mind my own business?"

"Of course not, Grandmother. I had told Ann how good you are at planning things like this. You always think of everything."

Ann breathed a sigh of relief. Richard's white lie seemed to ease Sarah's mind about whether or not she was being meddlesome.

Before long, both Richard and Ann had to get to their jobs, so they all got into Richard's car, and he drove Sarah home and Ann to the theater. Then he went back to his office.

After Richard had launched the moving company and had it running smoothly, his dad had voluntarily told him he should think about taking some time off. He said Richard had gone straight from a heavy work load at the university to a heavy work load at Buffington Nationwide Movers, and he didn't want him to burn out and become discouraged.

Richard's office was adjacent to Nelson's in the newly revamped corporate suite, so Richard decided to see if he could visit with his dad for a little while before he went to his own office. Nelson had some free time, so Richard sat down and began explaining about the closing of the show and the impending sale of the theater and all the things that had led him and Ann to decide on a Christmas wedding. He didn't know how his dad might feel about their spur-of-the-moment decision to get married, so he chose his words carefully.

"Ann and I have been thinking for a while that we would like to get married sometime around Christmas, but we just couldn't figure out how we could fit that in with her schedule of performances. She just couldn't afford to get out of her contract with the theater. Then when all this happened, it was like a gift had just landed in our laps, so we—"

Taking a long puff on his cigar and smiling from ear to ear, Nelson sent smoke curling across his desk. Then suddenly he broke into Richard's explanation, "Well, I'm very happy for you and Ann, and maybe I even helped things along a little bit."

When Nelson saw the puzzled look on Richard's face, he broke into laughter. "You really don't know what I'm talking about, do you?"

"No, I'm afraid I don't," Richard said seriously. "Would you like to explain it to me?"

"I'm the one buying the theater."

"What? You? What on earth are you going to do with that

building? No telling how much you'll have to spend to use it for anything except a theater, and what do you need with a theater?"

"Oh, I don't need a theater, but my buying it gave Ann enough time off for a wedding and a honeymoon, didn't it?"

Richard couldn't believe what he was hearing. His dad had been pushing him to get married and had been dropping little reminders almost every day, but for him to go so far as to purchase the theater where Ann was performing just to make it possible for her to have some time off—well, that was really wild! Was this wedding that important to him? It was unbelievable! He didn't know whether to thank him or tell him what a stupid business decision he'd made, but he knew he wouldn't do the latter.

"Ann was told the sale was pending. Has it been finalized?" Richard asked.

"Indeed, it has. The title deed was signed over about two hours ago."

"Well, what *are* you going to do with the building? I'm sure you have *some* plan in mind."

"I certainly do have a plan in mind. I'm going lease it back to Pinwheel Playhouse. I've already talked with David O'Hara, chairman of the board of directors."

CHAPTER 24

"*I* can hear the wheels turning in your brain, Dad. I have no doubt you have planned this to the last detail, but I don't get it. Aside from getting some time off for Ann, just what do you hope to gain by making this purchase?"

"Maybe I'm becoming more civic-minded. I've been to that theater on several occasions, and it really could use some sprucing up. I know it's known for that somewhat antiquated look, but it can exhibit that ambiance without being run down. I want to do some remodeling and upgrading. Then it will reopen, and no, I won't increase the lease amount above what they were already paying. When I talked with O'Hara this morning, he was very excited about my proposal. He said he would have to bring it to the board of directors next Monday, but he could foresee no negative response.

"Why do you think I've been pushing you to take some time off? You do need to get away from work for a while, but you also need to take time off for you and Ann to get married and go on a honeymoon."

"Well, that's a new one. All I've heard from you my whole life is that you don't believe in vacations. Work was your number one priority, and I got the feeling you expected that from everybody else too, especially me. You must be turning into a softie."

"Certainly not! I'll keep things going with the moving company while you're gone, but when you get back, it will be all yours again. When we have time, we also need to talk about some other things I've been thinking about for Buffington Transport. Right now, though, I want you to concentrate on your wedding and honeymoon. The honeymoon is one of my wedding presents to you."

"One of? What does that mean?"

"Just what it sounds like it means, but we'll talk about that after you return from your honeymoon."

"If everything clicks just right," Richard announced, "we will probably be having the wedding on Christmas Day at Grandmother's house."

"Christmas Day? Well, I guess that will blip out Christmas dinner. Why can't you get married on some other day?"

"That's what Ann and I had originally planned, but Christmas Day was Grandmother's idea. She said we can make the wedding and Christmas all one big celebration, and everyone who attends the wedding will also be a guest at the dinner. After she put forth that idea, we got to thinking about it and decided it was a pretty good one."

"Well, if Mother said it, I'm not going to argue with it. She can be a daunting foe."

Richard chuckled quietly when he remembered how his grandmother had *never* let his dad boss her around. He might not have agreed with her, but he knew better than to argue with her. "I'll have to get back to you later with details about the wedding when I know them."

"Richard," Nelson called after him as he turned to walk out the door, "I want you to know you're doing good work. I'm proud of you. You have an instinct for knowing what to do to grow a business, and not everyone has that. It's as if you were born to be head of Buffington Transport, Incorporated someday."

Richard looked at his dad and voiced an almost inaudible thank you. He left the office with conflicting feelings mounting inside him. He wanted to do a good job, not only to please his dad but also to please himself. He wanted his dad to be proud of him, but he also wanted the privilege of making his own decisions. He didn't want to be forced into a lifetime commitment to Buffington Transport, Incorporated, and he knew his dad well enough to know his comment was a step in that direction.

His mind reached back into his childhood and echoed his dad's admonitions: *Don't say you don't want to play football; you'll do it and you'll work hard at it. What do you mean, you want to stop taking piano lessons? You'll continue. No, I won't listen to your excuses; you* <u>*can*</u> *win that debate.* Now that he was grown, his dad had moved from the dictatorial phase into the enticement phase.

Looking at life in the here and now, he was completely happy with his role at Buffington Transport. He thought he might like to travel the trail his father and grandfather had blazed. Maybe he would always feel that way, but he wasn't sure, not yet. At this stage of his career, he still needed time and space to explore his own feelings. He knew he was locked in for ten years, and after that—well, he'd have to wait and see.

When Ann arrived at the theater, she walked straight to the bulletin board to see if Austin had called another meeting. He had. All the cast and crew were antsy to know their fate, and when Austin announced the building had indeed been sold, a mournful groan emanated from the group.

"Don't let this discourage you," Austin implored. "The sale of the building doesn't really matter. We knew we were going to be without a theater whether it sold or not, but I am confident we will have a place to call home very soon. Just put your best effort into the next few weeks, and don't let this weaken your performance. I want you to leave the audience clamoring for more. It will lift your spirits and bolster the confidence of our patrons. We don't want to lose our fan base during what we hope will be a brief interim."

Richard was at the theater to take Ann to eat and then home after the show. He could hardly wait to tell her about his conversation with his dad, and as soon as they got into his car, he launched into an account of what had happened: "I had a very enlightening talk with Dad this afternoon. You won't believe who bought the theater or what he plans to do with it."

Ann listened, mouth agape, as Richard's recounted his bewildering conversation with his dad. She put forth several questions about the deal, none of which Richard could answer.

"I don't know any details. All I know is that O'Hara seemed

pleased with Dad's proposal, and that he had no doubts the board would approve it. You know, I got the feeling Dad is sincerely interested in helping improve the appearance of that theater. That's certainly a side of him I've never seen before," Richard chuckled. "The astonishing thing about this, though, is his reason for buying the building. He bought it so you, Miss Ann Jernigan, would have enough time off for us to get married and go on a honeymoon, and he's paying for the honeymoon! What do you think about that?"

"I'm amazed! You don't mean that was his *whole* reason for buying the building?"

"Yep. At least, I haven't gotten him to admit to any other reason."

"No ulterior motive? I don't understand why he would be in such a hurry for us to get married?"

"If he has an ulterior motive, I don't know what it could be. This is certainly not a profitable business deal for him. Neither do I understand his reason for the rush unless it's just that he knows we are anxious to be married and he wants to help things along."

"Okay. Well, I guess we'll just have to graciously accept his help and his gift of a honeymoon. I still can't believe he would do such a thing," Ann giggled, "but I'm grateful for it. I'll make a point of thanking him and letting him know how much I appreciate it."

"Come to think of it, I didn't really thank him. I was so stunned, I didn't know what to say. If you're coming to the office to thank him in person, come to my office first, and we'll go together."

"You know, Richard, I think maybe your dad is changing. For the past several months, I've seen a side of him that is . . . well, *different* . . . in a good way. He seems kinder, less confrontational. Do you know what I mean?"

"Yes, I do know what you mean." Richard couldn't deny he had also seen a change. What he didn't tell her, though, was the feeling that came over him when he heard those words: *It's as if you were born to be head of Buffington Transport, Incorporated someday.*

CHAPTER 25

On the last Wednesday of October, Austin Rice called another meeting with The Pinwheel Players and stage crew. He walked slowly into their midst, hands in pockets and shoulders drooping as he examined the stage floor and mumbled something under his breath. Everyone was reading his body language and fearing the worst. Ann was baffled since she knew Nelson had bought the building and leased it back to Pinwheel Playhouse—at least, that's what Nelson had told Richard. What could be causing Austin to look so glum?

After what seemed like an eternity of suspense-filled silence, Austin took a flying leap to the top of a three-step stairway stage prop. He stretched out his arms and yelled, "Ladies and Gentlemen, this is *still* our theater!" At first, everyone just looked at him in disbelief. Then suddenly, as if a light bulb had come on in their collective brains, they broke into wild cheering and revelry. The good news made them forget all about the mean joke Austin had just played on them, and he was the man of the hour.

He went on to explain that they would have a hiatus from November 30 until January 13, during which time the theater would be refurbished. When they returned to work, they would need to be ready to do quick auditions and then launch into rehearsals for *Island Dream*. Austin didn't want to open with an inferior performance, so they would have to work hard and fast to meet their grand re-opening on the March 1.

Ann breathed a sigh of relief. For a moment, she thought maybe something had gone wrong in Nelson's deal with the board of directors, but evidently, his contract stipulations had been welcomed with open arms; otherwise, Austin wouldn't have shared this news with such enthusiasm.

———— ☼ ————

Because of Ann's busy schedule of shows, she had asked Sarah to take charge of the preparations for the wedding, and Sarah relished the task. "If you can arrange for decorations, food, and whatever else you think of, I will, of course, bear the financial responsibility," Ann told her.

"Don't be silly. I'll take care of everything. It will be my wedding present to you."

Ann laughed at Sarah's delight in volunteering to *take care of everything*. "That's the grandest wedding present I can think of, Sarah."

Sarah threw herself into arranging for the decorations. She and Maggie Finley, her florist friend, created a stunning melding of the two occasions. Sarah and Olivia worked together on planning the menu, with Olivia having the final say. Olivia was adamantly against having the meal catered, but she finally gave in to having the meat prepared by a professional chef. She also agreed that having Ginny do the serving and cleaning up would be a big help.

Time seemed to fly by, and by Thanksgiving, Sarah had everything arranged. The traditional Buffington Thanksgiving meal was an early lunch since Ann had to be at the theater by 2:00 p.m., but after lunch, Ann and Sarah found a few minutes to get their heads together about the wedding. When Sarah said she would take care of everything, she meant *everything*. Ann was amazed at all the planning she had done. It was going to be a glorious occasion!

"Sarah, I hope doing all this isn't putting too much of a strain on you."

"Certainly not! This is a tonic for me. I'm loving every minute of it."

Ann felt it *was* a tonic for Sarah, and that it was something she would think back on and enjoy over and over again.

Ann had called her daddy and asked him to send the wedding dress her mother had worn almost thirty years earlier. It wasn't the traditional floor-length wedding dress with a train, but rather an unpretentious ankle-length white taffeta. Ann thought it would be perfect for their home wedding.

As she tried it on, goose bumps rose on her arms and crept onto her neck, and she felt a strange awareness of her mother's presence. "You wore this very dress, Mother," she whispered. Warm tears bathed her cheeks as she looked at herself in the mirror, and for a few fleeting seconds, it was her mother looking back at her, a smile of approval on her lips. Ann lingered a while before the mirror, allowing herself to savor the deliciousness of this moment.

Ann and Richard had to cram a lot of work into the first three weeks of December. Richard was trying to do as much as he could to leave the moving company in good shape for his dad to take the helm.

Ann had to give Mr. Yancey, the telephone company, the postal service, and others notice that she would be moving out her apartment to a new address, effective January 10. She also had to do all her Christmas shopping and buy appreciation gifts for the three people who were making her wedding special—Charlie for being her maid of honor and for Sarah and Olivia for their labors of love.

Ann and Richard had discussed going to Niagara Falls for their honeymoon. However, after Nelson told Richard he had a surprise for them regarding their wedding trip, they were hesitant to make any plans of their own. They wondered how long it would be before Nelson would reveal his *surprise*.

During the second week of December, Nelson took them out to eat and presented them with hotel reservations and roundtrip airline tickets for Honolulu, Hawaii. They would fly out of LaGuardia the afternoon of December 26 and back to New York on the January 5. Furthermore, he had made a wedding night hotel reservation for them at the luxurious Emory-Banks Hotel, and he had arranged limousine service to the hotel following the wedding and to the airport the next day.

They appreciated the fact that Richard's dad was interested in making their wedding and honeymoon special, but in Ann's opinion, it would be special with or without Nelson's help. She wondered if it had dawned on him that they might like to make their own plans, even if it meant settling for something less spectacular than Hawaii and a chauffeur-driven limousine. It didn't really annoy her though; it was just something she wondered about. To be honest, they were both delighted to be going to Hawaii, so they accepted Nelson's generous gift with grace and gratitude.

CHAPTER 26

On Sunday before Christmas Day, Daddy, Aunt Lil, and Uncle Ben arrived. Daddy had already told Ann he would like to host a dinner on Monday evening for the wedding party and all the Buffingtons. "Since Richard's grandmother won't let us pay for the decorations and food, I feel I'm shirking my responsibility," Daddy explained. "This dinner will give everybody a chance to get better acquainted."

Ann made reservations for eleven people at Plumlee's, a restaurant with good food and a unique design—private dining rooms of varying sizes for all patrons. Ann arranged for table decorations, and she and Richard had their appreciation gifts all wrapped and ready to present to Bill, Sarah, and Olivia. Charlie was unable to attend, but Ann had already given Charlie her gift.

Guests gathered in the dining area and mingled as they partook of hors d'oeuvres and punch. Finally, Paul Jernigan interrupted their visiting, "I want to welcome all of you and invite you to find a seat around the table. We aren't using place cards, so you may sit wherever you wish. You'll find menus on the table, and I think our waiter is ready to begin taking orders."

After everyone had ordered, Paul asked Ann to introduce all the guests for the benefit of those who did not know one another. After she made the introductions, the room once again filled with the hum of cheerful chit-chat and laughter.

Paul Jernigan intentionally sat next to Sarah. "I'm glad to finally get to meet you Mrs. Buffington," Paul Jernigan said, "We've heard a lot of nice things about you, and I want to thank you for being so good to my Annie."

Before Sarah could answer, Ann came and stood between her daddy and Sarah. She put an arm around each of them. "I'm glad you two are getting acquainted since you are two of the most important people in my life."

"I'm happy to meet you Mr. Jernigan," Sarah said. "You should be proud of this young lady. She's exceptional in every way, but I'm not telling you anything you don't already know."

"You're right, she *is* exceptional, and it seems to me she's marrying an outstanding young man. I know you have made her feel welcome in your family, and I appreciate that."

"To me she *is* a part of the family. I just fell in love with Ann almost from the first day we met. I couldn't love her more if she were my own blood. I think she's perfect, and if she isn't, I don't want to know about it."

Ann gave Sarah a hug, "I'm far from perfect, and you know it, Sarah."

"What? You had me completely fooled!"

They all laughed as Sarah continued with her witticisms throughout their conversation.

After dinner and the presentation of gifts, visiting continued for a time, Then Nelson, Sarah, and Olivia said their good-byes and thanked Paul for the delicious meal and an enjoyable evening. Others soon followed suit, leaving Ann and Richard alone with Daddy, Aunt Lil, and Uncle Ben. The five of them lingered for a while.

"Mother's wedding dress is a perfect fit, Daddy. Wearing the dress she wore for your wedding means so much to me."

"I know, sweetheart, and she would be happy you want to wear it."

"I showed the dress to Sarah, and she thinks it is perfect."

"Well, Annie, you look like a lady in love," Daddy declared, looking across the table at her.

"I am. Can you believe I snared this handsome guy?"

"That's a crock!" Richard guffawed, "I'm lucky that this beautiful lady would have me."

"Well, I think you both did all right," Daddy teased, "but you're going to have to give her a lot of love, Richard, to equal what she's accustomed to. She had four parents, you know, and we all showered her with love; and maybe we spoiled her just a little bit."

"I'll take that as a challenge, Mr. Jernigan," Richard chuckled. Then he grew more serious. "I know you're trusting me to take good care of her, and I promise you I'll do that. She certainly won't be without love or attention."

On Christmas Eve, Reverend Conner met with Richard and Ann at Sarah's house and talked through the ceremony with them. They practiced getting into place, and they would give verbal directions to Charlie and Bill. Everything would be fairly simple, and that suited Ann. She wanted the wedding to be informal, relaxed and enjoyable for everyone. Because of Charlie's schedule, they decided to have the wedding at 10:00 a.m., followed by lunch at 11:15 and the cutting of the wedding cake as soon as possible after that.

Daddy had booked a hotel suite with a sitting room flanked by two bedrooms, and Ann stayed there with them on Christmas Eve night. She and Aunt Lil slept in one bedroom, and Daddy and Uncle Ben shared the other. To Ann, this night with them seemed symbolic of her transformation from their little girl into a woman with her own family. It was a special time of remembrances and partings wrapped into one. She knew it was a time that marked a change in their lives as well as in hers.

Christmas morning dawned bright and beautiful following light snowfall during the night. Ann threw back the curtains and looked out over the city set ablaze by the morning sun, and she couldn't contain her emotions as she laughed aloud at the breathtaking perfection of this day.

"I see you're still as giddy as you were last night. Did you sleep all night with that smile on your face?" asked Aunt Lil.

"Of course, I did. I'm still incredibly happy! Have you looked out this window? We couldn't have ordered a more gorgeous day!"

The long-awaited time finally arrived. At precisely 10:00 o'clock, Olivia began playing softly on Sarah's old pump organ, and Richard and Bill moved forward to stand beside Reverend Conner. Charlie came down the stairs and took her place. Then Olivia broke into the wedding march, and Ann slowly descended the stairs and joined Richard.

Reverend Conner asked Richard and Ann to face each other and join both hands for the ceremony. As they exchanged marriage vows, Ann's heart swelled with joy; then they sealed their vows with bands of gold. Laughter and cheers erupted as Richard kissed his bride, and the merriment continued with hugging and kissing, congratulatory hand-shaking and back-patting.

Soon Olivia tapped the side of a glass to get everyone's attention. "We'll be serving lunch in about five minutes, so you may begin moving into the dining room."

Everyone was in a festive mood. Even Reverend Conner's offering of thanks for the food carried a celebratory reverence. Throughout the meal and the serving of the wedding cake, everyone seemed to enjoy visiting and getting better acquainted, especially Charlie Patton and Bill Lambert, who sat next to each other at the table.

Ann and Richard excused themselves and changed into more casual attire before the guests sent them off in a hail of rice. With the festivities ended, the guests began to go their separate ways.

When Richard and Ann arrived at the Emory-Banks Hotel, they were given royal treatment. The doorman recognized them—how, Ann couldn't imagine—and motioned to another uniformed young man take their luggage and escort them to their suite. An envelope was passed from the doorman to the other man, and they bypassed the registration desk.

Once they were inside their suite and away from peering eyes, Richard took Ann in his arms. Then he asked, "Are you truly happy, Ann?"

His words puzzled her. "What kind of question is that? You know I'm happy."

He lowered his head and was silent for a moment. "I think you are, but I needed to hear you say it. You know we would have been married several months ago if it had been left up to me, but I wanted to give you time to be sure."

Ann smiled and answered, "I'm sure I love you with all my heart, Richard, and I meant every word of the vows we took."

From that moment, their hearts melded, and their love grew deeper. They were cocooned in their own secluded world—a enchanted realm nesting them in the sanctity of oneness.

CHAPTER 27

*H*awaii was glorious! Its beauty was even more spectacular than they had imagined, and all the food seemed bathed in a scrumptious medley of fruity tropical flavors. They vowed they would return someday, maybe for an anniversary, but for now, they were happy to be home.

To their surprise, Nelson met them at the airport. When they saw him standing alongside others welcoming the incoming flight, Richard's first thought was that something must be wrong at the business. Ann was concerned about Sarah. Discounting some urgent situation, Richard could think of no reason for his dad to be there. Giving personal attention to this type thing was out of character for him. Besides, it wasn't as if they were strangers to LaGuardia and needed help.

When Nelson spotted them, he waved and briskly walked toward them.

"Dad, you didn't have to meet us. We could have taken a taxi. Is everything all right?"

"Of course, everything's all right. I just wanted to pick you up," he said as he hurried them along to pick up their luggage. He seemed preoccupied and antsy. If everything was all right and he just *wanted* to pick them up, why did he seem so eager to whisk them away from the airport. He gave the impression he had something important to do. Ann concluded she would never understand Nelson's moodiness and unpredictability.

Richard and Ann tried to converse with him after they left the airport, but he had little to say. When they reached the street where they should have turned to go to Richard's apartment, Nelson kept going straight.

"Dad, I think you missed the turn."

No answer.

"Dad, you need to turn around. You drove past the street."

"Oh, we'll get there. I'm just going a different way."

It seemed they were going toward Sarah's house, so they looked at each other, shrugged, and decided to go along with whatever he had in mind. When he turned onto the street where Sarah lived, Ann whispered to Richard, "Maybe they're having a welcome home party for us." Richard grinned and nodded, but Nelson drove past Sarah's house and parked in front of a large two-story in the next block.

"Let's get out and go in for a little visit."

"Dad," Richard chuckled, "It's been a long time since we left Honolulu. We're not exactly presentable to be making a social call, particularly when we don't even know the people. Who lives here, anyway?"

"You'll find out. Just get out of the car, and let's go up to the door."

Baffled and somewhat annoyed by this strange directive, Ann and Richard exchanged uneasy glances. When they reached the door, Nelson rang the doorbell. An immaculately groomed woman, maybe in her forties, opened the door. "Come on in," she said, "I've been expecting you."

"Ann and Richard, this is Ruth Sensibaugh," Nelson said. "Ruth is a realtor who is going to show you through your home. This is a wedding gift." Then he pulled two sets of house keys from his pocket and handed a set to each of them.

Seeing the astonished looks on their faces, Ruth sensed they needed a time of privacy, so she excused herself and made her way to another part of the house.

"What on earth!" Richard exclaimed. "You can't be serious! Dad, you didn't need to do this. We have a place to live—not as fabulous as this, I'll admit—but adequate for our needs."

"Yes, Nelson," Ann added, "Richard's right. The wedding trip was beyond our wildest dreams and now this luxurious home in addition to that—well, it's just more than we can fathom. I would feel guilty accepting it."

"You have to accept it. It's a done deal. It's bought and paid for. It's yours."

Suddenly Richard grabbed his dad around the shoulders and hugged him forcefully. "I'm just in shock, Dad. Thank you so much. It would have taken us years to afford a house like this."

Nelson walked along with them while Ruth showed them through the house that would soon become their home. Ann appreciated Nelson's gift and felt it was something he truly wanted to do for them, but she couldn't keep from wondering why it wouldn't occur to him that they might want to choose their own home.

Despite the feelings churning inside her, she found herself falling in love with the house. As she studied the rooms, she envisioned the many possibilities of how tastefully they could be decorated. She knew it would take a long time to acquire enough furniture for every room, but they didn't need to be in a hurry. She would rather do it slowly and buy quality items they could cherish for a lifetime than to throw together pieces that wouldn't do justice to their surroundings.

After their tour of the house, Nelson drove them to Richard's apartment. As he was helping them unload their luggage and carry it inside, he casually commented, "Oh, by the way, I opened an account at Barrett's Home Furnishings. I did a lot work for Wendell Barrett a while back and didn't charge him, so he wants to repay me by selling us all the furniture you need at what it costs him. I don't think we can beat a deal like that, and Barrett's has quality furniture. I want you to go down there and pick out everything you need to make your guests ooh and ah the minute they walk through your front door."

Will this never end? Ann wondered. *How many more surprises are yet to come?* "Nelson," she said, "I don't want to seem ungrateful, but you are doing too much. Think of the ways you could benefit the business with this money you're spending on us. I feel we are taking advantage of you, and I don't like that feeling."

Before Nelson could reply, Richard chimed in, "Yes, Dad, you *are* doing too much. We have enough furniture to get by—not enough to furnish every room, but in time, we will."

Nelson put an arm around each of them. "Look, the business has had a good year, and right now the moving company is really taking off. I can afford to do this, and I want to do it. You've worked hard, Richard, and you've done a fine job. I want to reward you. Call it a bonus if it will make you feel better, but please indulge me."

What could they say after such a touching declaration? Finally, after what seemed like eons, Richard blinked away tears, looked at his dad, and croaked out two simple words: "Thank you." Then he hugged him again, smiled, and remarked, "I think it's the other way around; you are indulging us. I understand your request, though, so we gratefully accept all you have done and are doing for us."

"Yes, we do," Ann interjected, "and, most of all, we appreciate your gracious attitude in doing it."

When Nelson had gone, Ann and Richard looked at each other and laughed. "I can't believe this!" Richard exclaimed.

"Well, that makes two of us," Ann said. "How do you like the house?"

"I really like it, especially that huge room upstairs. I'm not sure what it's supposed to be, but I think it's crying for a pool table. What do you think?"

Ann giggled, "I might have known you would think of that."

"I'm serious. How about it? Maybe the builder intended it to be a game room."

"It can be whatever you want it to be, honey. Since everything I'll need will be downstairs, I'm sure I'll seldom go upstairs except to clean. That room can be your hideaway when you get tired of being with me."

"Are you kidding? I'll never get tired of being with you. You haven't said how *you* feel about the house. Do you like it?"

"I love it, Richard. At first, I'll admit I felt cheated that we didn't get to choose our own house, but after Ruth showed us around, I was captivated by it. Did you notice that the master bedroom has a little sitting room adjacent to it? That will make a perfect little nursery when we need one . . . you know . . . maybe in a few years."

A strange expression came to Richard's face. "Do you really want children, Ann?"

"Well, not right now . . . but someday . . . yes, I want children," she stammered. "Don't you?"

"No, not really. I like things just the way they are, with just the two of us. We both have extremely demanding jobs. I thought you were so dedicated to your profession that you felt as I do— that children would just get in the way of our careers. Besides that, children come with a hefty price tag, and that goes on for a long time. But if you're one of those women who feels life isn't complete without children, then we'll have children," he shrugged.

Richard's words stabbed her heart. It was an attack she didn't see coming. Her pain wasn't caused by the fact that he didn't want children but rather by the manner in which he spoke of them. It was as if he thought of them as family pets or as commodities that could be evaluated in terms of dollars and cents. She took no comfort in his cavalier willingness to have children. How could they dare bring children into the world with Richard feeling as he does? She wanted her children to have a father who would cherish them, be sensitive to their needs, and take pride in their accomplishments. Every child deserves loving parents.

A knot formed in Ann's stomach, and she couldn't force words from her mouth. She turned and walked into the bedroom of the apartment that had belonged solely to Richard. He had cleaned out closet space and other storage areas to accommodate her belongings, so she robotically began unpacking her bags and putting things away. Suddenly she stopped and sat down on the bed. *We talked about everything in the world, everything <u>except</u> children. Why didn't we talk about children? If we had, would it have made a difference? Probably not. I love him too much!*

CHAPTER 28

*T*he house was ready for occupancy, so they wasted no time moving their scant furnishings and other belongings into the home they had come to love. They had only a week before they both had to go back to work, and they wanted to be totally moved in by that time.

When they went to Barrett's to look at furniture, they were overwhelmed by the vast selection. They decided to go the route of traditional décor, comfortable yet stylish, with a few period pieces thrown in to create an interesting eclectic balance.

Ann tried to be frugal, but Nelson had urged them to buy *everything* they needed and wanted and not to skimp on quality. Barrett's had to order Richard's pool table, but everything else was in stock. They bought furniture and accessories to completely furnish the house except for one small upstairs room. Ann didn't feel they needed four bedrooms at this stage of their lives, and this little room tucked away in a remote section would make a good storage area or hobby room. It would remain empty for now.

From the apartment, they moved bedroom furniture, a sofa with matching chair, and two accent tables. The bed, night stand, and chest of drawers furnished one of the spare bedrooms, and the living room pieces and tables fit nicely in the sitting room off the master bedroom.

When Barrett's delivered the furniture and put it in place, Ann was thrilled with the results. She and Richard busily worked at hanging pictures, changing out a few of the window treatments, and putting bed skirts between the box springs and mattresses. Then Ann made the beds and topped them with coverlets and throw pillows she had bought to coordinate with the colors of the walls and window coverings in each room. Miraculously, they finished two days before they had to go back to their jobs, and when they walked through the house to take stock of their handiwork, they liked what they saw.

Ann decided they should invite Nelson, Sarah, and Olivia for dinner at their house before she had to get back in the thick of things at the theater. It would be a small way of thanking them for everything they had done, and it would also be an opportunity for them to see the house. She wondered if Sarah and Olivia knew about Nelson's gift. They probably suspected it when they learned she and Richard were not living in Richard's apartment as they had planned to do.

On Saturday evening before Ann and Richard had to return to work on Monday, they hosted the small dinner party. Sarah and Olivia arrived ahead of Nelson, and the minute Olivia walked through the front door, she exclaimed, "This is an absolutely gorgeous home!" She looked around the entryway and into the living room and added, "And somebody did a beautiful job decorating it. Did you use a decorator?"

"No," Ann replied, "Richard and I just put our heads together and this is the way it turned out. We wanted it to be attractive, but most of all, we wanted it to fit our lifestyle."

"Well, that's the most important thing," Sarah interjected, "since you're the ones who will be living with it every day. But I agree with Olivia; it is tastefully decorated."

When Nelson arrived, Richard gave them the grand tour while Ann did other last-minute meal preparations. They started downstairs and worked their way up. When their tour brought them back downstairs and into the kitchen, Nelson gestured a thumbs-up and voiced his one-word opinion: "Perfect!" he shouted.

Following dinner, they answered questions, mostly from Olivia, about their trip to Hawaii and the excitement of coming back to a new house.

"Well, it isn't really a *new* house," Richard explained. "My understanding is that it was built thirty-two years ago, but it's new to us and we love it."

"It has been well-maintained, though," Nelson put in. "I had it thoroughly checked out."

"*Well,*" Ann thought, "*if Sarah and Olivia didn't already know Nelson was the one who had purchased the property, they must have figured it out by now.*"

As the three of them were leaving, they told Ann how delicious the meal was and stressed again their delight with Richard and Ann's new home. "I'm very happy for you," Sarah declared, "and I have a very selfish reason for loving your house—it's close to mine, so you can come see me every day!"

The theater was all abuzz on this first day back to work. Everyone was excited about *Island Dream*. The only problem was that the musical offered few speaking parts for women, so most of the females would be cast as part of the chorus.

After giving painstaking consideration to her options, Ann decided she would audition for Rose Marie DePue, the female lead role. She knew it would be a gamble. If she didn't get the part, she would be part of the chorus—or even worse—relegated to the pool of back-ups.

Today was a day for getting organized, and auditions would start tomorrow, beginning with those for the lead roles. The work day was abbreviated, and performers were free to leave after they had signed up for an audition and had done whatever preparation they needed to do. Ann had arrived at the theater at 9:30 a.m. and was ready to leave by noon. She decided to call Charlie to see if they could get together for lunch. She hadn't seen or talked with her since the wedding, and she was anxious to tell her all about Hawaii and the house and to find out how things were going with her.

The timing was perfect. Charlie was getting ready to leave her apartment when Ann called, so they agreed to meet in at Frankie's, an old-fashioned hot-lunch café. Ann was already seated when Charlie came through the door, and she could see from a distance that she was all smiles and had a bounce in her step. She plopped down in the seat opposite Ann and immediately began the interrogation. "Okay, was Hawaii beautiful? Was the weather warm and wonderful? Was your hotel fabulous? Did you have the honeymoon suite?"

"Charlie, Charlie," Ann laughed, "It's so good to hear you chattering away like this. I know you have been going through a rough time with your job, so I take your enthusiasm as a sign you're feeling better about things. Am I right?"

"Yes, you're right about that, and there's more. I'll tell you all about it, but you have to answer my questions first."

"I can answer all of them with one word—*Yes*. Everything was perfect! But I have more news—Richard's dad bought us a house and even furnished it, and Charlie, it isn't just some little early-marriage starter home. It's huge and fabulous! I feel like I'm living in a castle!"

"You can't be serious! That's incredible! I can't wait to see it."

"I don't have anything the rest of today. What about you?"

"Sorry, but I have to be at the theater by 3:30 this afternoon," Charlie moaned.

"Okay, but you'll need to come over soon. Now tell me what's going on with you."

"Well, one thing is that things have smoothed out at work, and I'm feeling a lot better about how the other cast members feel about me.

"But that's not the only good thing that's happened. You know I met Bill Lambert at your wedding. He took me to the theater when we left Mrs. Buffington's house that day. Then he came back to the show, and we went to eat afterwards. We've had several dates since then, and I really enjoy being with him, and Ann, I think he feels the same about me."

Ann was stunned by Charlie's revelation, and she couldn't keep from thinking about her own negative attitude toward Bill. However, she didn't want to extinguish the flicker of romance Charlie obviously felt existed between her and Bill. "Oh, that's great. I had no idea you two had hit it off so well. Are you saying you think this might be a serious relationship?"

"At this point, I really don't know, but I do think that's a possibility. Wouldn't it be something if I married Bill," she giggled. "Friends married to friends. What fun we could have together!"

"Yes, that would be wonderful wouldn't it?" Ann muttered.

CHAPTER 29

"Hi Daddy, I feel ashamed that I haven't called you since we got home. A lot has happened since we last talked, and it suddenly dawned on me that you don't have my current phone number and don't even know how to get in touch with me." She gave him their telephone number and continued, "Is Everything all right with you?"

"I'm great, sweetheart. You sound chipper. I take it married life is agreeing with you."

Ann laughed, "You could say that. I know this isn't a legitimate excuse, but the reason I haven't called is that life has been a whirlwind here lately. The day we got back from Hawaii, Nelson met us at the airport and whisked us to a house he had bought for us as a wedding gift. Daddy, it's a beautiful home just a block down from Sarah. And—you won't believe this—he also bought us all new furniture. We have two spare bedrooms, so when you and Aunt Lil and Uncle Ben come to visit, your rooms will be waiting for you."

"Wow! That's some wedding present! I hope you thanked him," he teased.

"We were just amazed. I think our reluctance to accept his gifts hurt his feelings a little bit, but we've thanked him dozens of times since then.

"I have more good news, Daddy: I auditioned for the lead female role in *Island Dream* and got it! Five others tried out, so I feel honored to have been selected for the part. I would like to think," Ann giggled, "that I bowled them over with my talent, but I really think the fact that I had played the part in community theater and was familiar with the music was the clincher for me. We won't have much time to prepare before opening night."

"I'm so proud of you, Annie. Isn't it quite a leap from the dance troupe in *Flapperville* to the leading lady in *Island Dream*?"

"It is, and I'm humbled by it. I wanted so badly to be successful, but I never dreamed I could go this far this fast."

"We may be using those bedrooms pretty soon then. We can't miss *this* performance. When does it open?"

"March 1, and I have a feeling that's going to get here before I'm ready for it. If I don't call as often as I usually do, it will be because rehearsals are going to be long and hard. I will probably be exhausted every day when I get home."

"That's okay, honey. You're a busy little girl—sorry—young woman. You just squeeze me in when you can. I just wish your mother were here. She would be so proud of you."

"You know, Daddy, sometimes it's almost as if she *is* here. It seems I can feel her comforting me when I'm discouraged and smiling at the good things that have happened in my life."

As they continued sharing their hearts and clinging to cherished memories, Ann felt a closeness to her daddy that melted away the years. Their relationship had evolved to a new dimension of maturity and understanding.

By January 20, rehearsals had begun. The Players worked tirelessly, and gradually imperfections were corrected, and little missteps and errors were ironed out. Ann felt good about how it had all come together under the direction of Maxwell Markowitz. Everyone—cast and crew alike—had worked hard to make it what they considered an extraordinary show, and they had done it in record time. They were ready!

Daddy, Aunt Lil, and Uncle Ben wanted to be there for opening night, so Ann had purchased preferred seating for them. Almost all seats offered a good view of the stage, but she wanted to give them the full theater experience. Their seats were on the third row behind the orchestra pit.

Opening night finally arrived, and Ann developed an unwelcome malady called *stage fright*. Through the years, two or three other times she had suffered mild, short-lived episodes but had always gotten herself under control. This time was different. It started with jitters about noon and by early afternoon, she had a headache, queasiness and a tightness in her throat. In her dressing room two hours before show time, she tried meditation, deep breathing exercises, and listening to soft, soothing music. Nothing seemed to work.

As the minutes ticked away, she began to panic. Hot tears rolled down her cheeks, and she found herself in the grip of a negative, debasing self-assessment: *After all my hard work and this big break, I'm going to blow this opportunity. I will embarrass myself and my family. The audience won't like me, and I can just imagine what horrible things the critics will have to say. The house is supposed to be packed—a house packed with hostile patrons. This just can't be happening!*

Suddenly, a loud bang against the window high on the wall of her dressing room interrupted her thoughts, and she looked up to see a bird fluttering feverishly in an obvious attempt to get inside. It flew a few yards away only to return and slam against the window pane a second time. She thought she saw it drop to the ground, so she used a nearby step stool to lift herself high enough to see the area beneath the window. She spotted the bird, a ball of puffy gray, squatting in the snow that had collected there. It appeared addled and sat perfectly still except for a slight quivering. Then in a sudden flurry of energy, it burst into flight and was gone.

Strangely, this diversion seemed to restore Ann's confidence. *That little bird just learned a lesson*, she mused. *She learned not to be fooled by something that isn't what it appears to be. Her senses played a trick on her, but she refused to let that false perception defeat her. She gathered herself and courageously spread her wings and took to the air. After all, birds are meant to fly.*

After those hours of paralyzing fear, the shackles of terror fell away. Ann took the stage, relaxed and poised. She could honestly say she relished that first performance. From somewhere deep inside, she felt herself growing and stretching to meet new challenges. Her confidence level had skyrocketed after that first taste of success on opening night, but she knew she could take nothing for granted. Botched renderings could sneak up on even the most seasoned performers, and she knew she had to stay focused and put all she had into every show.

Island Dream closed after six months. With glowing reviews from critics as the run drew to an end, Charlie and several of the Pinwheel group told Ann she should turn her attention to bigger things. Zach Minelli expressed the same opinion. He told her he felt he could get her an audition with a larger venue. She was flattered and excited by their confidence in her, and she placed her career in Zach's hands.

The next day after her contract with Pinwheel ended, Ann called Charlie and asked her to come over about mid-morning of the following day. She told her she would put together a chicken salad and they could have a private, relaxing lunch without the hustle and bustle of a restaurant. In an earlier conversation, Charlie had hinted at something that had piqued Ann's interest and she wanted to ask Charlie about it.

Charlie arrived bearing her usual exuberance and a bouquet of flowers. After several minutes of giggling and chit-chat between the good friends, Ann mentioned the conversation they'd had two days earlier that had been left dangling, at least for Ann. "Charlie, when we were talking on the phone the other day, you said something puzzling. I think your words were, 'I may not even be doing theater much longer.' What did you mean by that?"

"Oh, that . . . well . . . it's true." She looked at Ann and her lips parted in a big smile. "Ann, Bill asked me to marry him, and I accepted. I wasn't going to tell you yet. Bill wanted us to get with you and Richard and tell the two of you together, but I've been so anxious to tell you, I was about to burst. You'll just have to play dumb when we make the big announcement."

"Charlie! I'm . . . I'm thrilled for you," Ann said. "When is the wedding?"

"We don't know yet. Several things will figure into that decision, both at Bill's end of the line and at mine. Bill's dad is really sick and has been given only a few months to live. Bill just can't leave him right now."

"Oh, I'm sorry. But I still don't understand. Do you mean you're quitting your career because you're getting married? Richard and I seem to be balancing our professional and personal lives just fine, but I guess that doesn't work for everybody."

"I have no doubt we could do that, but I don't want to. I'll be honest, Ann, I'm getting a little burned out. I think I just want to stay home and be a wife and eventually, a mother. I might do some teaching in my home, but I'm just tired of fighting the competition and trying to please everybody when *everybody* can't agree on what they expect of me."

When Charlie left to get to her rehearsal, Ann's thoughts turned again to the news that Charlie and Bill were getting married. The longer she chewed on her feelings about Bill, the larger the mouthful of bitterness became. *Richard and Charlie must be seeing something in him I have missed,* she told herself. *Bill must have changed, and I'm the only one who hasn't been around him enough to see it. I still have his phone number; I think I'll call him and see if we can meet.*

Under Richard's leadership, Buffngton Nationwide Movers had climbed to one of the top three among all New York City based moving companies. Richard had made THE ONE YOU CAN TRUST the company motto, and he stood behind it.

He maintained rigid expectations of his employees. It was his belief that, in the long run, it was better business to pay more and get principled workers than to have lawsuits dogging him because of inferior service. His strategy seemed to be paying off. Buffington wasn't the least expensive choice for customers, but the company was rapidly gaining a reputation for integrity, reliability, and trustworthiness; and most customers were willing to pay extra for that peace of mind.

Richard and his dad seemed to be bonding as never before, and it was all due to Richard's success. Nelson had always expected Richard to excel at whatever *he*, as a prudent father, decided his son should do, and he hadn't been shy about showing his disapproval and disappointment when Richard failed to measure up. Now—maybe for the first time in Richard's life—Nelson was ecstatic over his son's performance, and he strutted around proudly declaring Richard's genius and innate understanding of the business world to all who would listen. Of course, overtones of his own savvy for having fathered and trained such a prodigy also crept into his assertions.

CHAPTER 30

"*I* hope I haven't inconvenienced you, Bill. I just felt we needed to talk. I haven't seen you since the wedding, and even then, we didn't really visit."

"Yes, I know," he laughed, "but you were a little preoccupied that day. I'm glad you called though. I've been wanting to visit with you too."

"Charlie told me about the wedding plans."

"Yes, and it was your wedding that brought us together in the first place, so I guess I need to thank you for the opportunity to meet her. She's just the girl I've been waiting for, Ann. I didn't know I could love anyone as much as I love her."

"Well, she loves you very much, and I hope you two will be as happy as Richard and I have been." There was a long pause before Ann redirected the conversation. "I feel a little bit awkward discussing this with you, Bill, but since you're Richard's best friend and you are marrying *my* best friend, I just feel I need to get to know you better.

"As you know, I was very upset by what you said about Richard when we ran into each other last October, and I'll admit I came away with some hard feelings toward you. Later, when you apologized, I just couldn't accept your apology. I don't really know why. I guess I still wasn't sure I could trust you. Well, you and Richard have patched things up, and Richard feels you two are even closer than you were in high school. Charlie, of course, knows nothing about any of this rift. To her, you're just her knight in shining armor, and I want it to stay that way.

"I'm bringing all this up now because I don't like having this negative attitude toward you. If Richard has accepted your apology and now considers you a good friend, then I should accept your apology too. I don't want to keep harboring these bad feelings."

"I'm glad to hear you say that, Ann. I knew you resented me and didn't really believe I was sincere when I apologized, but I *am* truly sorry for the things I said and for the pain I caused you and Richard.

"You know, when I look back on my life, I'm ashamed of what I see—a teen-ager who drifted right on into manhood trying to bolster his own ego by making other people look foolish. That's a humiliating thing to have to admit, but I'm trying to reinvent myself. I want to be a man people will trust and respect, and I've had to start by learning to respect myself.

"You really struck a nerve when we talked that day and you pinned me down about whether or not I was being truthful. The more I thought about what you said, the more I could see how fouled up my attitude was. I realized I was not only hurting other people, but I was hurting myself as well.

"I'll tell you what has helped me more than anything, and I hope you won't think this sounds sanctimonious or pretentious. I went to talk to the pastor of my church. I hadn't attended church since I was about fifteen years old and my mom and dad quit making me go.

"The pastor now is a different guy from the one who was there when I was a kid, and he and I really hit it off. He's a little bit older than I am, but we have a lot in common. He quit going to church during his teen-age years too," Bill chuckled. "His advice sounds simple, but it isn't really that simple, at least not for me. He suggested I set aside a special time every day to read the Bible and pray. We talked about a lot of things, but in a nutshell, he said, 'Just tell God what you've told me and ask Him to help you be the man *He* wants you to be.' So that's what I'm trying to do."

Ann was deeply touched by Bill's openness in discussing his personal pilgrimage. She instantly sensed a depth of sincerity and honesty in him. As she listened to him, it was as if a weight was being lifted from her. She hadn't even realized what a burden she'd been carrying and how heavy resentment and bitterness could be.

"Bill, what you've just told me doesn't sound sanctimonious at all—just the opposite. It sounds like the honest admission of a man humbly asking God to help him right a wrong. I would call that courageous, not sanctimonious."

"Thank you, Ann. It means a lot to me that you believe me. Well, enough about that," Bill declared as he leaned forward and rested his arms on the table. "Richard tells me your acting career has really taken off."

"It does seem to be going in the right direction for now. However, in this business, success turns on the whims of the audience. I've been very fortunate and am thankful for the breaks I've had. And many of those breaks have come through the efforts of my good friend Charlie."

Ann paused and looked at Bill with new eyes. "I'm so glad we had this talk, Bill. You know, I've always taken pride in being fair-minded; in fact, some people think I'm too trusting. Lately, though, I've been seeing something in myself I don't like. I tend to be judgmental, and I have no right to judge the heart of another person. I judged you, Bill, and I'm sorry for that. Maybe I'm the one who needs to do some changing. I'll say this though—I don't think you're the same man as the one who said all those things about Richard. I knew that deep down you had to be a good guy because Charlie can spot a charlatan from a mile away," she teased.

Bill laughed, "How well I know! I'm not sure she didn't put me in that category the first couple of times we went out, but I know she trusts me now. She told me she'd been engaged to a guy a while back and that he turned out to be a big disappointment. I guess it was hard for her to trust any man after that."

"Yes, it was, and I wasn't sure she ever would. I'll be honest with you, Bill. When Charlie told me the relationship between you two was getting serious, I was afraid for her. I didn't want her to be hurt again, but you've convinced me you really love her."

They parted, and Ann walked away with an almost euphoric relief of the guilt-laden grudge she'd been harboring against Bill.

The next day, Ann was eager to tell Sarah about her conversation with Bill. She knew she could tell Sarah anything and she would understand, but she didn't want to go into the details of Bill's scandalous stories about Richard. Therefore, she mentioned only that Bill had said some things about Richard that he later recanted, and that he had admitted to being jealous of Richard back in their high school days.

"Over the months, my anger at Bill just kept building. It grew into bitterness, and that feeling was just killing me inside. It was like a sore that refused to heal. As Bill and I talked yesterday, though, all that bitterness just melted away, and I can't tell you how good it felt."

"Well, that story had a good ending. I'm glad you resolved your differences. It sounds like Bill had a lot of fences to mend, and maybe not all of them with you and Richard. I can understand why you felt about him as you did. But you know, we're all human, and we all let those human weaknesses creep up on us. I'm glad Bill was able to overcome his jealousy and his tendency to lie about other people. Lying and jealousy are twin brothers. They're like poison ivy and poison oak—they sort of reach out and grab people, and the victims don't even know they've been infected until it's too late. I'm proud of you, Ann, for handling that situation with Bill Lambert the way you did."

"What do you mean? I didn't handle it well at all! That's why I felt so guilty."

"You did exactly what needed to be done. You opened Bill's eyes into his own soul. You helped him see what he had done and how damaging it had been to other people and to himself. You didn't do it in a mean-spirited way, but in a way that encouraged him to correct the problem."

"Yes, but it took me a year to finally accept his apology, and because of my stubborn refusal to take him at his word, we both suffered. I told him I'd been too judgmental and that I needed to correct my ways just as he had corrected his."

"I understand what you're saying, Ann, but you're judging yourself too harshly. You weren't *gloating* over Bill's misdeeds. You may not have even thought of it in these terms, but you wanted what was best for Bill, not just what was best for you and Richard. I'll say again, you handled it well."

CHAPTER 31

"Richard, if Zach has any luck in getting me into a show, it will probably blip out our opportunity to celebrate on our anniversary. How would you feel about taking a long weekend and driving up the coast to New Haven for an early celebration? One of the girls at Pinwheel told me about a really nice bed and breakfast up there. Is your schedule too busy for that, maybe next weekend or the one after that?"

"I think we can do that. I'll just need to get someone to take over for me for a day or two. Dad might do it, but if not, there are a couple of other guys that can competently handle things. How about leaving on Thursday and coming back on Sunday?"

"If you can swing it, that would be great."

The next day, Richard called Ann from his office. "I mentioned to Dad about taking Thursday and Friday off next week, and he was all for it. He even volunteered to cover for me while we're gone. I guess I caught him in a good mood," Richard laughed. "Anyway, I wanted to let you know so you can begin making plans."

"That's wonderful, Richard. I'm so ready to get away for a while and have you all to myself. I'm selfish, you know," she teased.

Ann had noticed that for the last several months, Nelson had seemed to be more considerate and less self-absorbed. After what she considered her shameful misjudgment of Bill Lambert's penitence, she didn't want to make the same mistake with Nelson. Therefore, she dismissed her twinge of doubt about Nelson's motive for so willingly approving Richard's request for some time off.

With the top down on their red convertible, Ann and Richard

soaked in the delightful August day. The sun's rays toasted their skin, but the car's momentum sucked the ocean air across their bodies, cooling them and filling them with a sense of total tranquility.

"I love the smell of the ocean; it relaxes me and helps me leave everything else behind and enjoy the beauty of the scenery," Ann said dreamily.

"Me too," Richard smiled, putting his arm around her and drawing her close to his side, "especially when I'm with my sweetheart. This was a great idea. I'm glad you suggested it."

It was a leisurely trip up the coast. They couldn't get into their room at Oceanside Inn until 2:00 p.m. anyway, so they pulled into a restaurant and lingered over a scrumptious lobster feast. They requested seating on the covered deck where they could feel the gentle ocean breeze, hear waves lapping at the shore, and see whitecaps dancing in the sunlight.

The Oceanside Inn, a spacious two-story Victorian, was operated by two beyond-middle-age sisters named Elizabeth and Martha who lived at the inn in a downstairs private suite. Elizabeth was a spritely little woman who walked with short staccato steps and whose smile spoke a language all its own. Wearing a long Victorian-style dress, she welcomed Ann and Richard to the inn. A young man named Edward, also dressed in Victorian garb, carried their bags to their room. Edward appeared to be in his mid-thirties, but he had a naïve, childlike demeanor. When Richard handed him a five-dollar bill, he took it with both hands, shyly lowered his head, and smiled at Richard. He did not speak.

They decided to go for a walk before dinner, which was to be served at seven. After browsing in some little shops, they walked down to the beach. Sunbathers and children with sand buckets dotted the shore, and above the ocean's rumble, swimmers could be heard laughing and playing.

They sat down on the beach and dug their bare feet deep into the cool, wet sand. "This brings back memories, doesn't it?" Richard asked.

"I was just thinking the same thing. When I close my eyes and feel the sand between my toes, I am in Hawaii."

They basked in this time together, away from responsibilities and worries. It was just the escape they needed. As Ann bathed herself in memories of their honeymoon, she decided their love was even deeper than it had been eight months ago. Life was good.

After dinner, as they sat on the little balcony outside their room, Richard interrupted what had been a time of quiet relaxation: "Ann, you will be surprised to hear me ask this, but how would you feel about us starting a family? I know you have this Broadway thing dangling, but maybe we should start thinking about having a baby. I know how you love children."

Bolting up from her reclined position, Ann almost shouted, "Richard! I thought you didn't *want* children. Are you saying what I think you're saying?"

"Yes," he chuckled. "How do you feel about it? Would it jeopardize your career?"

A surge of excitement gripped her. He actually wanted a child. She was elated by this sudden admission.

"I'm all for it!" she giggled. "My career is important to me, but nothing takes priority to this!"

Driving away and bidding farewell to New Haven and their blissful second honeymoon, Richard turned to Ann and asked, "How soon will we know?"

"Know what?" Ann asked, puzzled by his ambiguity.

"Whether or not you're pregnant." Richard stated emphatically, his tone suggesting the meaning of his question should have been clear to her.

"Probably within the next month," she giggled, "but Richard, it can sometimes take several months. Just because we want to have a baby doesn't mean it will happen right away. Until two days ago, I had been on *the pill* ever since we married. I'm not sure, but I think that could delay things. We'll just have to wait and see what happens. If you're thinking I should tell Zach to forget about my career for a while, I don't want to do that yet. I could probably work for two or three months after I become pregnant, and that would give the theater plenty of time to find a replacement."

"I just don't want you to get yourself into something you can't get out of, and I don't want you to do anything risky . . . you know . . . like . . . you could fall or something."

Ann giggled again at his somber warning, but this manifestation of his protective male instinct warmed her heart.

CHAPTER 32

*I*n September, Zach called to say Ann had a chance for a part as a member of the chorus in *Mr. Showman*, but she would need to get in to audition as soon as possible. The musical had been running for over a year at the Regal, but with long-running Broadway shows, turnover in the chorus wasn't unusual. Zach said that *if* the show had an exceptionally long run, it could mean she would have a chance to move another rung up the ladder.

Ann was thrilled when she learned she had been chosen for the part. She threw herself into her work, and the choreographer gave her some time to rehearse with the group before she took her spot in the show. It was challenging, but she usually worked best when the pressure was on, and she soon felt she was ready.

For four months, she focused on her role with the chorus. Then one blustery evening in January, she received a call from Zach. "Ann, *Mr. Showman* has a spot opening up in the dance troupe. As you know, it's a much more select group and would give you more exposure. I think you have a good chance for it if you're interested."

Ann shrieked her elation, "Of course, I'm interested! How could I pass up an opportunity like this?" She began attending the rehearsals of the dancers, and three days later, moved from observer to participant. She couldn't believe it! She had, as Zach had predicted, moved *another rung up the ladder*.

Patti Santiago, the choreographer for the ten-member ensemble, told her she would be phased into performances as she continued rehearsing with the dancers. Ann worked diligently at perfecting the intricate routines so she would be ready when her time came. She felt honored to have been chosen for the part and hoped her performance would meet the expectations of the woman who had lovingly been dubbed *Patti Perfect*.

Richard had become impatient that Ann hadn't become pregnant, and his anxiety bewildered Ann. It seemed he had done an about-face in how he felt about children. Less than a year ago he had told her he didn't want children, that he was happy with things as they were. She wondered what had brought about this change in his thinking. It didn't matter, though. She was thankful for it.

One morning during the first full week of rehearsals with the dance troupe, Ann woke up nauseated. She told Richard, "I can't call in sick. I just can't risk losing this part, and Patti Santiago is a real stickler when it comes to being present and punctual."

"You mean you are going on to work although you're sick?" Richard asked. "That sounds risky. I hope your stomach settles before you have to start dancing. I'll get breakfast at Sammy's Café so you can rest a while longer."

Ann slept for another hour or so. Then she dragged herself out of bed, showered, dressed, and forced down half of a piece of dry toast. By the time she was ready to leave for rehearsal, her nausea was almost gone.

The next morning and the one after that, it was the same— nausea the minute she opened her eyes. She had already decided her sickness wasn't due to something she had eaten, and she had strong suspicions regarding its source. By the third morning, she felt sure. "Richard," she muttered while they were still in bed, "I am sick again, and I think I know why. I'm pretty sure I'm pregnant."

Richard propped his head up on one elbow, looked at her with a big grin on his face and shouted, "I knew it! I *just* knew it! I wish it wasn't Saturday so we could call for an appointment with Dr. Anderson. We'll do that first thing Monday morning," he said. Richard immediately began tossing out names he thought they should consider—all male names. When Ann mentioned some names for girls, he seemed almost offended. Richard was adamant that this baby had to be a boy. Ann didn't care. She was filled with joyful anticipation, boy or girl, it didn't matter.

Ann's appointment with Dr. Anderson was on Thursday, and Richard announced, "I'm going with you in case you forget to ask him something important."

"I *am* a grown woman, you know, and I think I have a reasonable degree of intelligence."

"I know, but you'll need some moral support," he insisted.

She circled her arms around his neck and smiled up at him. "I want you to go. I need you with me." she said. His desire to go with her had triggered in her an overwhelming yearning to be enfolded in his arms. Standing on tiptoes, she drew his head forward and planted a lingering kiss gently on his lips. "I love you, Richard. I love you for being a sensitive, caring husband."

Dr. Anderson couldn't tell by the examination whether or not Ann was pregnant. Based on what she had told him, he thought probably she was, but he would do a rabbit test, and he should be able to give them the results by Monday. They left the doctor's office disappointed that he was unable to immediately confirm their hopes. "I guess we'll just have to wonder for another four days," Richard moaned as he opened the car door for her.

"We've waited all these months; surely we can wait four more days," Ann laughed, but she, too, was eager to put an end to the uncertainty.

As Richard drove her to the theater, she turned pensive: "You know, it's funny—a few months ago, the thought of becoming pregnant would have scared me to death. In theater, absence *doesn't* make the heart grow fonder. In fact, by the time I have this baby, I'll probably be nothing more than an eraser mark on a page of Broadway history. The strange thing is that I'm at peace about it. Until recently, my career was the most important thing in my life, next to you, of course," she said, squeezing Richard's arm, "but the minute I found out you wanted a baby, that all changed. I want this baby! No matter what happens with my career, I *long for* this baby!"

"Well, that makes two of us, and Dad and Grandmother are going to be elated when we tell them. I guess we'd better hold off on that until we know for sure."

Back at home after rehearsal, Ann was in a quandary about what to do about breaking the news to Zach. She dickered back and forth between telling and not telling but ultimately decided a few days would make no difference. Those four days were an eternity of misery—waiting, wondering, knowing yet not knowing.

When Ann got home from rehearsal on Monday and walked into the living room, Richard was sitting on the sofa reading *Time*. A huge bouquet of red roses was on the coffee table before him. He looked up and laid the magazine aside. Then he stood and folded his arms across his chest, his typical cat-who-ate-the-canary look.

"Okay, what's the occasion? Did I forget something?" she asked. He was always reminding her of the date of this or that memorable occasion. He was much better at remembering those dates than she was.

"Read the card with the roses and you'll know."

She slipped the card from the envelope, and he watched her facial expression change as she read:

> Roses are Red;
> Violets are Blue;
> We are pregnant!
> It's definitely true!

Under different circumstances, she would have laughed at his corny version of this little verse, but today its message captured her heart. She flew into his arms. "Oh, Richard," she cried as the tears began to flow. "I'm going to have a baby! I was almost sure of it, but I can't describe how it feels to *know*!" As suddenly as the tears had come, they dried up. "Wait a minute. How is it you were given the test results? Why wasn't I contacted?"

"I knew you'd wonder about that. I called Dr. Anderson and asked him to let me know first. I told him I wanted to make it a special time of celebration if the test was positive, and I wanted to be the one to comfort you if it was negative. Thank goodness it was positive! I didn't look forward to having to disappoint you."

CHAPTER 33

Ann called her daddy first, and despite his typical laid-back reaction, she knew he was thrilled for them. "Well, I can't retire yet and move to New York, so I guess I'll be spending a lot of time riding on airplanes," he commented. "I don't want my grandson to grow up not knowing his grandpa."

"I think you just let it slip that you're in Richard's camp; you want a grandson."

"That would be all right, but I'd settle for another little girl just like you."

"Oh, good," she giggled, "I don't want everybody except me to be disappointed if this baby is a girl. Anyway, I wanted you to be the first to know. I have some other calls to make, so I'll call you again later when we can talk longer. I love you."

"I love you too, and I'm looking forward to being a grandpa. You take care of yourself, sweetheart."

When she got off the phone with her daddy, she called Aunt Lil, Charlie, and Zach, in that order. Aunt Lil cried quiet tears of happiness. Charlie let out a deafening scream. Zach said, "Hmmm," and she could hear the wheels of his brain grinding out how he should handle this unexpected change in her career.

She and Richard had decided to ask Nelson and Sarah out to a nice restaurant and find some novel way to make the big announcement. Ann suggested they ask Olivia to join them: "She was so gracious in preparing that wonderful meal on our wedding day," Ann put forth, "I feel we need to include her in this special time also." Richard agreed.

They decided to make a date with the three of them for Sunday evening. Olivia would be at Sarah's house anyway, so Ann and Richard could pick them up and they could all go to the restaurant together. Nelson would meet them there.

On Saturday morning, Ann called the little flower shop owned and operated by Sarah's friend Maggie. She wasn't sure she would get an answer on a weekend and was about to hang up when she heard Maggie's cheery "Finley's Flowers." She explained to Maggie the little surprise they were planning and asked if she could do a tabletop arrangement appropriate for the occasion. Maggie was a tiny ball of creative energy who talked fast and had a delightful laugh. She was always bursting with ideas, and she gleefully suggested, "I have just the thing—a miniature baby buggy. I'll fill it with delicate fern and baby's breath and stick two or three toy blocks in with the foliage. It will be perfect.

Ann called the restaurant and spoke with the manager. He agreed to reserve a table for them in a somewhat secluded area and to have the special floral arrangement placed on their table before they arrived at 7:00 o'clock.

As Sarah got into their car on Sunday evening, she asked, "Well, what's the special occasion? Family gatherings are usually at my house."

Ann and Richard looked at each other. Sarah was suspicious, but Richard nonchalantly replied, "Does there have to be a special occasion for us to take the people we love out to dinner?"

Sarah cackled, "Absolutely not! We could do this every week, couldn't we, Olivia?"

"I'd have no problem with that—that is, if Richard wants to foot the bill every time," Olivia replied.

Sarah delighted in Olivia's spunky reply since she rarely participated in family bantering. Maybe at age fifty-six, she was learning to relax and have fun.

Nelson was waiting in the foyer when they arrived. They joined him and exchanged chitchat for a few minutes before Richard approached the Maître d, who flashed him a knowing smile and led them to their table. After they were seated, Sarah piped up, "So this isn't a special occasion, huh?" She looked across the table at Richard and Ann and added, "Would you like to explain this pretty little centerpiece?"

"Ann will do that, Grandmother, after we've ordered."

"It seems self-explanatory to me," Nelson chimed in.

Nelson was sitting next to Sarah, and she held her little clutch bag in front of her mouth, leaned in close to him, and whispered, "Hush, Nelson. I've already said too much. We don't want to *completely* spoil their surprise."

They gave their attention to the menu for a while. Then after the waiter had served their beverages and taken their orders, Richard unfolded his six-foot-two-inch body and proudly stood to his full height. He paused, and then, as if he were introducing the guest speaker at a banquet, he announced, "Ann has something to tell you, something we hope will make you as happy as it has made us." With that, he sat down. The three of them looked at Ann in silent anticipation.

Remaining seated, Ann said, "As Nelson said, the centerpiece is a giveaway. Last Friday we learned that our family size will increase, by only one we hope," she giggled; "however, if it turns out to be more than one, we'll be happy with that too."

The three guests laughed softly and beamed with approval. "When is the baby due, Ann?" Olivia asked.

"We think it will be the first week of October. Maybe we'll know more when we see Dr. Anderson again."

"How exciting!" Sarah exclaimed. "What fun it will be to have a baby in the family! I'll be sure I have a high chair in time for our Easter meal."

"Well, this is great news!" Nelson exclaimed. "I told Richard you guys had better get busy so we would have a new Buffington to take over the family business when he retires."

"Oh, you're always thinking of *business*, Nelson. For heaven's sake, let us all enjoy this great news without listening to you plan the child's future," Sarah admonished.

"It was just a comment, Mother. I'm not trying to plan the child's future. That would be a bit premature; besides, I'm leaving that job to Richard."

As if a curtain had dropped on time, Ann's mind couldn't move beyond Nelson's perfunctory declaration. Or maybe it was much more than that. Maybe it was the first step in a premeditated, clandestine deal cooked up by Nelson and Richard—or more accurately—cooked up by Nelson and carried out by Richard.

On their way home from the restaurant, Sarah and Olivia thanked Richard and Ann for the good time and the wonderful meal. Sarah again told them how happy she was about the baby and that she could hardly wait for October. "I'd better speed up my knitting. I have blankets and all sorts of things to make. Olivia, you need to buy me some yarn in soft pink and blue and other pastel shades."

Richard seemed to be enjoying the light-heartedness of the occasion. He chatted away with his grandmother and his aunt, laughing and teasing all the way to Sarah's house.

Except for polite responses to their congratulatory expressions, Ann was silent. Her mind was busy trying to decide how Richard really felt about this new addition to their family. Ever since their New Haven trip, she had been convinced he truly wanted a child they could love and nurture to become confident and responsible in finding his own direction in life. She had assumed they agreed about these key issues of child rearing. Now she had doubts. Had his plan all along been, as Nelson had implied, to produce and groom a new Buffington to take over the family business?

CHAPTER 34

Ann didn't want to jump to conclusions, and she didn't want to approach Richard with doubts and accusations, so she chose not to say anything to him about the questions that were torturing her: *Was Nelson responsible for Richard's sudden interest in starting a family? Did Richard want them to have a baby so he could satisfy his dad's desire for an heir to someday take over the family business?*

The love she felt for this child flooded her whole being, and she needed to know Richard shared that love. He seemed excited about the baby, so maybe she was making something out of nothing. Maybe it was as Nelson had claimed—that his statement about having someone to take over the business was just a casual comment and not intended to be taken seriously.

After several weeks of wrestling with the feelings Nelson's words had stirred inside her, Ann decided to discuss her concerns with Richard. One night after they had gone to bed, she snuggled into his arms. Then she whispered, "I love you, Richard, and I love our baby. Even though I haven't seen him or held him in my arms, I love him. Do you feel that way too?

"Of course, I do," he affirmed. Then he grinned, "Does this mean you're conceding the baby is a boy?"

She pulled away from his embrace and retorted, "Oh, be serious, Richard, you know what I mean. I'm not joking."

"Yeah, I know what you mean," he laughed, "but you left yourself open for that, and I couldn't resist teasing you."

"I guess I just need to be reassured that you love our baby the way I do."

His countenance softened. He looked at her silently for a moment, seemingly giving serious thought to choosing his words. Then, in what was almost a whisper, he said, "At this stage, I'm sure your love for the baby is different from mine. After all, he's part of you; he's growing inside your body. But I *do* love our baby," he said sincerely. "My love, though, is more in thinking about what he will bring to our lives after he is born. I look forward to having a little boy who will hold onto my finger when we go for walks. I envision taking him to the park and the zoo, to teaching him to fly a kite and ride a bicycle. That's the kind of love I feel. I guess it's a love of anticipation. Do you understand?" He asked the question as if he thought his explanation wouldn't pass the love test and that she would be disappointed. But he was wrong.

She smiled at him, placed her hand on his face and kissed him softly on the lips. "I love you," she whispered as she snuggled closer into his embrace and pressed her cheek against his chest.

Bewildered, he lifted her head and looked at her. "Are you crying? I didn't mean to upset you. I was just trying to explain to you how I feel. I hoped you would understand."

"I do understand," she sobbed. "That's why I'm crying; these are happy tears. Oh, Richard," she cried, "I know you truly *want* our baby in the same way I do. I could hear it in your voice. You made a good point about why my love is different from the kind of love you feel. I should have thought of it myself—that carrying this baby inside me would naturally create a maternal bond that would be mine and mine alone. But that doesn't mean you love the baby any less than I do; it just means you love him in a different way."

"Well, I'm glad we got that settled," he sighed.

"Your timing wasn't the best in the world," Zach said, "but I'm happy for you. I just wish you could have stayed with the show long enough for them to see just how talented you are."

"I know I've let you down, Zach. You worked so hard to get this opportunity for me, and you brought me more success than I dreamed was possible. I'll forever be indebted to you."

"You're making it sound like we're at the end of the journey," he frowned. "That's definitely not the case. I'm expecting you, young lady, to get back into shape as fast as you can after you have this baby. Then I'm going to put you right back out there." He relaxed and was once again the fatherly Zach she had known. "I'll tell you, kiddo, you're more talented than you think you are. The thing you have that most upstarts don't is poise. Nothing is mechanical with you. Whether you're dancing, singing, or speaking, everything just flows naturally. You seem totally at home on stage."

"Wow! You're a great morale builder. Coming from you, those words mean a lot. You make me want to get back into action as soon as I can, but right now I don't know how soon that will be. I don't think it will take me long to get back into shape physically. I just don't know how soon I'll feel comfortable entrusting my baby to somebody else."

"I know. You're not the first I've had to follow down this road, and I'm sure you won't be the last. You just do what you feel is right for you. When is the baby is due?"

"Dr. Anderson says October 10. He did concede there was room for error, though. I think his words were, 'Babies have their own timetable.' I guess we'll wait and see."

"Hmmm, let's see. Today is April 3, so we still have a good six months to think about how to jumpstart your career after the baby decides to take the stage," Zach reasoned. "I'm glad you could meet with me today so we could talk things over, and I'll get right to the main thing I want to talk to you about. In negotiations with the people at the Regal, your contract is up on April 17. Under the circumstances, of course, it won't be renewed. You could stay with the chorus two more weeks if you want to. However, your replacement is ready to go and could step in at any time. It's up to you, but you need to let me know today so they'll know what to do about putting the new girl in. As I told you on the phone, everyone at the Regal wishes you well."

"I didn't expect to feel this way, Zach, but I can honestly say I'm ready to let go of the theater for a while and just concentrate on family. Richard is concerned that I might hurt myself, and I guess that's possible, but I'm not worried about that. I just don't see that my continuing to work would make any contribution, and I think it would be better for everybody if I just end it now. Can we work it that way? I mean, can you cancel the contract effective immediately?"

"Of course, I can. You've already given notice. It's easy to cancel a contract when all parties agree. I'll tell them today that you won't be back, so you can go clean out your stuff and that will end it. Is that what you want to do?"

"Yes, it is. I'll do that today." Zach seemed relieved, and she got the impression the theater had been putting pressure on him to move the date up for ending her contract. She could understand their need to cut her loose. It didn't make sense for her to continue to work when they already had someone ready to replace her. Anyway, she welcomed her immediate dismissal. Her work was physically demanding, and she felt she needed to take care of herself first and then worry about other obligations.

"Zach, I'd like to change the subject for a minute. I'm concerned about Charlie. Has she said anything to you that would indicate she's discouraged with her career?"

"Yeah, well, I don't know if I'd call it discouraged. I think she's just losing interest. You know she's planning to get married, but I don't need to fill you in on that. I think Charlie just doesn't want to spend her life being part of the chorus in off-Broadway theaters. I've learned never to judge what a young person might or might not be capable of doing, but I honestly don't think Charlie will ever hit the big time in musical theater. Don't get me wrong; she's very talented. She just isn't committed enough to pour her heart into it, and heart is half the battle."

"I didn't want to put you on the spot, but Charlie is my best friend. I don't want to see her give up on something unless it's for the right reason. Charlie was serious about another guy a while back; in fact, they were engaged to be married, and he broke it off because he couldn't compete with her career. I was afraid she might give up the theater so something like that wouldn't happen with Bill. But Bill Lambert is a good guy. I haven't always thought so, but that's another story. Anyway, I don't think he would demand she give up her career."

Zach stood to his feet. "I need to run now, but I want us to keep in touch. Just because I won't be representing you for a while doesn't mean I don't care about you. Keep me posted on things, especially when the baby comes." Zach was noted for putting an abrupt end to things. He had accomplished his mission, so he patted her hand and made a hasty exit. She watched him walk away, as it turned out, for the last time.

CHAPTER 35

April and May were happy months for Ann. Winter's biting chill had softened into spring, and the whole world was waking from a long sleep. Spring had always stirred something deep within her and renewed her zest for living. This spring carried a special kind of excitement—a vivid consciousness of the new life growing inside her body.

She stopped to visit with Sarah almost every day when she went for her morning walks, and she continued her weekly rendezvous with Charlie. She felt good. The morning sickness was gone, and eagerness was building inside her as each day crept closer to October. Most days were filled with the usual household tasks and with looking through books and magazines to get ideas about decorating the baby's room. She did go shopping one day to buy sheets and blankets for a bassinette and crib, onesies and other tiny outfits for the baby, and miscellaneous items to surround their little one with comfort and loveliness.

Near the end of May, Richard had to make a week-long business trip to Washington D.C., so she decided to take this opportunity to transform the small room adjacent their bedroom into a nursery. Her daddy had told her he wanted to buy whatever furniture she needed for the nursery, so she made a trip to Barrett's where they had bought furniture for their house. She purchased a bassinet, a baby bed, a chest of drawers, and a changing table, along with enough wall paper to cover the walls of the little sitting room that would become the nursery.

While she was shopping, Mr. Barrett, a friend of Nelson's, saw her and recognized her from their earlier dealings. He quizzed her about when the baby was due and about how much wall paper she needed. She described the little room with the wainscoting half way up the wall and gave him the measurements of the room. Then he surprised her by telling her he had the paper in stock and would send someone out the next day to do the papering. When she inquired about the cost, he smiled and said, "Consider it a baby gift." With that he was off on other business.

The men who came to hang the wallpaper also delivered the furniture. By the middle of that afternoon, the paper was on the walls, and the furniture was in place. The cordial young men had even moved the existing sitting-room furniture to the empty room upstairs, something she thought she would have to ask men from the moving company to do. What she had thought would take a week to complete was finished in one day.

When she surveyed her handiwork, she was pleased with what she saw. She had transformed a lifeless sitting room into an adorable nursery. Richard would be proud of her. She could hardly wait for him to get home.

She made a big to-do about showing him the nursery. She blindfolded him, led him into their bedroom, and turned him so he would be facing what had been the sitting room. When she removed the blindfold, he was silent for a moment. Then he asked, "So what do we do when he isn't a baby anymore? This can't be a permanent arrangement."

"Of course not," Ann responded, "it isn't intended to be, but we need to have the baby close to us for the first few months, maybe even for a year or so. That's something we'll just have to take a step at a time. Since this is the only downstairs bedroom, we need to consider at what point it will be safe for him to sleep so far away from us."

She had fantasized that Richard would laugh and kiss her, pick her up, whirl her around, and tell her how wonderful the room looked and how proud he was of her; but he didn't do that. In fact, his reaction seemed cold and indifferent, even negative. She tried not to show how deeply his insensitive rebuff had hurt her. "Do you like the nursery?"

"What? Oh, yeah, it looks really nice, but why change it for no longer than we'll be using it for that?"

"Because I want it to look like a nursery, and I enjoyed doing it. I love the way it turned out, and I was hoping you would too."

"Oh, it's beautiful," he said, tossing the words into the air. He paused and his reaction suddenly changed from disinterest to reprimand. "But Ann, what do you think you're doing? You're supposed to be taking it easy. Isn't that why you took Zach up on getting you out of your contract early? You shouldn't be out running around on shopping sprees and carrying heavy bundles and being on your feet all day. I just hope this little project doesn't cause you to lose the baby. I suppose you even climbed up on a ladder and put that paper on the walls." His tone was accusatory, scolding.

A lump rose in her throat, but she swallowed hard and forced herself to remain calm. She didn't know how to answer his flagrant accusations that she had acted foolishly and had risked the life of their baby. When she finally found her voice, she responded firmly, "No, I didn't. I wasn't on a ladder at all, and I didn't spend nearly as much time shopping as you seem to think I did. With the exception of a few baby clothes, I carried no *bundles*. Everything was mailed or delivered. Richard, do you honestly think I would knowingly do anything that would endanger the life of our baby?"

"No, I don't think you would *knowingly* do anything. That's just it. You didn't *know!* You didn't *think!*"

With those remarks, he walked out of the room and left her standing there in disbelief. A sudden flash of anger replaced the hurt she had felt earlier, and she ran after him, caught his arm with a firm grip and pivoted him to face her.

"Wait, Richard. We have to settle this. What is *really* bothering you? Is it that I did this while you were gone? Just three weeks ago, we talked about turning the sitting area into a nursery. 'I'll leave all that up to you' is what you said. Is it because of the amount of money I spent in what you disdainfully referred to as my 'little project'? If it's the money, don't worry about it. My dad wants to buy the furniture as a baby gift, and Barrett's did the wallpapering free. The only cost was for the wallpaper itself, the pictures and the teddy bears, and I'll pay for all that with money I have earned. It won't cost you a dime. You're off the hook."

By the time she finished speaking, she was choking on her words and tears were blurring her vision. She knew she had been sarcastic and belittling, but she didn't care. She wanted to hurt him as deeply as he had hurt her. She wanted him to know how it feels to be treated like an inept, ignorant dolt. On every other occasion when he had questioned something she had said or done, she had absorbed the verbal assault and had excused his accusations as misunderstandings. This time, though, she couldn't dismiss his insensitivity so easily.

Richard seemed stymied by this unexpected onslaught. He looked at her in bewilderment, as if he couldn't comprehend what had just happened between them. Silence dropped like a curtain, and Ann walked away.

CHAPTER 36

A nn went to bed earlier than usual. She felt tired and heartsick after what had transpired between her and Richard. A part of her wanted to go to him and apologize for becoming angry and saying those hateful things—to have him snuggle her in his arms and make the whole thing go away. She knew she would do just that if this were the first or second, or even the third or fourth time something of this sort had happened. But ever since they had returned from New Haven, these fiery rejections of her opinions or decisions seemed to come from out of nowhere. Typically, Richard was a cheerful, easygoing man and a loving husband, but sometimes something seemed to trigger a sudden change in his temperament, and that troubled her.

To avoid any further risk of conflict, she pretended to be sleeping when he came to bed. He quietly slid into bed next to her, and for what seemed like forever, they lay there back-to-back, each wide awake. Ann was suffering her own private torment, and she wondered if it was the same with him. Finally, he turned and spoke softly, "Ann, are you awake?"

At first, she thought of keeping up her pretense; then she answered, "Yes, I'm awake," but she remained with her back to him, a clear signal that *this time* she wasn't surrendering. He reached out and tenderly touched her shoulder. A shiver went through her and she could feel herself giving in. She detested conflict and couldn't bear having this rift between them.

When she turned to face him, he took her in his arms and held her tightly. Then he whispered, "I'm sorry, Ann. I know I hurt your feelings when I didn't show an appreciation for all the work you had done on the nursery. I was just astonished that you could have accomplished all that in just one week. I guess I jumped to some inaccurate conclusions. I love the nursery, and you did a beautiful job of decorating it."

She pulled away from his embrace and looked into his eyes. "Richard, this isn't about how you reacted to the nursery. Yes, I was disappointed that you didn't show any appreciation for what I had done, but that isn't the real problem. The real problem is that you don't trust me. You evidently think I am either indifferent or ignorant, or maybe both, when it comes to protecting myself and our baby. And I don't know what other inadequacies you see in me. Maybe you think I'm a spendthrift. Maybe you feel left out that I didn't include you in my 'little project.' I don't understand your attitude.

"Somehow, we're getting our signals crossed, and I just can't be happy if I am constantly afraid of being blamed for saying or doing something you think is wrong. From our earlier conversation, I thought I had your go-ahead in turning the sitting room into a nursery. I had calculated how much it would cost and had planned to talk with you about it, but that was before Daddy told me he wanted to buy the furniture. I guess I never mentioned that to you, and I probably should have. Maybe that would have eliminated all this confusion and dissention between us."

"I understand, sweetheart. I know I sounded like I was accusing you of doing something wrong, and I'll admit that I had a lot of questions as to how you could do all that without overly exerting yourself and without spending a lot of money.

"I guess when you said you wanted to turn the sitting room into a nursery, I thought you meant putting a baby bed and a chest in there. It never occurred to me that you would want to do anything to the walls. When you showed it to me, all I could see was a big dollar sign with all that furniture and wallpaper. It's not the money, though. I don't mind spending the money if that's what you want, but I'll admit it still doesn't make a lot of sense to me to do all that for no longer than we'll be using it for a nursery." He drew his mouth into a crooked half smile and chuckled, "Since I knew you had helped Uncle Ben paper their house while you were living with them, I even had visions of you teetering on a ladder, stretching and straining, trying to put that paper on the walls."

Suddenly, she erupted in laughter at his comical description. His explanation made sense to her, and she understood how seeing the nursery for the first time must have been like having ice water thrown in his face. "I'm sorry, Richard," she declared, relieved to know all this hullabaloo had been due to a giant misunderstanding. "I hadn't thought about how different our ideas for the nursery might be."

The storm had ended. They were back in each other's arms, each apologizing for the painful verbal exchange between them. Ann went to sleep in a state of blissful exhaustion.

"Sarah, it was just awful. We both said things we regretted saying, and it all could have been avoided. It was just a stupid misunderstanding. I guess I'll have to start giving a detailed explanation of everything I'm doing and why I'm doing it."

Sarah sat forward and took a sip of her coffee. "Spats are a part of married life, Ann, and they *can* strengthen the bond between a husband and wife if they are handled properly. However, a lot of marriages have been ruined because the couple couldn't get beyond their differences. I'm glad you and Richard talked about it and were able to resolve the problem. You have to get these things out in the open; otherwise, they harden into stone. Then the marriage is in *real* trouble."

"I know, but the thing that bothers me is that we were both angry. At first, I was just hurt by some of his insinuations. Then the pain changed to anger, and I started blurting out things I knew would hurt him, things I *wanted* to hurt him so he could see how he had made me feel. I'm so ashamed now of the way I acted and the things I said."

"It's okay to feel remorse, Ann. Painful as it is, it's good for us.

It shows we have a conscience. I think it's the good Lord's way of slapping our hands and telling us we need to straighten up. I'm sure Richard is sorry for what he said too."

"Sarah, I'd like to talk with you about something, but I'm hesitant to bring it up. I'm afraid of hurting you, and I certainly don't want to do that. It's just that you're the only one I feel I *can* talk to about this." Ann looked at Sarah and tried to speak, but the words wouldn't come.

Finally, Sarah spoke up, "Ann, you know you can tell me anything." She paused. "This is about Richard, isn't it?"

Ann nodded a painful yes. She searched Sarah's face for encouragement to continue. "As you know, we had such a marvelous time in New Haven. It was truly a time that strengthened and deepened our love for each other." She hesitated, struggling to bring herself to speak the next words. "After we came home, though, I started noticing that from time to time Richard seemed . . . I don't know . . . negative, impatient, distant. That behavior has escalated recently, especially since we found out I was pregnant.

"Sometimes, for no reason at all, he becomes angry, and most of the time I have no idea what he is upset about. Much of the time when he's like that, he is either blaming me for something or he's criticizing something I've said or done. I want to be understanding, but when I ask him what is bothering him, he just sloughs it off. Most of the time, he's the same happy, carefree person I've always known him to be, but about the time I relax and think everything is all right, he goes into another one of these negative moods. I don't want to worry you with this, Sarah, but I don't know what to do to improve the situation. I thought you might have some suggestions."

Sarah was slow to respond, "I wish I had a solution for you, Ann, but I don't. I'm going to use a term that may not make sense to you, but it's the first thing that came to my mind as you were describing Richard's behavior. *Buffington Syndrome* is my name for it. I saw it in William's father and in William. Joan experienced it with Nelson. I was praying to God that Richard wouldn't fall prey to it also. It has always mystified me how bright, successful men come to a point in life when they feel it necessary to control everything and everyone around them, especially their wives and children.

"You'll have to deal with this in your own way, Ann, but I chose to stand up to William. I told him I resented his overbearing manner with me and Nelson and Olivia. I respected him and tried to please him, but I didn't let him rob me of my individuality. I refused to honor his wishes if they violated my own sense of right and wrong. That's where I drew the line, and he knew I wouldn't cross it. I don't mean to imply that William wasn't a good husband and father. In many ways, he was exceptionally considerate of us. We had a lot of good times. I learned to do two things—to dwell on the kind, attentive side of William and to look forward to the good times."

Ann leaned forward and took Sarah's hands in hers, "Sarah, you said you didn't have a solution, but you just gave me the answer I have been searching for. I just hope I can live my life as graciously as you have lived yours. I can't imagine your ever getting angry and becoming vindictive the way I did last night. I have to learn to approach things in a calm, responsible way and not allow my emotions to dictate my behavior. I love you, Sarah, and I don't know what I would do if I didn't have you to let me air out my problems."

"Oh, I've been known to lose my temper, maybe a time or two," she chuckled. "The only advantage I have over you is age. Over the years, I've come to see the futility of anger. It never accomplishes anything. In fact, it's one of the most destructive things I can think of because anger crowds out understanding and patience. Ann, you and Richard are the hope of the future for me, and I pray it will be a bright future. But it will take work from both of you to keep it that way."

CHAPTER 37

"**R**ichard, are you going with me to see Dr. Anderson today? My appointment is at 10:00 a.m."

"I won't be able to make it, honey. I have a meeting that will last until about 12:30. If it were not a luncheon meeting, I'd plan on meeting you for lunch. I guess you'll have to handle this one on your own," he grinned.

"I'm anxious to see what Dr. Anderson has to say. It doesn't seem to me that I'm showing very much to be approaching my eighth month. Don't you think I should be bigger by now?"

Richard slid some papers into his briefcase. Then he laughed and quipped, "Do you really expect me to know the answer to that? You're the only pregnant woman I've ever paid much attention to."

"I know," she giggled, "but I thought you knew everything. I guess I'll just have to depend on Dr. Anderson's expertise."

He crept up behind her, wrapped his arms around her and cradled her bulging tummy in his hands. "I don't have to know everything to see that you either have a baby inside you or you swallowed a pumpkin seed."

He kissed the back of her neck, and she turned and put her arms around him. "I love you, Richard, and I can hardly wait for our baby to get here."

Dr. Anderson had brought Richard into the world and had become the Buffington's family physician when he took over his father's practice shortly after Nelson and Joan were married. They all trusted his skill and loved him as much as they had loved his father before him.

It was August 27, 1959, when Ann entered Dr. Anderson's office. At that time, the date didn't seem important. It was just another office visit—another check-up. But that was all about to change.

Dr. Anderson finished the examination and asked Ann get dressed and meet him in his office. "Did Richard come with you?" he asked.

"No, I'm alone today."

He was returning the phone to its base when Ann walked into his office. When he looked up at her, he was wearing the expression of a man weighted down with some heavy burden. "Ann, I took the liberty of calling a colleague—an obstetrician—to have a look at you. He is willing to make time for you this afternoon at 1:30 if that will work for you."

Dr. Anderson's words stupefied Ann, and she had trouble processing the implication of what he had just told her. "Yes . . . that . . . that will be just fine," she stammered.

"Good, I think we should take advantage of the fact that he can see you this afternoon," Dr. Anderson said, jotting on a note pad as he spoke. "His name is Dr. Adam Scott, and his office is in this building, suite 332." He ripped the sheet off the pad and slid it across his desk to her. "Richard needs to go with you."

Suddenly Ann was gripped with fear. She felt the breath being sucked from her body, and a thousand thoughts were racing through her mind as she struggled to understand. "What do you mean? Is something wrong with the baby?" She looked at him pleadingly.

"I don't know, Ann. That's why I'm sending you to Dr. Scott. He's better equipped to make a diagnosis than I am."

"But you obviously have some reason for your concern. If you think there's something wrong with the baby, I'd rather hear it from you than from a doctor I don't know."

"Ann, I'm not a specialist in prenatal development, but I've been keeping a close check on the size and movement of the baby. You are about six weeks away from delivery, and you say you are feeling slight movement at irregular intervals. By now, you should be feeling a pattern of more robust movement, and the occurrences should be much closer together. Also, the baby is smaller than would be expected at this stage, and I'm concerned about the heartrate. I wish I could tell you everything was fine, but, Ann, nothing is gained by ignoring a potential problem. But don't panic. Let's wait and see what Dr. Scott has to say.

"Would you like to use my phone to call Richard and have him meet you? Maybe the two of you could go have some lunch and then go to Dr. Scott's office. I can call him for you if that would make it easier."

"Well, Richard is . . . I . . . I think he said he will be tied up until . . . maybe until 12:30. I don't know . . . I'm not sure where to—"

"Let me call him, Ann. I'll be able to locate him." Dr. Anderson interrupted. He reached across and patted her hand that was resting on his desk. "I'll give him Dr. Scott's suite number and he can meet you there."

Dr. Scott looked to be in his sixties with graying hair, a fleshy face, and a built-in smile. He greeted Ann in the examining room, "I'm Dr. Scott, Mrs. Buffington. Dr. Anderson is not only a colleague but a good friend. Sometimes we do favors for each other." Following the examination, he patted her arm and said, "That wasn't too bad, was it? Meet me in my office after you are dressed." As he turned to leave the room, he instructed his nurse assistant, "Mr. Buffington is in the waiting room. Please show him to my office."

Richard sat in one of the two wingbacks in front of the doctor's desk and began surveying the assortment of books and pictures on the bookcase behind the desk. When Ann entered the room, he stood and slid her chair back for her to be seated. "Ann, what's this all about? All Dr. Anderson told me was that he was sending you to an obstetrician for a second opinion and that he thought I needed to be with you—second opinion about what? What's going on?"

"I'm just as shocked as you are that he sent me to this doctor. I asked him to explain why he felt I needed to do this, and he told me the baby was smaller than it should be at this stage, that I should be feeling more movement, and something about the baby's heartrate. That's all I know. I don't know what it all means, but I'm—"

Before she could finish, Dr. Scott walked into the office. He was still wearing the smile when he introduced himself and shook hands with Richard. He took his seat across from them and commented that there appeared to be complications with Ann's pregnancy. Basically, he was telling her the same thing Dr. Anderson had told her. He, like Dr. Anderson, seemed hesitant to discuss the seriousness of the problem.

"Dr. Scott, what does this mean?" Ann asked.

His smile was replaced by a furrowed brow, and he looked at them sympathetically. "I'm afraid, Mr. and Mrs. Buffington, there is a problem with the development of the fetus. Based on my examination and tests Dr. Anderson has done, I feel strongly that your baby will have some degree—possibly an extreme degree—of physical and neurological underdevelopment and impairment. It is possible that your baby's senses of sight, sound, and touch will be affected by these developmental problems. After the baby is born, tests can be done to determine sensitivity in these areas, and at that time, Dr. Anderson will probably recommend that the baby remain in the hospital and be placed in an incubator for a while to allow the organs to develop more fully."

Ann gasped and began sobbing, "Can't anything be done?"

"I wish something could be done, Mrs. Buffington, but I'm afraid the medical world doesn't understand genetic anomalies of this nature well enough to treat the resulting conditions."

"How sure are you about this, Dr. Scott?" Richard inquired. "Would it do any good to take Ann somewhere else—maybe the Mayo Clinic?"

"You can go to other doctors—and there are many fine ones—including at the Mayo Clinic, but, Mr. Buffington, your wife can't travel the distance to the Mayo Clinic this late in her pregnancy. I understand your need to explore every possibility, and I'm not discouraging that, but you're running out of time."

Then Richard dropped a bomb, and Ann felt her whole world crumbling. "What about an abortion, Dr. Scott?"

"In New York, Mr. Buffington, abortion is illegal under almost all circumstances. Furthermore, it is too late in the pregnancy for that."

Richard stood to his feet. "But that's inhumane!" he shouted, bringing his fist down on the doctor's desk. "To bring a child into the world when you know he can't have a normal life is immoral! It's cruel! You can't do it!" He was beside himself. He blamed the legal system, the world of medicine, Dr. Scott personally, and even his own Dr. Anderson who had seen him through a half-dozen childhood illnesses and a broken arm.

Dr. Scott tolerated Richard's tirade patiently, yet firmly. He stood and moved toward him. Then he gently put his hand on Richard's shoulder and eased him back into his chair. "You must calm down, Mr. Buffington. You're not helping yourself or your wife by reacting in this manner. You need to go home and discuss this between yourselves. I'm sorry I can't be more precise, but medical science simply doesn't have the tools to foresee the exact nature or full extent of your baby's limitations. Dr. Anderson will instruct you about how to take care of your infant. I will also be available for consultation.

"It's never easy to deal with the kind of shock you've had today. You're feeling helpless right now, but you will come to grips with this and will figure out how to cope with the difficulties that lie ahead. This baby could even become someone who strengthens and blesses your lives and your marriage in a way you can't imagine right now."

CHAPTER 38

O rdinarily they would be engaged in lively conversation as Richard drove the route to their house, but on this day, traffic noises and the hum of the engine were the only sounds. Ann couldn't find words to express how she was feeling. She was suffering her own private misery, and the only comfort she could find was in her self-appointed isolation. It wasn't that she didn't want to share her sorrow with Richard; it was that she couldn't. From his reaction in Dr. Scott's office, she got the impression that to him the news about their unborn baby was an inconvenience—maybe even a burden—but not a *sorrow*.

Ann replayed the discussions in the offices of the two doctors. They both seemed certain she would deliver a baby whose body and mind would, for some unknown reason, be defective—*abnormal*—a word they had carefully avoided. She wanted to scream, *Why? Why an innocent baby?*

In the chaotic jumble of all that had transpired, she could hear Richard saying, "What about abortion?" He had spat the words into the air without compassion or any hint of feeling or caring about the baby or about her. Earlier, he had said he loved the baby. How could he so cavalierly bring up the possibility of abortion? How could he consider ending the life of another human being, especially that of someone he *loved*?

He pulled to the curb in front of their house. Then, in an expression seeming to blend sympathy with resolve, he reached over and clasped Ann's hand: "I'm sorry, sweetheart," he said, "but it's going to be all right." Words that should have been comforting brought a pang of fear. She heard determination in his voice, as if he had made up his mind to rescue them from this crisis. What did he have in mind? What did his "I'm sorry" mean?

"I don't understand, Richard. Are you sorry we've just been told our baby will not be *normal*—that all our plans and expectations for him have just been shattered? Suddenly, she began to tremble. Tears coursed down her cheeks as she asked, "Are you apologizing for suggesting that abortion could be a way to end what has turned out to be a tragedy?" She couldn't halt the words that were flowing uncontrollably from her mouth. She continued her interrogation, conscious of the sarcasm in her voice and of the crass accusations she was aiming at Richard. She loved him and needed his support and understanding, but his suggestion of abortion reflected no concern for their baby or for Ann's physical and emotional wellbeing. She felt estranged from the person she needed most.

Finally, her verbal grilling came to an end, and she quietly sobbed herself back into her world of solitude. Her body felt lifeless and limp, like a damp cloth that had been squeezed until nothing more could be extracted from it. "Are you going inside?" she asked flatly.

"Yes. I'll call Dad to tell him I won't be coming back to work today."

He helped her from the car, and when she was standing, he put both arms around her. "We'll get through this, Ann," he whispered. "It hurts right now, but we'll get through it." They walked slowly to the front door.

Inside the house, he asked, "Do you want to lie down? Maybe if you could go to sleep for a little while, you would feel better."

"Yes, I think I'll do that. I have a headache. Would you bring me an aspirin? Dr. Anderson said it would be all right for me to take an aspirin occasionally."

When she walked into the bedroom, she did something that came naturally every time she entered—She looked toward the little nursery. This time, she paused and wistfully surveyed the tiny room. She trailed her hand along the side of the bassinette. Then she went to the baby bed, picked up the baby bear, and hugged it to her chest.

She sat down on the side of the bed and smiled as she thought of the infant she carried inside her. Gently touching her abdomen, she whispered, "I'll take good care of you, little guy. No matter what, I'll take care of you."

She was still clutching the bear under her chin when Richard came into the room carrying a glass of water and an aspirin. She swallowed the tablet, and Richard took the glass from her. She lay back on the bed, and he covered her with a blanket. Then he sat down on the bed beside her and leaned over and kissed her forehead. "Now, try to get some sleep," he said. "I'll be in the living room if you need me. I love you, Ann." He closed the door behind him as he left the room.

After a while, the headache subsided and she drifted into an uneasy sleep, waking occasionally and remembering the painful events of the day. When she was fully awake, she tossed the blanket aside, slipped her feet into her shoes, and opened the door to the hallway. As soon as she stepped into the living room, she heard Richard's voice and realized he was engaged in an intense telephone conversation.

"She's terribly upset right now. I'll have to wait a while to talk to her about it. I know it's important . . . yes . . . yes, I know. I'll look into it as soon as possible . . . maybe in a few days. I don't know. I have to approach this cautiously. Dad, for heaven's sake, she's very fragile! Please don't push me on this!"

When Richard turned and saw Ann standing in the room, the color drained from his face, and he quickly brought his conversation to an end. "Yes, I'll be in the office tomorrow. I'll talk to you later." He rushed to Ann. "Do you feel better after your nap? Headache gone?"

"Yes, the headache is gone, and I do feel better. I think the aspirin and the nap helped. Were you talking to your dad just now?"

"Yes, when I called to let him know I wasn't coming back to the office today, I told him about the visits with the doctors. He had someone in his office and couldn't talk, so he wanted me to call him back later and give him more detail."

"From what I heard, I thought you might have been arguing with him. What was that all about?"

He nervously replied, "We weren't arguing. We were just discussing what Dr. Anderson and Dr. Scott had said. But you need to get that off your mind and stop worrying about it."

"I can't get it off my mind. I spent a lot of time thinking about and planning for our baby before today, and now I can't think about anything else. The big difference between then and now is that my focus has changed. *Our* focus has to change. We face challenges we didn't know about until today. My concern is that we don't know exactly what to expect; therefore, we don't know how to prepare, but I'm sure Dr. Anderson will help us with that."

"Ann, I . . . never mind . . . we'll talk about this later. What do you want to do about dinner? Do you feel up to going out?"

"No, I don't want to get out again. You go ahead without me; I'm really not hungry."

"But, Ann, you have to eat."

"Okay, just bring me something. I don't really care what it is." Her frustration was obvious. "I'm sorry," she said. "I didn't mean to snap at you."

"It's okay, honey. "You're still upset because of the news we got today. I won't be gone long. Will you be all right?"

"Yes, I'll be fine." She looked up at him and saw a drawn, troubled man, and she was stabbed with pity for him. She knew she had been rough on him, and she knew he was trying to comfort her. What she didn't understand was why he didn't seem to be grieving the way she was grieving. Why had he suggested abortion?

When Richard arrived at Marlow's Café, he placed his to-go order and then went to the pay phone to call Bill Lambert. "Hi, Bill. Yeah, we do need to get together—maybe next week. Hey, Bill, I'm at a pay phone waiting for a food order. Ann and I got some shocking news earlier today, and Ann is really upset." Richard went on to explain what the doctors had told them. After listening to Bill's sympathetic response, Richard got to the point of his call. "I know Ann will want to bring the baby home to take care of it, but that just isn't going to be best. Could you talk to Charlie about helping me convince Ann to place the baby in a home? This baby will need to be with professionals who are trained to take care of children with these kinds of problems? I'm pretty sure Ann isn't going to listen to me, but I think she will listen to Charlie.

"Well, no we haven't asked the doctor about it, but I just know we can't take care of a baby like that at home. I asked the obstetrician about the possibility of an abortion, but he said that wasn't an option. Well, it's good to visit with you, buddy, and we'll get together next week. I think my order is ready, so I'd better go."

CHAPTER 39

When Richard went back to work the next day, he went straight to his dad's office as Nelson had instructed him to do. Vicki was told they were not to be disturbed, and Nelson got straight to the point, "When do you plan to talk to Ann about making arrangements for the baby?"

"That's a little bit premature, Dad. Ann is upset enough already, and I don't want to add to that until we know more. I do plan to talk to her and get her moving in the direction of an institution, but I'm going to have to take it easy on that, maybe even wait until after the baby is born."

"Richard, you can't do that! Do you realize what you're suggesting?" Nelson asked. "You would have to take the baby home for a while, and that just won't work! Once Ann takes that baby home, she will never want to give it up. No, it will be much easier to make prior arrangements for the baby to be taken immediately to foster care and then on to an institution."

"Dad, I agree with what you're saying, but, I can't just snatch the baby away like that. Ann would never agree to it, but she will agree to do whatever is best for the baby. I just need time to help her realize the baby will be better off with people who are equipped to take care of his needs."

Nelson's demeanor softened, and he replied calmly but commandingly, "You're setting yourself up for a lot of heartache for both you and Ann. You will ultimately have to put the baby in an institution, and the longer you put that off, the more difficult it will be. You have to take charge of things, Richard, even if it makes Ann unhappy for a while. She'll get over it."

The next morning, Ann still felt drained of energy, so Richard told her he would go out for breakfast. She could stay in bed and rest. But by the time he left for work, she was wide awake and her mind was flooded with thoughts about the baby and about all the people she needed to contact. She had gone into the kitchen and was pouring a glass of orange juice when the phone rang. When she answered, she heard Daddy's cheerful voice, "Good morning, Annie. How are you, hon?"

"Oh, Daddy," she said, "I was planning to call you later. Things are not going well," she stated matter-of-factly. Her strength crumbled, and her voice became a soft whimper as she struggled to tell him about yesterday's nightmare.

"Oh no, honey, I'm so sorry. I wish I were there to put my arms around you and help you through this. I am planning to fly out there when the baby is born anyway. Why don't I try to get a flight for tomorrow? I've built up a lot of vacation time."

Again, Ann slipped on her mask of self-control, "No, Daddy, I'm all right. I'm emotional right now because I'm telling you about all this, but I'm really doing okay." Her voice became restrained, resolute. "I've come to grips with our baby's condition, and Daddy, I think I love him more now than I did before we received this terrible news. I think knowing how fragile and dependent he will be has somehow given me a deeper, more responsible love. I feel he is trusting me to take care of him, and I'm not going to let him down."

As soon as Ann ended her conversation with her daddy, she called Charlie. She was surprised to learn that Charlie already knew about her visit with the two doctors and was planning to call Ann after she was sure she would be awake. Charlie was sympathetic and supportive, but Ann knew that would be Charlie's reaction. She knew she could always count on her good friend.

Then she called Sarah. She thought it was strange when she didn't get an answer at Sarah's house. Even if Olivia had taken Sarah for an appointment, Ginny should be there to answer the phone. Ginny was always there from 7:00 a.m. until 6:00 p.m. every Monday through Friday. Ann waited a minute or two and then called again— still no answer.

She remembered having heard a siren close by when she was trying to call Sarah the first time, and she was seized by sudden fear. She rushed out to the sidewalk and looked down the street. As she walked toward the flashing lights, she realized the ambulance was indeed parked in front of Sarah's house. She hurried toward it as fast as she could and arrived on the scene just in time to see the medic holding the door for Nelson to get into the back of the ambulance. Ginny was standing on the sidewalk wringing her hands as it drove away, sirens blaring.

"Ginny, what happened?" Ann cried, trying to catch her breath.

"Oh, Ann, Mrs. Buffington had a heart attack. That's what the men with the ambulance said. She just slumped over in her chair, and I called Mr. Buffington. I guess he called the ambulance. Ann, she looked so bad!" Ginny cried.

"Go back inside, Ginny, in case the phone rings. Someone needs to be there to answer it. I'm going back home, but I want you to call me if you get more information. I will try to get in touch with Richard."

Ann had almost reached the house when Richard pulled up to the curb and got out of the car. He ran to Ann and breathlessly gasped the words, "I'm on my way to the hospital. Do you want to go with me?"

"I certainly do," she replied, and they both rushed to the red convertible.

When they reached the emergency room, Nelson intercepted them. "Richard . . . Ann, it's very bad. They're working with her right now and sent me out of the room. I don't know if she will make it, Richard. We have to prepare ourselves for that possibility."

Ann felt the weight of another layer of anguish on top of the recent report about the baby. A feeling of helplessness engulfed her as she stood listening to Richard and Nelson discussing the gravity of this unexpected calamity. Olivia came hurrying into the room, and they filled her in on all that happened.

Ann quietly made her way to a nearby chair and sat down. When Richard realized she was no longer beside him, he went to her. "You look pale, Ann. Are you feeling sick?"

"I'm okay. I just feel weak and trembly. You need to go back to your dad and Olivia; they need you."

"Dad and Aunt Olivia are all right." He took her hand and lifted it to his lips, "Are you sure *you* are all right?" he whispered.

"Yes, I am." She paused and then sobbed, "No, that isn't true. I'm not all right. This is such a shock. She seemed to be doing so well. I'm having trouble grasping this, and I'm frightened. I don't know how I can get through the days ahead without Sarah."

Just then, Dr. Anderson appeared in the room, and all four Buffingtons rushed to meet him. "Let's sit down," he said, leading them to a private corner of the waiting room. He waited for everyone to be seated in the circle of chairs. Then he sat down next to Nelson. "I'm sorry, my friends. We did everything we could, but she slipped away from us. I was hoping and praying, as I know you were, that we could pull her through this, but we just couldn't make it happen. If you want to see her—and that's strictly up to you—the nurse will come out in a few minutes and let you know when it's all right for you to go back there."

Dr. Anderson stood and shook hands with each of them, expressing further condolences and inviting them to feel free to call him if they had questions. When he came to Ann, he gave her hand a little pat and said softly, as if his words were meant for her alone, "Hang in there. Life isn't always this difficult. Brighter days *will* come."

A curtain had dropped on time, and they all looked at one another in disbelief. Just a few hours ago, she had been knitting a baby shawl. How could it have happened so suddenly? They watched Dr. Anderson walk down a long hallway until he turned a corner and went out of sight. Maybe they expected him to return with some further word. But nothing more could be said. Nothing more could be done. Their Sarah was gone.

CHAPTER 40

The day of Sarah's funeral was a dreary, lifeless day. The family gathered at the gravesite in a soupy fog and a suffocating stillness—a silent dirge that hushed even the singing of the birds. It was as if all nature had paused to mourn the loss of a gallant lady.

Ten days later, Hollis Wilhite, the family attorney, drew the family together for the reading of Sarah's will. Surprisingly, Nelson seemed to accept all stipulations, even Olivia's acquisition of Sarah's house. After Wilhite had read the will to them, he pulled another document from his briefcase and told them there was more.

"Last month, she called to tell me she had written out something she wanted to change in her will. She said she was mailing it to me. After I received it, I wrote the codicil and even read it to her over the phone to make sure it was what she wanted. She verbally approved it, but she never executed it. It cannot be legally enforced without her signature, but I am presenting it to you. If you really want to respect her wishes, this codicil should be honored."

With that explanation, Wilhite presented the document stating that the sum of $100,000 be designated to fund a trust naming Richard and Ann's unborn baby as the beneficiary. It went on to stipulate conditions related to the distribution and use of the trust assets, and it named Richard and Ann as co-trustees of the trust.

Ann and Richard silently exchanged questioning glances. Then Nelson looked at Olivia and asked, "Sis, do you have any objections to endorsing the codicil? This will be my grandbaby, so I'm in favor of it, and I think Richard and Ann are too."

"I think we should do what Mother wanted," Olivia replied, "and even if she hadn't made that change, I would be in favor of it. After all, we're family, and we have to help one another. The way the codicil is written, Richard and Ann will have control over its use, and they are sure to need it in the days ahead."

"Then that settles it. I need your signatures on some documents, and we'll be finished," Wilhite stated.

The meeting had taken place at Sarah's house, and after Hollis Wilhite left, they remained seated for a few minutes reflecting on the times when this house had been the hub of all family activity. As they were all leaving, Ann went to Olivia and thanked her for her gracious acceptance of the unauthorized addition to the will. "I was touched by the things you said, Olivia. You have a good heart. I could see and hear so much of Sarah in you as you were speaking."

"That may be the nicest thing anyone has ever said to me," Olivia said. "Thank you."

A few days later, Richard and Ann were discussing the change Sarah had made to her will. "It's almost as if she sensed that something might be wrong with the baby," Richard commented.

"I was just thinking the same thing," Ann replied. "She couldn't have known at that time about the baby's condition. We didn't even know. In fact, the day she had the heart attack, I tried to call to let her know I was coming over. I wanted to tell her what the doctors had said, but I didn't get a chance to do that. Did you talk to her about it?"

"No, but Grandmother always had an uncanny ability to sense things. I think she sensed something about the baby that made her take this action, and we will need that money in the days to come. Of course, if we place him in a state-funded institution, we may have little expense, but we will have doctor bills. I'm sure the costs will go far beyond what our insurance will cover."

"A state-funded institution!" What are you talking about? We are *not* putting our baby in an institution," Ann railed.

"But Ann, that may be what is best for the baby. If his condition is as severe as Dr. Anderson seems to think it will be, we can't take care of him."

"Oh, yes we can—*I can*. I love this baby, Richard, and I want to be able to show him that love every day of his life."

"Be reasonable, Ann. He won't even know you're his mother. If his mental limitations are as great as Dr. Anderson described, he won't be aware of his surroundings or people or *anything*. We can't let this situation destroy our lives. What about your acting career? You *are* planning to get back into it, aren't you?"

"This *situation*, as you call it, has placed a responsibility on us, Richard. Our baby didn't ask to be born, and he certainly didn't ask to be the victim of cruel developmental imperfections. We're responsible for his being conceived, and when he is born, we will be responsible for taking care of him. That's what I plan to do. My acting career ended the minute I learned about the special care our baby will need."

Richard seemed stunned by her adamant refusal to acquiesce to his line of thinking. "Ann, you're being irrational," he shouted. "We can't take care of this baby here in our home!"

"That's insane! Many people have done and are doing just that!" Ann's voice grew shrill as she fiercely defended her conviction that their baby would need to live in an environment saturated with love and emotional bonding with his parents. "How can you possibly think of turning our baby over to strangers? No matter how well-trained or well-intentioned they are, they cannot love and cherish him the way we can."

By this time, the atmosphere was thick with hostility as their anger rose to the level of a frenzied unleashing of their feelings. Richard's face glowed crimson, and his lips quivered. Ann, her fists clinched in defiance, staunchly resisted his efforts to sway her thinking.

"You're being unreasonable," he screamed, and he stormed out the front door.

When he was gone, Ann felt sick and numb. Her heart ached, and she wanted to cry, but the tears wouldn't come. This dissension between them had crept in like a thief and had snatched away her most cherished possession—a loving, harmonious family. It seemed clear to her now that Richard's love had conditions. He was in love with an ideal—a fantasy of fathering a flawless child. And when the ideal was shattered, his love hardened into cold acquiescence to making physical provisions for their baby and nothing more. Could she be wrong about what she saw in him? Was he refusing to become personally involved in meeting the emotional needs of his own child?

She was hurt and angry, and her anger intensified her determination to stand up for what her heart told her was right for their baby. She would not allow Richard or Nelson or anyone else to goad her into robbing her baby of the love and tenderness of his mother. She hoped Richard's attitude would change after the baby was born—that seeing and holding his baby would help him look beyond the imperfections and see an innocent child who needed loving parents.

Without warning, she felt a gripping pain in her lower abdomen—a cramping that gradually subsided and then returned. She suspected this was the beginning of her labor, but this shouldn't be happening for another month. It was too early. Maybe it was a false alarm. She had no idea where Richard was or when he would return, but she told herself not to panic—that this would be a long, drawn-out process. She lay down on the bed and waited, dozens of questions flooding her mind. *If only I had my mother or Sarah here to give me advice*, she thought. Over the next few hours the spasms of pain gradually grew closer together and became more intense. Finally, after six hours—when the episodes were seven minutes apart—she decided she should first call a taxi and then call Dr. Anderson.

Suddenly, Richard came bursting through the front door. "Ann, where are you, Ann?" he called frantically.

Before she could answer, he bolted through the bedroom door, dropped to his knees beside the bed, and cradled her face in his hands. Tears were coursing down his cheeks. "I'm sorry, darling. I shouldn't have allowed myself to become so upset with you. Will you forgive me?"

As he was speaking, she grimaced and clinched her teeth to keep from crying out in pain. "Richard, it's time to call Dr. Anderson," she gasped.

"Oh, sweetheart, I'm sorry; I'm so sorry," he repeated over and over. She realized he didn't comprehend what she had said to him.

"Richard! Call Dr. Anderson *now* and get my suitcase from the top shelf of the closet. It's packed and ready to go. It's time for you to drive me to the hospital." The urgency in her voice seemed to jar him into action.

Richard drove to the emergency entrance of the hospital, and a nurse was waiting with a wheelchair for Ann. She whisked her away and told Richard to have a seat and that someone would come for him before long. A little later, another nurse came and escorted him to Ann's room. She told him Ann was progressing nicely and would soon be going into the delivery room. He could stay with her until then.

At 12:14 a.m. on October 8, 1959, Joy Marie Buffington made her debut onto the stage of life. She weighed three pounds, two ounces and was destined to impact many lives in a way known only by God.

CHAPTER 41

Paul Jernigan couldn't make it from Dallas to New York in time to be present for the birth of his granddaughter, but he arrived well ahead of her dismissal from the hospital. Due to her low birth weight and underdevelopment, she was placed in a neonatal incubator for eight days. When she was dismissed from the hospital, she was still a shriveled, delicate-looking little thing. She was completely bald except for a thin tuft of downy black hair and on the top of her head. Her tiny face resembled an old man with squinty eyes and pursed lips, features that were altered only by an occasional yawn or grimace and then quickly returned to their usual appearance.

Paul spent three weeks with his daughter and granddaughter after they brought Joy home. During that time, he served mostly as an errand boy in assisting with the day-to-day routine of bathing, dressing, and caring for their fragile little baby.

"Daddy, I have watched you as you've helped me take care of Joy. What do you think?"

"What do you mean? I think she's beautiful!"

Ann smiled, "I know you do. I can see how much you adore her. What I'm asking, though, is have you noticed how listless and unresponsive she seems to be?" Worry lines creased Ann's brow. "I guess it's too soon to expect her to show signs of being aware of other people and things around her, isn't it?"

"I don't know, honey. It's been too long since you were a baby for me to remember all that. I would say, though, that it *is* too soon. But, sweetheart, you have to just let her be who she is. She doesn't have to be like all other babies. She's ours and we love her just the way she is."

Ann ran to her daddy, threw her arms around his waist, and pressed her head against his chest. "Oh, Daddy, I love you," she cried. "I know she won't be like other children, but I do want her to know she's loved. It's important to me to make her understand how much I love her."

One day, Ann accidently knocked over a glass of water, and the icy liquid splashed onto Joy's face and chest. They both rushed to her, and Ann picked her up and cuddled her while Grandpa Paul dried her with a soft towel. She frowned, whimpered softly, and was soon sleeping soundly again. She even slept through the changing of her wet gown.

"Daddy, does it seem unusual to you that Joy didn't start screaming the minute that cold water hit her. Maybe I'm trying to overanalyze everything she does, but it just seems to me she should have shown more reaction. What do you think?"

"Honey, quit torturing yourself. Don't get hung up on what's *normal*. Just relax and enjoy her. Grow with her and be thankful for the happiness she brings to our lives."

Occasionally soft wheezing sounds or gurgling noises emanated from the bassinette, and Ann couldn't keep from asking, "Do you hear that, Daddy? Are those the kinds of sounds babies usually make?"

"Babies make all sorts of funny little noises," he chuckled. "I remember when you were a baby, your mom and I were often amused at the sounds you made. Sometimes when you were sleeping, you whistled—a pure as a crystal whistle." They both laughed. It was so good to have Daddy here with her, reassuring her and encouraging her to relax and enjoy being a mother.

Richard had been strangely absent ever since they had brought Joy home from the hospital. Without advance notice, his busy schedule required him to leave home early every morning and not return until late every night. Ann noticed that Richard seemed to be deliberately avoiding any interaction with her dad. He showed only passing interest in her, and he never went near Joy Marie. It was as if he was making a point of rejecting Joy's presence in their home.

Two days before Paul was due to return home, he brought up the subject of Richard's absence. "Sweetheart, I hate to leave you here to take care of Joy all by yourself. With Richard gone so much, I think you need someone to come in to help you."

"I think I can manage, Daddy. You've helped me through the most difficult time. Many mothers take care of several children. Surely, if they can do that, I can take care of my one little Joy." Ann sat down on the sofa beside her daddy, clutched his hand and leaned her head on his shoulder, "You've been a lifesaver, though, and I'm really going to miss you when you leave."

"Ann, I don't want to stick my nose into your business, but is everything all right between you and Richard? He seems . . . I don't know . . . different . . . distant." Ann became quiet, and then she began to sob quietly. She tried to hide her tears from her daddy, but he had struck a nerve. "Honey, I don't want to meddle, but I can't leave here without knowing you're all right."

She threw herself into her daddy's arms. When she could finally get words to come, she cried, "I don't know what to do, Daddy. Richard wants to put Joy in an institution. According to him, we can't take care of her. He thinks she needs to be in a place where caregivers are trained to take care of children with *abnormalities*.

"I can't do it, Daddy. I just can't," she sobbed. And then the whole sordid account of the last few weeks came gushing out—of Richard's suggestion of an abortion, the arguments they had about placing Joy in foster care and then in an institution, and his refusal to have anything to do with their baby girl.

Paul put his arms around her and whispered, "Annie, Annie; I'm so sorry you're having to go through all this. You know, I vowed never to take sides in any disagreements between you and Richard, but I just don't understand this! How can he not love his own child? Have you considered the two of you going to visit with Dr. Anderson about this?"

"I did ask Dr. Anderson about it before we brought Joy home

from the hospital. I didn't mention to him that Richard thought we couldn't take care of the baby at home. I just asked him if he thought Joy's condition was so severe we should consider placing her in an institution. He was definitely against it unless something unforeseen develops. He said she would be much better off with parents who love her and can give her special attention."

"Do you think Dr. Anderson could change Richard's thinking about this?"

"No, Daddy, I don't. I don't think Richard will listen to anyone except Nelson, and I feel strongly that Nelson has colored Richard's thinking. I don't understand why they feel the way they do. I know this sounds terrible, but I've wondered if Richard considers Joy a nuisance—just someone who gets in his way."

"Do you want me to stay longer, sweetheart. I can arrange that if you need me."

"No, you have your work, and I'll be all right. She smiled and declared, I'm thoroughly enjoying being a mother."

When her daddy left New York, Ann felt a gnawing pain in her heart. He had been right. She couldn't do this by herself. She needed Richard. She needed his support emotionally as well as physically. Her heart cried out, *Oh, Richard, please love Joy as much as I do. Love her and love me enough to help me.* Ann realized the caregiving would never end, and that as Joy grew older, it would be even more difficult for her to administer the multitude of tasks required in taking care of her fragile child.

As soon as Paul went home, Richard moved into a spare bedroom. He told Ann it was so he wouldn't disturb her with his early exits and late returns, but she knew something was very wrong. The closest he ever came to showing any affection for her was to give her an occasional quick kiss on the cheek, and even that seemed lacking in emotion. He treated her like an object he no longer needed but couldn't bear to toss away, and he was unwilling to talk about what had become a miserable relationship between them. Time crawled by as Ann waited for him to show interest in his daughter—and in *her.*

Thanksgiving came and went, and Nelson and Richard nixed

the traditional Thanksgiving meal Olivia offered to prepare. Nelson's explanation—and, of course, Richard's too—was that gathering at Sarah's house without Sarah would be a sad occasion.

With Christmas only two weeks away, Ann asked Richard if they would be participating in the Christmas meal Olivia wanted to prepare for the family. The only answer he gave was, "Probably not," and she knew he was waiting to take his cue from Nelson.

"Richard, we have to talk about this *wall* between us. I've been hoping you would open up and tell me what is bothering you, but it doesn't seem you are going to do that. We can't go on like this, with this rift between us and with your total disregard for Joy. I love you, and I want us to be a family, but I'm beginning to think you no longer love me. Do you love me, Richard?"

"It isn't that easy, Ann. It isn't that I don't love you; I just want things the way they were, and I want you the way you were. If you want to know what the problem is, I'll tell you what it is. It's your stubborn refusal to see that we can't keep this baby in our home!"

"This baby! You talk about her as if she were a stick of wood. She's a living, breathing part of us, Richard. She's our daughter, and this is her home too."

"No, it isn't! And if you insist on keeping her here, then we can no longer be together. I don't want to lose you, Ann, but I won't be party to this pretense that she's all right. She has a serious problem! She isn't all right, and she never will be! Why can't you see that?"

"No, she will never be 'all right.' She will always require care, and that's exactly what I plan to give her. For as long as she lives—and, according to Dr. Anderson, that may not be very long—I will cherish every minute of every day of her life. She may not be what *you* consider normal, but she isn't the one with the problem, Richard. You are the one with the problem!"

Just then, as if charged by some invisible force, Richard flung his right arm upward across his body and, with the back of his hand, sent Ann reeling to the floor. Stunned by the assault, she lay there unable to move, a chasm of outrage separating them. Then, as he had done a few weeks earlier, Richard stalked from the room and out the front door. Suddenly, her mind was seized by an image of a girl lying on the ground in Central Park.

Ann's brain became numb. She couldn't take in the reality of what had just happened, but one thing was clear to her. She couldn't allow her daughter to be exposed to the threat of Richard's aggression. She didn't want to be in the house when he returned, so she hurriedly packed bags for herself and Joy. She retrieved her stash of emergency cash, and then she called for a taxicab. She decided to go to the airport and chance getting a flight to Dallas. She would call Daddy from there.

As she boarded the plane with her daughter, the past three years zipped through her mind like slides being flashed on a screen. She wondered if Richard was really capable of genuine love. Sarah had been right—Nelson had a hold over him that tainted his whole being. If Joy were not a factor, Ann would do everything in her power to help him overcome Nelson's grip, but she couldn't risk her daughter's safety.

It was almost midnight when Ann's flight taxied into Love Field. When she spotted Daddy waiting for her, she noted his worried expression and the cloud of weariness that enveloped him. As they drove from the airport to Bonner Valley, she tried to explain her sudden decision to come home, but her heavy heart and cluttered mind made it impossible for her to express her feelings. Finally, she said, "Daddy, maybe tomorrow I'll be able to tell you all about this, but right now, I just can't talk about it. I'm tired and confused and not even sure I did the right thing. But I did what I thought was best—no—what I *had* to do. For now, let's just let it go at that."

"That's okay, honey, you tell me when you feel up to it. From the sound of your voice when you called, I knew something bad had happened, and I've just been praying you and Joy were all right. Maybe tomorrow you'll explain that bruise on the right side of your face."

Ann touched her hand to her cheek and felt a hard knot. Until then, she hadn't even noticed the puffiness and diminished vision in her eye. "He hit me, Daddy, and I left because I didn't know if he might hurt Joy." Her words were flat and unfeeling as if she'd thought about them for a long time and was now devoid of any emotion in uttering them.

She felt safe now, and a deep sense of belonging spread over her. She cradled Joy in her arms and threw back the wrap that had shielded her baby's face from the cold night air. She stroked her tiny hands and kissed her forehead. There was comfort in holding her, protecting her, loving her.

CHAPTER 42

When Ann walked into her old bedroom in Daddy's house, she was surprised to see a baby bed at the foot of her bed, completely ready for Joy with sheets and blankets and even a little wind-up music box hanging over the side. "I was thinking I would have to put Joy in bed with me," she said. "When did you get the baby bed?"

"As soon as I got back from New York. I thought you might come for a visit sometime, and I wanted to be prepared."

"You could see this coming, couldn't you?" She kissed his cheek and said, "I love you so much, Daddy!"

"I just want to take good care of my two girls."

Ann looked at him just in time to see him wiping pearls of moisture from his cheek. She knew they had much to discuss, but tonight wasn't the time. "I'm exhausted, Daddy, and I'm sure you are too. As soon as I change Joy, I'm going to get some sleep. Thank you for everything, and we'll have a long talk tomorrow."

The next day, Ann explained to her daddy why she had left New York. She painfully recounted how Richard had knocked her to the floor and that she had fled because she was afraid he might harm Joy. She told him about the battles she had fought to keep Joy with her and about her suspicion that Nelson was forcing Richard to insist on placing Joy in an institution. She even disclosed her conversations with Sarah concerning the strange power Nelson has over Richard. Paul wrapped his daughter in comforting words the way he used to wrap her in a warm blanket. When their conversation ended, she felt renewed—not without pain and sadness—but purged and relieved.

Two days passed, and another, and then another. Ann heard nothing from Richard. She had thought he would call Daddy's house when he realized she and Joy were gone. She expected him to be remorseful and to beg her to return and give him a chance to show her how sorry he was for his behavior. She had steeled herself against being too soft, too forgiving, too willing to jump back into an unstable, even dangerous, situation.

But Richard didn't call. She didn't know what to think about his sudden absence from her life. Could it be that he didn't want her back? Maybe he was glad she was gone. Whatever the circumstance, she had to talk to him. She had to know where she stood.

For two days, she tried to call him, first at the house and then several times at his private office number. Finally, she called the corporation number.

"Buffington Transport, Incorporated. This is Vicki."

"Vicki, this is Ann. Is Richard in his office?"

"Yes, Ma'am, he is. I'll put you through."

At the sound of her voice, Richard hesitated and then asked, "How are you, Ann?" He said it with a noncommittal politeness he might use in speaking to a casual acquaintance.

His detached, impersonal manner stymied her, but she managed to reply, "I'm fine."

"Well, I guess that makes two of us," he shot back, a cold wind chilling his words.

"Richard, I don't like having this conversation with you on the office phone where someone else could listen in, but since I can't seem to catch you at the house or on your private line, I have no choice. I don't know what's going on with you, but you aren't the same man I married two years ago. When I left last week, you were out of control. I would never have believed you would hit me, and when you did, all I could think of was that you might harm Joy too. Surely you can understand that. I can't come back until I know things will be different."

She waited for a reply but heard only a deep breath being exhaled, and then silence. She couldn't understand why he offered no response. He should have shown anger or regret or *some* emotion. "Richard, did you hear me?"

"Yes, I heard you. So, you're saying this is all my fault, right?"

"No, I'm not saying that. I haven't always handled things as I should have. Sometimes I've been very angry at you and have intentionally said things to hurt you, but I've never even come close to hitting you. I've somehow managed to keep my anger in check. It worries me that you became angry enough to hit me." Her tone softened, "Richard, I would like for us to work out our differences, but I just can't come back until I know Joy will be safe. Another thing I can't do is put Joy in some sort of *home*. I know that's what you want, but what you're asking of me would tear my heart out. I can't do it! She's our baby, and I want her in our lives, not just every now and then when we go visit her or take her home for a day or two, but every day of her life."

"Well, I guess that leaves us at an impasse. I can't accept your terms. I was planning to call you maybe next week when things are worked out. I've talked to Hollis Wilhite about filing for divorce, and he's drafting documents for Joy's support and an equitable division of property. Don't worry, you and Joy will be provided for. Believe it or not, I take my responsibility for Joy seriously. I want her to have as good a life as possible, and I'm willing to pay for that to happen. We should be able to take care of all this without a lengthy court battle. I'm giving you total custody of Joy, and you'll have a nice financial settlement. I have an appointment waiting for me, but I'll get in touch with you when I know more."

She heard the click of the receiver. They were no longer connected, not on the telephone and, evidently, not in life. Their conversation left her with a hollow feeling. She had been confident of his love for her. She thought he would never want to be without her and that he would eventually come to share her love for their daughter. *How foolish and naïve I have been*, she thought.

———— ✺ ————

"Ann! He hit you? Why? What happened?" Charlie's voice rang with disbelief.

"I know this comes as a shock to you, Charlie. I'm still in shock myself. A year ago, nobody could have convinced me that Richard would ever hit me, and I would have laughed at the suggestion that he would want a divorce. I thought Richard and I had a strong marriage that could survive anything. But ever since we found out about Joy's health issues, things have been different between us. I didn't say anything to you about it because it was hard to talk about. It was just too private for me to share with anyone. I also kept thinking we would get beyond our *misunderstanding* and things would smooth out between us. I guess I took a lot for granted."

Ann and Charlie were on the phone for over an hour. It was painful for Ann to divulge the most sensitive details of what had transpired between her and Richard, but as she did so, a catharsis washed over her, releasing her from the snare of doubt and despair. What emerged to replace her negative self-assessment was a dignity in who she was and what she could become. She couldn't live the rest of her life feeling defeated and broken and useless.

She didn't know how much Joy would ever comprehend, but if there was even a small chance that she could sense her mother's emotional strength or weakness, Ann felt she had to remain positive and resilient. She couldn't permit her daughter to be further maimed by having to live in a negative environment. As for Richard, she felt sorry for him. He was missing out on something beautiful, something life-changing and edifying, and he didn't even know it.

Richard called Ann three days before Christmas to explain what he and Hollis Wilhite had worked out. Wilhite had already put a copy of the divorce contract in the mail for her to review. She could note any changes she wanted to make and mail it back to him. Wilhite would call her about the court date when he knew it, and Richard would pay her roundtrip air fare to LaGuardia and back to Dallas.

Richard thought she would probably want to fly back to Dallas the same day, but if she did need to stay overnight, he would arrange and pay for her to stay in a hotel near the airport. He hoped they could come to an agreement as quickly as possible.

"Well, you seem to have given a lot of thought to this, Richard, but I need to get the rest of my things out of the Manhattan house. I need time to box them for shipping."

"I can take care of that," Richard volunteered. "I plan to sell the house and most of the furniture unless there's something you want. I don't need a big house like that, and Dad suggested I get a smaller place. In fact, I've already moved out, so all the personal items left there belong to you. I can have my guys go pack it all up, and we can tag it on with another load we have going to the Dallas area."

"I guess that would simplify things. In addition to my personal items, have them pack the pictures and teddy bears from the nursery, as well as all of Joy's furniture."

"I'm just trying to be helpful, Ann. I know you don't like being away from Joy."

"Yes, you're right. I don't want to be away from her. Aunt Lil would love taking care of her, but I don't like leaving her." *How sad,* Ann thought, *that he has no interest at all in seeing his daughter. His idea of help is not for me to bring Joy with me and bring Aunt Lil along to help with her. He would rather I leave Joy in Bonner Valley, away from him and his world.*

Daddy, Ann, and Joy spent Christmas Day with Aunt Lil and Uncle Ben. Aunt Lil prepared their traditional Christmas meal, and after they had eaten and exchanged gifts, they sat before the fireplace and shared memories of past Christmases. It was a peaceful yet sad day for Ann. Her thoughts drifted back to Sarah and to the beautiful wedding Sarah had hosted for her and Richard two years ago today. How much things had changed since that day!

Two months later, Ann boarded a noon flight from Dallas to New York City to officially end her marriage to Richard. Aunt Lil had come that morning prepared to spend the night and take care of Joy. Nelson had used his clout to arrange for a 9:00 a.m. hearing with the judge for Richard and Ann to execute divorce papers. The whole thing took less than an hour, and Ann was in the air headed for home by 12:30 p.m. She wondered if she would ever see or hear from Richard again.

CHAPTER 43

*B*onner Valley hadn't changed much since 1956 when Ann had moved to New York. It was still a sleepy little town of about 5,000 souls where almost everybody knew everybody else and everybody else's business, or at least some version of it. The town knew about Ann's brief stint on Broadway, and they were in awe of the hometown girl who had hit it big. They lauded her success, but they admired her dedication to her baby daughter even more.

During her first few months back in her home town, she sequestered herself and Joy from everyone except Daddy, Aunt Lil, and Uncle Ben. She said it was because she didn't want to unnecessarily expose Joy to any contagious illnesses that might be making the rounds, but her real reason was that she didn't know how people in town might react to Joy. She didn't want their pity, and she couldn't bear having them scrutinize her daughter in search of evidence of abnormalities. They wouldn't intend to be rude, but there were bound to be a few people whose curiosity would make her uncomfortable.

Just a few weeks earlier, her conversation with Daddy, and then with Charlie, had given a big boost to her sense of wellbeing. She thought she had put all the pessimism and self-pity behind her, but here she was, once again mired in feelings of inadequacy. She was still reeling from Richard's rejection and weeping bitter tears over her failed marriage. Her busy days went by pretty well, but at night when she was alone with her thoughts, she looked back at a pathway strewn with pieces of her broken heart. She tried not to worry about what the future might bring, but she couldn't escape the concerns she had about what would happen as Joy grew older.

By March of 1960, with the divorce behind her, Ann settled into a routine of daily activities in the house that held many beautiful childhood memories. Daddy had updated the kitchen (including the installation of a dishwasher, his contribution to promoting a germ-free environment), and he had purchased a new washer and dryer to make it easier for Ann to keep up with the daily laundering of diapers. Mazie, his housekeeper, continued to come once a week to clean and do the laundry and ironing, thus freeing Ann to give her attention to Joy's needs.

Ann had some good days when she felt optimistic and confident in her ability to deal with the obstacles that came her way. But she also had bad days when a raging river of uncertainty swept her away as she struggled to grab onto something stable enough to pull herself to safety.

She considered herself a colossal failure as a wife, but she didn't know how she could have handled things any differently. The thing that gnawed at her most, though, was why a merciful, loving God would allow an innocent child to suffer. From the time she was a little girl, she had been taught that God loved her and that she could trust Him to take care of her, even if she didn't always understand why things happened as they did. During her college years, she had drifted away from those teachings and from the closeness she had once felt to the Lord.

During the months since Ann's return to Bonner Valley, prayer had become a constant with her. If she couldn't find peace in the Lord Jesus, then she had nowhere else to turn, but she was not finding the comfort she longed for. The Lord seemed unapproachable and distant. She repeatedly cried out, "Why, Lord? Why is all this happening? Am I being punished? Please speak to my heart. Let me feel your presence and know you understand what I'm going through." But her prayers seemed futile, and she began to lose heart. Even more devastating, she began to lose faith.

"Are you deaf, God, or do you just not care that I am suffering?

Joy is pure and innocent. Why is she suffering?" Ann's exasperation had made her audacious and accusatory. Her prayers gradually became utterances without any expectation of results—meaningless rituals without reverence. Gradually, her frustration turned to anger and bitterness.

Why do I bother to pray? She wondered. *Maybe I can't feel the presence of God in my life because there is no God! Maybe he doesn't really exist, and all these years I've just been deluding myself.* She felt herself falling into an abyss of helplessness and hopelessness, yet she wanted to believe. Something deep within her compelled her to believe. *This can't be,* she thought. *Without faith, life is meaningless. If God doesn't exist, we're all just helpless creatures drifting around in a chaotic world without purpose and without hope!*

Aunt Lil came every Thursday morning to pick up Ann's grocery list; then she would return with the groceries, visit with Ann and cradle Joy in her arms for a while before she went home. One Thursday, Ann was having an especially difficult time with the questions that continued to haunt her: *Why has this happened to Joy? Why can't Richard love his daughter? What does the future hold for Joy? Why isn't God answering my prayers?*

Aunt Lil sensed her mood and asked, "Ann, what's wrong? You seem a little down today."

"I'm feeling all right, Aunt Lil. I just become frustrated sometimes. Well, maybe frustrated isn't strong enough; maybe angry describes it better."

"Tell me about it. What's making you angry?"

"I guess if I'm honest about it, I'm angry with God. I love Joy, and I love her just the way she is, but that doesn't keep me from wondering why she has to be this way—completely lacking in the ability to enjoy life. And what about her future? If she outlives me, what will happen to her then?" Tears began to roll down Ann's cheeks. "Aunt Lil, I've prayed and asked God to help me understand all this and to know how to give Joy a good life. Why isn't he answering my prayers?" Ann cried. "I feel so helpless!"

Aunt Lil sat down beside Ann on the sofa and put her arm

around her. Ann snuggled into her aunt's embrace. "Oh, Ann, it's natural for you to have these questions. I can't say I know what you're going through because I haven't walked the valley you're walking, but I do know a little bit about loss and heartache. When our little Benny died at the age of two, it ripped the heart right out of me, and I thought the sun would never shine again. But time gave me a different perspective. After a while, I was able to find pleasure in the memories. Instead of being depressed because he was taken from us, I began to rejoice over the time we had with him.

"I know your situation is different from mine, but believe me, honey, God knows about every heartache and doubt you have. Just trust Him. Even when you think He isn't listening, trust Him.

"Ann, I think one of your problems is that your world is too shut off from everybody except family. You need to get out and see people. Every time I go anywhere, especially to church, people ask about you. They would love to see you, but they know you have your hands full, and they're afraid of being a bother. They don't want you to think they don't care; they just don't know what to do about calling you. I think you're going to have to take the first step. Why don't you plan to go to church with your daddy this Sunday, and I'll come stay with Joy."

"That's very sweet of you, Aunt Lil. In some ways, I would enjoy doing that, but I just don't know if I'm up to facing everybody. I have gotten cards from several people, and I guess I should have called them. How could you stay with Joy? I thought you taught a Sunday school class."

"That doesn't make any difference. I'll come over here after Sunday School and you can go on to church with your daddy."

Ann's face brightened at the thought of seeing some of the people who had been dear to her all her life. "If you're sure you want to do that, I guess it would be good for me to get out every once in a while. Yes, I would enjoy going to church."

"Then it's settled, I'll come over as soon as I get out of Sunday school—and I just had another idea—I'll bring my pot roast and we'll all eat lunch over here. I'll leave Ben at church and he can come home with you and Paul. How does that sound?"

209

"I would love that. This brings back memories. We used to eat Sunday lunch together all the time when I was growing up. I'll make a dessert.

Paul and Ann arrived at the church in time to visit with several people before they went into the sanctuary. Even after they found Uncle Ben and took their seats beside him, several people came over to speak to Ann, lovingly embrace her and tell her how happy they were to see her. She hadn't realized how much she had missed the kindness and warmth of these gentle people. Their gestures of care and concern warmed her heart.

Following the singing of hymns, Brother Craig slowly walked to the pulpit, greeted the congregation, and led in prayer. Then he read his text—Psalm 139:1-14. His message celebrated the Lord's omniscience, omnipresence, and omnipotence; and he challenged the congregation to acknowledge and honor their all-knowing, ever-present, all-powerful God by trusting Him to guide and empower their lives. As was his custom, he closed his message with a brief summary of the main points of his message:

"Our God is omniscient. He knows everything about you; He knows about your disappointments, your failures, your heartaches, and He also knows about your dreams and ambitions. God is omnipresent. He is in *all* places *all* the time; He is *always* with you, *always* listening. Even when you feel He is ignoring your cries for help, He hears and understands your needs. God is omnipotent; He has the power to give you the spiritual resources to become all He wants you to be. Don't rob yourself of God's blessings and cripple your ability to be your best self. Yield your heart and your will to Him. If God was willing to give Jesus, His only Son, to purchase your freedom from sin, shouldn't you show your gratitude by honoring Him with your life?"

When Ann walked out of the church building on that warm spring Sunday, she carried with her a new perspective of all that had happened and was happening in her life. She felt her fractured spirit beginning to heal. A deep peace settled over her, carrying with it a hope—even an expectation—for something more than a mundane existence for Joy.

She thought back to her conversation with Bill Lambert several months ago, and she remembered what he had said about setting aside a time every day to pray and read his Bible. For weeks she had been praying and asking God to help her through this difficult time, but it occurred to her that she had been *talking to* God, but she wasn't letting God *talk to* her. Maybe God was trying to answer, but she wasn't listening. She decided to start reading her Bible and giving God a chance to speak to her.

One day she picked up a Bible that had belonged to her mother and began thumbing through it. The satin ribbon was marking Psalm 147, and her eyes were drawn to an underlined verse: "He healeth the broken in heart, and bindeth up their wounds." The words gripped her. Was it just coincidence that she had turned to this verse? She didn't know the answer, but she did know these words had spoken to her heart.

Day after day, as she continued her time of Bible reading and prayer, she marveled at how the doors of her mind and heart opened to the voice of God. She began to see things about herself that she'd never seen before—twisted thoughts and attitudes that had crept in while she was busy making what she thought was a good plan for her life.

"Dear Lord," she prayed one day, "no wonder I couldn't feel your presence with me. I was praying out of anger and self-pity. I was demanding answers and solutions. I still don't understand all that has happened or why Joy is having to suffer, but You know all about it. You have trusted me to take care of this special child, and I trust You to lead me in knowing how to do that. You understand her far better than I do. I pray that in some unfathomable way, You will help me give her a meaningful life. Give me the ability to make her understand that I love her. Amen."

Joy was growing and gaining weight, but otherwise, she remained the same. Ann usually laid her on her back after bathing her each morning, but since she was unable to roll to her side, Ann would reposition her many times throughout the day and night. Joy seemed totally unaware of people or activity around her. When she was awake, her eyes wandered around the room, focusing on nothing, and her dainty face was void of expression. Ann worried because she had no way of knowing if Joy was comfortable or uncomfortable or even whether or not she was in pain. Dr. Matheson, the pediatric neurologist in Dallas, thought Joy was probably comfortable most of the time. "I feel sure she has diminished sensory perception and, therefore, doesn't experience pain in the way we think of it."

Except for the check that came every month from Richard, Ann and Joy were completely cut off from the Buffingtons. Ann and Olivia had called back and forth a few times, but since Olivia had remarried and had a busy life with her new husband, even that had come to a halt.

Charlie was now Ann's only link with New York, and the two friends still talked at least once a week. Ann knew their long-distance friendship was expensive, but it was an indulgence she granted herself as one of the staples she needed in her life. In late May, Ann boarded a flight out of Love Field and went to Seattle and be Charlie's matron of honor. She had left Joy in Aunt Lil's capable hands while she made the overnight trip.

One June morning, Ann had to run to answer the phone before it stopped ringing.

"Hello, Ann. This is Hollis Wilhite. I'm the Buffington family attorney, and I met you when the family came together for the reading of Sarah Buffington's will."

"Yes, I remember you Mr. Wilhite."

"I'm calling at Richard's request. As you know, the trust for Joy Marie was created before she was born, but she is clearly identified as the beneficiary, with you and Richard as co-trustees. Richard is now placing trusteeship solely in your hands, Ann, since you are Joy's caregiver. He is, however, maintaining the right to oversee the use of the trust assets. He wanted me to let you know he will honor your judgment in using the $100,000 for your daughter's benefit, and that he will not question expenditures from the trust so long as they are paid to third parties and not directly to you. He further stated that the trustees of the Sarah Buffington estate (Nelson and Olivia) will honor the trust throughout Joy Marie's lifetime, but upon her death, any and all remaining balance will revert to the estate. I have prepared a document for you to sign, which I will mail to you. You will need to sign it in the presence of a notary public and return it to me. Do you have any questions about any of this?"

"No, I understand, and I will take care of it as soon as I receive the document."

Although Ann knew it was necessary to legally safeguard the assets held in a trust, she somehow felt annoyed at the wording of the document she was asked to sign. Did the Buffingtons really think she would abuse her trusteeship? Her own integrity wouldn't permit her to exploit them, and Richard should know that.

When she told her daddy about the call from Hollis Wilhite and how it had made her feel, he chuckled and said, "Ann, not everybody is like you. Given your circumstances, many women would feel they had earned every penny of that trust and would pay themselves a nice caregiver's fee." She hadn't thought of it in that way, but it didn't change her feelings about it. Ann wanted them to know they didn't have enough money to pay her for loving and taking care of her own daughter. Her heart wasn't for sale.

CHAPTER 44

As the weeks and months went by, Ann felt herself bonding with her daughter in an unusual way. Her fears about Joy's wellbeing hadn't disappeared, but a peace had settled over her. She still didn't understand why God would allow a child to endure the limitations Joy would be subjected to in this life, but instead of blaming God, she acknowledged His goodness and praised Him for trusting her with this special gift.

A great deal of ambiguity existed within the medical community concerning the brain function of children in Joy's condition. Therefore, Ann had developed her own manner of caregiving. She refused to assume Joy was completely unaware of what was going on around her, and she treated her as if she were healthy and whole. She continually talked to her and sang to her. Every day when she held Joy's head against her cheek, she whispered into her ear, "I love you." She made feeding, bathing, dressing, and even diapering happy times filled with laughter and play. Every morning after Joy's bath, Ann gently massaged her arms and legs and lovingly caressed her delicate hands and feet. Whenever she nestled Joy on her shoulder, she made a habit of stroking her head and back.

One day, Ann laid Joy on her lap with her feet pressing against Ann's stomach. She took both Joy's hands in hers, kissed them and said, "You aren't a mistake, sweetheart. God doesn't make mistakes, and He planned you just the way you are. You are a special blessing from God." Joy's eyes opened wider than usual, and for a fleeting second, seemed to focus on Ann's face. A thrill surged through Ann's whole body, and in that brief moment, she sensed a glimmer of recognition in Joy's eyes. *I think she knows I'm her mother and that I love her. Please, Lord, don't let this be just my imagination or wishful thinking. Help her to know me.*

Ann longed for Joy to repeat this spark of perception, but it didn't happen. Her eyes still explored the empty space above and around her. Her face was still void of expression as she lay in her bed like a beautiful doll. But Ann refused to be discouraged. *Even if I never again see that look of awareness in her eyes, I believe that somewhere in the depths of her soul she knows me.*

On October 8, 1960, Joy Marie's first birthday, Ann hosted a birthday party, complete with a cake topped with a single candle. A cluster of balloons reached for the ceiling above Joy's portable crib. At the appropriate time, twelve guests sang happy birthday to Joy and joined in blowing out the candle on the cake.

Then, as if time had been caught up in some science fiction time machine that rapidly peeled away month after month, another year had passed and then another. On Joy's third birthday, someone unexpectedly showed up shortly before time for Joy's party. Grace Garrison had been best friends with Ann's mother from the time they were little girls, and now Grace had moved back to Texas from California. Grace's husband had died, so she decided to return to her home town. Someone had told her about Ann's situation, and she wanted to see Ann and Paul and little Joy. Grace had been the RN in charge of the neonatal ward at the local hospital until she and her husband moved to California. Ann's mother had credited Grace with saving Ann's life when she had stopped breathing shortly after she was born.

"Grace! Oh, my goodness! What a wonderful surprise!" Ann cried when she answered the door and saw the face of this dear friend. Ann threw her arms around Grace. "Come on in this house, Grace, and just let me look at you."

"Ann, you look just like your mother. When I look at you, I see her, and I hear her in your voice."

"What a nice compliment! Grace, it's been at least ten years since I've seen you. Are you still living in California?"

Grace briefly explained the circumstances that brought her back to Bonner Valley. Then she looked around and noticed the balloons and birthday cake and began apologizing, "Ann, I'm so sorry I came barging in without calling first. I've caught you at a bad time. I'll come back someday, and we'll have a nice long visit."

"Don't you dare leave! It's my daughter's third birthday party, and I can think of no one I'd rather have here to help us celebrate than you. Please say you'll stay. Daddy will want to visit with you too, so you can't go running off."

Ann led Grace into the bedroom where Joy was lying in her bed. She was dressed in her special birthday outfit—pink pants and a matching top with lace trim outlining the collar and cuffs. A pink ribbon secured a lock of black hair on top of her head. She was awake.

"Oh, Ann, she's a beautiful little girl. I just wish Eve were here to see her. She would love her dearly, and she would be so proud of you for the marvelous way you take care of her.

"You know, Ann, after we moved to California, I was head nurse for three years in the neonatal unit of a hospital. There, as here in Bonner Valley, children with congenital impairments would occasionally come through our unit. I developed a special interest in these children, and I did a lot of reading and even attended some classes about children who suffered from physical and neurological underdevelopment. After a while, I quit my job at the hospital and started doing private nursing in homes with special needs children. It turned into a very satisfying career. Your little Joy brings back so many precious memories of those little ones. They captured my heart, and it was hard for me to leave them."

Grace continued relating her experiences with the children whose lives had impacted hers, and as Ann listened, a thought that had been circulating in her brain for months was crystalizing into a plan. "Grace, if you aren't in a hurry, please stay for a while after the party so we can visit. I want to talk to you about something. Do you think you can do that?"

"Certainly. I have nothing else to do, and I'd love getting to visit with you and Joy. I don't know your routine, Ann, but is it all right if I pick her up?"

"Sure. Our guests will begin arriving in about 15 minutes, so I was going to move her to the portable crib in the dining room anyway. You can do the honors."

It was obvious to Ann that Grace was perfectly comfortable holding Joy. "I want to hold her for a few minutes," Grace said, "but I'll put her in the crib before your guests come. I get a sense about children—what's comfortable or pleasing and what's not—by holding them, and I want to see what *vibes* I get from Joy."

When the party was over and all the other guests had left, Paul visited with Grace for a while; then he excused himself, and Ann and Grace were left alone.

"Grace, I don't know how much you know about my adult life, but I went to New York to try to make it in musical theater. I was doing pretty well, but when Joy came along, I knew I couldn't continue that life. My husband wanted us to put Joy in an institution, and when I refused to do that, he became abusive—but that's another story. Anyway, I left and came home to Texas, and that's a short summary of my life after I left Bonner Valley in 1956.

"I've said all that as a background for the next thing I want to discuss with you. For the past few months, I've been considering doing some teaching—voice lessons and possibly dance—before I get so out of practice I can't do it anymore," Ann giggled. I don't know how much interest there would be. I'd just have to spread the word and see what happens.

"The thing that's been holding me back is my concern about Joy. I'm not sure I would feel comfortable dividing my attention between teaching and taking care of her. I worry that my teaching would distract me and keep me from giving adequate attention to Joy. I also worry about not doing justice to my students because of my uneasiness about Joy. Do you understand what I mean?"

"Of course, I do, and I think you're right to be apprehensive. Have you considered having someone take care of her while you teach?"

"Until you arrived today, I couldn't think of anyone I would trust. What about it, Grace, would you be open to doing that? I don't know what you usually charge for in-home care, but I feel pretty sure I can match it."

"I was hoping you would ask me," Grace said, "I would love to. I'm as free as the wind, Ann, and I can work around any schedule you have in mind. The money isn't a big factor. We can work that out so it won't put you in a bind."

"It won't put me in a bind, Grace. You set your fee and I'll pay it. It will be paid out of a trust that was set up for Joy by her great grandmother, Sarah Buffington."

"Well, then I guess that's settled," Grace said. "You just let me know when you want me, and I'll be here."

"I'll begin putting out the word that I am available for private voice lessons," Ann stated. "I'll see how that goes, and then branch out from there. I don't really have room to give dance lessons here at the house, so I'll have to give more thought to that."

"Well, I need to go, honey, but it's so good to see you again and to get to know that precious little girl of yours. You've given me something to look forward to, and just when I needed it." Grace took a note pad from her purse, jotted her phone number on it, and gave it to Ann. "I bought the Crocker house over close to the schools. Do you know where it is?"

"Yes, I do. Sula Ramsey used to live next door to the Crocker family. She and I were good friends in elementary school before she moved away, and I was over at her house a lot." Ann began laughing: "I remember going to a party Sula had in her back yard, and Mr. Crocker yelled over the fence for us to be quiet. It was only 8:00 p.m., but we were disturbing his sleep. Sula called him *Mr. Cranky*."

A far-away, pensive look came to Ann's face. "Those were good times, and it makes me sad when I think about my Joy never having experiences like that."

Grace took Ann's hand in hers. "Honey, I understand how you feel, but don't you think God is capable of handling that problem? If Joy could speak, she might have some amazing stories to tell—secrets between her and the Lord Jesus. Maybe we're the ones who are in the dark."

"Oh, Grace," Ann laughed, "I think if Mother were here, she'd tell me the same thing. I'd forgotten how much alike you two were. You thought the same way about a lot of things. Ann threw her arms around Grace and cried, "I'm so glad you're back in Bonner Valley. I need you!"

CHAPTER 45

The week before Thanksgiving, the phone rang while Ann was relaxing following a busy morning. It was Charlie, and she was bursting with exuberance: "Ann, guess what! Bill and I are moving to Bonner Valley! Bill is taking a job as a field representative with a pharmacy group in the Dallas area. Do you know a good real estate agent? Can you recommend a good motel where we can stay while we look for a house? We're flying to Seattle to have Thanksgiving with my parents and back to New York on Friday to pick up Bill's car; then we're driving to Bonner Valley on Saturday and Sunday. We should get there sometime Sunday afternoon."

"Charlie, how wonderful!" Ann cried. "I can't believe this! You don't know how much I've missed you, and it will be so great to have you right here in Bonner Valley. Yes, I know a good real estate agent and yes, I know a good motel—right here in our house! We have plenty of room, so we're expecting you to stay here until you can move into your own place."

"We won't impose on you for that long," Charlie laughed, "but if it's okay, we will stay with you for two or three days while we look for a house."

"Well, the original offer still stands if you change your mind."

Ann gave Charlie directions to the house. "If you get lost, just call and Daddy will come lead you here. Be careful driving. The weekend following Thanksgiving isn't the best time to be out on the highways. I'm so excited! Oh, by the way, when you get to the house, pull into the driveway; that will make it easier to unload your bags."

"Okay, Ann. Oh, I can't wait to see you and Joy!"

It was dark when Charlie and Bill arrived at Paul Jernigan's house on that Sunday evening, but Ann's directions guided them there without a hitch. Ann was watching the driveway and saw their headlights as they drove in. She ran out the front door and into Charlie's arms; then she gave Bill a hug, and they all went inside.

In the family room, the fireplace glowed with embers and sent the aroma of cedar throughout the house. Paul sat reading *Newsweek* with Joy beside him in her portable crib. When Charlie and Bill entered the room, Paul stood and extended his hand to Bill, "It's good to see you again, Bill." Then he greeted Charlie with a hug. "Well, young lady, you are radiant. I take it you don't mind being transplanted in Texas.

Charlie giggled, "I'm so excited to be here. This is my first trip to Texas, but I really look forward to a warmer climate. Of course, my real reason for wanting to move here is this gal," she laughed as she gave Ann a little squeeze.

Paul and Bill carried luggage in from the car, and they all sat down to roast sandwiches, salad, and cherry pie. Soon, Bill began to show signs of weariness, leading Paul to offer, "Bill, I know you're bound to be tired from that long drive. Anytime you want to go to bed, don't feel you have to stay up. We'll have time to visit tomorrow."

"Thanks so much, Mr. Jernigan, I may just do that. I did almost all the driving. Charlie is so excited about seeing Ann that I'm sure she will want to stay up and visit a while, but they don't need me."

"Your room is waiting for you," Paul said. "Let me show you the bathroom and where to find things," Paul said as he led the way down the hallway. "Just make yourself at home. If you need anything else, let us know. By the way, Bill, you can call me Paul."

"All right, Paul. We really appreciate your hospitality. I'll see you in the morning."

"You bet. Hope you sleep well."

"I don't think I'll have a problem with that," Bill laughed.

"I'm turning in too," Paul said, "and I'll see you gals in the morning. It's good to have you and Bill here, Charlie."

After Ann and Charlie cleaned the dishes and put everything

away, Ann took Joy from the portable crib to her bed. Charlie and Ann dressed for bed, and then Charlie joined Ann in her bedroom where Joy was now sleeping. They sat down on the sofa nested in front of a bay window. For almost two hours they quietly shared and reminisced, laughed and cried.

"You remember I told you on the phone I was teaching voice lessons to five high school girls. Well, that number has almost tripled. I now have thirteen, and I'm really enjoying it. I couldn't do it, though, if I didn't have Grace to take care of Joy. Grace has been an answer to prayer. She is an absolute treasure!

"I could probably handle a few more students, but I want to be able to spend most of my time with Joy. Six of the lessons are on Saturday, so that's my busiest day. The others come between 2:30 and 4:30 on various week-day afternoons. It's working out well for them and for me. I would really like to start some dance classes—group sessions, not private lessons—but I just don't have room to do that here at the house."

"Have you thought about renting a place, maybe something you could turn into a studio for both vocal and dance lessons?"

"I've *thought about* a lot of things, but most of them are just dreams that will never become reality."

"Bounce your ideas off me. Maybe we can figure out a way to make them become reality."

"Well, I'd love to have a theater arts school, complete with a theater—nothing too elaborate, but with a stage versatile enough for a variety of performance genre. I'd like it to have a seating area large enough to accommodate the families and friends of the students. You're the only person I've told about this big dream, Charlie, because it will never happen. I don't have the resources to build something like that, and there's certainly nothing to rent in Bonner Valley that could be adapted for use as a theater."

"Ann, it's never going to happen as long as you have that negative attitude about it. Nobody's going to dump a studio in your lap. You have to plan for it. You have something unique to offer this community—your own theater experience. As the word continues to spread, you'll have students coming from every little town around here. Your reputation will pave the way, girl! Your business will grow, and your profits will grow. Then maybe you can afford to build that studio."

"I think you're oversimplifying the situation, Charlie. I'm just trying to be realistic. I can't afford to gamble on something that may not pay dividends. Joy's future is financially secure, but I need to be able to support myself. Of course, living here with Daddy is a big help, but I still need to watch my spending."

"Well, I still say you shouldn't write it off yet. Wait and see what happens. You might be surprised at the possibilities."

"I'm just not a risk taker, Charlie. Maybe I was prone to be like that when I was younger, but I'm not in a position to take chances now. I have to consider how things will affect Joy."

"You don't have to be a risk taker. Just be open to the possibilities; be a visionary."

"Charlie," Ann laughed, "you're such a *lifter upper*. Whenever I get stuck in a rut, you always dig me out. Everything you said, I needed to hear."

CHAPTER 46

$\mathcal{T}$he morning dawned clear and cold, but the sunshine warmed the day to a balmy sixty degrees by noon. Last week Ann had called Midge Tumulty, Bonner Valley's only real estate agent, to make an appointment for Charlie and Bill to look at houses, so as soon as they had eaten breakfast, they were gone. Daddy had gone to work, and Ann had fed Joy and performed her ritual of bathing and massaging. Joy was now sleeping, and Ann was rethinking last night's conversation with Charlie.

Ann couldn't see how she could ever earn enough money to build a school of theater arts, but Charlie's positive attitude had given her a fresh perspective. Ann tucked her dream into the shadows of her mind, but from time to time, she drew it into the light and twirled it around on the dancefloor of her consciousness.

Grace came at 2:00 p.m., ready to watch Joy so Ann could give her undivided attention to a string of lessons starting at 2:30. A few weeks earlier, Grace had suggested that she could prepare supper for them while Ann was teaching. She could do what Ann had to do—bring Joy into the kitchen with her while she was cooking. That would give Ann more free time in the evenings. Ann liked the idea, so it became a part of their routine. Grace always ate with them, and then Grace would help Ann clean up the dishes.

As Ann was visiting with Grace about the menu for their evening meal, Charlie came bouncing into the living room, Bill not far behind her. "Ann, we found the perfect house," she bubbled. "It's an older home out at the edge of town, so we want to get somebody to inspect it to make sure it's in good shape. Midge is taking care of getting it inspected, but it looks great and has gobs of room. The downstairs alone makes our apartment in Queens look like a doll house," she laughed.

"I'll bet you're talking about the old Parsons house. Which direction from town?"

"North, unless I'm all turned around," Charlie answered.

"It *is* north," Bill affirmed. "It sits up on a hill on five acres of land with lots of trees. It's inside the city limits, but it has a real country feel about it. I think I'd really like that."

"I feel sure it's the old Parsons place. What do you think, Grace?"

"It does sound like it," Grace mused. "Is it a two story with an elegant staircase leading to the second floor from a long, wide hallway?

"Yes, that's it!" Charlie exclaimed.

"Oh my, that house was a showplace in its day," Grace reminisced. "I remember people talking about it when I was a child. It was built back in the late 1800s, and it had indoor plumbing, even way back then. It seems I remember that it was originally something other than a residence, but I'm not sure about that."

"It has a modern kitchen and two roomy bathrooms, one upstairs and one downstairs," Bill explained. "I think Midge said those areas had been renovated fairly recently, and they do look a lot newer than the rest of the house."

"One of the rooms downstairs is what got my attention," Charlie interjected, "but I won't even attempt to explain. You'll just have to see it to understand."

"Well, here we are chatting away, and I haven't introduced you," Ann said. "Grace, these are my dear friends Charlie and Bill Lambert; Charlie and Bill, this is my sweet Grace I've talked about so much."

"Ann has talked a lot about you two, so I feel I already know you," Grace said. "I'm so happy to finally meet you. Well, I need to go see about my little doll, so I'll see you folks later."

"Oh," Ann gasped, glancing at her watch, "my first student will be here any minute, and I need to get things ready. I'll be finished about 5:15. Just relax a while; you've had an exciting day, and I want to hear all about it later. We'll have dinner when Daddy gets home about 5:45, so don't stray too far if you get out again."

That evening after dinner, Grace shooed Ann and Charlie out of the kitchen and told them she would do the cleaning up tonight so they could visit and be with Joy for a while before she went to sleep.

"Ann, I would like for you to go with me to look again at this house Bill and I saw today," Charlie said. "I know how busy you are, but I really want you to see it."

Ann was puzzled by Charlie's insistence, but she didn't want to disappoint her. "Sure, Charlie. I'll ask Grace to come early tomorrow if that would work with Midge's schedule. Have you told to her you want to look at it again?"

"Yes. I told her I'd like to show it to you, and she said to give her a call when we wanted to go. I'll call her first thing in the morning."

"Let me check with Grace. If she can come early tomorrow, you can call Midge tonight. I've known Midge Tumulty for years. She won't mind if you call her at home."

Within a matter of minutes, it was all set. Tomorrow at 12:30 p.m., Midge would take Charlie and Ann to the house that Midge had confirmed was indeed "the old Parsons place."

The next day as they drove to meet Midge, Charlie dropped some hints she hoped would spark Ann's curiosity and interest, "I guess you wonder why I'm so anxious to show you this place. I want you to see something special about it." As they pulled into the circle drive, Charlie added, "You'll just have to see it for yourself. I want to know if you see the possibilities I see."

Midge greeted them as they got out of the car, and the three of them walked together up the broad stone walkway leading to the front door of the plantation-style home. As they stepped inside, Ann gasped at the magnificence of the sight before her. "Oh, Charlie, I had no idea this house was so beautiful."

"Isn't it gorgeous? But, Ann," Charlie gestured with a tilt of her head, "what I want you to see is at the end of the hall."

Charlie led the way as they proceeded to the end of the hallway that dead ended into paneled double sliding doors. Charlie opened the doors into a vast open space. When the entire area came into view, Ann was in awe of the spaciousness before her. "What on earth?" Ann muttered, more to herself than to Charlie. She couldn't imagine what the builder had in mind when he left so much seemingly useless space.

"I know what you're thinking, Ann. I thought the same thing— Why? But there is an answer." Midge had wandered into the kitchen, and Charlie called for her to join them. "Midge, tell Ann what you told me about this part of the house."

"The house was built by a doctor as a tuberculosis sanitarium for women. He and his family lived upstairs, and the hospital was downstairs. He filled this big room with hospital beds. The beds were lined up along this wall facing those three sets of double French doors that open onto the veranda. You saw the veranda at the front and along one side of the house. Well, that veranda wraps across the back also. The doctor wanted his patients to be able to see outdoors and to have access to the veranda so they could go outside into the fresh air. Those big casement windows at each end of this area were put there to draw fresh air indoors."

Charlie looked at Ann and giggled, "That explains it, doesn't it?"

"Yes, it does, but it seems luxurious for a hospital."

"Well," Madge put in, "the story is that he believed two ingredients needed by his patients were missing from traditional hospitals and sanitariums—a beautiful, cheery atmosphere and lots of fresh air. That's what he tried to supply. His mother was one of his patients, and most people think that's probably why the sanitarium was for women only.

"Different owners have used this room for different things—a billiards room, a party room, a playroom for kids—but none of them ever changed it," Midge explained.

"It all depends on what people want in a house, and this one has exactly what I want!" Charlie exclaimed. "With the exception of coming downstairs to use the kitchen, the upstairs is more than adequate for living quarters for Bill and me; therefore, I have a great idea for what we can do with all this space," Charlie declared, making a sweeping gesture across the length of the room. "Ann, it would make a wonderful dance studio! It even has hardwood floors. What could be more perfect?" Charlie continued with more ideas pouring from her brain. The only problem she saw was that there was no audience space for group performances. Finally, she paused and spread her lips in a knowing smile as she waited for Ann's reaction.

"Are you saying you want this big house so you can start a school of dance?"

"Yes, but not *just* a school of dance. I thought your dream was a theater arts school."

"Well, that's true, but I don't feel I can make that kind of investment right now. You said I need to save with that as a goal, and you're right. That is what I need to do."

"Not necessarily," Charlie rebutted, "Ann, I'm trying to tell you I want you help me turn the downstairs of this house into a school of theater arts. I know we'll have to build a clientele—or at least, *I* will—but I think we can do this. If we team up, it will be less expensive for both of us. How about it?"

"But, Charlie, in a partnership, partners go halves on the expense, and you and Bill are the ones buying this house. What about my financial obligation? Would I pay rent or what?"

"Well, maybe you could pay a percentage of your earnings; that would work for me. How about you?"

"Oh, I don't know, Charlie. It isn't just the financial part of it I have to consider. Working here would take me away from Joy more, and I'm not sure I feel at ease about that. Can you give me some time to think and pray about it?"

"Of course. That's what I want you to do. Ann, Bill and I are probably going to buy the house whether or not you agree to go in with me on the theater arts thing, so don't feel you are spoiling anything for me if you don't feel comfortable doing this. I thought it could be a good thing for both of us, but I want you to feel good about it too."

"I know, Charlie, and I'm really interested. Your offer if very tempting, but I just have to make sure. I know you understand."

"I certainly do. Ann, you're the best friend I've ever had, and that friendship is more important to me than any of this. You just think and pray, and whatever you decide will be all right."

"Thanks, Charlie. I'll let you know something in the next few days.

CHAPTER 47

Over the next week, Ann pondered Charlie's proposal. One minute she would think this opportunity was God's answer to her prayers, and the next minute, she doubted her instincts. She was hesitant to jump into something when she had no assurance of how it would all turn out. What kind of response could they expect in a small town like Bonner Valley? Would there be enough interest to make it financially feasible?

Every day, this decision was the focus of Ann's thoughts and prayers as she read her Bible and asked God to lead her to do the right thing. How could she know for sure whether or not this was God's will? One day, her devotional reading took her to Hebrews 11. She read about those Bible heroes—Noah, Abraham, Isaac, Moses, and many others—who trusted God even though they couldn't see the final outcome of their actions. Suddenly, she was struck with a truth so obvious that she couldn't imagine why it had evaded her until now: *It requires no faith at all to follow the path God lays out when you know where the path is leading. You exercise faith only when you don't know what's waiting at the end of the road, but you go down that road anyway.* She was leaning toward accepting Charlie's offer, but she wondered if she might be mistaking her will for God's will. She couldn't afford to make a mistake.

The week after Charlie and Bill had first looked at the house, the inspection report came back revealing the need for a new roof and a few minor repairs. The owner was willing to take care of all that and throw in an interior paint job if Charlie and Bill would agree to close the deal quickly. Since Bill had recently sold the Manhattan property he had inherited following the death of his father, he was able to pay cash for the house and acreage, and Midge was able to expedite the paperwork.

Finally, Ann gave Charlie an answer. The more she had thought and prayed, the more convinced she had become that this was what she should do, so she allowed her faith to take her down that nebulous path. The day after the closing on the property, Charlie approached Ann with the idea that she and Bill wouldn't require any financial outlay from Ann until they had tested it out for a year. "I don't want to put you in an uncomfortable situation, Ann, so let's just try it for a while; then, if you want out, you won't have lost anything."

"No, Charlie, that isn't fair. You will have utilities and other expenses, and in a big house like this, that can really add up. I insist on bearing my part of the load."

"Well, Ann, I figure it like this: You'll bring your clientele along with you, and when your students see what I'm doing, it will be good advertisement. I need you, Ann, so my *unselfish* proposal is as much for my benefit as for yours."

Ann giggled, "Oh, Charlie, you aren't a very good liar, but I appreciate the effort. No, dear friend, I'll pay a percentage of my earnings just the way we discussed. What percentage do you suggest?"

"Oh, that . . . well . . . I hadn't really given it much thought. How about ten percent?"

"Charlie, you're cheating yourself," Ann giggled. "How about twenty-five percent? And I'm not sure even *that* is fair."

"Well, if you're sure you want to do that, it's okay, but you don't have to. Ann, I'm so happy you decided to do this!"

In January, Charlie and Bill moved into the august old house, which swallowed their meager furnishings in one gulp and begged for more, but Charlie was too busy getting the word out about her dance classes to worry about decorating.

Later that month, calls inquiring about her dance classes began to trickle in, and by the end of February, the trickle had become a flood. Within three weeks, Charlie was teaching two classes of modern dance, one of tap dance, and one of ballet. She had a total of twenty-four students, all beginners. She had her hands full, and she was loving it.

Ann's students seemed to enjoy coming to this elegant house shrouded in the mysterious ambiance of the past, and they became enamored with the school as a whole. The program that had started as a dream in Charlie's brain had taken on a powerful persona of its own.

In late spring, Grace began taking Joy to the studio two or three days a week in the afternoons. She would usually push her around the big veranda in her buggy where a breeze was almost always felt if there was a breeze anywhere. Although Grace couldn't really see visible evidence of it, she sensed that Joy enjoyed being outdoors. It was just one of her many instincts about Joy, and Ann had learned not to take Grace's instincts lightly.

As the weather turned from warm to hot, Grace began taking Joy inside. Sometimes she would roll her stroller into the vocal studio where her mother was teaching. Although Ann had been told Joy might be deaf, Grace was adamant that Joy either recognized her mother's voice, or sensed her mother's presence.

Other times, Grace would keep Joy in the big room where the dance lessons were in progress. One day, Grace was watching the dancers, Joy beside her in her buggy. Suddenly, Grace saw something, but she wasn't sure what it was. Out of the corner of her eye, she thought she detected a slight motion, maybe an involuntary jerk, in Joy's buggy. When she looked at Joy, she was calm and still, but her placid face seemed different, changed in a way Grace had never seen before. Instead of the usual wandering of her eyes as she searched the space before her, she seemed to be following the movements of the dancers. The doctors had said Joy was either blind or saw only shadows, but Grace had worked with enough children to know this wasn't her imagination. She had witnessed some spark of brain activity brought about by Joy's sensing or *seeing* the dancers. She could hardly wait to tell Ann.

That evening as Ann and Grace were cleaning up after supper, Grace told Ann what she had witnessed. "Her eyes were following those dancers, Ann. I just know it."

Ann was stunned, but she didn't doubt what Grace had told her. She thought back to a time when she felt she had seen a glimmer of recognition on Joy's face—a fleeting moment when she was sure she and Joy had made eye contact. "What does it mean, Grace? Are you saying the doctors have been wrong all this time—that maybe she just got off to a slow start but is getting better?"

"No, that's not what I'm saying. I don't think anyone really knows what she does or doesn't feel or understand. The doctors have even admitted as much. The thing I'm saying is that *if* she is responding to music and dancing, let's give her more exposure to it. If that stimulates her brain and brings her pleasure, shouldn't we give her that pleasure? I don't want you to get your hopes up, honey. I don't think this really changes anything in the long run. I just think it gives us a new way to give her something good in her life."

By July, with two recitals behind each of them, Ann and Charlie had begun rehearsing a special program to present to the parents of their students. Ann had written a musical adaptation of *The Three Little Pigs*, and Charlie had worked out the choreography. Together they had written an entire musical score for their version of the story. To give each of the forty-eight students equal standing (with the exception of the four students who played the pigs the wolf), they divided them into eight groups, four chorus groups and four dance groups. Each group represented the personality of one of the four characters. Since the musical had no speaking parts, Bill Lambert would serve as narrator.

Two weeks before the performance, Ann and Charlie called all the parents to see if the students could come the next two Saturdays for all-day workshops—free, of course—in which students would be working on scenery, costumes, make-up, and staging. They received overwhelming cooperation. Several parents offered to donate supplies or services and even volunteered to help on the two days of the workshops.

The workshops were a huge success. The students enjoyed learning to build scenery, to design and make costumes, and to apply stage makeup. They got a taste of all that goes into making a production come together, and they began to tune in to their individual strengths. They came to understand that theater involves much more than performing, and Ann and Charlie emphasized that they should take pride in perfecting their strongest abilities.

Realizing it would be impossible to accommodate an audience inside, they decided to set up chairs on the lawn, and the large veranda became the stage. The plan was not without challenges—finding enough chairs and transporting them, moving the piano to the veranda, working around the large support columns on the veranda, and configuring the props to allow free movement on the stage. The problems about the chairs and the piano were quickly resolved by parent volunteers, and Ann and Charlie knew they could work out the staging obstacles. They were beginning to smell success!

The one big question still looming before them was something beyond their control—the weather! They had no way of knowing what the weather would be like on August 24, so the understanding with the students and parents was that if it was raining or seriously threatening rain, the program would be postponed until the following Saturday.

August 24 dawned bright and clear, and the two entrepreneurs, who now made a practice of starting every day's work in a fellowship of prayer, thanked their heavenly Father for the calm, beautiful day.

Following the musical, some of the parents served punch and cookies, and everyone enjoyed refreshments as they visited. Reaction to the musical was explosive.

"Can you believe how well those kids did on those dances? I never dreamed they would have learned so much in this short amount of time!" Diane Weaver exclaimed.

Margie Musgrove was heard to say, "Those kids should be on Broadway. Those little voices sounded like angels singing."

"I don't think angels sing about a wolf huffing and puffing, Margie," her husband chortled. "but I'll admit they did a fine job. I laughed until I cried when that one little pig kept trying to catch the wolf's tail. They certainly put a new twist on an old story."

"Those little guys in the pig and wolf costumes were adorable.

They acted those parts to perfection. Even though they didn't have speaking parts, you could read their body language," one astute parent declared.

"Well, I knew it was really going to be *something*. Our Cindy had told me all about it. She's taking both voice lessons and tap dance, and she just loves it!" Louise Beecher announced, and in Bonner Valley, Louise Beecher's endorsement carried weight.

In conversations all over the yard, people were using expressions such as "wonderful," "so much talent," "a lot better than any recital," "magnificent," "so impressive!"

Ann and Charlie were bombarded by their students, all giggly and full of energy, asking one question after another: "When can we do another one of these?" "Will you write us another one, Miss Ann?" "Next time, may I be one of the characters?" "I want to design the scenery; my dad's an architect, and he'll help me."

After the parent volunteers had carried all the chairs away, taken down all the scenery, and cleaned up the refreshment table and after all the students and guests had left, Ann and Charlie sat down on the steps, looked at each other, and began laughing.

"We hit a home run!" Charlie shouted.

"Yes, we did!" Ann agreed. "We couldn't have asked for a better performance. The kids worked their hearts out, and it paid off."

"You know, the kids are going to expect us to keep writing stuff they have fun doing," Charlie laughed. "I think we mopped ourselves into a corner."

By this time, they were both slap-happy tired and decided to call it a night.

CHAPTER 48

On Monday, Ann and Charlie were interviewed by a reporter from *The Dallas Daily*, and an article featuring their school and their production of *The Three Little Pigs* showed up the following Sunday. The show was the talk of the town, and Ann and Charlie were inundated with calls from people inquiring about enrollment, some living as far as sixty miles away.

In October, Joy had her fourth birthday as family and close friends gathered to celebrate. Then fall turned to winter and winter to spring. With their business thriving, Ann and Charlie decided to recruit one or two more teachers to help with the overload and to broaden the scope of their curriculum.

They brought in a young woman who had just graduated from Southern Methodist University that spring with a major in drama and a minor in speech. Her name was Joanna Langston, and she proved to be an effective teacher in helping students develop stage presence. She also opened up a class in elocution and served as speech coach. On her recommendation, they hired a young man who had been in SMU with Joanna, and Trent Overholt joined them as vocal coach for the male students and as tap dance instructor. Charlie turned the two tap dance classes over to him, thus freeing her to create another much-in-demand class in modern dance.

Grace continued to bring Joy to classes and rehearsals, and it was her firm belief that this atmosphere of music and dancing brought Joy a level of pleasure she experienced nowhere else. The students began to notice Joy, to talk to her, and lovingly stroke and pat her.

They knew she was unable to show any response; nevertheless, they adopted her as a little sister.

One day, a ten-year-old male student came to Ann and asked if it would be all right for his mother to bring his little sister to visit the classes. "Well, Miss Charlie is the one you should ask about that, Chad, but I think it would be all right. How old is your sister? Would she be interested in taking a class?"

"She can't be in a class. She's five, but she's sick . . . well, not *sick* exactly, but . . . you know, she's like Joy. When I told Mom that I'd heard Miss Grace say she thought Joy liked visiting the classes, she wondered if Emma could visit."

Ann was touched by the boy's sincere inquiry and by his concern for his sister. "Well, of course, your mother is welcome to bring Emma. We will be happy to have them."

In the weeks that followed, Chad's mother, Carolyn Butler, brought Emma to visit regularly, and she and Grace concluded that something about the atmosphere of the studio had a calming effect on both Joy and Emma. According to Grace, at times it also seemed to kindle a subtle energy in Joy. It was nothing physically perceptible, with the possible exception of eye movement. It was more something Grace sensed. Carolyn observed that the music and dancing seem to settle Emma and make her less agitated.

A germ of an idea took root in Ann's mind when Grace shared with her the similarities she saw in Joy's and Emma's response to the dancing and singing. *Maybe there are other children who could benefit from visiting the classes. If so, should we open our doors to them?* The more Ann thought about the possibility that exposure to music and dancing could be a type of therapy for these special children, the more she felt drawn to make it available to them.

One evening after the students had left for the day, Ann mentioned to Charlie the dream that was building in her. "I just can't get it out of my mind, Charlie. Grace seems convinced that Joy and Emma find pleasure in the music and motion. If she's right, we have a ready-made situation for offering that type therapy. How would you feel about opening our classes for mothers to bring their special children to assess whether or not they think it would be beneficial for them?"

"I knew you were thinking about this, Ann, because I know your heart for children, especially those with special needs. You know I share your concern, and I like your idea of allowing them to visit. However, I'd like to make a couple of suggestions before we put the word out about this: First, ask them to sign up for certain time slots on certain days of the week, with no more than six or seven people visiting at one time. That way the room won't become too crowded. Second, require that the child be accompanied by no more than two people. Of course, one of those should be an adult and the other should be of an age and temperament to understand how to behave in a setting such as this. If we have children attending who are disruptive, we can't do justice to our students."

"Yes, you're right, Charlie. Those are good suggestions and things I hadn't thought about. That will be a good way to handle it. Then you are suggesting they could continue to come on a regular basis if they feel it *is* beneficial?"

"Sure. Why not? Isn't that the whole idea? It would be a shame to have them decide their children are receiving something helpful and then not make it available to them. Anyway, unless there are a lot more people who need this kind of service than I think there are, we should be able to accommodate everybody by scheduling the visits. I don't think six or seven people at one time would be too many, so depending on how many days of the week they want to come, we should be able to take care of ten to fifteen children each week, along with the parents who bring them. See, I've been doing some figuring too," Charlie declared as she flashed a wink at Ann.

"Thank you, Charlie, for being so understanding and for caring about them the way I do. I felt a little bit guilty even to suggest such a thing. I don't want to impose on you, but I appreciate so much your willingness to go along with my instincts about this."

"Stop that! I'm not doing it to pacify you. I'm doing it because it's what I want too."

"I know you are, Charlie. By the way, I've decided to dub all these children as *special*. I detest the label *handicapped*. And all the other terms are just as bad, so when we put the word out about opening up the classes to them, we'll just refer to them as *special* children or—maybe for the sake of clarification—children with *special needs*."

"I love it!" Charlie exclaimed. "After all, that's what they are. It's the perfect description."

By the end of summer, six families were bringing their special children to visit the classes, including Carolyn and Emma. As word spread to other parents, the six grew to be eight, the eight to twelve, and the twelve to fifteen. And requests to visit continued to come. "I hate to turn any of these people away," Ann moaned, "but we just don't have space for any more people to visit. I've even asked the parents who were coming three days a week to cut back to two days, but it still isn't enough. Just pray with me, Charlie, for some solution to this."

"You know I'm already doing that, and Bill is too. I guess Grace has rubbed off on me. At first, I thought she was just imagining Joy's response to the music, but I've seen it also when you would have your vocal students rehearsing with the dancers. And I certainly can't argue with all those parents who insist the atmosphere of the studio has made a difference in their little ones. It seems no one knows exactly how to describe it, but they're convinced it's true. I'm just amazed at the number of parents requesting this service."

October was a busy month, so Ann decided to celebrate Joy's birthday at the school as a part of a regular teaching day. She set up a refreshment table near the entrance to the dance studio, and Aunt Lil and Uncle Ben served strawberry punch and chocolate cake to the guests. It was a come-and-go affair where friends, students, and the complete list of special children and their families cycled in and out. Daddy enjoyed greeting the guests and visiting with a few old friends. Grace kept an eye on Joy.

The dance classes and vocal students were practicing numbers for a fall musical that would be presented later that month, so the big dance area was abuzz with human depictions of leaves falling from trees and sent tumbling along the ground by gusts of wind. The parents of the special kids were captivated by the performance, and Ann watched carefully to see if she noticed any response from Joy. Suddenly, her heart did a flip-flop when she saw Joy's eyes briefly following the dancers before returning to their usual wandering movement. *Now I know what Grace has been talking about. Joy did see and respond to the dancing*, Ann thought. *I just can't let all those other children down. Lord, help me find a way to make this gift available to them!*

CHAPTER 49

The fall musical, *Freddy's Fall Frolic*, was based on a story Ann had written over a year ago. Charlie and Ann collaborated on the musical score, and Charlie worked out and directed the choreography. Joanna helped students with speaking parts, and Trent coached those who were doing the tap-dance routine. The students enthusiastically threw themselves into the show. They loved the vocal music and dances, and they were eager to show an audience what they could do.

They also loved the story about the young sapling named Freddy. Freddy is facing his first fall and winter, and he is afraid because of the things he has heard about trees losing their leaves. He is proud of his leaves and wants to keep them. Furthermore, he doesn't know he will grow new leaves, so he thinks they will be lost to him forever. It is only when fall comes and he sees leaves—his own mingled with those from many other trees—swirling through the air and skittering along the ground that he learns to delight in their beauty and playfulness. The lively animation, crisp dialogue, and stirring vocal selections combine to carry forward the theme of learning to see beauty and purpose in circumstances that may, at first, seem ugly and frightening.

A month ago, the students and their parents had pitched in to help with making costumes and building scenery, and the kids had worked tirelessly in learning the vocal and dance renditions. Now the spectacle had come together, and it was show time!

Due to the popularity of their earlier musical, it seemed the whole town turned out for this one. Again, the veranda was the stage, with action spilling over to ground level, and chairs were placed on the lawn for the audience. This time, the parents knew what to do. Without any prompting from Ann or Charlie, they literally took over setting up for the performance.

During the refreshment time following the show, Ann and Charlie mingled with the guests. They especially wanted the parents of the special kids to feel welcome and to meet some of the other parents. Ann was visiting with the parents of a special little girl named Ali when Bonner Valley's mayor came up and joined the conversation.

"Hello, Jim," Ann said, "I didn't realize you were here. Did you come to see any particular student?"

"No, I just came to check out all the good things I've been hearing about your school. You know, if you ran for mayor right now, I think you'd beat me," Jim jested.

"That's very flattering," Ann chuckled, "but I assure you, you have nothing to worry about." Then she made introductions. "Jim, I want you to meet Cynthia and Gary Reed," she said, gesturing toward the Reeds. "Cynthia and Gary, this is James McMasters, the mayor of Bonner Valley. The Reeds are new to our little city," she informed Jim.

"Well, I'm very happy to meet you," the mayor declared, a big smile lighting his tanned face. "What brings you to Bonner Valley?"

"I teach science at the high school," was the reply from the soft-spoken man who looked to be in his mid-thirties.

"I knew your name sounded familiar. I remember your being introduced at the start-of-school picnic. I speak for the whole town when I say we're glad to have you and your family as part of our community. We hope you'll enjoy living here."

"Thank you, Sir. We like Bonner Valley very much," Gary replied.

"Cynthia and Gary have an infant son and this special little girl named Ali," Ann said as she hunkered down beside the stroller. "Hi, Ali. I hope you enjoyed the dancing and singing today. It was especially for you and the other children." Ann stood and explained, "Ali is the same age as my Joy and they both seem to enjoy the atmosphere of the school. Therefore, Cynthia brings Ali here two days a week."

"I heard about your invitation for children to come visit your classes," Jim said. "Do you really feel it helps them to be around the music and dancing?"

"Yes, I do. I'm convinced it can be therapeutic. I say *can be*. I'm certainly no expert. I just know what I see in my daughter and in some of the other children who visit our classes."

"How many do you have coming to visit?"

"Fifteen children, and of course, they all have to have someone to bring them and stay with them."

"That many!" said Jim. "I never dreamed we had that many children living in this area who would need this sort of therapy."

"Well, they don't all live around here. Many of them live in communities scattered throughout the northern and eastern parts of Texas. Some drive quite a distance."

"Wow! It sounds like you and Charlie are providing a much-needed service to a lot of folks."

"They certainly are," Cynthia Reed interjected. "When we first moved here and I heard about this therapy, I'll admit I was a little bit skeptical. Now I know firsthand that it really works. I can see a difference in Ali when we come for visits. Ann, I hate to end our conversation so abruptly, but we have a sitter with our little Ethan, and we need to get back to him."

"By all means, you need to do that, but thanks so much for bringing Ali today. I'll see you and Ali on Tuesday, Cynthia. Gary, you could come along too."

Gary smiled and said, "I'd really like to do that sometime. We enjoyed the musical today. Bye, Miss Ann. Mayor McMasters, it was good to meet you."

"And it was nice to meet both of you," the mayor replied. "By the way, everybody calls me Jim. Let me say again how happy we are to have you in Bonner Valley."

After the Reeds walked away, Jim picked up where he had left off: "Well, I think Cynthia affirmed my statement. You and Charlie are helping a lot of folks."

"Not as many as we'd like, but fifteen is all we have room for.

This big old house is wonderful for our classes, but it just wasn't built to accommodate an audience. It's okay for recitals where students are doing solos or duets, and we can control how many students are involved, but it just doesn't work for a group performance such as this. Now that we are bringing visitors in to observe the classes, we desperately need more space. I suppose what we really need is a theater with a fairly large seating area. It would certainly beat this make-shift stage and chairs on the lawn," Ann laughed.

"Why couldn't you use the high school gym like everybody else in town does? It wouldn't work for your daily classes, but when you give programs like this, it would accommodate the audience, and you'd have the whole basketball court for your stage."

"Oh, no. I'm not going to do that. There are too many risks of damaging the floor with this type program. We could cover it with something, but that would be expensive and take a lot of work. Even if the school approved it, I wouldn't be willing to take that chance," Ann replied.

"I see your point," Jim admitted. "Well, there has to be a solution to the problem. We'll just have to put our heads together and work on it. After seeing today's musical, I see what everybody's been raving about. I think you and Charlie are bringing something out of these kids that even they didn't know they had in them. Keep up the good work. I'll see you later." With that, Jim made his way through the crowd and to his car.

CHAPTER 50

The last week of October, Bill Lambert had to make a business trip to New York City, and since he and Richard hadn't been in touch recently, he decided to call him and ask if they could have dinner together while he was there.

Before Bill left for New York, he told Ann he was anxious to see Richard because he was concerned about him. "After you left, I tried to visit with him several times, but our conversations seemed strained and uncomfortable. I think he was afraid I would bring up his behavior toward you and Joy. He was aloof and seemed changed. He had lost that appealing charisma and had become more stilted, more like his dad, I'm sad to say."

"Oh, I pray that isn't true," Ann lamented. "I had hoped Richard could find the strength to be his own person and not let Nelson dictate his life. The Richard I knew prior to Joy's birth was a man who cared about other people's feelings. That's why it seemed so out of character for him to hit me. Bill, I think he is extremely conflicted inside, and I, too, am concerned about him.

"I have no way of proving it, but I think Nelson is responsible for Richard's rejection of Joy. In fact, the more I've thought about it, the more convinced I have become that Nelson has planned Richard's life from the time he was born, even his marriage to me and the birth of our baby. He wanted an heir to the Buffington *empire*, and for some reason, he thought I measured up to his standards of a wife for Richard. When Joy failed to meet his expectations, however, and I wouldn't stick her in a home somewhere, he decided both of us had to go."

"I think you're probably right, Ann. Ever since our elementary school days, I've watched that man pull the rug out from under Richard's personal ambitions and force him into activities he hated. I thought it would be different after you two were married, though, because I knew Richard was deeply in love with you. He's going to be all right now that he has Ann, I decided—no more kowtowing to his dad's demands. I guess the hold his dad has on him is stronger than I had thought. When I get back from New York, I'll let you know how things went."

"I hope you bring back an encouraging report."

"I hope so too. Pray things go well between us. Like you said, I think Richard is very conflicted, so ask God to reach into his soul and pull out the Richard we knew when you and he first married. Maybe *that* Richard is struggling to make a comeback."

Bill paced the sidewalk as he waited outside the restaurant. "He should have been here fifteen minutes ago," Bill mumbled, "I hope he hasn't decided not to show up." After another five minutes of pacing, Bill caught sight of Richard briskly walking toward him.

All smiles, Richard grabbed Bill in a masculine embrace, slapped him on the back, and declared, "It's good to see you again, Billy Boy. How's life been treating you?"

Surprised by Richard's burst of enthusiasm, Bill returned his eager greeting, and the two friends walked into the restaurant, laughing and talking. It was as if there had never been a breach in their relationship, although Bill had felt a definite rebuffing by Richard back when Bill and Charlie had refused to help him convince Ann to place Joy in an institution.

After they were seated, Richard declared, "I'm so glad you called. I've had you on my mind recently and was planning to call you to see how things were going with your job and to see if you still like living in Texas."

"Well, I really like my job and I love Texas. Everything moves at a slower pace in Texas, and that suits me just fine. Charlie really enjoys living there. Of course, she loves living close to Ann. The two of them are in business together."

Richard seemed astonished. "Really? What kind of business?"

"They own and operate a school of theater arts. It has really caught on, and they're doing very well with it."

"That . . . that's great," Richard stammered. His smile faded and he appeared to be drawn away into a preoccupation with something distant and mysterious.

Just then, the waiter came to take their order. Richard snapped out of his trance, laughed and said, "We've been busy visiting and haven't looked at the menu. I think I'm ready to order, though. Do you need a little more time, Bill?"

"No, I'm ready."

Throughout dinner, they discussed their work, reminisced about happy times, and laughed at silly things that had happened when they were growing up—a class field trip that went awry, Halloween pranks they had pulled, Boy Scout hikes and campouts. Bill carefully avoided the Central Park incident, as well as Richard's conduct with Ann that caused her to take Joy and flee to her daddy's house in Bonner Valley.

"I think you'll be interested to know that both Ann and Joy are doing well. Ann has found something to replace musical theater. She loves teaching, and she and Charlie are making a real impact on life in Bonner Valley. Ann went through a rough time, but she seems happy now. Apart from some minor setbacks, Joy is growing and thriving."

Richard's obsession with something far away returned. He paused and then finally responded, "What? Oh, yes, I am happy for them, but I don't see how Ann can work and take care of Joy at the same time."

"That's another great thing that has happened. Ann has reconnected with her mother's best friend, an RN experienced in the care of children with special needs. Grace Garrison has been an answer to prayer for Ann. She takes care of Joy while Ann is working. She is like one of the family."

"I see. Well, I guess that's good," Richard stated flatly. "However, I got the impression—in fact, Ann told me—she wanted to take care of Joy *herself*. She said she wanted to *bond* with Joy—an impossibility, of course—and that she didn't trust anyone else to give Joy the personal attention she needs. I knew that couldn't last. I knew she would get tired of the constant care she would have to give Joy. I tried to tell her that, but she wouldn't listen. Well, I guess this proves I was right all along in thinking Joy should be placed in a home. It just isn't natural for a person never to grow beyond infancy, and no parent can stand up to that kind of pressure on a prolonged basis."

"Richard, I think you misunderstand the situation. Joy is still Ann's first priority, and Ann is still Joy's primary caregiver. Ann's arrival time at the school is 10:15 a.m., and she's home every evening by 5:30. She feeds, bathes, and tends Joy's other needs every morning before she goes to work, and she often goes home on her lunch break to see Joy. Except for those hours when Ann is at the school, she is almost always with Joy, and even then, Grace often brings Joy to the school for visits. If you're thinking Ann started teaching to avoid the responsibility of taking care of Joy, you're wrong. Her teaching fulfills a need in her and also benefits the community of Bonner Valley. I think you're looking at it all wrong."

Richard didn't reply to Bill's comments. Instead, he changed the subject. "Did you get your asking price for your dad's house in Manhattan?"

"Yes, I came out all right on it. Houses are much less expensive in Texas than in Manhattan, so the income from Dad's house almost completely paid for the house and five acres we bought in Texas. The house is way too big for us, but Charlie and Ann use the downstairs for their school, and we live in the upstairs."

"It sounds like you put up all the money, and Ann's just riding on your coattail in this school thing. Doesn't she have any financial responsibility in the partnership between her and Charlie?"

"Of course, she does. We offered to test the thing out before she paid anything, but she wouldn't do it that way. She pays Charlie a percentage of her income. It's a good arrangement for both of them."

The two men continued to visit for another hour or so before Richard stood and announced he had to prepare for a 6:00 a.m. meeting and needed to be on his way. "I've really enjoyed our visit, Bill, and if you get to New York again, give me a call and we'll get together. Give Charlie my regards." He picked up the check from the table, "This is my treat."

Bill stood, and as the two men shook hands, Bill said, "I invited you, so I'll pay the bill."

"No, I really want to do this," Richard insisted.

"It isn't supposed to work that way, but thanks. I'll look forward to next time when it will be my turn to buy. It's good to see you again, Richard. I'll give Charlie your regards, *and* I'll tell Ann you are happy she and Joy are doing well."

Without acknowledging Bill's comments, Richard smiled and muttered, "Have a good trip home." Then he walked away from the table and exited the building.

CHAPTER 51

The next morning, Bill flew back to Dallas, and the following evening, Ann invited Charlie and Bill to dinner. "I don't know what to tell you," Bill reported. "He was cordial and seemed happy. He was like his old self in many ways, but there was something different about him. I guess the best way to describe it is he seemed defensive, like he was afraid I would bring up forbidden subject matter. When I mentioned you and Joy, I got the impression he wanted to hear what I had to say but was reluctant to show too much interest. He seemed glad you and Joy were doing well, but then he became edgy when I mentioned the theater arts school. He reacted negatively to your working. I didn't understand why that would matter to him."

"He's evidently still harboring hard feelings toward me," Ann stated. "Otherwise, he would have shown some regret for what happened between us. I'd think he would have confided in you if his attitude had changed. Did he show any interest at all in Joy?"

"No, not really, except to say he was glad you and Joy were all right. I'm not sure he would have mentioned you or Joy at all if I hadn't volunteered information about you. I don't want to hurt you, Ann, but I know you want me to be honest."

"Yes, Bill, I do, and you don't have to worry about that. I'm beyond being hurt by Richard. As long as he is allowing Nelson to call the shots in his life, nothing I do will seem right to him. I guess I just keep hoping he will go back to being to the wonderful guy I married. Thanks for bringing me up to date on things."

"Well, I look at it this way," Charlie interjected. "He's the one losing out by turning his back on you and Joy."

"Thanks, Charlie. I think so too."

———— ☼ ————

One Monday morning about two weeks later, Ann had just finished her routine with Joy and had placed her in Grace's care. She was ready to leave for school when the phone rang.

"Good morning, Ann. This is Jim McMasters. I hope I'm not calling at a bad time."

"No, it's fine. I'll be leaving for school in about five minutes, but I have a little while."

"This won't take long. My reason for calling you is to see if you and Charlie could come to my office for a visit sometime soon. There's nothing urgent about it. I just want to talk to you about something. I know you have lessons and classes almost all day on week days, so if it would work better to meet on a Saturday, I can do that."

"You've aroused my curiosity, Jim. Can you tell me what this is all about?" Ann inquired.

"I'd really rather speak with you *and* Charlie together, so let's set up a time to meet."

"Okay, I'll see what will work for Charlie, and I'll talk to Grace about staying with Joy."

"Good. When you work something out with them, give me a call."

"I'll do that," Ann said. "I'll try to call you tomorrow."

"Sounds good. Thanks, Ann."

When Ann told Charlie about Jim's call, they decided they wanted to see him as soon as possible to find out about the mysterious *something* he wanted to discuss with them. After affirming that Grace could come early on Wednesday morning, Ann called Jim and asked if 8:00 a.m. would be all right.

"That will be a good time," Jim replied. "I'll arrive early and be watching for you in case you get here before Tommy unlocks the outside doors."

As they were approaching the building, Jim swung the door open and held it for them to enter. "Good morning, ladies, you're right on time. My office is the second door on your right. Just go on in. We have a break room across the hall. Could I get you some coffee or tea?"

They both declined his offer. "Please sit down," he said, gesturing to two upholstered chairs. He sat down and smiled at them across his desk—clean except for a telephone, a desk calendar, and a pen and pencil holder that doubled as a nameplate.

"I know you ladies are wondering why I want to visit with you, but before I get into that, I want to tell you how impressed I am with the work you are doing with those kids in your classes. I've been visiting with a lot of people in town, and I don't think you realize how much your school means to this community. You've sort of breathed new life into an old town that has always put sports first. Not that there's anything wrong with sports, mind you, it's just that you've awakened us to the fact that the young people of this town have a lot more talent than any of us realized. They just needed somebody to pull it out of them, and you ladies are doing that. The main thing, though, is that you're giving them confidence in themselves; you're helping them learn they're good at something they didn't even know they could do.

"Another thing I'm impressed with is what you're doing with those children you refer to as *special*. I've never heard of anything like it, even in big cities. I think you're breaking new ground in offering something like that. Even if it isn't a recognized therapy, the parents who are bringing their children to your school are certainly excited about it. That's a part of what I want to discuss with you.

"I've had a lot of people talking to me about building a theater, and that's all because of your school. They recognize you need a place to present recitals and musicals, but all of us also want you to have enough room to accommodate the needs of all those families asking to visit your classes.

"Some people have asked me about bringing it to a vote of the city. Others have suggested that we try to get enough private donations to build it. I'm on the side of the private donations, for this reason: If the money comes from city coffers, the theater will have to be a public venue, and that would mean you two ladies couldn't use of it for your private school. However, if it is built with private funds, a lease agreement could be worked out that would give you exclusive use of the facility."

Charlie and Ann exchanged glances. "Are you serious?" Charlie asked. "Do you mean it's possible that we might have access to a *real* theater for shows *and* for the school? I can think of nothing that would make me happier!"

"But do you really think people will donate enough money to build a theater?" Ann asked. "It will cost a bundle to do it right. A theater is unlike a lot of other structures."

"Ann, you know that most folks in Bonner Valley are just ordinary people of ordinary means, but there are a few who have managed to strike it rich with oil or gas or cattle. The man who's really pushing this thing is Doyle Davenport. Doyle raises cattle, but he's also a successful home builder. He knows about the cost of building, and he knows how to cut costs without cutting quality. He's already been looking into the cost of a building that will seat two hundred. He could probably pay for the whole thing all by himself, but he has talked to two other men in town who share his enthusiasm and his means for getting things done. I met with the three of them, and they agree that we should pay for the theater with donations, but listen to this—They aren't making it public knowledge, but they want to cover whatever amount is still needed after all the donations have come in. To answer your question, Ann, yes, the people will donate enough money to build a theater!"

"I can't believe this is happening," Ann cried, "and I still don't understand something. Just because the theater is being built doesn't mean it will be ours to use as if we owned it. Some of those donors may have other ideas about the use of it."

"That won't happen, Ann, because the people behind the

building of this theater will make it clear to everybody that their donations will be used for your school," Jim said, "but I think I'm safe in saying that most of the people who donate will be doing so because they're behind you in what you're doing. You ladies have made all of us come to appreciate the professionalism you have brought to live theater right here in our little city, and you have opened our eyes to the needs of those special kids and their families. The town wants to show gratitude for that."

"What a beautiful thing for you to say, Jim," Charlie smiled. "Thank you."

Ann was silent for a few minutes. Then she whispered, "Jim, what Charlie said sums up how I feel too. I had no idea . . . I . . . I'm very humbled by this."

"As I said earlier," Jim reiterated, "we will have to work out an agreement, but I know the lease amount will be held to a minimum. Everybody wants to make sure you ladies stay around here and keep doing what you're doing."

CHAPTER 52

O n the last Tuesday in November, Bill Lambert had an early morning visitor who came to tell him some downed electrical lines had created a power outage for part of Bonner Valley, including Bill and Charlie's house and, of course, the Stage One School of Theater Arts. The outage would take several hours to repair, and it had interrupted both electrical and telephone service.

Since Charlie had no phone service, she drove to Ann's house to inform her of the situation. With Thanksgiving only two days away, they decided to close the school until after the weekend. They put their emergency plan into action with their pre-established telephone chain and attempted to contact all the students, at least those who weren't affected by the power outage. Charlie went back home to intercept anyone who might show up at the school. Ann called Grace and told her the situation. Then she settled in for a stay-at-home day with Joy.

Ann had just finished feeding Joy her lunch when the phone rang. When she answered, a familiar voice greeted her.

"Hello, Ann. This is Richard. How are you?"

He sounded aloof and businesslike, so she knew right away this wasn't a friendly call. She answered, "I'm fine, thank you. How are you?"

"I'm okay—a little bit puzzled right now—but otherwise, okay."

"Oh, and what are you puzzled about?"

"I'm wondering why you find it necessary to work instead of staying home and taking care of Joy. Can you explain that?"

Ann was stunned. How could he possibly question how she took care of her daughter? With the exception of the child-support check he sent every month, Richard had totally ignored Joy. If he'd had his way, Joy would have been placed in an institution long ago. The trust set up by Sarah had met Joy's needs, but that wasn't Richard's doing. Suddenly a fiery dart of anger shot through her, but she remained calm and unemotional in her response.

"It's good to know you are concerned about Joy. I wish you could see her, Richard. She will never be able to do what many other children are capable of doing, but she makes her own special contribution. She is an inspiration to many people here in Bonner Valley."

Richard was mute. She knew he had expected her to lash out at him for meddling in her affairs, and to be honest, that was exactly what she felt like doing. She was proud of the way she had held her tongue and hadn't let him dupe her into becoming argumentative. It was her hope that her benign response would help avoid a confrontation. As his silent umbrage dragged on, however, her self-satisfaction was gradually burned away until her pride lay in a heap of ashes at her feet.

"You didn't answer my question. Why do you feel it necessary to work? You've done an about-face in what you told me earlier: You said you wanted to take care of Joy yourself—that you wouldn't trust anyone else to take care of her. What happened to your feelings about that?"

"I haven't changed. You misunderstood me then, Richard, and you misunderstand me now—or maybe I should say you *misinterpret* my attitude. For several reasons, I don't feel comfortable placing Joy in a home for special-needs children. For one thing, such institutions assume that children with Joy's degree of disfunction are completely insensitive to their surroundings, and I have serious doubts about that. Another reason I don't want her living in an institution is that I can't see how the caregivers could possibly meet her emotional needs. I don't doubt that most of them are dedicated, capable professionals, but I don't think their work load would permit them to give adequate personal attention to each child.

"Taking care of Joy is the most gratifying thing in my life, but a while back I began to feel that sharing my knowledge of the world of musical theater would meet a need in our community as well as in my own life. At first, I thought about teaching voice lessons here at the house, but doing that would divide my attention between my students and Joy. I knew I couldn't feel comfortable with that unless I could find someone I trusted completely to help me with Joy. Grace Garrison was the answer to my prayers. I've known Grace my whole life. She's experienced in taking care of children with special needs, and she loves Joy almost as much as I do. I don't understand why you have a problem with this, Richard."

"Oh, I don't object to what you're doing. I just don't think you can justifiably spend money from Joy's trust to pay someone to take care of her. That sounds to me like you're spending Joy's money to make life easier for yourself."

Ann tilted her head back, looked up at the light fixture dangling above the dinette table, and burst into laughter, "Oh, Richard, is *that* what this is all about? Money?"

"Do you find that amusing?"

"Not in the sense you mean," Ann retorted. "Maybe satirical would describe it better." "You're not concerned about Joy; you're concerned about how I'm spending the money in her trust. Because of your resentful, pugnacious attitude toward me, you are willing to compromise what is best for her."

Richard's caustic laughter blasted through the receiver. "Now it's my turn to be amused. Do you really expect me to believe that you feel having this . . . this Grace person take care of Joy is better for her than taking care of her yourself?"

"That's exactly how I feel," Ann shot back. "Receiving care from both Grace *and* me gives Joy the best of two worlds. I have my special times with her every day: I feed her, bathe her, massage her, talk to her, tell her how much I love her, sing to her—all things you consider foolish and futile. But Grace has an uncanny gift for seeing Joy's needs in ways that have eluded me. Grace might be compared to a personal trainer for an athlete. She brings out the best in Joy, and she has vastly improved her quality of life. I invite you to come here, Richard, and observe how Grace works with her. I think you would be impressed."

After a long pause, Richard lashed out, "You're good at rationalizing things to suit yourself, aren't you, Ann? According to whose evaluation has Grace improved Joy's quality of life? Yours? I checked the trust account this morning. To date, you have spent $11,907.77. That seems exorbitant to me. I want an accounting for everything you've paid out of the account. I've been busy and haven't given as much attention as I should have to keeping up with the trust. I didn't realize you were using it for unnecessary services."

A dizzy, sick feeling gripped Ann as she listened to Richard attack her integrity. "I'll be happy to supply you with payment documentation. I've kept careful records. Aside from what I've paid Grace, all other payments were made to medical institutions and providers. I can assure you, though, that both of the physicians who see Joy on a regular basis will attest to the contribution Grace has made to Joy's life."

"Oh, I'm sure you'll be able to persuade them to verify what you've told me. It's easy to get medical professionals to see it your way when it benefits them."

"Are you suggesting what it sounds like you're suggesting—that I would *bribe* Joy's doctors to endorse Grace's contribution to Joy's wellbeing? You know I would never do such a thing! Furthermore, both Dr. Cooper and Dr. Matheson are men of high ethical standards who would be offended at even the suggestion of such a thing.

"What has happened to you, Richard? You're turning into someone I no longer know. I think you're treading on dangerous ground by making such ridiculous accusations, and I refuse to have this discussion with you."

Richard laughed and snapped back, "Oh, I'm not the one on dangerous ground, Ann. If I were you, I'd walk carefully. I'll be in touch."

She heard the click of the receiver. The battle had ended, and

Richard had struck the last blow. He had left her wounded and bleeding, but the war wasn't over!

When Daddy came home that evening, one look at Ann told him she had been crying. "What's the matter, honey? Is Joy all right?"

"Joy's just fine, Daddy. I wish I could say the same about myself. Richard called today and made vague threats about the money I've spent from Joy's trust. You probably remember that Sarah died before she could sign the codicil establishing the trust. When Hollis Wilhite, the family attorney, told the family about Sarah's desire to create the trust, Nelson and Olivia were both in favor of honoring Sarah's wishes. Now . . . oh . . . I don't know . . . I . . . I'm just afraid of what Nelson and Richard might try to do. Richard is on a vindictive rampage, and I've had a bad feeling ever since he called today."

Paul Jernigan walked over to his daughter and put his arms around her. "Ann, I'm sorry you've had to go through this, but don't let Richard's bullying get you down. That's exactly what it is. He's acting like a schoolyard bully. Let's just wait and see what happens. Then if he gets tough, we'll get tough right back. And anyway, you have something more valuable than the Buffington money. You have your integrity and a whole town full of friends who will vouch for the fine mother, teacher, and Christian woman you are."

"I appreciate your vote of confidence, Daddy. Ever since Richard called, I've been feeling like a spineless weakling. I needed your pep talk.

"I have dinner ready, and I'll go ahead and feed Joy while you're getting washed up."

Ann pulled Joy close to her chair and locked the wheels of her stroller. As she placed a bib around her, she smiled at her and said, "I love you, sweetheart, and I'll always take care of you. Nobody is ever going to hurt you."

CHAPTER 53

*F*ollowing his November meeting with Ann and Charlie, Mayor McMasters had called a January town hall meeting. *The Bonner Valley Sentinel* announced the time, place, and topic to be discussed, and Doyle Davenport had fliers made and placed them around town.

The high school gymnasium was packed, and conversations hummed from one end of the bleachers to the other. When Jim walked to the microphone, a hush fell over the crowd. Mayor McMasters gave those gathered for this occasion basically the same information he had given Ann and Charlie, minus the part about the generosity of Doyle Davenport and friends.

"I suppose the first thing we should do," Jim stated, "is find out how all of you feel about building a theater, so raise your hand if you would like to speak to that question."

Sherman Horton was the first to speak: "I think we've got to build a theater, Jim, if we're gonna hold onto that school. I think we're mighty lucky to have Ann Marie Jernigan . . . I mean Buffington and that other young woman come to a little town like this and start up a school like that. From what I hear, they charge a lot less than they could if they was in a big city. Millie . . . you know . . . my twelve-year-old granddaughter . . . well, she's like a different person since she's been taking voice lessons. She used to be so shy she blushed every time anybody spoke to her, but now we can't shut her up." Laughter rippled through the crowd and Sherman decided he'd said enough.

Evelyn Oaks' hand shot up. When Jim acknowledged her, she voiced her agreement with Sherman and made some additional observations: "I like what you said about building it with private donations. One thing I don't understand, though, is who will hold the deed to it. Will the city still own it? And, if so, won't it still be off limits for these ladies to use as a school?"

"Those are very good questions, Evelyn, but I don't know how to answer them. Phil Jenkins, our city attorney is here; maybe he can give us an answer."

Phil almost leapt to the microphone, his body language telling everybody he had looked forward to this moment. "Evelyn, I'll get to your questions, but let me lay some ground work first. I could discuss building permits and legal stipulations for buildings of this type, but those issues are premature at this stage. Therefore, let me simplify things by explaining what I think would be the most logical and effective way to handle this particular situation.

"I suggest the theater be paid for with private donations rather than city funds, but some steps should be taken before we begin taking donations:

(1) A non-profit corporation recognized by the Internal Revenue Code should be formed.
(2) Articles and by-laws stating the purposes and rules of the corporation should be drawn up by an attorney-at-law.
(3) Officers for this corporation should be selected in compliance with the articles and by-laws.

"The duties of these officers would be to oversee the building and management of the theater or to employ others to do so. As donations are taken, a designated officer should keep detailed records of the tax-deductible donations.

"This corporation would not have to answer to the city concerning the use of the building; therefore, it would have the power to grant exclusive use to the Stage One School of Theater Arts. Ann Buffington and Charlotte Lambert have already agreed to this plan. They would lease the building, and the income derived from the lease, as well as any future donations, would be held in escrow for maintenance, insurance, and other expenses. There are some other details that would have to be worked out, but basically, that's it. In my opinion, it would be a sensible and safe way to handle it. Did I answer your questions, Evelyn?"

"Yes, you did. Thank you, Phil."

When the town hall meeting ended, it was clear that virtually everybody in town was in favor of building a theater and funding it through the non-profit corporation suggested by Phil. Phil explained that his contribution to the project would be to draft the necessary documents and obtain the required approval for the suggested entity. Phil explained, "Upon approval by the proper authorities, the corporation would operate for the purposes discussed. It would simply follow city building codes, pay the required fees, and file timely reports."

The town looked to the mayor to get the ball rolling, so Jim authorized Phil to move forward with the corporation by appointing the requisite officers and submitting the substantial set of records for approval. The mayor then recused himself of any further involvement. "I don't think I'd get any flak for it," he told Phil, "but I just don't want people to think I'm using professional clout to push my personal interests; I do have some strong opinions about this."

"I know," Phil replied, "So do I, but the officers will soon take over, and I will simply be the paper-pusher. I'm headed back to the office right now to get started. Maybe I can expedite approval so we can move forward with this project."

The officers Phil appointed set a tentative timeframe for citizens to donate to The Theater Company, Inc., the legal name they had given the non-profit corporation. They made it clear they would, of course, continue to accept donations beyond this timeframe, but they were hoping to get enough money together to break ground by spring and have the building enclosed before winter.

The next day after the newspaper came out informing the town that donations were being accepted, Henrietta Jacobs showed up at Doyle Davenport's office. The frail woman moved gingerly to take a seat in the chair Doyle had positioned for her. Henrietta's late husband, Andrew, had retired years ago after serving as a much-loved principal of Bonner Valley High School for over twenty years. Early in their marriage, Henrietta had given birth to a special son, their only child, and had given him constant care for the thirteen years of his life. She looked up at Doyle and, through her tears, said to him, "I've walked the road Ann Buffington is walking, and I want her to have a place to help those children. I don't have any money, but I have this land if you can use it."

"Are you talking about that five acres you own up by the high school?"

"Certainly. That's all I have except for my house I live in."

Word got out that Doyle lifted her from her chair, almost squeezed the breath out of her tiny frame, and kissed her right on the mouth. Then he shouted, "Not only can we use it, Henrietta, but your land is the perfect location."

Davenport, president of The Theater Company, along with the other officers: Felicia Prescott, Thurston Holmes, Chester Wilbanks, and Leonard Case chose architect Calvin Newton to design the structure. Ann and Charlie co-chaired a committee to work in an advisory role with Newton, and within six weeks, the plans were displayed and discussed at another town hall meeting.

In mid-January, Ann received another call from Richard. From his frosty first words, she knew she was in for another vicious skirmish. "I want you to know, Ann, that I have talked with Hollis Wilhite about terminating Joy's trust. Since you haven't honored the stipulations of the trust, you should no longer have access to it.

"That's interesting. In what way have I not honored the stipulations of the trust?"

"You shouldn't have to ask that after our discussion last month. You are using the trust to pay for baby-sitting services. I don't think that falls under the category of medical expense."

"Grace isn't a *baby-sitter*, but we have had this discussion,

Richard, and nothing will be gained by discussing it further. You will never understand the importance of Grace's contribution to Joy's life, so there's no need for us to go into all that again."

"I didn't call to argue with you, Ann. I just called to say you might want to rethink using money from the trust to pay someone to take care of Joy while you pursue a career."

"You know, Richard, I have a copy of a notarized document I signed in which you relinquished trusteeship of Joy's trust account. You placed that responsibility solely in my hands to be handled at my discretion. The only condition you placed on my spending was that expenditures must be made to third parties and not to me personally. I have not violated that requirement."

"I didn't accuse you of paying money to yourself; you're too smart for that, but you are using money from the trust to pay for something that benefits you rather than Joy—something that relieves you of the burden of taking care of her. I think a judge would see it that way."

Ann's anger flared, "How dare you refer to the care I give Joy in that manner! I'm sure taking care of Joy would be a burden to you, Richard, but it is no burden to me. She is the light of my life! And what does Hollis Wilhite say about all this?"

"He's looking into it."

"You mentioned terminating the trust. Since Olivia and Nelson were the ones who had to sign the document accepting the codicil Sarah had requested, I would think they would be the only ones who could request a reversal of that decision."

"Actually, Dad was the one who asked Hollis to check on it, and I'm sure Aunt Olivia will go along with whatever Dad thinks best. She doesn't do very well at making decisions on her own."

Ann wasn't surprised that all this upheaval over Joy's trust had started with Nelson, and she was sure Nelson had delegated Richard to deliver the verbal attack on her character. Ann remembered what Sarah had told her about the tension that existed between Nelson and Olivia, and she doubted that Olivia would "go along" with terminating the trust.

"Okay, Richard, you've delivered your message. I've been duly warned that Joy's trust may disappear. You and your dad can pull all the strings you want to make that happen, but you are violating Sarah's wishes in doing so. If Sarah were alive today, she would love her great-granddaughter, and she would defend her right to have a specially trained nurse working with her. She would never condone your selfish denial of what is best for Joy or your scornful attitude toward me. You can try to convince yourself otherwise, but you and I both know what I'm saying is true."

Ann sensed that Richard was pleased with himself for having put her on the defensive. She could envision his giving Nelson a blow-by-blow account of how he had pinned her to the wall with his verbal agility—how he had made her squirm under the threat of losing the assets derived from the Joy Marie Buffington Trust. Richard, like Nelson, now seemed to measure every aspect of life in terms of monetary value, and she was saddened at the person he had become. *How could he have changed this much?*

Richard stammered something about needing to get off the phone because he had a meeting to attend. Then he said a hasty good-bye. He had done his duty. Nelson would be proud of him.

CHAPTER 54

*T*he drafting of the plans for the theater building were moving forward smoothly, and Ann and Charlie were becoming more excited each time they met with architect Calvin Newton. A dream was coming true before their eyes, at least on paper.

At the theater arts school, the students were working on something new and different from anything they had done before. April 7 would mark the thirty-fifth anniversary of a deadly tornado that had virtually swept the town of Bonner Valley off the map. The composition Ann and Charlie had written dealt with community spirit and neighbor helping neighbor. They thought it would be an uplifting reminder to the people of Bonner Valley of how their plucky ancestors had faced and overcome the aftermath of a tragedy. The presentation was planned for the last Saturday in April, with the hope of warm weather and no storms.

In February, Richard called again. "I thought I should bring you up to date on some things," he said. "Dad and Aunt Olivia have asked Hollis Wilhite to petition the court to have the trust terminated on grounds that the codicil had not been signed by Grandmother. We feel relatively sure of being successful in this action, so maybe you should start thinking about how you will handle things financially. We can probably work something out so repayment of the money you have spent from the trust won't be too difficult for you. After all, you have a lucrative profession now, and I'm still paying child support." His voice carried a confident, almost gleeful tone. He seemed to find great satisfaction in the power wielded by his words.

"You're very sure of yourself, aren't you, Richard? It is hard for me to believe that any conscientious judge, after hearing all the facts—not just your version of the facts—would rule to take away funding for the care of child with special needs. Even more unbelievable is your willingness to violate your grandmother's desire to provide for your child. But then, over the past few years, I've come to realize I don't know you at all anymore. I don't know what happened to that compassionate, lovable man I married.

"Well, I guess it's time for me to retain a lawyer. I'll do everything I can to protect Joy's rights, Richard, so get ready for a fight. I will always take care of Joy's needs, even if the trust Sarah intended for her is taken away, but I will not permit you to completely disassociate yourself from her as if you had no responsibility for her care. I can't force you to love her, but I will do everything in my power to force you to acknowledge her!"

Without giving Richard a chance to say anything else, Ann concluded, "Please tell Hollis Wilhite he will be hearing from my attorney." She put the phone back on the base, sighed deeply, and prayed a silent prayer: *Lord, please help me through this. You know I'm ignorant about legal matters, but I want to do the right thing for Joy. I ask you to give me guidance, wisdom, and a gracious spirit.*

It was a Sunday afternoon, and her daddy had heard her side of the conversation. "Well, I don't know what Richard said to you, but it sounded to me like you held your own." When Ann told Daddy the *news* Richard had broken to her, he walked over to her and put his arms around her, "I'm proud of you, sweetheart. You handled that very well, and you are doing what you have to do. You'll need a New York attorney. Do you know one?"

"No, but I know someone who does—Bill. I'm going to call him right now."

"Hi, Charlie. Well, the other shoe finally dropped, and I need a lawyer. I know Bill used an estate lawyer when he was settling up things after his dad passed away. Is he someone Bill would recommend? Good. Let me talk to him.

"Hello, Bill. I need a New York attorney. How did you feel about the estate lawyer you used?"

"Ann, he is wonderful. His name is Matthew Worth. He's young but very sharp and extremely articulate. I think you'd like him. I have his telephone number right here if you want it?"

"Yes, that would be great. I want to get on this as soon as possible. I'll try to reach him tomorrow." Ann went on to tell Bill about Richard's phone calls and the attitude he had reflected. "I detest getting into this sort of thing, and I dread the thought of appearing before a judge and having to lay my soul open to a total stranger, but I feel it's something I have to do. With my part in the cash settlement from the divorce, plus Richard's child support check and my earnings, I think I could make it. I just resent having Richard treat Joy with such disregard, and I'll do everything I can to keep him from robbing her of something that is rightfully hers."

"You hang in there, Ann, and if you need any character witnesses, you know you have plenty of those. Although Richard is a friend, he is wrong in this, and I'll speak up for you if I'm called on to do that."

"Thank you, Bill. I hope it doesn't come to that. I know having to choose sides is difficult for you."

"It's hard for me to see Richard behaving in this way, but making a choice isn't hard. I have to go with what my heart tells me is right. You know you can call on Charlie and me for anything, and if it's possible, we'll do it."

"Thanks again, and I'll let you know how my conversation goes with Mr. Worth."

"I'll look forward to hearing what you have to say. Bye, Ann."

On Monday, Grace came took over the early morning routine with Joy so Ann would have time to make the call to Matthew Worth before she had to leave for school. At 8:00 a.m. (9:00 a.m. in New York) she called the office of Matthew Worth. She thought she might have to wait for him to return her call, but his receptionist put her through.

"This is Matthew Worth."

"Mr. Worth, my name is Ann Buffington. I need a good lawyer, and you were recommended to me by Bill Lambert. Do you have time to listen to an explanation of my situation?"

"I remember Bill—a nice guy. I have an hour before my first appointment. Give me a brief, general description of what you need; then I can tell you if I can help you."

She did as he suggested, telling him about Joy's deficiencies and about the codicil establishing the trust for Joy's benefit. She explained that Sarah had died before she could sign the codicil but that the beneficiaries named in her will had agreed to its terms. Then she told him that the Buffington family attorney was representing them in an action being brought against her to terminate the trust.

"Let me ask a couple of questions, Mrs. Buffington: How long ago was the will executed, and was the codicil executed at that same time?"

"The will was executed in September of 1959," Ann replied, "and yes, the codicil was presented and a document was signed by the beneficiaries, Nelson Buffington and Olivia Lovelace, on that same day. Olivia has since remarried, and her name is now Perchinski."

"If it was executed that long ago . . . well, we can discuss that later."

As they continued to converse, Matthew Worth asked more questions, probing her relationship with Richard and with the Buffington family. She felt a sympathetic response from him—more than that—she sensed a compassionate understanding.

"Mrs. Buffington, do you mind if I call you Ann? I like using first names. Please call me Matthew."

"I like using first names too."

"Ann, I am very touched by your story. I have a twin sister, and what you have told me today could have been her speaking about her own experiences. She too has a child who is much like your daughter Joy, and she was also in an abusive relationship. I will happily take your case, and I will fight for your rights and the rights of your daughter. I'll contact Hollis Wilhite and let him know I'm representing you; then I'll get started building our case. I will have further questions as I begin work on this, so please give me your phone number."

Ann gave him her number and then asked, "Matthew, do you have any idea how soon I can put this horrible experience behind me?"

"Well, that depends on several factors," Matthew stated. "This will be a bench trial and, therefore, not as lengthy as a jury trial, but it may require investigation and preparation equal to that of a jury trial. Building a case will include researching applicable state statutes and legal precedents. Discovery—the process by which attorneys for each side obtain information from each other—can take two months or more. Getting a court date can also take a while, but the trial itself should take no more than two or three days. As you can see, all this takes time, but I'll keep you informed about the progress."

Ann hesitated before speaking, "I guess I didn't realize how complex this would be. I'm sure it will require hours of work on your part, and I can only imagine the cost of such litigation. I apologize for my ignorance in this type thing, but could we work out a type of payment plan?

"Ann, I am in a position to take on certain pro bono causes. I hope you will give me the satisfaction of defending you in an issue that is close to my heart. In the end, if Richard is ordered to pay my fees, that will be fine; I will accept payment. If not, I choose to move ahead without my usual retainer or hourly fee."

Ann was astonished. "I don't know what to say or how to thank you. Ordinarily, I wouldn't accept such a generous, self-sacrificing gesture, but the stakes are too high for me to let my pride interfere. Thank you so much, Matthew."

Matthew chuckled, "I'm doing it as much for myself as for you. From what you've told me so far, this is a case I think we can win, and I relish the thought!"

When Ann returned the phone to its base, she smiled and silently prayed, *"Lord, thank you for leading me to this caring man. Please bless him and guide him in his work."*

Ann was excited as she told Bill and Charlie about her telephone visit with Matthew Worth. "I'm not going to let myself become too optimistic, but he did give me a good feeling about my legal footing."

"I felt certain you would like him," Bill said, "but I didn't know about his sister; I had no idea you two would have that kind of identity. I know he will work hard for you, Ann. For one thing, he's just that kind of guy, and from what you've said, I get the feeling he has a special interest in your case."

CHAPTER 55

atthew Worth called Ann several times over the weeks following their first conversation, each time gathering more information for their case. He requested she send him copies of receipts and cancelled checks for all expenditures from the trust, and he wanted copies of Joy's medical records.

He also asked for documents and diplomas verifying Grace's educational background and nursing experience, especially her experience in working with children with congenital disorders. "Tell Grace," Matthew said, "to contact the parents of some of her former patients and ask them to write letters of commendation for her work with their children. It would be extremely helpful if at least one parent could travel to New York to testify.

"Both you and Grace need to be prepared to testify, and I've also contacted Dr. Anderson, your physician in Manhattan, to apprise him of the situation. He knows he will be called to the stand."

"From some of the things Grace has told me about the relationships she has built with some of the families in California," Ann commented, "I think they will be willing to write the letters, and she may feel she can ask one or two of them about traveling to New York. I'll speak to her about it and see what she thinks."

Grace contacted the families of all four of the children with whom she had worked. She explained Ann's situation to them and asked them to write letters commending her work with their children. She mailed each family a stamped envelope addressed to Matthew Worth. Later, she received a call from Greg and Laura Potter, parents of one of her "little darlings," as she called them. "Grace," Greg said,

"I want you to know I'll be happy to fly to New York to testify, if you need me to do that."

"Greg, you must have ESP. We *will* need you to testify. I will give your name, address, and phone number to Ann's attorney. We don't even know the court date or any details, so it will be better for him to contact you about it. I don't know if he will mail you an airline ticket or just how that will be handled, but I'm sure he will give you all that information when he contacts you."

"No, Grace, I will bear this expense. I really want to do it this way. I can never repay you for all you did for us, but I want to do this for you and Mrs. Buffington."

"Greg, won't that be a financial burden on you? You don't owe me anything."

"I can afford it, Grace, and I want no argument about it. Just tell the attorney to let me know when I should be there. I'm my own boss and have no constraints on my time."

Ten weeks after Ann's initial call to Worth's office, he called her to let her know he had evaluated all the material she had provided, including the letters from Grace's prior employers. "The discovery process is progressing as I had expected," Matthew assured her. "Greg Potter's testimony will be extremely beneficial to our case, and I will call him about the court date as soon as I know it. At that time, I will also apprise him of what to expect when I call him to testify."

When April 24, 1965, appeared on the calendar, Ann was glad she could be present to see her students through the performance of *After the Storm*. Because of its historic significance, people came from miles around to see the show, some of them survivors of the horrific natural disaster. The performance was widely applauded, and the students of the Stage One School of Theater Arts were beginning to feel like celebrities.

Plans for the new theater progressed rapidly, and on Saturday afternoon, May 8, Ann and Charlie were given the honor of jointly turning the first shovel of soil on the site one block north of the high school—the plot of ground donated by Henrietta Jacobs.

A week after the groundbreaking, Matthew phoned: "I got a call from Hollis Wilhite yesterday, and we agreed that the case is ready for trial. He is going to contact the judge's bailiff for a court date. We may not have much advance notice about the date, so keep your schedule flexible."

Three weeks later, Matthew called to tell her the court date had been set for July 8, and that she and Grace should fly out a day early. I'll arrange for your hotel accommodations and travel from the airport to the hotel. I'll probably pick you up from the airport myself," Matthew told Ann.

On July 7, Ann and Grace packed their bags and Paul took them to the airport to catch their 6:40 a.m. flight. Aunt Lil and Uncle Ben moved in with Paul so Aunt Lil could give Joy around-the-clock care. "Don't worry about her, honey," Aunt Lil told Ann, "you know I'll take good care of her, and I'll love doing it."

"I know, Aunt Lil. I don't worry about that. It's just that this will be only the second time I've been away from her overnight, and this will probably be over more than one night. I'm going to feel like a part of me is missing. I guess I just have to place that in God's hands along with everything else. Please reassure her that I'll be back soon."

"I will, but please stop worrying, honey. She will be all right. You just take care of things in New York, and remember you're doing this for her."

"Yes, I know. Thank you so much, Aunt Lil. I don't know what I'd do without you."

The next morning, in the ubiquitous gray of predawn, Daddy drove through the entrance to Love Field. Ann's mind flashed back to that morning in 1956 when he had brought her here to send her off on her own. She had become an adult, and he had grudgingly granted her the freedom to fly away like a bird that had just found its wings. Could her zealous pursuit of musical theater have taken place only nine years earlier? How long ago it seemed!

This time, the flight was on time, and Daddy stayed and watched his daughter board the plane. Reluctant to leave, he continued to watch as the last passenger walked through the tunnel. He observed the activity of the workmen on the ground and watched as the plane backed away from the terminal and taxied into position. Then his eyes followed it speeding down the runway and lifting into the air, carrying a part of his heart into the distance. He was alone, but if people had been nearby, they might have heard him whisper, "Lord, take care of my little girl. Give her courage and wisdom and guidance in everything she faces in this grueling ordeal."

Matthew Worth had told Ann he would be carrying a sign with M.W. printed on it when he met her and Grace at the airport. She scanned the gathering of people, all eagerly watching for a familiar face to pop into view, and soon she spotted the M.W. held above the heads of the crowd. She and Grace approached him, each carrying a small suitcase and a shoulder tote. "Are you Matthew Worth?" Ann asked.

"Hello, Ann," Matthew chuckled, "It's good to meet you in person." Then he turned his attention to Grace, "And you must be Grace Garrison." Without giving her time to affirm his statement, he added, "Ann has told me a lot of nice things about you, Grace."

"It's nice to meet you too, Mr. Worth," Grace replied, "I feel as if I already know you."

Matthew took a suitcase from each of them and asked, "Do you have other luggage in the baggage claim area?"

"No, this is it," Ann answered. "We're hoping we won't be here long."

"That is my hope too," Matthew said. Their chit-chat halted as Matthew escorted them through the airport.

"How was your flight?" he asked as he held open the front and back passenger doors to his Chrysler sedan.

"No problems," Ann replied. After Matthew slid into the driver seat, she continued, "The plane wasn't crowded until after our plane change. Grace was reading, so I had time to think through things and prepare my mind and emotions for the unpleasant task ahead."

"Don't let this rattle you, Ann. I'm the one who will be dealing with the opposition. Your job is to remain calm and poised and answer questions when you are called on to do so. By the way, Ann, I need to go over some things with you before tomorrow, and I think over dinner tonight is the only time we'll have to—"

"Mr. Worth," Grace interrupted, "I know you need to confer with Ann privately, so you two go ahead and have your working dinner. I'll eat in the hotel restaurant and go to bed early. Greg Potter is staying in this same hotel, but he doesn't get in until later tonight. I'm supposed to meet him for an early breakfast in the morning."

"Thanks, Grace, I don't want you to feel left out, but I see you understand attorney-client privilege," Matthew said.

"Oh, I don't feel left out; I'm an early-to-bed-early-to-rise kind of person, and this arrangement suits me just fine."

Matthew parked in the hotel parking garage, escorted the ladies into the hotel, and helped them get settled in the room they were sharing. "I'll pick you up at 6:30 for dinner, Ann. Maybe you'll have a while to rest before then."

"I'll wait outside the hotel entrance for you, Matthew, so you won't have to bother with parking," Ann offered.

After Matthew left, Ann grew serious, "Grace, thank you so much for helping me through all this! Your testimony is extremely important to our case, and I appreciate your contacting your former employers and asking them to write those letters. I'm just shocked at Mr. Potter's offer to come at his own expense to testify, and you're the reason for that! Another thing—Thank you for sparing Matthew the embarrassment of having to ask you to let us have a private dinner." Ann hugged Grace and added, "I love you dearly, Grace."

Grace smiled, "That feeling is mutual, Ann. You're the daughter I never had."

Later, as Matthew pulled Ann's chair away from the table, he chuckled, "When I made this reservation, I requested a table in a private area, but as you can see, we may not have much privacy. I don't like discussing business within earshot of nearby tables. I guess we'll have to speak softly."

"Do you really think anyone will know or care what we're discussing?"

"You never know. I think some people make a hobby of eavesdropping, and they find attorney-client confidentially especially enticing."

"I guess that's true," Ann laughed.

After they had ordered, Matthew said, "Let's get our discussion out of the way now so we can enjoy our food when it arrives. Ann, I don't know what to expect from Richard's lawyer. I don't really know Hollis Wilhite, but I haven't heard anything bad about him.

"I think we have a good case, and you have certainly done nothing that could be interpreted as a breach of the terms of your trusteeship. However, we need to be prepared for whatever accusations they bring against you. You may have to listen to some pretty distasteful claims, but I'll handle those. As I told you earlier, don't let them rattle you. Remain in control of your emotions, no matter what is said by the opposition.

"I don't know who the judge will be, and the judge is an important player. After all, judges are human. No matter how impartial they try to be, they are inevitably influenced by their own experiences and convictions."

Platters of grilled shrimp, baked potato, and broccoli were set before them. It seemed Matthew had said all he planned to say—at least, for the time being. "Well, this looks scrumptious," he declared. "This is the first food I've had since toast and coffee early this morning,"

"It does look wonderful," Ann agreed. "Come to think of it, I haven't eaten much today either."

When they had finished their meal, Matthew clued Ann in on a few other items, and they left the restaurant. Before they parted for the evening, Matthew reminded her, "We appear before the judge at 10:00 a.m. I'll pick you, Grace, and Greg Potter up at 9:00. If you have any questions, now's the time to ask."

"I can't think of anything. I suppose I'm as ready as I'll ever be."

It was 9:10 when Ann got back to her hotel room, and Grace was sound asleep. Ann was physically exhausted, but she was anxious to know how things were going at home. Daddy answered the phone. "Hey, hon, Lil and I were just saying we hoped you would call tonight. Is everything going all right so far?"

"It is. Matthew Worth is taking good care of us. We had dinner and discussed the case, and he's picking us up in the morning. The trial is scheduled for 10:00 a.m., so say a prayer for us that things go well. Has everything gone all right there today?"

"Things are fine here. Lil is keeping Joy right on schedule with everything." He paused, and Ann could hear Aunt Lil's voice in the background. "Lil said to tell you she's spoiling your little girl; she's rocking her to sleep," Daddy chuckled.

"Tell her I approve. I'm just jealous that I'm not there to do it. I'm going to say good-night and go to bed, Daddy. I'm really tired. I'll call tomorrow."

As Ann returned the phone to its cradle, a strange sense of loneliness and isolation swept over her. Her arms ached for Joy, and she couldn't remember ever feeling so homesick. Then she did something she hadn't done since she was a little girl—She got on her knees beside her bed. She prayed every night, but tonight was different. She was coming to the Lord with a special need:

"Lord God, I'm one of Your fickle children. I'm prone to worry when I should trust, doubt when I should believe. I have no right to ask for victory in this court battle unless it's your will. You haven't called on me to understand, only to obey. Grant me complete trust— the kind of trust Job exhibited when he said, "Though He slay me, yet will I trust Him." I do trust you, Lord, whether in victory or defeat, to bring me through this dark tunnel with a stronger faith than when I entered it. Give Matthew Worth an alert mind and an eloquent voice. Give the judge a heart of compassion. Give me the graciousness to accept the verdict of the judge, whatever it is. As a postscript, Lord, I pray that you will speak to the hearts of Richard and Nelson. Transform their indifference toward Joy into an appreciation for her special worth as one of your children. Open their eyes to her beauty. I love You, Lord, and I place my life in your loving care. Amen"

CHAPTER 56

*M*atthew, Ann, Grace, and Greg Potter arrived fifteen minutes early and were seated outside the courtroom where the judge was hearing another case. Two other people straggled in and took seats. The three Buffingtons and Hollis Wilhite arrived and sat across the room. Nelson and Hollis pretended not to see Ann. Richard made brief eye contact and then looked away. Olivia approached Ann, her body language messaging deep remorse. "I've missed you, Ann," she said softly. "I wish we were seeing each other under different circumstances." She glanced back over her shoulder at three grim faces and six eyes shooting daggers in her back; then she whispered, "I want you to know this wasn't my idea."

Ann smiled and said, "I know, Olivia, I know. Thank you. It's good to see you."

Olivia walked back and took her seat beside Nelson.

The door to the courtroom opened and two men and a woman exited. Soon an officer of the court called out "Buffington vs Buffington," and Matthew glanced down the hall, hoping to see Dr. Anderson. All parties involved entered the courtroom as the officer held the door open for them and closed it behind them. Everything was quiet except for the shuffling of papers and the murmur of voices as the judge spoke softly with another officer.

Judge Charles Allen Chandler looked to be perhaps in his mid-sixties with graying hair and half glasses sitting far out on the bridge of his nose. Ann thought he looked rather ordinary—unintimidating but businesslike. Glaciers melted as they waited for him to speak. Finally, he recognized the attorneys and gave a summary of the business at hand. "I see we are dealing with two issues, related but separate: The first is a petition to terminate the Joy Marie Buffington Trust, and the petitioners are Nelson Buffington and Olivia Perchinski. The other matter is a claim against Ann Buffington by Richard Buffington alleging that Ann Buffington has abused her authority as trustee of the subject trust. The pleadings pray for reimbursement of any and all funds transferred from the trust by Ann Buffington."

He called on Hollis Wilhite to present his case. Wilhite stood and first claimed the illegitimacy of the trust on the grounds that Sarah Buffington had died before signing the codicil. He elaborated on the generosity of Nelson Buffington and Olivia Perchinski in carrying out their mother's wishes by approving the codicil and establishing its terms.

In his opening statement and via testimony from Richard and Nelson, he launched into a biting, degrading picture of Ann's irresponsibility. First, he attacked her for refusing to honor her husband's judgment that their severely handicapped baby girl should be placed with people who were trained to give her proper care. "It is clear," he put forth, "that Ann Buffington was and is acting irrationally and was and is perhaps mentally and emotionally unbalanced."

Next, he accused her of leaving her child in the care of Grace Garrison, a family friend, while she pursued a career—a career that operated on an erratic schedule and which often required her to put her career interests above her family responsibilities. "The main criticism of Ann Buffington, however, is *not*," Hollis Wilhite stated emphatically, "that she has given priority to her career over the needs of her daughter. The main criticism is that she has used and is using assets from the Joy Marie Buffington Trust to pay Grace Garrison to take care of Joy Buffington while Ann Buffington herself is involved in vocational activities."

When Wilhite finally finished, he sat down, having made audacious allegations against Ann, none of which he had even attempted to prove.

Ann couldn't believe her ears. If the situation were not so serious, she would have found these insane criticisms laughable. Her head was spinning with conjecture—*Surely, Judge Chandler won't accept these claims just on the word of Hollis Wilhite's witnesses. He has to have proof!*

Finally, it was Matthew Worth's turn to rebut the allegations. After the testimony of Richard and Nelson, Matthew cross-examined each, pointing out lack of detail and lack of proof in their accusations, but he reserved the majority of his attack for his own case.

"With regard to the petition to terminate the trust," Matthew asserted, "Mr. Wilhite seems to be looking at the trust exclusively as a financial arrangement. From my client's view, it was much more than that—It is and has always been a monetary expression of the love of a great-grandmother for a great-grandchild she would never see. The fact that Sarah Buffington did not sign the codicil making this trust a part of her will does not alter the fact that it was her desire to do so. To terminate this trust would be to nullify the wishes of its benefactor by parties whose concern seems to be purely materialistic." Matthew continued, "Not only should this trust be upheld for the reason I have just mentioned, but more importantly, Nelson Buffington and Olivia Perchinski affirmatively created the trust in September of 1959, over five years ago, and the time to contest the codicil has long passed." Worth then presented a brief clearly supporting his legal position.

Matthew looked directly at Judge Chandler and confidently declared, "Your Honor, as to the first portion of this matter, termination of the trust, I respectfully demur to the evidence and urge the court to enter judgment against the plaintiffs and in favor of my client, Ann Buffington. Since the statute of limitations for contesting the subject trust has expired, the claim of the plaintiffs must be dismissed." Matthew returned to his seat.

Judge Chandler shifted his weight, leaned forward, tilted his head down, and peered over his reading glasses. He pinned Hollis Wilhite with a piercing glare, and without further review, stated sternly, "I have read the brief submitted by counsel for Ann Buffington and cannot, Mr. Wilhite, understand one reason why we are here today on this claim. Clearly, the time to contest the codicil and the trust arising therefrom has expired. That portion of your case is dismissed. Court is recessed until 1:00 p.m. when we will take up Mr. Worth's case on the second matter concerning the allegations of improper acts by Ann Buffington as trustee."

Back in the court room following the lunch break, Judge Chandler reconvened the proceedings by calling on Matthew Worth to continue with his defense. Matthew stood and addressed the court, "Your Honor, as you indicated earlier, the issues being decided by this court are related—so much so, that I find it impossible to completely separate them. Therefore, although the petition to terminate the trust has been dismissed, I would like to address some of the allegations brought against my client during that phase of the proceedings. This is necessary if I am to defend my client adequately against the claim that she has abused her role as trustee of the Joy Marie Buffington Trust."

Judge Chandler nodded his approval, "You may continue, Mr. Worth."

Matthew called Ann as his first witness and, with systematic examination of his witness, refuted the prosecution's allegations concerning Ann's psychological health. Matthew wanted the court to see Ann as an intelligent, rational young woman who loved her daughter and was committed to her wellbeing. But he also wanted the court to hear some things about Richard—things that could come only from Ann.

"Mrs. Buffington, you have indicated that your husband was vehemently against taking your daughter home from the hospital— that he wanted her to be taken directly to foster care. How did he act toward her after it became evident that she was in your home to stay?"

"After we took her home, he ignored her. It was as if she didn't exist. He wouldn't even look at her."

"Now, Ann—this may be painful for you—I would like for you to tell the court what transpired between you and Richard on December 9, 1959."

"Richard and I had drifted apart due to our disagreement concerning Joy's care, and almost every time we spoke, our conversation ended in a quarrel. On the date you mentioned, Richard became so angry that he hit me and knocked me to the floor. Then he stormed out of the room. Before I could get up, I heard the front door slam. I was stunned, but it instantly came to my mind that I had to take Joy and leave. I didn't want him to find us there when he returned. In his state of mind, I was afraid he might harm Joy, and I couldn't risk my daughter's safety. I quickly packed bags for Joy and me, and we flew to Dallas that evening."

Matthew continued, "Ann, as you observed Richard's lack of concern for your baby and his behavior toward you, would you say he was behaving rationally?"

Ann calmly replied, "If I had felt he was behaving rationally, I would never have left, but his emotions, not his mind, were dictating his behavior. He was driven by anger. No, he was not behaving rationally."

Matthew concluded his examination of Ann with a final question: "Ann, what is your response to the accusation that you were and are behaving irrationally?"

"If loving my baby and wanting to keep her with me is irrational, then I plead guilty. But I think I have enough intelligence to know how to take care of my little girl. It is my contention that I am capable of meeting her needs in a more loving, responsible, and reliable manner than anyone else in the world."

Ann had convincingly presented herself as a level-headed, conscientious mother who wanted only what was best for her child. Therefore, considering the attitude Judge Chandler had already exhibited toward Hollis Wilhite's case, Wilhite made quick work of his questioning, hoping to avoid further admonishment from Judge Chandler.

Matthew had noticed that Dr. Anderson was now seated in the courtroom, so he announced, "I now call Dr. William H. Anderson to the stand." Dr. Anderson's identity and significance had been clarified during the pre-trial discovery process as Ann Buffington's primary care physician when she was living in Manhattan.

In answer to Matthew's question concerning the advice he gave Ann on October 14, 1959, Dr. Anderson replied, "I remember Ann's situation well; nevertheless, I referred to my records to check the advice I had given her at that time. It was as I recalled: I advised her against institutionalizing her newborn baby daughter. I told her it was my firm conviction that even babies who are physically and mentally incapacitated are more likely to thrive in the environment of a loving family than in a place where they would receive less individual attention. Over these years, my thinking about this has not changed."

In addition to supplying information about his own treatment of Ann and Joy while they were his patients, Dr. Anderson had agreed to review Joy's other medical records. He testified that the expenses paid by Ann from the trust were unequivocally medically necessary and that the charges for all services and products were reasonable. At that time, Matthew submitted copies of receipts and other records of funds spent from Joy's trust. Every expenditure, with the exception of those made to Grace Garrison, was to a medical provider or establishment.

Hollis Wilhite's attempt to discredit the experienced physician was a dismal failure and brought groans even from Nelson and Richard. After a series of sustained objections, Wilhite threw up his hands in a gesture of frustration and ended quickly with "no further questions."

Ann was tempted to look at Richard and Nelson, but she wouldn't allow herself to do so. She knew they were livid at having Matthew Worth, young whippersnapper that he was, make the older and more experienced Hollis Wilhite look foolish and inept for not having done his homework.

Judge Chandler interrupted the proceedings by announcing a fifteen-minute recess for people to refresh themselves. Then he disappeared from the bench, and the courtroom emptied.

CHAPTER 57

*F*ollowing the break, everyone reassembled, and the judge reconvened by calling on Matthew Worth to resume his defense.

Matthew's third witness was Grace Garrison. A stately, self-possessed Grace walked slowly to the witness stand. After she was sworn in, Matthew stated, "Mrs. Garrison, the court is aware that you and the defendant are long-time friends. Because of that friendship, the plaintiff claims you are nothing more than a baby sitter to Joy Marie while Ann is outside the home with her career. What do you have to say about this allegation?"

"I would say anyone who makes that claim certainly doesn't know anything about me. I am an RN with special training in pediatrics. I was in charge of pediatric nursing in the Bonner Valley City Hospital for fifteen years and in Thorp Hospital in San Diego, California, for three years before my career took a new direction. I then became a home care nurse for children with special needs. I am working with Joy Buffington because I have a professional service that benefits her."

"Mrs. Garrison, in your professional opinion, is Ann Buffington shirking her responsibility as a mother by placing her in your care for a portion of each weekday?"

"Definitely not! Anyone who makes such as assertion lacks understanding of the physical and emotional demands placed on the primary caregivers of such children. Ann Buffington is an extraordinary mother, but she, like every other human being, needs some variety in her life. Her teaching career makes her a better mother than she would be if she devoted twenty-four hours of every day to taking care of Joy Marie. Helping young people discover and develop their musical talent brings a dimension to her life that gives her an added sense of accomplishment. That sense of accomplishment rejuvenates and energizes her in the care of her daughter."

Matthew handed Grace some papers documenting her employment with the two hospitals she had mentioned, along with copies of several awards of commendations. "Mrs. Garrison, I have placed in your hands copies of documents that have previously been marked as Defendant's Exhibits one through six inclusive. Would you please identify these documents?"

Grace identified the first two as proof of her employment with the aforementioned hospitals earlier in her career. She paused.

"And exhibits three through six?" Matthew prodded.

Grace modestly identified these documents as various professional recognitions and awards she had received. At Matthew's prompting, Grace read the source and nature of each of these awards.

"Why did you resign as head nurse in the pediatric unit of the prestigious Thorp Hospital in San Diego?" Matthew asked, "Were you unhappy in your work there? Did you feel any pressure from your employers to resign?"

"Oh no, they were happy with me and I was happy with them; in fact, after I resigned, they asked me to reconsider. I worked with an exceptional group of medical professionals, and it was a comfortable situation for me both professionally and financially. However, during my time there, I developed a special concern for disabled children, especially children with cognitive issues. I began independently to study the research about children who are trapped inside imperfect bodies and who suffer diminished mental capacity. The more I read and studied, the more I felt I wanted to be more intimately involved in helping those children. Finally, after learning that many families needed in-home care for their special-needs children, I decided to combine my newfound knowledge with my pediatric training and enter that field of nursing."

"How long ago did you make this change, Mrs. Garrison?"

"I started doing home care nursing in 1953—twelve years ago.

Matthew handed Grace another document and explained, "Mrs. Garrison, I am placing in your hands Defendant's Exhibit seven. Please identify this exhibit and tell the court the significance of the three sets of figures reflected in this document".

Grace studied the exhibit for a moment. Then she responded that it offered documentation of her monthly salary with three different employers at different times during the past twelve years—her last payment stub dated August 1, 1952, from Thorp Hospital in San Diego; a cancelled check dated August 31, 1962, from Mr. Roger Hampton of San Diego; and a cancelled check issued just last month from Ann Buffington. Grace explained that Mr. Hampton was her last employer in California and that she took care of his son Greg.

"Isn't it true, according to Defense Exhibit seven," Matthew stated, "that your salary was reduced by your decision to become a private nurse, and that it was cut even further by your move to Texas? Over a twelve-year period, it would seem your salary should have increased, but yours has decreased. Do you have any regrets about your decision to go into private nursing?"

"Definitely not. I loved and still love every one of those children, and my work with them has brought me more satisfaction than any type nursing I have ever done. I had a yearning in my heart to have one-on-one interaction with these children, and in working with them, I believe I have developed an insight into the nature of their needs and desires. I know that sounds strange, and I don't know how to explain it myself, but it is true. I believe I am capable of giving children with special needs something that makes a difference in their lives."

"And what about your decision to return to Texas? If you were still living in California, wouldn't your salary as a private nurse be quite a bit more than the salary you are earning in Bonner Valley, Texas?"

"Yes, I would be earning more money if I were still in California, but, Mr. Worth," Grace explained, "I didn't move back to Texas looking for a job. I moved back there thinking I might retire and begin drawing my retirement benefits, but God had other plans for me. I feel about Joy Marie the way I felt about all the other children I took care of—She needs the skill I have to offer. But beyond that, Ann and Joy Buffington are like family to me. My work with Joy is a way I can honor the memory of Eve Jernigan, Ann's mother and the best friend I ever had."

Matthew Worth then narrowed his line of questioning to inquiries addressing Grace's effectiveness with Joy Marie. Grace related how she took Joy to the theater arts school for visits two or three days each week and about her observations of Joy's responsiveness.

"Finally," Grace stated, "Ann and her business partner, Charlotte Lambert, decided to open the classes for other special-needs children and their caregivers to visit. They wanted to let the caregivers see if music and the movement of dance had the same effect on their children as it had on Joy. Many of these visitors experienced positive results, and the program has snowballed into what many of the parents call *therapy sessions*."

"Mrs. Garrison," Matthew stated, "You are an educated, intelligent woman with the remarkable ability to sense the needs and responses of children who are unable to verbally express themselves. I suspect you are also pretty good at picking up inuendoes in the speech of people in general. This is what Mr. Wilhite said about Ann Buffington's career, and I quote: 'The main criticism against Ann Buffington is not . . . that she has given priority to her career over the needs of her daughter. The main criticism is that she has used and is using money from the Joy Marie Buffington Trust to pay Grace Garrison.' What do you think that statement suggests?"

"Well," Grace replied, "It seems Richard Buffington is less interested in his daughter's welfare than he is in how the money from her trust is spent."

Hollis Wilhite sheepishly declined cross-examination.

Next, Matthew called Greg Potter, an employer of Grace Garrison while she was living in California. She had served as a private nurse to his son who suffered from multiple congenital disorders. Grace's service with little Nate Potter ended when the child passed away in

1957. Matthew let the court know that Mr. Potter had voluntarily traveled, at his own expense, from California to New York City to testify in this trial.

"Mr. Potter, please tell the court about your association with Grace Garrison."

"I speak for both myself and my wife," Greg Potter stated, "when I say we want to do this for Grace and her current employer, Mrs. Buffington. Grace has a unique gift of relating to children like our Nate. She was able to draw responses from him that we would never have thought possible. We had a second child, Nate's older sister, who also loved Grace. Two years ago, we lost our daughter in a freak accident at school. Grace was kind enough to fly back to California for Amy's funeral although she had already begun working for Mrs. Buffington. I tried to reimburse her for her airline ticket, but she wouldn't accept it. This is an opportunity for us to show our gratitude to this gracious lady—the most dedicated and valued caregiver we ever had for our son—and to Mrs. Buffington for encouraging her to take time off to come to be with us during that difficult time."

Hollis Wilhite had no questions for Greg Potter.

Matthew Worth summarized, "The uncontroverted evidence clearly shows that all expenditures from the Joy Marie Buffington Trust, including payments made for the services of Grace Garrison, were necessary and reasonable for the quality care of Joy Marie Buffington."

Judge Chandler again addressed Hollis Wilhite. "Mr. Wilhite, do you have anything further to say about this issue?"

Wilhite took a deep breath and launched into an oration he hoped would even the score in what, so far, had been a lop-sided competition. "Yes, Your Honor, I would like to reaffirm our claim that Ann Buffington abused her authority as trustee of the Joy Marie Buffington Trust. It was only through Richard Buffington's leniency that she has had singular access to the trust. He relinquished his trusteeship in order to simplify his former wife's use of the account. He trusted her to be judicious and transparent in using the funds available to her, but at no time did she give an account of her spending to him or to anyone else. It was by accident that he learned through a friend about her career and the subsequent hiring of Grace Garrison.

"Despite the argument presented by the defense," Wilhite continued, "no *proof* has been presented that Grace Garrison's services are necessary—or even beneficial—for Joy Marie Buffington. All we have is the word of Ann Buffington and of Grace Garrison herself. In the final analysis, Your Honor, this is still a matter of her word against his word. Since Sarah Buffington, the benefactor of this trust, is not present to express her disapproval of the manner in which the trust has been and is being used, I feel it is safe to assume that her sympathies would lie with her grandson rather than with someone outside the family."

Wilhite's words stung Ann to the core of her being. The extraordinary woman she had admired and loved so dearly—her special friend who had treated her like a granddaughter and with whom she had had many deeply personal conversations about life and love, disappointments and failures—*Her* Sarah was being summoned from the grave to strip Ann of her credibility and integrity.

Judge Chambers sat silently for several minutes, his head lowered. Finally, he spoke: "I have arrived at what I believe to be a fair and reasonable decision on the second portion of this case, and it is my hope that all of you can leave this room feeling you have learned something about fairness and justice and even a little bit about mercy. I want to challenge all of you—particularly the plaintiffs—to think about your stance in this case. I'd like for you to look inside yourselves and see what you find there; then look around you and see what you find there. That may seem to be a childish, frivolous injunction, but if you do it sincerely and with the right attitude, you might be surprised at what it reveals.

"Although the first portion of this lawsuit has been disposed of, I feel compelled to point out a few things to the plaintiffs. Mr. Nelson Buffington, I know you are a shrewd and successful businessman. Most people in Manhattan know the Buffington name. I can't see what's inside your heart and mind, but I think I can make some fairly accurate assessments about your life. You live in a nice house, drive a nice automobile, and wear nice clothes. You don't have to worry about where your next meal will come from or whether you will have enough money to pay your bills each month.

"The petition you made to this court has everything to do with money and nothing to do with your need. I believe it was your mother's desire to establish this trust, and you must have thought so too. Otherwise, why would you and your sister have signed a document to make it a part of her will. I don't understand the motive behind your desire to terminate this trust. How can you possibly be at peace in your heart if you aren't sure your granddaughter will receive proper medical attention? If you'll look inside yourself, Mr. Buffington, you might find hostility toward your former daughter-in-law. If you do, I suggest you get rid of it. Animosity serves no good purpose. Then look around you and see how fortunate you are. Doing these things might make you a more grateful, happier person.

"Mrs. Olivia Perchinski, you have been a silent participant in these proceedings. The fact that Mr. Wilhite did not call on you to testify leads me to wonder if you are truly sympathetic with the action for which you and your brother petitioned the court. If your heart was not in this, I admonish you to gather the strength to follow your own conscience and not let anyone sway you from what you believe to be right.

"Now, Mr. Richard Buffington—as for your lawsuit to revoke Ann Buffington's trusteeship of the Joy Marie Buffington Trust and to recover money she has already spent from the trust assets—I cannot, in good conscience, rule in your favor. One of two things must be true: Either you aren't concerned about your daughter's medical needs or you trust your former wife enough to know she will find a way to provide those needs with or without benefit of this trust. If your daughter's needs don't concern you, then you aren't much of a man, and you certainly aren't much of a father. From all I've heard today from both sides of the aisle, your resentment for your former wife runs deep. I hope you won't allow that resentment to deprive your daughter of the best life possible for her.

"I will admit to you, Mr. Buffington, that I have trouble with your value system. Obviously, you do not want a relationship with your daughter. You were offended that your wife insisted on bringing your less-than-perfect baby into your home. It seems to me you would have appreciated and admired your wife's desire to give your daughter a home where love and attentiveness would be a priority.

"I say to you, Mr. Buffington, what I said to your father. Look inside yourself and examine your motive in taking this action. If you find bitterness toward your former wife, I advise you to dig out that root of antagonism and replace it with understanding and mercy. Then look around you and count your blessings. Having followed your father into a thriving business, you probably lead a charmed life financially. Why is it so difficult for you to show some benevolence to the mother of your daughter?

"My judgment in the second portion of this lawsuit is for the defendant. Restitution of funds paid from the Joy Marie Buffington Trust is denied, and I uphold the defendant's right to continue as sole trustee of said trust. "This court is now adjourned."

Ann was speechless! She couldn't believe this dramatic turn of events. With tears streaming down her cheeks, she grabbed Matthew Worth and hugged him, sobbing the words, "Oh, thank you, Matthew, thank you!"

"I'm not surprised we won," Matthew said, "but I'm amazed at the stern thrashing Judge Chandler gave them. I have a feeling they're feeling like whipped dogs right now, and I hope they are. They needed to hear everything he had to say."

Grace told Ann she would see her later at the hotel. She and Greg Potter were having dinner together so they could visit a while before he took his flight back to California.

Ann and Matthew made their way to Matthew's car in silence, the judge's decision still echoing in Ann's mind. As they were driving away, Ann asked, "Matthew, did you have any say-so in who the judge would be?"

"No. Cases are randomly appointed to whichever judge is available. We just got lucky."

"I'm not so sure it was luck, Matthew. I prayed that God's

will would be done in court today, and that he would direct the proceedings. I think that's what happened."

"Maybe so, Ann, I hadn't thought about it like that. Would you like to have dinner before I take you back to the hotel?"

"I appreciate the offer, Matthew, but I have a lot to do tonight. I'm anxious to get home, and I need to make airline reservations for Grace and me; I'm hoping to get an early flight tomorrow. I also need to call home. I'll just get a sandwich or something at the hotel."

From her hotel room, Ann made two phone calls, first to the airline and then to her daddy, "Can you pick us up tomorrow at 2:08 p.m. I have good news! I'll give you all the details when I get home. How's my baby? Is Aunt Lil still making it okay?"

"They're both fine, sweetheart. You mean it's all over?"

"It's all over," she giggled, "and it's an amazing story. I love you, Daddy. As a matter of fact, I love the whole world right now!"

"And you're just going to leave me dangling like this?" Paul Jernigan pleaded.

"Yep. I want to see your face when I tell you all about it. Now, I'm going to grab something to eat. Then I have to shower, pack, and get to bed early. I just hope I can sleep. I'm exhausted, but my brain is still spinning."

In the backseat of the taxicab on their way to the airport, Ann and Grace chatted like school girls. After their exuberance had mellowed into silence, Ann silently prayed:

Heavenly Father, I am thankful for our courtroom victory, but a part of me feels bad for Richard and Nelson. Speak to them and instruct them, Lord, in accordance with Your will. Give them understanding of how rich and meaningful their lives could be if they would open their hearts to You. Lord God, You are the Master Conductor! I thank you and praise You for directing the symphony of my life.

CHAPTER 58

A nn's life soon got back to normal. After weeks of harassment and accusations from Richard, the phone calls had stopped, and she felt as if a crushing weight had been lifted from her.

The Stage One School of Theater Arts continued to grow, and by October of 1965, Charlie had forty-two students in her dance classes, and Trent was teaching tap to another fourteen. Joanna taught one class in elocution and another in improvisation. From 10:30 a.m. to 5:00 p.m., Monday through Friday, Ann was busy with private voice students, but Trent took the Saturday students so Ann could have the entire weekend with Joy—a time she treasured and tenaciously guarded.

Last spring, Daddy had decided to enclose the back patio and wall it with large windows that could be opened to allow fresh air to flow through the room. He had always enjoyed gardening, and this year he had taken a special interest in fall plants. The flowers and foliage were gorgeous, creating an outdoorsy, relaxing atmosphere in the new sunroom. Ann thought it would be a great place to have Joy's birthday party, but she decided to make it a small gathering of family plus Grace and Charlie and Bill.

The party was on Saturday, October 9, the day after Joy's birthday. Ann served sandwiches and other finger foods in addition to chocolate layer cake topped with six little heart-shaped pink candles and the words *Happy Birthday, Joy* in fancy pink script on chocolate icing. Ann held Joy in her lap, and Grace held the cake in front of her as they all sang the happy birthday song to her and collectively blew out the candles. Joy's countenance remained inscrutable, her eyes searching beyond the cake.

When Grace handed Ann a piece of cake, Ann scooped up a morsel of the cake and icing with a spoon. "Yum, Yum," Ann hummed as she moved the spoon to Joy's mouth. Joy pushed her tongue out over the icing, and drew it slowly into her mouth. Then Ann heard a sound coming from Joy's mouth. It was a soft *muuum*. "Grace! Daddy! Did you hear that?"

"Yes! shouted Grace. She was trying to say what you said, Ann! She was trying to say *Yum!*"

"I heard it too! Daddy exclaimed."

Aunt Lil, Uncle Ben, Charlie, and Bill were over near the windows admiring the show of plant life in the back yard; they were oblivious to what had taken place until they heard the commotion. Everybody gathered around Joy poised to hear her repeat the sound—but they were unrewarded.

Ann pulled Joy close to her and whispered in her ear, "I love you. I think you already know that, but I want to keep telling you. I want so much to make you understand it."

Construction on the theater went quickly, and by November. the structure was weathered in. Thanksgiving and Christmas came and went, and the chill of January and February passed. The trees budded and jonquils, daffodils, and other spring plants pushed their heads up through the crusty soil. On May 16, 1966, Ann received a call from Doyle Davenport. "Ann, we're finishing up. We just have a little more carpet to lay. As soon as the men complete the work and get things cleaned up, I want you and Charlie to do a walk through with Felicia, Thurston, Chester, Leonard and me. I'm thinking that will be next week, so if you girls can clear a time, we'll do that. Then it will be time to dedicate this building and get you moved in." Ann could hear the ring of satisfaction in Doyle's voice, and as he talked, she pictured that big grin for which he was noted.

"What wonderful news, Doyle! I can hardly wait to see it. You know, I'm still mad at you for making it off limits to Charlie and me until it's finished. Since we're so close to the completion of things, though, I forgive you. Thanks so much for calling. We'll be ready whenever you say."

———— ✸ ————

The next day after Doyle's call, Ann was in the middle of a voice lesson when Joanna opened the door and came in without knocking. The look on her face and urgency in her voice spoke for her: "Ann, Grace is on the phone. She says she must talk to you right now."

Ann flew off the piano bench and ran to the phone. "Grace, what's wrong?"

"I have Joy at the emergency room, Ann. Get here as soon as you can."

Ann grabbed her purse and called over her shoulder to Joanna, "Tell Charlie I had to leave." When Ann entered the emergency room she cried, "Grace, what happened? Where is Joy?"

"Ann, I don't know what happened. She just started making choking noises and then began to turn blue. Dr. Cooper has her on a ventilator. She's still in the emergency room right now, but they're going to move her to intensive care." Grace led the way to Joy's bed.

Ann gasped as she pushed the curtain aside and walked into the cubicle. Her whole body ached at the sight of Joy's tiny body lying in a massive bed, a snarl of lines and tubes surrounding her and a noisy machine pumping air into her lungs. Tears streamed down Ann's cheeks. All she could do was hold and stroke Joy's hand, but she longed to wrap her baby in her arms, to sooth her and tell her she loved her.

Soon Dr. Cooper entered the small area. "She's very sick, Ann. She's having trouble breathing because her lungs are filling with fluid, and a thick mucus is forming in her throat. She doesn't have the strength to cough up the mucus, so we removed it with a suction device, and that will have to be repeated from time to time.

We're afraid of aspiration if we try to give her anything by mouth; therefore, we're feeding and keeping her hydrated with an IV. I put a medication in the IV that I hope will eliminate the fluid and mucus. If she doesn't get better over the next twenty-four hours, I'll try a different medication."

Ann asked the doctor to step outside the cubicle with her. Fear was written in every line of her face, and her eyes still glistened with tears. "Dr. Cooper, am I going to lose her?" Ann asked forthrightly.

"Ann, doctors may fool themselves into believing they know when a person's life will end, but they don't. Only God knows that. I learned that lesson by being wrong several times." Ann smiled at him and thanked him. Then she went back to Joy's bedside, and Dr. Cooper went his way.

"Grace, would you call some people for me. First, call Daddy if you haven't already, and he can call Aunt Lil and Uncle Ben. Then call Charlie; tell her I'm not sure when I'll be back. She can let my students know I will be out indefinitely. Doyle Davenport also needs to know what's going on. You'll find some money for the phone in my purse."

"I'll take care of it, honey. You just stay with Joy," Grace said as she squeezed Ann's hand.

Three nurses came into the room and announced they were moving Joy to a hospital room and that Ann could wait in the hall and then follow them. "A room? I thought she was going to intensive care."

"Dr. Cooper thinks she'll be better off in a private room," nurse Thompson explained. "He is assigning a nurse to give special attention to Joy. The nurse will be checking on her about every half hour and will respond immediately in case of an emergency."

The room was spacious with a large window looking out on a lawn that was on its way to being green. It had a recliner and two other chairs, so Ann had a much more comfortable arrangement than would have been possible in intensive care. Besides that, she wanted to stay with Joy around the clock, and she was sure that would not be permitted in intensive care.

The next day, Dr. Cooper told Ann he was changing the medication. "This one doesn't seem to be working, but don't be discouraged; maybe the next one will."

The days dragged into the second week, but Ann refused to leave the hospital. Grace had brought her clothes and other things she needed, but the thought of being away from Joy, even for a little while, made Ann uncomfortable.

Paul had been in and out every day since Grace had called to tell him Joy was in the emergency room. On the second Saturday of Ann's constant vigil, he tried to persuade his daughter to let him relieve her so she could go home and rest for a while, but she still wouldn't leave. "I'm glad you're here, Daddy, but I just can't go home and leave her here."

When Dr. Cooper walked into Joy's room on that Saturday morning, his demeanor betrayed his concern. "Ann, the medications don't seem to be helping. I called Roger Matheson, her pediatric neurologist in Dallas, and he has agreed to come to Bonner Valley today and see her. Because of his specialty, he's better equipped to treat children with congenital disorders than anyone in North Texas."

Tears began to well in Ann's eyes, and her daddy went to her and put his arms around her. "Honey, Dr. Cooper is doing everything he can."

"Yes, I know he is. I was just hoping she would have shown some improvement by now. I don't know which hurts worse—the thought of losing her or seeing her as she is now with that machine helping her breathe and surrounded by all those wires and tubes. If she could only tell me what she's feeling. I just want to know she isn't in pain.

"Oh Daddy, I'm so scared. I know if she doesn't respond to any of the medication or treatment, if the only way she can live is to be on this ventilator, then—" Ann began to weep openly, releasing the fears she had held inside from the moment Joy drew her first breath over six years ago. "If she doesn't improve soon, I know Dr. Cooper is going to ask about removing the ventilator. I don't think I can do that, Daddy."

"I know, honey," Daddy said, "but let's don't run ahead of God.

We've known from the time she was born that someday we would probably have to let go. Don't you think the Lord knows everything you're going through right now? Knows everything Joy is going through? She's in His loving arms, and He will take care of her and of you."

"I know you're right, Daddy. All of this is in God's hands.

At about 2:15 that afternoon, Dr. Matheson knocked softly and entered Joy's room. "Hello, Ann," Dr. Matheson said as he approached her with an outstretched hand. "Dr. Cooper has discussed Joy's situation with me, and he's taken all the right steps. Let me just take a look at Joy, and then we'll talk." He examined her, quietly consulted with the nurse as he looked over the chart she had placed in his hands, and studied the information generated by the machine beside Joy's bed.

After a while, he walked away from the bed. He greeted Paul and Grace. Then he cradled Ann's arm and guided her to a chair. He pulled another chair close to hers and sat down beside her. Taking both her hands in his, he spoke quietly, "Let me explain what's happening. She has been in a coma since shortly after Dr. Cooper saw her several days ago. What started with a respiratory problem may now be affecting other parts of her body. I'm afraid her kidneys, and maybe some other organs, are beginning to fail. About all we can do is to keep her comfortable. I know this is hard for you, Ann, but I have to be honest with you. You need to prepare yourself for the reality that she may not pull out of this."

Ann began to sob softly and suddenly appeared to crumple in her chair. Daddy and Grace rushed to support her, and Dr. Matheson stood and folded a blood pressure band around her arm. "It's going to be all right, honey," Daddy said lovingly, "we talked about this. We want what is best for Joy."

Ann didn't speak. Dr. Matheson's words had brought her fears into focus. She was no longer dealing with a blur of possibilities but with a face-to-face encounter with facts. Her hope was slowly being suffocated.

CHAPTER 59

On June 2, 1966, after being on a ventilator for seventeen days, Joy Marie Buffington threw off all the imperfections that had shackled her, and she entered the home waiting for her with the Lord Jesus.

Her death certificate gave cause of death as kidney failure, but according to Dr. Cooper, "Her whole body decided it was too tired to keep holding on, so it just let go." Ann was with her to the end and felt a strange bonding with her daughter in those last moments. As Joy drew her last breath, in some mysterious unspoken language of the soul, Ann felt Joy being released from the burden of a broken body. A deep sense of peacefulness engulfed Ann. In her heart, she knew everything was all right. Joy was in a happy place.

When Ann called Richard to let him know Joy had passed from this life to her heavenly home, he offered his condolences and inquired about the funeral service. Ann began giving him the details of the arrangements, but before she could finish, he interrupted her. "I won't be coming to the service, but I do want to know where I can send flowers. I have to go to a meeting, Ann, but thanks for calling." The conversation was over, and a chill went through Ann's body. Richard reflected no more emotion than he might have if he'd just witnessed someone stepping on a bug.

The church was overflowing on the day of Joy's funeral. Ann wished Richard had come, not because his presence would have brought her any comfort, but to show him how many people loved Joy and treasured their memory of her. Seating was reserved for students of the theater arts school. However, when the students saw adults standing along the sides, one-by-one they gave their seats to other people. By the time the service started, students were lining the wall all along one side and around the back of the church auditorium.

— ◯ —

A week following the funeral, Doyle Davenport called Ann and asked if she felt up to doing a walk through at the theater.

"Yes, I'd like that Doyle. I still haven't started back to work so I can meet anytime, but I'll need to see when Charlie can be free."

"I was going to ask you to do that. I want the two of you to give your approval as soon as possible so we can sign off with the contractor. I've been putting him off, but Howard's a good friend and he understands the circumstances. He did a great job; I think you'll be pleased."

Since many of Charlie's students were taking a break for the summer, her schedule was flexible. "How about tomorrow morning about 10:00 o'clock in front of the new theater?"

"That sounds good to me," Ann said. "I'll call Doyle and set it up."

Ann and Charlie had seen the outside of the building, of course, and since they had worked with the architect, they were familiar with the layout; however, they had seen only a mock-up of the interior. When Doyle unlocked the main entrance, they walked into a breathtaking foyer, a large central area with plenty of room for people to visit. They scanned the beautiful entrance, noting the ticket/concierge counter near the rear wall, flanked on each side with two sets of double doors leading into the auditorium. Restrooms and water fountains were located to the right and left just inside the front entrance.

The auditorium boasted wrap-around seating, complementing a semi-circular extended stage area. Row height and staggered alignment of the seats ensured a good view of the stage from virtually anywhere in the auditorium. Lighting, sound equipment, and acoustical enhancements were all state of the art.

In addition to rehearsal rooms, dressing rooms, and bathrooms, the backstage area housed storage rooms for props, costumes, and various types of equipment.

"Doyle, I'm flabbergasted by this!" Ann cried. "I know all this was extremely expensive; I don't know how in the world you raised that much money!"

"We just announced that we were taking donations, and the donations began pouring in," Doyle laughed.

"You know, Doyle, I'm never at loss for words," Charlie said, "but this has left me speechless! This far exceeds my expectations. It seems larger than I thought it would be. How many did you say it will seat?"

"Our original plan was for a capacity of 200, but for whatever reason, Howard decided the size of the overall building called for a larger audience area, so he upped it to 230. He didn't mention that until we had already signed the contract, but he said the miscalculation was his, so he didn't charge us for the extra seats.

"There's one other thing I want to discuss with you ladies—We need to schedule the dedication. The Theater Company will take care of planning it, but we need to make sure the two of you can be there since you're going to figure into the program. Do you have any suggestions?"

"The sooner, the better, I'd say," Charlie laughed, and Ann nodded her agreement.

"I brought my calendar with me," Doyle said, "and I was looking at Sunday, July 10, at 2:00 p.m. How would you feel about that?"

Almost simultaneously, Ann and Charlie said, "That sounds great."

Dignitaries from several Texas cities were in attendance for the dedication, and the first three rows of the middle section were reserved for these and other special guests. Mayor Jim McMasters acted as the master of ceremonies. He welcomed everyone, recognized special guests, thanked donors, and read congratulatory telegrams. Then he introduced the speaker, Dr. Logan Horner, an educator whose Aunt Henrietta had donated the land on which the theater was built.

Following Dr. Horner's speech, a large stone covered with a purple velvet drape was wheeled onto the stage and placed in front of the lectern. The mayor asked Ann and Charlie to come forward and stand beside the stone. "For most of you, Ann Buffington and Charlotte (Charlie) Lambert need no introduction," Mayor McMasters said, "but for those who don't know them, they own and operate the Stage One School of Theater Arts. When they started their school, I'm sure they had no idea how successful their business would be. It didn't take long for them to outgrow the studio they are using now. But the growth of their classes isn't the only reason they need more space. To understand why they outgrew their present location, you have to know the whole story, which I will tell you after these ladies remove the drape from the stone. Now, ladies, the audience is going to count to three with me, and on the count of three, I want you to lift the drape and let it fall to the floor."

Ann and Charlie did as he directed, and for a split second, a hush fell over the audience. Then the momentary silence was followed by a collective gasp as the inscription came into view. When Ann and Charlie stepped forward to read what had been chiseled into the stone, they both burst into tears.

Joy Marie Buffington
Theater of the Performing Arts
In loving memory of
Joy Marie Buffington
1959-1966
and
Wayne Allen Jacobs
1926-1939

The mayor cleared his throat, "Now for the rest of the story: When Ann Jernigan Buffington moved back to Bonner Valley where she had grown up, she brought with her little Joy Marie, her precious daughter. Most people would refer to Joy as *handicapped*, but Ann doesn't like that term. Instead, Ann refers to her daughter as *special*. Grace Garrison, Joy's nurse, began to notice a difference in Joy when she would take her to visit the studio where her mother was working, and Grace and Ann decided the music and dance were a therapy for Joy.

"Ann and Charlie began inviting other parents to bring their *special* children to the studio to see if they too might benefit from the musical atmosphere, and many of these children *did* respond. Soon, Ann and Charlie were inundated with requests to visit the classes—many more than they could accommodate. That's when the people of Bonner Valley decided we needed a theater that would give Ann and Charlie plenty of space for visitors and, at the same time, give them a place for their students to perform. This theater is the result of that concern."

As a final comment, Mayor McMasters said, "Not long ago, Joy Marie Buffington went to live in Heaven, but she will never be forgotten. She was the inspiration, the catalyst, that caused a lot of us to look at life in a different way, and that's what ultimately led us to see the need for this building. For that reason, we have named this theater the Joy Marie Buffington Theater of the Performing Arts.

"You notice the theater is dedicated to the memory of two people, Joy Marie Buffington and Wayne Allen Jacobs. Wayne Allen Jacobs was the *special* son of Henrietta and Andrew Jacobs. Most of you know Henrietta, and many of you remember when Andrew was the principal of Bonner Valley High School. Henrietta donated the land on which this theater now stands, and we felt it proper that we dedicate this theater to the memory of the two young lives who inspired this undertaking. This stone will be placed on the lawn in front of the building as a reminder of the special impact these children had on all of us."

The audience didn't know whether to applaud or remain silent out of respect for the memory of these two children, but they didn't have to wonder long. When Ann began to applaud, the entire crowd followed her prompting. Ann walked over to Jim McMasters and asked to speak to the audience.

"Of course, you may do that, Ann. I want you to," Jim said.

Ann walked to the microphone, and the audience stilled. "Charlie and I are deeply humbled by this show of appreciation for our work here in Bonner Valley. Many of you are not aware that the Bonner Valley schools allowed students (with permission from their parents) to miss gym class one day a week to come for their lessons with us. The administration's benevolence in doing this has been extremely helpful to us and to many of our students. We think it would be a disgrace for us to keep this beautiful facility all to ourselves. I know the high school music and speech classes have no auditorium in which to perform, and that they have had to make do with the gymnasium, which is an ideal place for young voices to get lost up in the rafters." A knowing surge of laughter rippled through the audience before Ann continued. "We see no reason that we can't share this theater with the community, especially with the public schools. Surely, we can cooperate with one another in scheduling programs.

"I personally want to thank you for memorializing my daughter in such a beautiful way, and I'm sure Mrs. Jacobs is as grateful and pleased as I am that you have honored our children with this dedication. Thank you so much."

The audience dispersed, wiping their eyes and feeling a sense of warm community spirit.

CHAPTER 60

Summer turned to fall, and Ann and Charlie had moved their school to the new theater. The program thrived, and parents of special children no longer had to be scheduled for a time to visit. A side door of the theater was always unlocked during school hours, and parents could come and go as they pleased. Near this side entrance was a wheelchair ramp and parking for the handicapped. Ann was still in a state of disbelief that the people of her home town had seen fit to build this magnificent structure.

Saturday, October 8, was a bleak day for Ann. It marked what would have been Joy's seventh birthday, and she thought back over previous happy celebrations with singing and cake and candles and balloons and *Joy*. After spending the morning feeling a knife twisting inside her and a deep emptiness that nothing could fill, Ann decided to go for a walk. Daddy told her he could go with her, but she said she would like to be alone this time; she knew he understood. "Maybe later we can pick up Grace and go to the cemetery," she said.

An early cold front was fueling a biting north wind, so Ann draped her muffler around her neck and pulled the hood of her parka over her head. She made her way to the city park where strong gusts were snatching leaves from the trees and sending them tumbling and swirling.

From a bench near the pond, she watched little whitecaps bobbing ducks up and down and listened to the swoosh of trees being tossed by an angry, raucous wind. She had always enjoyed the fall of the year. Even on raw, dreary days such as this, she had found a type of comfort. On this day, however, every nerve of her body empathized with the plaintive cries of nature. Engrossed in her memories, she was indifferent to the icy fingers that had pulled her hood from her head and had sent her muffler flying.

At first, the cold air felt good on her face and neck; then she began to shiver. She ran to retrieve her muffler, and as she did so, she noticed the colorful leaves skittering along the sidewalk. She smiled as she remembered the story about Freddy, the little sapling.

Freddy wouldn't have been afraid to lose his leaves if he had known he would grow new ones, Ann mused. *Life is a cycle. Leaves fall away—sometimes prematurely—to make way for new ones; but the fallen leaves exhibit a unique, often spectacular, beauty that marks the fulfillment of their destinies, and our memory of that beauty lives on long after the leaves have crumbled into dust. It is the same with people. From beginning to end, our lives are appointed. Joy lived exactly the amount of time she was created to live, and she left a legacy of hope. With her responsiveness to music, she altered the way a whole town thought about children who appear to be completely lacking in appreciation for the world around them. The end of her life was like one of these leaves—a beautiful reminder of how God used one special life.*

Walking home and reflecting on her pilgrimage over the past ten years, Ann began to pour her heart out to the Lord:

"Ten years ago, I was so out of step with you, Lord, that it didn't even occur to me to ask what you wanted for my life. You indulged me by permitting me to pursue what I thought was my destiny, and you blessed me beyond my wildest dreams in that pursuit.

You permitted me to be married to a man I thought was my soul mate, and you tolerated my bitterness when that world came crashing down.

You even allowed me to shake my fist at you and accuse you of cheating Joy out of a normal life.

When I boldly demanded answers, you patiently waited for me to come to my senses, just as the prodigal son did after he had shamefully squandered his inheritance. I shiver, Lord Jesus, when

I think about my impudent and irreverent behavior. I acted like a spoiled child having a temper tantrum; yet, despite my arrogance, you still loved me.

You transformed my flagrant, sinful rebellion into a desire to help young people discover the best that is in them, and you gave me a heart for bringing a new dimension to the lives of special children like my Joy.

Lord God, forgive me for being presumptuous, and give me a humble heart. I praise you for who you are—holy and righteous. Only you could take my human blunders and turn them into blessings.

Thank you, Jesus, for loving me and for giving me your Holy Spirit to comfort and guide me. I love you and trust you to help me conduct my life in a way pleasing to you. Amen."

As Ann reached the front porch, Daddy opened the door for her. "Well, you were gone quite a while. I was beginning to worry. Are you feeling better?"

"I do feel better. I had a conversation with Jesus, and that always gives me a new perspective on things." she said as she smiled up at him.

"You have some company," Daddy said.

Ann quickly removed her parka and muffler and followed her daddy into the living room. Their pastor and his wife, Brother and Mrs. Craig, stood to greet her. "We just came by to bring something to you, Ann. We didn't intend to stay very long, but your daddy insisted you would be disappointed if we didn't wait for you."

"I certainly would have been," Ann declared.

Brother Craig handed Ann a small white box and encouraged her to open it. "We remembered that today was Joy's birthday, and we felt this little remembrance might be appropriate."

"How thoughtful of you! Well, please sit down while I open this."

The couple returned to their seats. Ann opened the box and removed a little pink Bible, the cover inscribed in gold with the name *Joy Marie Buffington*. "This is precious!" Ann cried. "I will always treasure it. You must have known I needed a boost today."

"We hope it will be a little reminder of how God blessed you when He entrusted you with the care of one of His special children," Brother Craig said. "The ribbon is marking a passage I underlined. We hope you find it comforting." Brother Craig stood, took Ann's hand and gently patted it. "We really do need to leave now, but you know we are praying for you, and we are available if you need us."

"Thank you both so much. You've made a difficult day a little less painful," Ann said as she put an arm around each of them and drew them to her in a loving embrace. "You couldn't have done anything that would have been more meaningful to me."

When the guests were gone, Ann picked up the little Bible and lifted the ribbon to reveal the marked page. Brother Craig had underlined the last part of Psalm 30:5. She read it aloud for Daddy to hear. "Weeping may endure for a night, but joy *cometh* in the morning."

Ann's eyes filled with tears as she looked at her daddy. "Do you think that word *joy* could also be spelled with a capital letter?"

"Yes, honey, I think it could be," Daddy replied as he wrapped her in his arms.

"I miss Joy terribly, Daddy, and I still don't understand a lot of things. I just can't believe God plans for bad things to occur in the lives of innocent children like Joy. I do think, though, that he sometimes chooses not to intervene with the natural course of things. God could have miraculously altered whatever biological malfunction caused Joy's condition, but in His wisdom, He had a different plan for her.

"I don't pretend to understand the mind of God, but I trust Him to know what is best. Our Lord doesn't make mistakes, and He had a reason for allowing Joy's afflictions. He used even her imperfections to touch the lives of other people. I don't know what kind of person I might be if she hadn't come into my life.

"Brother Craig didn't know it, but something he said expressed my feelings about my relationship with Joy: She made me feel blessed—honored that God trusted me enough to give me this special little girl, even if it was just for a little while.

"It's taken a long time for me to come to this, Daddy, but I think

I now understand God's plan for my life. My destiny isn't to be on stage; it never was. That phase of my life was just a preparation for what God really wants me to do—to give hope to the parents of children like Joy and to encourage and help musically inclined young people to cultivate their talent.

"I may never overcome this sense of loss. I don't know about that, but I do know my night of paralyzing sadness has ended, and when the Lord is finished with me here on this earth, I look forward to a morning of eternal *Joy!*"

Printed and bound by PG in the USA